BESTSELLING ROMANCE AUTHORS PRAISE SHIRL HENKE'S ROMANCES:

"Terms of Love is a sexy, sensual romp that will keep you enthralled from first page to last. Without a doubt, Shirl Henke at her best."

—*Katherine Sutcliffe*

"Rigo is my kind of hero. *Return to Paradise* swept me away!"

—*Virginia Henley*

In *Paradise & More,* "Shirl Henke goes big time with a grand and glorious novel of Columbus's Spain and the swashbuckling New World. I couldn't stop reading!"

—*Bertrice Small*

"A riveting story about a fascinating period. I highly recommend *Paradise & More."*

—*Karen Robards*

"Warm, savvy and perceptive, Shirl Henke's wonderful plots and characters never let you down!"
—*Maggie Davis, aka Katherine Deauxville, Maggie Daniels*

THE CRITICS RAVE ABOUT SHIRL HENKE'S ROMANCES:

In *Return to Paradise,* "Shirl Henke once again demonstrates why she is one of the top authors of the genre!"
—Romantic Times

"Return to Paradise is a story you'll remember forever...definitely a book you'll keep to read again and again!"
—Affaire de Coeur

"Shirl Henke brilliantly captures the passions and prejudices of Spaniards and Apaches in *Night Wind's Woman."*
—Romantic Times

Shirl Henke's novels are "immensely satisfying...historical romance at its best!"
—Romantic Times

"Another of Shirl Henke's wonderfully intricate and extremely well-researched tales, *Paradise & More* is a sumptuous novel!"
—Affaire de Coeur

"Shirl Henke mesmerizes readers with the most powerful, sensual and memorable historical romances yet!"
—Romantic Times

BRIDE FOR SALE

"So that's how you see our marriage?" Rhys said. "You're going to whore for your precious family? For the money? Well, darling, you sure do charge a handsome price. If I live to be seventy, I figure it'll cost me about a thousand each time I take you."

Tory slapped him hard in pure reflex, stunned at his crudity. "How dare you—"

"I'll dare a lot, Tory, darling. I'll make you beg...." He let her go then, let her back away from him, trembling with fear.

"This is a farce, Rhys. You don't want me here." She gestured to the bead-tasseled bed. "You want a hostess, an ornament, something to show off to your new business associates."

Now his face took on a new expression, the slow, killing smile of a predator. "No chance of that, darling. I want you there, now. If this decor reflects how soiled you feel by marrying me, you'll just have to act the part—soiled dove. You, the whore. Me, the whoremaster."

TERMS OF SURRENDER

SHIRL HENKE

LEISURE BOOKS NEW YORK CITY

A LEISURE BOOK®

May 1993

Published by

Dorchester Publishing Co., Inc.
276 Fifth Avenue
New York, NY 10001

Printed in the United States of America.

For our friends at Romantic Times:
this book, written early in 1990,
would never have been completed without you.

TERMS OF SURRENDER

Acknowledgments

When we first decided to write a spin-off story from *Terms of Love*, my associate Carol J. Reynard and I decided to use not only the wonderfully colorful and exciting backdrop of Colorado, but to expand the scope to include the raucous silver boom of the 1880s in the southwestern part of the state. Of course, Cass and Steve Loring, Blackie Drago, and others from *Terms of Love* make cameo appearances in *Terms of Surrender*, but the story belongs to a roguish charmer from Wales and his lady, who is not at all accidentally named Victoria—for the Queen. The problems in characterization were unique, and I am once more indebted to Carol for helping me with Tory's development, as well as adding her usual "poison pen" critique to the whole story, without which I would be lost. She also handled all the background details regarding the elegant nineteenth-century furnishings in Dragon's Lair as well as double-checking my flora and fauna for the San Juan Mountains of Colorado.

As opposed to *Terms of Love*, where we used a great many historical figures and real cities, in *Terms of Surrender* we decided to create a fictional town, a composite of Ouray, Silverton, Lake City, and Gunnison, so that we could incorporate the most fascinating tales about all of them in our story. For the extensive research needed to create Starlight, Colorado, and its citizens, we are once more indebted to the Maag Library of Youngstown State University and most especially to the head of reference, Mrs. Hildegard Schnuttgen, the wizard of interlibrary loan.

Terms of Surrender is one of our most action-packed yarns yet, full of all sorts of mayhem—everything from fistfights to bushwackings, so we needed a "fight master" as well as a weapons expert to arm our good guys and our bad guys. My husband, Jim, blocked out the knife-fighting scenes and Rhys's exercises in boxing with various villains; he also howled with laughter at my execution of his instructions and corrected my tactical errors. A Western is not a Western without the right guns—be they long or short arms. We are once more indebted to our weaponry expert, Dr. Carmine V. DelliQuadri, Jr., D.O., for a job, as always, outstandingly done.

Chapter One

The Five Points, Winter 1873

When Barth got sick, Rhys learned to steal. Barth, with his twinkling green eyes and lilting Welsh voice, dead now all these weeks. Rhys had lost track of time since coming to New York. Each day blurred into the next. In the rabbit-warren alleys of Five Points, darkness and light were all the same. He shivered in his thin, coarse clothes as he hunkered in the shadows, remembering in spite of his promise to Barth that he would forget.

A year ago last spring it was, a sprightly golden day when he had left the coal mining town of Rhondda for the seaport city of Cardiff in Wales. With the sun warm on his back and the coal dust cleared from his lungs, Rhys Davies had walked briskly along the rutted trail, ignoring his blistered feet. Each step carried him farther from the pauper's grave of his sodden father. In Rhondda he was Tom Davies' boy, son of the town drunk, a scraggly orphan whose

13

mother had died when he was a toddler. Feeling the money in his pocket reassured him. In America no one would know about his past. In America he would become rich and powerful, then return for Tara.

Thinking of the mine owner's beautiful daughter had made the fourteen-year-old slow his step, but only for a moment. She was out of his reach now, but one day he would come back. *When he was rich*. Just then he heard the creak of an old wagon lumbering down the road.

"Want a lift, lad?" Barth had called out good-naturedly. That had been the beginning of their friendship. Like Rhys, Barth was on his way to Cardiff and thence to America. Like Rhys, he had toiled in the mines, but for much longer. At 37 he had the black cough bad, but he had saved enough money to see him to the fabled city of New York. Rhys' small stake had come from Tara, who was afraid of her father's retribution against her youthful sweetheart. She had pressed the cash into his hand and begged him to flee before her father's men beat him for daring to court the mine owner's daughter.

Such grand plans Rhys and Barth had made! The filthy, sweltering hold of the steamer crossing the Atlantic had not daunted them; New York did. It was much larger and richer than Cardiff, but the wide boulevards, four-horse coaches, and richly dressed pedestrians were far away from the New York where the new immigrants lived. A world away.

With what little money they had left between them after purchasing passage, Rhys and Barth rented a small room on East 4th Street, bare and cheerless but clean. Barth, whose English was passable, found a job as a liveryman and Rhys took on the ill-paying task of street sweeper. Evenings were spent on the banks of the East River gathering the mint

14

leaves that grew wild there. These they cleaned and bunched, then sold to fancy uptown hotels for extra money. As Barth scrimped and dreamed of better days, Rhys practiced his English.

The boy could still remember the day he had felt certain that Barth was going to die. Last fall when the winter winds began to shake around the corners of the shabby buildings on 4th Street, Barth's cough, quiet over the summer, resumed once more. During a bad spell at work he had spat up blood. The stable owner, fearful of the dread consumption, dismissed the Welshman. Within two weeks their savings were gone and the landlord evicted them. Winter grew fierce with icy rain that froze the thin clothes to their backs. Rhys' pitiful earnings as a street sweep were not enough for decent lodging, so they gravitated south, each room they rented more meager and cold than the one before it. The pair finally ended up in a dreadful alley called "Murderer's Row" in the basement of an old tenement given over to thieves and prostitutes. If Rhys thought the coal mines of Wales dark and dangerous, by comparison the Five Points of New York made them seem like paradise.

Their tiny room, with its chill earthen floor, quickly filled with water when the ice melted in the gutters outside. One drunk, passed out in the next cubicle, drowned in a foot of water as the thawed sewage slowly seeped into the basement. No one removed the body for a week. Mercifully, the weather again turned bitter cold and froze the corpse before the smell drove Rhys and Barth into the streets.

Barth coughed up dark, then bright red blood. Rhys tried begging from frock-coated bankers on Broadway, but the boy with the thick Welsh accent found them less than generous. A financial panic was in full swing, and the city's slums were overflowing with foreigners, whom many Americans blamed for their economic woes.

Rhys turned to watching the deft pickpockets work amid the elegant swells uptown and tried his hand at it. He barely escaped a caning on his first foray, but, desperate for food and rent money, he gave up his totally inadequate job sweeping and turned to practicing the art of thievery.

The open produce stalls run by Italian grocers were the easiest pickings, the German butcher shops the most difficult. The Welshmen ate a vegetarian diet most days. But one night Rhys got lucky and snitched a wallet and a gold watch. He and Barth would feast on a fat veal knuckle and a round loaf of pumpernickel.

Rhys burst into their room with his prizes to find Barth unmoving on a pile of filthy rags in the corner. One touch to the ice cold face told a boy long accustomed to death that his friend was gone. The stiff, quiet dignity of Barth's emaciated body racked the youth's soul as no other death ever had. He huddled with the body through the night, the veal and pumpernickel forgotten.

The following afternoon the old Irishman who managed the tenement came to collect his rent. He sent for the police to take the body away. Rhys, drained of grief, had watched numbly with dry eyes. He never learned where Barth was buried. Two days later the dazed youth had been evicted.

Huddled in the corner with the cold February wind scouring his hands and face, Rhys tried to forget that Barth was dead and he was alone. If only he could focus on Wales and Tara, but his limbs were cramped and his stomach growled, dragging him back to the present. He had not eaten all day. He stood up and searched the narrow patch of sky above the three-foot-wide alley. Full dark soon, it was time to be on the prowl.

Barth's fine dreams made Rhys bold. He cut across Worth Street to Broadway and began to stroll in the lanky, cocky manner he had adopted in defiance of the slums. He was too big to slide into the shadows easily, yet too young to be welcomed into the street gangs. Barth had taught him the basics of box fighting. Rhys Davies could give a good account of himself when cornered, but it was too dangerous to fight, if a fight could be avoided. He worked after dark, earning enough by pilfering to eat and even buy a pair of decent shoes at a second-hand shop on Chatham Square. Most immigrant children in the slums went barefoot in blistering heat and icy cold.

"If I'm ever to return for Tara, I have to get some money, real money, not just enough for food," he whispered aloud in the gathering darkness, practicing his English. He had a good ear and spent as much time as he could uptown, where the "real" Americans lived. He wanted to emulate their speech as well as lift their purses.

A sharp growl in his concave belly quickly banished grandiose thoughts about the future. Then he saw a man stepping from the doorway of a posh drinking establishment. Dressed in a thick fur coat and sporting an elegant hat, he weaved his way unsteadily down the street toward a hansom.

Timing was all. With a quick glance right and left, Rhys sprang into action, covering the distance on the sparsely populated street in a rapid zigzag until he bumped the larger, older man against a lamp post with a resounding whump. One deft hand reached inside the warm coat while the other appeared to be steadying the winded man. Rhys felt the bulge of leather in the left front pocket and expertly freed it.

Mumbling an apology, he raced off in the opposite direction, thinking himself well away. The sot was too far in his cups to miss his wallet until he arrived home and tried to pay the hansom driver. Suddenly a whistle shrilled in the night air.

Police! Seemingly out of nowhere a hand grabbed his frayed collar. Lashing out in blind panic, Rhys knocked it away. The cloth of his thin coat ripped, leaving the blue-uniformed man holding the scrap as Rhys rounded the corner, heading for the dark, narrow rabbit warrens of Five Points. When the six-story bulk of the old tenement loomed ahead of him, he slowed, clutching the wallet to his heaving chest. His lungs gulped in the cold, fetid air.

Within ten minutes he was haggling with old Mick Drewery for a night's lodging and a greasy meal. "I can pay, man, but you'll not be robbin' me," he protested as the Irishman impassively held out a meaty red palm for the half dollar he had demanded.

Rhys ignored the feel of a man brushing against him, thinking him intent on reaching the bar for a drink. Then the back of his neck prickled as a cold, scratchy piece of cloth was laid on his bare skin. "An exact fit if I do say so myself, boyo." The voice was thick with an Irish accent, low and musical, and it belonged to a policeman.

Rhys turned to the constable, a big man who stood solidly between him and the nearest exit, the incriminating piece of torn cloth once again in his hand.

"You'll be comin' with me, lad. No trouble now, hear?" Although he had a fat truncheon at his hip, the big man made no threatening gestures, just took Rhys's thin arm in a surprisingly gentle grip and ushered him from the saloon to where another constable waited nervously.

"Another waif for yer sister, Liam?" his partner queried sourly.

"Mayhap, then agin, mayhap not," was the easy reply.

Rhys felt his knees weaken as he thought of the crowded city prison where men, women, and children competed with the rats for rotten swill and lived in their own excrement. Five Points was a sewer, but at least he could walk out of it now and again.

As they escorted the morose youth down the street, the two uniformed officers seemed to be pondering what to do with him.

"How old might you be, boy?" the Irishman asked.

His short, thin companion snickered. "Old enough ta hold his own at the workhouse, I'll warrant."

Sensing animosity in the American and perhaps the smallest bit of Celtic kinship in the Irishman, Rhys looked at him and replied, "Fourteen last summer."

The Yankee constable gave a snort. "Ha! Likely. He's as big as me 'n' well done growin', Liam."

"Don't be gettin' too sure of that," Liam replied shrewdly, measuring the disjointed way the boy's hands and feet seemed fitted to his emaciated body. "I expect this one'll fill out a head taller."

Since Rhys at five-feet-nine was already taller than his antagonist, he sensed a frisson of anger flicker from the sour Yankee to the genial Irishman.

Feeling Rhys's bony arm, Liam asked, "And when is it you ate last?"

"Yesterday. I was just gettin' supper when you came on me," he replied defensively. He felt oddly embarrassed that anyone should know how poorly he survived.

"Gettin' yer supper with some decent man's money," the shorter policeman accused, patting the wallet he had taken from the boy.

"Be on with you 'n' return the money to that *dacent* man, Robert. I don't doubt he's sobbed himself into a thirst by now and'll be needin' his money to replenish his fluids," Liam replied with sarcasm.

"Yer a fool 'n' yer sister, too, takin' in this trash. He'll cut yer throat fer a loaf of bread." With a sigh of disgust, Robert took off, obeying his superior much against his will.

Rhys watched him depart, feeling mightily relieved. At least he was not bound for the workhouse. The Irishman had a sister who took in street children. Once, two richly dressed Mission Society ladies had visited him and Barth, bringing food. They were kind, he supposed, even if they did spout overmuch about being "born again." But he and Barth had been forced to move just after that and never saw them again. He forced himself to look up at the big, bluff man's ruddy face. "You takin' me to where them rich ladies make you pray before they feed you?"

Liam O'Hanlon let out a chuckle. "You might not be too far from the truth there, lad, but as to rich— the only Irish in New York who're rich've quit bein' Irish. It's a funny accent you have, boy. Where might you be from? You're not a Scot, are you?"

"I'm Welsh," Rhys replied in affront.

"Any kin in this country?"

"Not anymore. There was one . . . friend, but he's gone now." The boy put his head down and refused to volunteer more.

The constable considered Rhys as they walked. The neighborhood changed slightly as they moved up Broadway and turned west onto a narrow side street. Around the next block stood a white clapboard building, two stories high with a rambling, seedy look to it. Set back off the street, it boasted a tiny patch of yard in front and a vacant mud lot next door. On the wrought-iron arch above the front gate were the words St. Vincent's Roman Catholic Orphanage, Sisters of Charity of St. Vincent de Paul.

"Sisters! Yer sister's a sister?" Rhys croaked. In Wales, where the rich were Established Church and the lower classes Nonconformists, everyone looked with suspicion on popery.

"Frances Rose, the sainted woman, is both, yes, boyo. Me sister 'n' a nun besides. I think if you'll be givin' her half a chance, you'll like her."

On shaky legs Rhys climbed the creaking wooden steps. Even if they were papists, this place looked infinitely better than the workhouse.

As they walked through the front door, a squeal of delight erupted from little Sandra Ruth Burns who catapulted into Liam O'Hanlon's arms. Sister Elizabeth Mary peered down the long, narrow hallway toward the front of the building. "Your brother's back, Sister, and from the look of him, he's got a brute in tow this time," she said apprehensively. Ever since they'd taken in Evan Manion, the thin young nun had grown increasingly unhappy about the older boys Liam brought them.

Wiping her hands carelessly on her frayed blue-gray skirts, Frances Rose turned from the kettle of stew she was stirring and squinted down the hall, waiting for Liam. He handed Sandra Ruth a sweet and shooed her off. As he entered the bright light of the kitchen, his sister asked, "And who might we be havin' here?" She pulled a pair of bent spectacles from her pocket and put them on. They hung precariously on the end of her round, short nose.

"Go on, introduce yerself, lad," Liam coached sternly.

Although the room was warm, Rhys was aware of the even warmer flesh exposed on the back of his neck. He felt branded. "Rhys Davies, ma'am—I mean Sister, or whatever yer called," he added with a hint of defensive surliness as he stared at her imposing headdress with its starched winged coronet.

Sister Frances Rose O'Hanlon was a small, square woman with a bulldog face and steady gray eyes that could cut through diamond. Her mere presence in a room full of shrieking boys brought absolute silence in seconds. Feisty, stubborn, and shrewd, the nun had a heart as wide as the East River.

"I'm called Sister Frances Rose," she announced briskly, ignoring his rudeness. "This quaking aspen next to me is Sister Elizabeth Ann, and it's right pleased we are to meet you, Rhys Davies. Might you be wantin' a bit of this stew? I was just puttin' the finishing touches to the seasoning. It's for tommorow's midday meal, but a taste now wouldn't hurt. You look to be needin' some solid food," she added, answering her own question as she dished up a heaping bowl.

The fidgety thin nun, also wearing the intimidating starched cap and faded blue habit, motioned for Rhys to sit at the scarred wooden table in the center of the room. Wrinkling her nose at the aroma of his filthy clothes, Elizabeth Ann announced, "I'll see to some bath water," then left the room.

Sister Frances Rose placed the bowl before him. At first he gulped the scalding chunks of meat and vegetables, almost swallowing them whole, ignoring his burning mouth to assuage the even fiercer burning in his belly. Finally, noting two pairs of neat black shoes planted firmly on either side of his chair, he glanced up, first at the constable, then the nun.

"Ain't we to say a prayer or somethin'?" he asked, wiping his mouth with a filthy coat sleeve. "Them Mission Society ladies used to make me sing," he offered, looking nervously at the heavy plaster crucifix hanging across the room on one dingy whitewashed wall. He felt immediate kinship for the hapless figure on the cross.

Liam chuckled and Frances Rose joined in. "I think in this case the Lord can wait for his thanks until you're fed and bathed," she replied drily.

The bathing was not all that bad, especially considering that he had a full stomach to fortify him. In fact, when the small chubby boy named Paul brought him a pair of well-mended but clean pants and a soft cotton shirt, Rhys felt almost respectable. Some of the old dreams he and Barth had shared resurfaced as he dressed and slicked back his hair, a useless task. The unruly brown curls would never obey a comb. Sighing, he gave himself a final inspection at the cracked mirror in the small washroom and then followed Paul to Sister's office.

Liam had left. As Rhys looked at the book-lined walls and the saints' statues that filled the cluttered room, his nervousness returned. The toughlooking little nun stood up and from her full five feet inspected him. Seemingly approving what she saw, she nodded, and her starched white headdress flapped ever so slightly.

"Liam says you're Welsh and that you've been in this country scarce a year. You're all alone and live by stealing around the Five Points area." Frances Rose sat down behind her battered pine desk and motioned the shuffling boy to take a chair.

Rhys sat stiffly. "I stole to live, Sister. I had an honest job as a sweeper until Barth got sick . . ." The words poured from him, defensively at first.

Then the dam burst in a torrent, aided by a few shrewd prodding questions from the old nun. Rhys finished his tale by saying honestly, "I'm grateful for the clothes 'n' the food." He hesitated then, for she had asked little, and he had volunteered much. "Do I got to become a Catholic to stay here?"

A smile twitched at the corners of her jowly cheeks. "What faith was your family, Rhys?"

"Oh, the miners' families about Rhondda were Methodists, a few Presbyterians. My ma, she died when I was a mite, she was Methodist. My pa's only religion was what he found at the bottom of an ale bucket," he added bitterly. "Guess I ain't got no church."

"Did you learn to read and write in Wales?"

"A little, but only in the Welsh," he replied. "I was sent to work in the mines when I was eight." Again he looked at the books along the walls behind her desk. "All the men who were rich, who had the power, they were the readers."

"You want to have the power, and you believe to be gettin' it, you have to read books?" she asked, following his keen blue eyes as they roved around the room.

"Aye. I want to go home someday—to show Tara's father that I'm good enough for her—*rich* enough," he added emphatically.

Frances Rose nodded sagely. So that was the lay of the land, was it now? "Wales is a long way from here, Rhys," she said softly, remembering a childhood long ago in a green valley in the south of Ireland. "Few of us ever go home. Maybe the Lord has a purpose for you here instead."

"So I gotta become a papist," he said with a resigned sigh, not really all that upset about it. How bad could it be? "Do ya make us sing psalms

24

and memorize whole chapters in the New Testament like the Mission Society ladies?"

"Well, not right off, mind you. We'll leave the choir singing to the choristers for now, and before you can memorize anything, you'll be needin' to learn to read and write in English."

Rhys looked into her smiling gray eyes and said, "Sister, ya got a deal."

As it turned out, Rhys possessed a beautiful baritone voice and did sing in Sister Mary Joseph's choir, but not until he had overcome several obstacles at St. Vincent's, first among them one mean street tough named Evan Manion.

Like Rhys, Evan was a thief rescued by Liam's charity, but unlike Rhys, Evan had been a junior member of a gang and had quickly seen his opportunity to organize some of the younger boys at the orphanage into a coterie of admirers. At the end of Rhys's first week, after morning Mass, which he found fascinating, he followed the other boys from the church into the dining room and took his usual seat. After the prayers, he dug into his steaming bowl of hot oats and milk. When the children queued up with their empty dishes to place them on the table by the kitchen door, Rhys's bowl suddenly went flying, knocked from his hand by Manion.

As Rhys stooped to pick up the pieces, his face grew beet red in embarrassment. Then he glanced up at his tormentor. Manion was smiling. With blue eyes narrowed, the younger boy whispered low, "You done that apurpose."

"What if I did?" Evan answered flippantly, boldly sauntering away.

Sisters Frances Rose and Elizabeth Ann watched the exchange from across the room. "I told you those older boys from Five Points wouldn't work out. They're a terrible influence on the younger children. Why, yesterday I caught Frankie Lueger chewing tobacco! He was green as spring apples and told me Evan had made him do it," Elizabeth Ann said in outrage. Frances Rose only nodded and watched Rhys finish his cleaning up.

During the noon meal Elizabeth Ann came rushing into the Mother Superior's office with a squeal of hysteria. "They're fighting—that new Welsh boy and the Manion bully!"

Calmly Frances Rose stood up, picked up a solid hickory cane from behind her desk, and headed for the dining room. If she had any fears about the thin Davies boy holding his own with the heavyset Manion, they were quickly put to rest.

Rhys's instincts had been sharpened by his years on New York's streets. When Evan had again tripped him at lunch and this time sent him and his food flying, Rhys had come up covered with sticky gravy. Sisters or no Sisters, he had to act! He turned on his tormentor with several hard, fast punches. Rhys's lessons in box fighting, Barth's bequest, were yielding dividends.

"Quite a left hand, that one has," Sister Frances Rose said with smug satisfaction.

"You knew he could fight," Elizabeth Ann accused.

"Let's just say I was hopin' he'd be the Lord's instrument for a bit of chastisement." Frances Rose watched Rhys deliver a series of short jabs with his right hand, then knock Evan down with a powerful left. "Me own uncle Sean couldn't have done it better! He was a lefty, too."

Elizabeth Ann crossed herself in exasperation. "Your father a gambler, your uncle a box fighter, and your elder brother a hard-rock miner in that

26

Godless Western wilderness! How did you ever come to your holy vocation, Sister?"

"Maybe I had to join the order just to pray for all my dead relatives!" Frances Rose snapped. As she marched toward the boys now thrashing on the floor, their respective cheering sections parted like the Red Sea before the upraised arm of Moses. The room grew deadly quiet, and both boys became aware of the magnitude of their infraction. In the presence of the Wrath of the Lord, they drew apart and struggled to their feet to face her.

Rhys had a sore arm and a few cuts and bruises, but Evan was definitely in worse condition. His lip was split, his right eye blacked, and his nose was spurting blood. Sister Frances Rose calmly shooed the children away, sent Sister Mary Joseph for clean water and rags, then handed Evan a large napkin to stanch the flow of blood from his nose. "Probably broken," she said dismissively. On his flat homely face, it would scarce be noticed. Anyway, she felt certain he would get far worse scars in the future. "See Father Ryan tomorrow and make your confession," she instructed him.

Turning to Rhys, she motioned with her hickory cane for him to follow her. Once in her office, she looked at the miserable boy, who shuffled, certain of eviction from the only sanctuary he had ever known. "You have a natural way about you, Rhys Davies. All the young ones will be followin' you now, not Evan. Maybe it's not so good, you in the same room with the wee ones learning their letters. I think you should not be goin' to class."

"But I need to learn English readin'," Rhys protested.

"I can teach you readin' faster than the first primer allows. And in turn, you can sort of keep an eye on

27

Evan and a few other of his bully boys for me." A
slow smile spread across the little nun's face. "But
first, I think I'd better be teachin' you one or two
fine points about the manly art." The young Welshman simply blushed as Sister Frances Rose assumed
a left-handed boxing stance. "Now, lad, when you
follow a jab with your left, you have a habit of
dropping yer left hand just before you throw it.
Leaves you wide open for a straight right. Uncle
Sean, God rest him, would have knocked your block
off."

Education in the slums of New York, as in the
Welsh coal-mining districts, was mostly a luxury of
the rich. And Rhys did want desperately to be rich.
The clever old nun offered him his chance, and he
seized upon it like a drowning man clinging to a
lifeboat.

He read late into the nights, discovering a whole
new world filled with marvelous people, from Julius
Caesar to St. Francis of Assisi, from Christopher
Columbus to George Washington. But above all, he
loved tales of the West and its golden promise. Sister
Frances Rose herself fueled his ardor for striking out
toward the clean air of the Rockies. She told him stories and read him letters from her deceased brother
Rory, who had struck it rich in Colorado's gold-rush
of 1859 and endowed St. Vincent's Orphanage with
his fortune.

One day, as the young Welshman sat staring out
at New York's grimy skyline of distant church spires
and dilapidated tenements, Frances Rose watched
him from the door of her office. He had been with
them for four years now. Liam had been right about
his growth. At eighteen he stood over six feet, with
a broad chest and lean, muscular frame. The skin-

ny waif had finally grown into his hands and feet. Although big, he was graceful in his movements. The dancing lights in his dark blue eyes matched the enchanting lilt of his husky, melodic voice, which had never quite lost its Welsh accent.

"Dreamin' of that pot of gold again, are you?" she asked.

Rhys turned and looked pensive for a moment. "No, only thinking of how dirty the city is here and how clean it is uptown. I made a delivery for Mr. Cavandish this morning—to the Astors' house on Fifth Avenue at 34th Street. They had me carry the boxes in. Some fancy new glasses. I put them in their china pantry. Pantry! It was as big as our whole kitchen, nothing but floor-to-ceiling cabinets with glass doors, filled with pretties—even a cut-glass bowl big enough to drown in! Then one of Mrs. Astor's daughters came in. She was dressed in pale blue silk, Sister—silk before the noon hour!"

"And then you had to take the wagon back down the avenue to this," she concluded softly. "Was she as pretty as Tara, Rhys?"

His face grew puzzled for a moment, then he chuckled. "Even prettier, I think. Lordy, it's been so long since last I saw Tara . . ." He shrugged. "She's long wed by now. She was a full year older than me and her father's only heir."

"You've let your dreams of returning to Wales die, but what of other dreams, Rhys?" In recent months, as he took jobs outside the orphanage, she had sensed a restlessness in him. It was time to let go, but it saddened her.

He smiled and melted her heart. "Dreams I have aplenty, and it's you who's responsible for most of them."

"They must have another Blarney Stone in Wales,

29

you young rascal." The nun sat down at a small table with a threadbare ivory linen cloth on it. She deftly flipped and shuffled a deck of cards. "Now, tell me your plans while I deal us a hand of five-card stud, my favorite way—first and last cards in the hole."

"You always used to win," he said as if suddenly surprised by the fact that his companion was growing old.

She chuckled when she dealt the second cards, a deuce for him, a queen for herself. "What better way to teach an ignorant lad such as yourself mathematics? Look how well you've learned! Pay attention now. It's my bet. If I win this, you must go to Mass tomorrow—and make confession to Father Ryan tonight."

"Done," he agreed with an expansive wave of his hand.

"Am I just imaginin' you have lots to unburden to the good father, especially about that MacGregor hussy at the tavern down the hill?"

"Merely a few innocent beers with a friend," he evaded.

She snorted in disbelief. From worshiping fine ladies afar, Rhys had changed tack the past year. The girls of the city, pretty, young, and far too light of skirt to ever be suitable, found the handsome Welshman all too appealing. Just so none of those entrapped him in marriage! She looked at him with penetrating gray eyes and said, "I trust you'll be confessin' your 'innocent beers' to Father Ryan."

"Only if you've paired up that lady," he replied with a grin as he looked at her queen.

"There are more ladies in this deck than the likes you've been consortin' with here of late." She dealt the third card and they again bet. Frances Rose now had a trey with her six, no help for her queen in a five-card game. Rhys was a born gambler, just like her beloved father, with the same agile mind, the same expressionless face when he played. If only he had learned her father's love of the Church. But since the day of his baptism, Rhys's religious devotion was at first only to conform, then later to please her. She had accepted the fact with good grace, praying to St. Jude, the patron of impossible tasks, to locate just one religious bone in the youth's body. Now that she sensed that his time to leave them was near, she realized that his spiritual welfare was out of her hands.

Shrugging, she dealt their fourth card. Rhys had a jack and a three showing with his deuce. She drew another six and increased her bet. He called and waited calmly for the last card, down like the first one. Suppressing a snort of triumph, she looked at her last hole card—the queen of spades! Two pair. She raised.

He called her and raised. She saw his raise and raised again. He saw that and raised a second time. Even though they were playing for pennies, which always went into the orphanage's coffers, she became agitated. The devilish bluffer. She saw his last raise and called. He flipped over his down cards. Two more deuces!

Sister Frances Rose O'Hanlon decided that when St. Jude was too busy on Rhys's journey west St. Christopher, patron of wayfarers, would take up the slack. And if help did not come from the patron saints, the old nun thought wryly, *The devil does take care of his own!*

Chapter Two

Starlight, Colorado, 1879

Victoria Laughton was glad to be home. Her soft turquoise eyes swept over the comforting familiarity of her very own bedroom. After a year at Miss Jefferson's Academy in St. Louis sleeping with three other girls, this privacy was sheer bliss. Her hand trailed lovingly across the crisp lace edges of the starched doily on her bedside table, then moved to plump one of the blue silk pillows on her bed. The room was utterly feminine and delicate, much like the girl with her light blonde hair and porcelain complexion, tinged ever so discreetly pink at the tops of her high cheekbones. Her features were surprisingly well formed for one so young, patrician yet possessing an inner strength. Her mouth gave a hint of petulance when she was denied her way.

As the eldest child and only daughter of Stoddard Laughton, the leading banker in Starlight, Victoria

Elizabeth Laughton was seldom denied anything. Even Miss Jefferson's Academy had been her choice. Her mother favored a more prominent school in Boston, but the Southern romance of the Confederate widow's institution in St. Louis appealed to Tory. She prevailed on Papa, who wanted her closer to home. Together they carried the day.

"I have the whole summer to spend here," she fairly squealed to her empty room, whirling in a graceful pirouette that sent her ruffled skirts swirling about her slim ankles. There would be parties, dances, picnics—and lots and lots of young men to escort her. After the regimentation of boarding school, she could scarcely wait for the summer social whirl to begin.

Last year Mama had said she was too young, but lots of the girls at Miss Jefferson's had gentlemen callers after their first year at the academy. She had learned dancing and playing the piano—not to mention painting lovely watercolors and planning table settings and menus for elegant dinners. She was being schooled to become a proper wife for a prominent man. Her youthful heart sang as she considered how much fun the next years would hold. She would accumulate suitors and weigh the attributes of each against the others'.

Papa would have to be convinced that she needed a new wardrobe, but her mother would be a willing ally there. She had brought back a trunk of pattern books from St. Louis. This isolated little town, nestled in the splendid fastness of the southwestern Colorado Rockies, was so behind the times. "I shall become the fashion arbiter," she pronounced with youthful bravado and set out to speak to Hedda Laughton about her plans.

Sanders Laughton, like his elder sister, had been

sent away to complete his education at a fine prep school in Chicago. But unlike the naturally bright and vivacious Tory, who seemed to charm everyone and soak up book learning like a sponge, he had failed out after the first term. A second school, this time in Denver, had been tried. Again the slothful fourteen-year-old spent his time playing hooky. On Bock Beer Day, May 21st, he had been arrested for drunken conduct in the German-saloon district and again expelled. He was not glad to see Tory home, riding on a cloud of praise from her teachers. Everyone knew those dumb girls' schools were easier than a real course of study for men of business. But his parents were now making invidious comparisons between his performance and hers.

Still, Tory had always been his ally with Stoddard and Hedda. The siblings were only a year apart and as children had been close. He had always been able to persuade her to take the blame for his high jinks. Only when they were sent their separate ways this past year had his real troubles begun.

Hiding in the pantry, Sanders rummaged through the liquor cabinet with an occasional furtive glance over his shoulder. Snatching a bottle of sweet dark port, he slipped it beneath his coat. He liked it far better than the evil sour beers he'd been introduced to during his school days in Denver. It paid to have rich parents, he thought smugly as he headed for his room.

Cutting through the formal dining room on his way upstairs, he came upon Tory. It irritated him no end that at five feet two inches, his fine-boned sister was still as tall as he. When would he ever grow?

"Sanders, what are you doing here? I was looking for Mama." She noticed his pallor and the nervous way he ran his fingers through his baby-fine hair. This past year had been hard on him, the poor darling. "Are you all right? You look unwell," she said solicitously.

"I'm fine, just fine, Tory," he snapped. He felt the bottle beneath his arm slip a notch and knew he must get rid of her before she discovered his theft. "If you're looking for Mama, I saw her go into Papa's office a few minutes ago," he said slyly.

As she nodded and whirled toward the long hallway, he smiled to himself. Papa and Mama had been murderously angry when they had walked stiffly into the office. Tory had not been around the past months to see the rift between them. Spitefully, he hoped she would burst in on one of their "serious discussions" and be sent to her room with a severe reprimand as he had last week. Let her be the butt of their parents' ire for a change.

Victoria almost reached the study door in a headlong dash before her decorum lessons from Miss Jefferson's took over. A lady never rushes and is never out of breath. A lady always knocks and requests entry. She slowed her steps and straightened her shoulders, patting her hair to be certain it lay smoothly down her back. Then she raised her hand to knock.

The door was ajar just enough to admit sound from behind its three-inch walnut thickness. Her hand froze in midair as she heard her mother's voice, icy, cutting, and venomous—a tone unlike any Victoria had ever before heard from her cultured Bostonian Mama.

"You will remove that harlot from this town within the week, Stoddard. I do not ask this. I demand it. Either that or I shall take the children and return to Boston with them. I will not be publicly humiliated by your tawdry affair with a cheap entertainer!"

"You wouldn't dare. Think of the scandal of divorce," he replied disdainfully.

"The scandal of living in a community this size with your paramour is far greater," Hedda replied with frigid dignity.

Stoddard let out a mirthless chuckle. "What's your wish, my dear? To have me return to your bed? I thought not."

"It's one matter for you to vent your lusts discreetly, as do other gentlemen in town, but you've gone far beyond that, being seen escorting a cheap actress about the city, even dining in public with her. I will not be subject to gossip and humiliation!" Hedda's voice took on an edge of hysteria.

Stoddard retorted angrily, "Not nearly so humiliating as allowing me to touch that pristine ice castle you call a body. You'd hate that worse, Hedda."

"Don't threaten me, Stoddard. I've given you a son and a daughter—fine, beautiful children—your heirs. I've done my duty as your wife. Now I'll have my due respect, or"—she hesitated and then her voice became portentous— "I shall write Papa. As the United States Senator from Massachusetts, he has the full backing of President Hayes. If you ever hope to see your political ambitions realized, you won't cross me. Keep your disgusting carnal liaisons discreet or pay the consequences!"

Hearing her mother's voice grow louder as she neared the door, Victoria's frozen immobility broke. She bolted around the corner and raced for the servants' stairs. Blinded by her tears, she stumbled and scraped her shin on the rough wooden step, but did not feel the pain. Her world had just been torn apart. Her picture-book-perfect parents, the most elegant and congenial couple in all of Starlight's social echelon, were really a sham. Her father was infatuated with a harlot, and her mother was threatening to take her and Sanders off to gray old Boston! Shivering in fright, she threw herself across her bed and gave way to a torrent of weeping.

Sanders had watched from the end of the hall while Tory eavesdropped and then bolted off as if stung by a bee, practically falling up the back stairs. He didn't know what had set her off, but was disappointed that their parents had not caught her.

When Victoria sent word down that she was too fatigued to join them for dinner, Stoddard and Hedda allowed it. But when she failed to leave her room or eat anything on the tray sent up the following morning, Hedda grew worried.

"What is wrong with that girl? Mrs. Soames and Mrs. Everett are coming for tea this afternoon," she fretted to herself while the maid Bessie took the uneaten breakfast back to the kitchen.

"I think she's pouting because she heard you and Father fighting," Sanders said from his end of the lace-covered dining room table.

Hedda's fork clattered against her china plate as she skewered her son with icy aqua eyes. "What ever do you mean? When?"

The boy pretended innocence. "I saw you and Father go in the study like you always do before you 'discuss' something. She listened at the door for the longest time. I tried to get her to leave, but she shoved me away. Then she ran off crying like a banshee." He shrugged and excused himself from the table, watching her pale, bloodless hands clench and unclench on a linen napkin. His mother was so absorbed in her problem she had forgotten he was even present.

He wondered idly what the argument had been

37

about this time. Probably that actress from the Rose Theater. He had eavesdropped last week when Mrs. Goode had told Hedda oh-so-regretfully yet gleefully about his father's indiscretion. Well, now everyone in the house was on his mother's list, not just him. Whistling, he headed for the front door.

Hedda walked upstairs, gathering her courage to confront Victoria. She must compose herself first. Pausing at the top of the stairs, she rubbed her temples, careful not to disturb the perfectly coiffed pompadour of silver-streaked blonde hair. In her day, Hedda Lodge Laughton had been a beauty. At thirty-seven she was still striking in a brittle, cool way. Thinking of Stoddard and what his gross immorality had probably precipitated, she felt a surge of fresh anger infuse her.

Victoria was so immersed in her misery she didn't even hear the knock. When Hedda stepped into the room and softly called her name, Victoria turned from the window with a start. She had been gazing unseeingly out at the orchard behind their house. How badly her plans and dreams for the summer had gone awry! With a sob she launched herself into Hedda's arms.

Taking the child's tear-swollen face between her manicured hands, Hedda planted a cool, precise kiss on Victoria's forehead and then led her to sit on the edge of her rumpled bed. Making a small moue of distaste at the bed clothes, she said, "Victoria, you know a lady never lies abed and allows her room to become slovenly. You should have been up and dressed by now so Bessie could freshen the linens and straighten your room."

"I just couldn't face . . . everyone," the girl said forlornly.

Hedda knew that her worst fears were true. "So,

you eavesdropped at the study door yesterday like a common servant." She put her hand up for silence when Victoria began to protest. Walking imperiously toward the window, she gathered her scattered thoughts and decided on the direct approach, no matter how distasteful the task. The girl was fifteen. Perhaps it was just as well to get it over with a bit early.

Hedda turned and faced the child-woman crumpled like a lost waif on the edge of the bed. "It is unfortunate that you learned what you did yesterday," she began in a serene, detached tone, "but what's done is past. You need have no fear about scandal or leaving your home. Your father has amended his error."

"Then—then you and Father have made up? You love each other again?" There was a note of clear puzzlement in Victoria's eyes and voice.

Hedda's face became glacial. "Love. Pah! I shall have to pay more attention to the sort of drivel they allow you to read in school—and with whom you associate. Love is as mythological as those disgraceful Greek stories I found you reading last year."

"They were classical tales, Mother. Myths, yes, but not at all disgraceful," Victoria defended. Miss Wharton had given the girl a slim volume of Greek mythology, and she felt compelled to defend her beloved teacher. "Anyway, real love has nothing to do with mythology."

Hedda brushed that aside impatiently. "Pay attention to me! I'll tell you what is real, young lady. The kind of flowery sweetheart's love that every young girl daydreams of is very much a myth. Men, even those of the best class, do not give you bouquets and spout poetry to you in simple hopes of holding your hand." She paused a beat, then steeled herself

39

and asked, "What do you think a young lady must do on her wedding night?"

Victoria crimsoned in embarrassment. She really had no specific ideas about sex beyond a few chaste, stolen kisses boys had given her in the past year. But she had heard the muted whisperings of older girls at school, which always quieted when younger girls entered a room. She positively could not repeat any of *that* in front of her mother!

"I thought you abysmally ignorant, but it's just as well. I do not intend to go into any of the disgusting physical details. It'll be bad enough when the time comes. Only choose a man of discretion, and if you are clever and fortunate enough, he will quit his base rutting on you as soon as you are with child. It's a woman's duty to provide her husband a male heir, but if she endures his physical attentions beyond that, she's a fool."

Victoria looked at Hedda's flawless profile, the face tautened by stress into cold, harsh lines. The girl was hopelessly confused, yet her mother looked so forbidding. Gulping, she screwed up her courage and asked, "Is that why you and Father have separate bedrooms? Some of my friends parents sleep in one—"

"You are never to discuss sleeping arrangements— this family's or any other's—with any of your friends ever again!" Hedda interrupted with an imperious hiss. What had the child been discussing and with whom? Recovering her veneer of calm, Hedda instructed in reasoned, measured tones, "Men and women who are gentlemen and ladies never share a bedroom. That is how the lower classes live. Ladies do their duty and submit to their husband's needs until they produce children. Then a gentleman will seek to assuage his baser instincts elsewhere, not subject his wife to them."

Victoria was beginning to understand a few things. At least, she thought she was. "You mean there are some women who want men to . . . to . . ." She let her words fade in a misery of humiliation.

"Yes, but those women are not of our kind. They are uneducated, lower-class tradesfolk or, worse, harlots. A lady never enjoys being handled intimately by a man. It is simply a duty performed within the lawful bonds of matrimony."

"Then after that, husbands . . ." Victoria hesitated, unable to imagine her own father consorting with some dreadful Irish washerwoman or a harlot " . . . husbands take other women as lovers?"

"They discreetly visit places across town where there are women who can please them. Your father made a mistake, Victoria. He became infatuated with an actress, a vulgar, brassy young thing. He allowed people in Starlight to see them together in public places." She shuddered in fury, then said icily, "It will never happen again, I promise you. He has sent her away and will be most discreet from now on. Do you understand what I've been explaining to you? You are a lady and are expected to behave as such. In return you have the right to expect proper behavior from your future husband." She waited until Victoria nodded sadly. "Good. We will never speak of this subject again. I know I can rely on your common sense and ladylike behavior. Now bathe your face to take down that awful swelling, get dressed, and come downstairs. We're to have tea with several ladies from church this afternoon."

As Victoria watched her mother gracefully glide from the room, she felt numb. Her mind filled with a wild jumble of horrid images: her father, genial and indulgent, even if a bit stuffy and stern, the papa of her childhood, doing lustful, evil things with those awful women on Main Street! She had heard Sanders gossip about the red-light district. Then she was hit by yet another awful thought. Sanders would grow up to be like their father! Mother said all men had these base cravings. Trembling, she stood up, took a deep breath, and began to splash her swollen face with cool water.

That evening at the dinner table, Victoria observed her father and mother carefully. To her amazement, she could find not a hint of the chilling animosity she had heard behind the study door. They were smiling and gracious, directing bits of the polite dinner table small talk to her and Sanders as if nothing had happened. She was certain that Hedda had said nothing to Stoddard about her eavesdropping. Sanders was bored and asked to be excused before the dessert course, but that, like all else, was as predictable as snow in the Rockies.

Victoria tossed fitfully in bed that night. Rising early the next morning, she was starved, since she had been unable to eat much the preceding evening. She dressed quickly and slipped down the back stairs to beg a hot roll and a glass of fresh milk from their cook. Breakfast would not be served for at least another hour.

Just as she put her foot on the first riser, voices speaking in hushed whispers echoed up the bare narrow staircase.

Bessie the maid hissed, "She's leavin' on today's stage, I heard. I can't believe old man Laughton let her go so easy."

"Ha," scoffed the cook. "With her royal highness Mrs. Boston Royalty threatenin' him with her family tree? Flavia Goldstock's only an actress. The likes of them comes 'n' goes. She don't mean a fig to him. Now, his position here in Starlight and his place with the Republican Party in Denver, that means plenty."

The stage depot was a big brick building, two stories high with several professional offices upstairs above it. It was on Wheaton Street just off Main, a neighborhood where frock-coated businessmen drove to work and rough-looking stockmen and miners congregated to watch for the arrival of supplies. Wheaton Street was not an appropriate place for a fifteen-year-old girl to walk, especially unescorted. But some self-punishing instinct had led Victoria to slip out the back door of the modiste's shop on Vandementer Street and come to watch passengers purchase tickets for the afternoon stage to Denver.

She was nervous. If any of her father's friends saw her standing in the shadows of the alley and reported such to him, she would be in unthinkable trouble. *But I have to see her—to see if she's really leaving.* She also wanted to see what one of "those women" looked like.

Victoria despaired when the driver, a short, wiry man sporting a droopy handlebar mustache and an eight-foot blacksnake, came striding toward the coach and threw the mail sacks into the boot. He was leaving without any passengers! Just then a feminine voice with a decidedly Southern accent trilled out, "If you would be so kind, driver."

The little man turned and tipped his greasy battered hat, then took two heavy bags from a burly man standing beside the woman. As the little driver tossed the luggage into the boot with surprising ease, Victoria studied Flavia Goldstock, "actress."

She was tall and voluptuously proportioned. Her perfect hourglass figure was dramatically capped by a great mass of gleaming ebony hair, piled into artful curls clustered beneath a frilly concoction of a hat. Her red velvet dress was a bit heavy for the summer's day, but the immaculately made-up woman seemed impervious to heat.

Victoria could see that Flavia wore face paints, but not the gaudy sort she had expected. At least the actress did not look like the women on the lower end of Main Street who worked in the saloons! Everyone could tell what they were. As Flavia Goldstock was helped into the coach by the big man, Victoria caught her last fleeting glance. What would make a woman be so brazen as to perform on a stage? Or, worse yet, to lead men—good men like her father— to ruin their reputations by consorting with her? Did her father actually sleep in the same bed with that woman? Victoria almost gasped aloud in guilt for her rambling imagination.

"Look at her, bold as brass! After all her shameful capering on and off stage in a decent town," Charity Soams said.

Victoria jumped in horror as panic flooded her . . . Her mother's best friend stood just around the corner! The girl slunk back into the shadows as Esther Smithton, Charity's sister-in-law and another social arbiter of Starlight, spoke.

"Well, at least she *is* leaving without any further scandal. Not a man in town was safe with her around. They all went to the Rose Theater to see her perform Shakespeare. Ha! To strut about in boy's tights, that's what the performing really was!"

"I wonder what will become of her. She lost her manager here. Died of some heart ailment, they said," Charity whispered bemused.

Esther snorted, "Well, it's no worry for decent folks whatever befalls her, but the devil does take care of his own."

Chapter Three

Starlight, Colorado, 1884

The brisk spring wind whipped his coat collar against his neck, but the sun on his back was warm as the lone rider pulled his flat-crowned hat more securely onto his head. He was a big man, broad-shouldered and long-legged, dusty and tired after riding all the way from Denver southwest through the jagged beauty of the Rockies.

After turning his shiny black stallion down Main Street, he surveyed the crowd, noting through eyes half-closed against the gusty wind, that the town was large. A public lending library stood on one corner and a brick hotel on the other. A row of elegant gingerbread homes had welcomed him from the upper end of the street. He could hear the dull roar emanating from the saloons and sporting houses several blocks down. This was still the respectable section of Main. He watched a handsome open landau pulled by a pair of matched grays go by, the

46

horses as impeccably turned out as their driver. A squat glass-fronted frame building across the street caught his eye. The title *Plain Speaker* with the words "Michael Manion, Editor and Publisher" proclaimed it the city's newspaper. "A library, a newspaper, and a fine hotel. Maybe Starlight is more than another fly-by-night boom town, Blackjack," he muttered to the stallion as he looked at the well-dressed people. He'd learned to judge men and women from the cut of their clothes and the way they walked.

The town had promise, definite promise. Blackie Drago had been right. This was the place for him to begin building his new life. Working as a faro dealer in Denver the past five years, he had accumulated a sizable poke. How could he invest it to best advantage here? As he mulled another question, a sign in the barber shop window next to the newspaper caught his eye: "Went to bury my wife. Be back soon." Business must indeed be brisk!

Chuckling over the scrawled note, he considered the newspaper publisher's name and wondered idly if he was any kin to Evan Manion, who now languished in a penitentiary in upstate New York. Out West a man often lived down a bad family name left back east. The West was a place of infinite possibilities, but the stranger believed in playing the odds. He patted the money belt at his waist and reined in at a long row of saloons. This was his part of town . . . but only for the present.

Just as he swung one leg carelessly over Blackjack to dismount, a shot erupted from inside a small, dingy saloon across the street. Reaching for the Winchester '73 on his saddle, he pulled it free and stood beside his horse, watching the swinging doors of the Forty Rod Saloon. A tall, thin man dressed in miner's flannel and denims emerged with a Colt in one hand.

It slipped from nerveless fingers as the man slumped against the door frame, then dropped like a sack of wheat into the dusty street, stone cold dead. A dog yipped and broke free from his leash, intent on investigating the warm corpse pooling blood onto the earth. Dragging an old rope, he approached his quarry. Another shot whistled from the saloon and the yellow cur seemed propelled sideways as he was knocked into the street near the dead man's head.

His owner, a burly brute with wild black hair and a long, mangy beard came shambling up cursing at the top of his very considerable voice. The busy street had cleared like a chessboard after a checkmate. No one emerged from the saloon as the giant bellowed, "Ya shot my dawg! 'N' he wuz worth two o' my wives, that damned Ute and th' Frenchie— 'n' I et all four o' them! Git out here 'n' fix ta meet yore maker."

A woman's shriek from the saloon pierced the air. A short, pudgy man wearing the grimy remnants of a Confederate officer's uniform shoved her in front of him as he walked onto the street. He shot at the enraged animal lover but missed as the garishly bedecked whore tripped, bumping his arm.

Across the street, the stranger was slowly retreating, leading his horse toward an alley between two saloons, his rifle trained on the confrontation he hoped to avoid. The bummer fired again, but this time his liquor-fogged brain had as much to do with his missing the looming target as did his captive. He was dead drunk, one of the seemingly endless supply of rebel veterans who had drifted across the West for the past two decades, embittered, rootless, and often dangerous.

The giant lunged forward and grabbed the bummer with one meaty fist, tossing the woman aside as if she were a stick doll. Just as the contest looked as though it were over, another shot whizzed past the stranger, coming from the alley behind him. It grazed his hat, knocking it from his head. Crouching low, he spun around and leveled the Winchester on another bummer.

The second man, equally as drunk as his companion, took note for the first time of the stranger between him and the fight. "Didn't mean ya no harm, mister. Phil th' Cannibal's got my pard 'n' he's gonna do fer 'im if 'n I don't—"

A scream followed by a sickly crack interrupted the man's slurred speech. Phil of the voracious appetite had snapped the killer's back and dropped him unceremoniously to the dirt of the street. The whore, now on all fours, whimpering, began to back away from the enraged brute. Ignoring her, he turned toward the two men in the alley across the street and began to lumber in their direction.

"Where the hell's your sheriff?" the stranger asked. "More lead's been spread across this street than dug out of the Rockies." He turned from the drunk to the giant, sensing that the brute would not be swayed by sweet reason.

"Yew crazy galoot! Yew kilt Asa like yer dog would a damnblasted cat."

"Asa warn't worth my dawg on th' best day he lived. Neither er you." Phil took a step into the alley and Blackjack shied nervously. Ignoring the stranger, the giant continued toward his shivering victim, who began firing his Confederate Colt wildly. One shot hit the side of the building, sending a spray of splinters to speckle Phil's black beard. The next shot came perilously close to the stranger, still trapped between the combatants. The tall man ducked and swore, then swatted his valuable mount's rump to send him into the street, free of the impending fracas.

"Dammit, man, run, don't shoot if you can't bring him down," he yelled. The terror-glazed eyes of the bummer fixed on the man yelling at him. The drunk's gun swerved dead center on the stranger. The split second it took him to pull the trigger gave his unintended target time to fire. The bummer was flung backward onto a heap of trash.

Phil, now deprived of his prey, roared, "He wuz my meat! I kill my own varmints. Eat 'em, too," he added with a wolfish grin as he appraised the long, well-muscled frame of the younger man.

The stranger swung his rifle in an arc that brought the barrel into contact with the charging brute's jaw. The crack of splintering bone was unmistakable. As Phil began to sink to his knees in a daze, the "innocent bystander" retreated hastily from the alley.

"You killed Salk and cold-cocked Phil the Cannibal! Son of a bitch, handsome, some day's work." The purple-clad whore, a bit the worse for her contact with the reddish Colorado earth, sauntered up, boldly inspecting him. Before he could issue a disclaimer or remove himself from her odorous presence, several well-dressed men seemed to appear out of nowhere.

"Good day, sir. I am Willoughby Johnson, Mayor of Starlight, and this is Stoddard Laughton, President of the Union Trust Bank. We are in your debt, Mr.—?"

"Davies, Rhys Davies," the stranger said, a white smile slashing his tanned face as he shook hands with the two men. "As to being in my debt, I sincerely doubt it. I just got caught in the cross fire."

"He saved my life!" the whore interjected. Rhys backed off a step lest she attempt to reward him with an embrace. Both local men ignored her.

The stocky yet dignified banker, Laughton, said smoothly, "These ruffians have been a problem here of late. We recently lost our sheriff," he added, eyeing Rhys's Winchester '73 lever-action rifle and sizing up the tall, imposing figure of the tough-looking drifter. "We could use a man with your nerve."

"Pay's good. Thirty a week and your meals at the jail included—from Mrs. Winter's restaurant, best home cooking in town," the mayor boasted.

Rhys shrugged, "I'm not interested, gentlemen, even though I'm sure Mrs. Winter's food is excellent."

"We'll double the money," Laughton said with intensity.

The drifter turned and reached for the dragging reins of his horse. "Sorry, gents. I'm not a lawman," he replied with a grin. "Too often find myself on the other side. You better do something with Phil before he wakes up—looking for a snack," he added, retrieving his hat from the dust. With a flourish, he brushed it against his thigh and placed it on the back of his head.

He mounted Blackjack and rode farther down the street, leaving the mayor and the banker to deal with the carnage around them.

"Some place," Rhys muttered, his fingers ruffling across the ragged edge of his hat brim. "A man could get shot just looking for an innocent game of poker." He inspected the various establishments, deciding that one a good distance from Phil the Cannibal's vicinity would be preferable. There were many to choose from, some seedy and small, several larger and loud. One unimaginatively called the Beer Palace caught his eye. Although slightly run down, it boasted a room crowded with miners and stockmen. "All waiting to be fleeced," he said as he dismounted.

Rhys tied Blackjack to the hitching post and walked into the dim interior.

The place smelled of sawdust, beer, and unwashed bodies. The noise was deafening, the conversation and laughter punctuated by the tinny clank of a half-broken piano. Above the poor devil hacking away at the broken keys was a sign scrawled in red paint: "Please do not shoot the piano player. He is doing his damndest."

A big tropical bird with vivid yellow and green plumage squawked from his cage, oddly matching the forced gaiety of the whores plying their trade among the patrons. One woman dealing faro paused with a card in her hand to stare at the tall stranger filling the doorway. As he ambled into the room and leaned casually against the bar to order a beer, she watched the way his cool blue eyes scanned the room, especially the poker tables across from her. *A gambler, that one, and too damn pretty for any woman's good.* She winked at him as he glanced her way. He touched his fingertips to his hat brim in a fleeting gesture, then continued to peruse the tables as he sipped his beer.

Emmet Hauser watched the new man from beneath hooded eyes. He sat at his table by the stairs with his back to the wall where he could study all the patrons in his saloon. The owner was a big man, tending to corpulence, heavy-boned and solid. His square, pale face had a cruel, sullen caste, and his yellowish cat's eyes missed nothing. He, too, sized Rhys up as a gambler, but after checking his dusty, somewhat shabby clothes, he dismissed him. When Ginger misdealt and lost, having to pay off her table, he frowned in her direction. Stupid women, always mooning over handsome young men! Just as he stood up to walk over and reprimand the redhead, the stranger stopped at Ricky Barlow's table. Hauser sat back down to see what the gambler could do.

"Mind if I sit in?" he asked genially, his hand on the back of an empty chair.

"Help yourself," Barlow replied with a cursory glance at the travel-stained man. "The game's draw poker, jacks to open."

"What's the limit?" Rhys inquired as he folded himself into a crude wooden chair.

"Sky's the limit, stranger." Barlow laughed. Then when Rhys peeled off a roll of bills from a clip in his coat pocket, the youth's expression changed swiftly from easy dismissal to flustered amazement. "Come ta think on it, it's kinda cloudy today. Th' sky over Starlight's about a hundred dollars high."

A stocky old miner sitting across from Barlow chuckled, and a well-dressed young man with pale tan hair frowned. Saunders Laughton had been losing steadily all afternoon and saw humor in nothing. Nate Bridges, a prosperous rancher, glanced over at the hard-looking man with the bankroll and decided to watch him. Let young fools like Laughton and silver-rich old-timers like Able Courtney waste their money. What Barlow didn't win he was sure this new fellow would.

The game went smoothly for over an hour with Courtney, Bridges, and Davies winning occasional small pots. Barlow won more often, but since he was a professional who worked for Emmet Hauser, the locals expected him to be good. Gradually Rhys began to win more often, calling and raising Barlow, who grew increasingly nervous.

Rhys watched Barlow deal the first three cards around the table, then extended his right hand, palm up. "Let me see the deck."

Silence rippled across the room in widening circles. Soon every eye in the crowded saloon was on Barlow's table. "Call a man a cheat 'n' you better be able to back it up," one man called out.

"High-grading at this card table is serious as high-grading in my mine, son," Courtney said to Rhys.

"You got no call to ask to see this deck," Barlow said defensively, looking frantically for Hauser.

The saloon owner walked over to the table in several fast, furious strides, knocking people out of his way, but by the time he reached the table, Rhys had pried the cards from the dealer's fingers with one hand. His other held a .40 caliber pepperbox pulled from inside his coat. He flipped through the deck with speed and efficiency born of long practice, then turned over his three cards and asked the others to do the same. Courtney and Bridges obliged. Rhys flipped Barlow's over, but Laughton angrily refused.

"You got a pair of aces to match Barlow's?" Able Courtney asked with a knowing grin.

"No, he hasn't, unless there are six in this deck. We're two cards short, and I'd bet those aces are somewhere on Mr. Barlow, here," Rhys said quietly.

Sullenly Laughton turned over his cards, a jack, a deuce, and a six, as the gasps from the crowd rose and then hushed.

"Count the cards on the table," Rhys said calmly. Bridges quickly did so as the mine owner watched and nodded.

"Two short just like you said, 'n' both of 'em aces," Bridges said.

"Take off your coat." Rhys's voice was still cool but laced with contempt for the clumsy cheat he was about to reveal. He raised the pepperbox and shoved it in Barlow's face. "Now."

Hauser gave no indication of what he expected his hapless employee to do. He had warned the boy not to get too greedy, but had always thought Ricky clever enough to get away with palming cards. The place was crowded, and he knew that Courtney and Bridges—not to mention several others in the room—would back the stranger. He would not interfere unless Barlow was so stupid as to attempt to involve him. His looming presence beside the boy's chair was sufficient to silence the sweating, trembling dealer.

When Barlow stood up and began to take off his jacket, the sleeve cards slid to the floor, slowly as snowflakes drifting on a still evening.

"By damn, stranger, yer right," Able said as he reached down for the pair of aces. "He'd o' had four aces! 'N me with nary a thing but a pair of jacks. You figger this out just now?"

Rhys smiled. "I've been watching him palm cards and feed them back to all of us for the past hour."

"Oughter hang th' bastard," someone in the back of the crowd yelled. The sentence was echoed across the room, but Hauser put his hand up for quiet, then walked around the table to Rhys.

"I hired him to deal honest. I'll see to it he gets put in jail."

"I understand you have no sheriff," Rhys replied, the gun never wavering from Barlow.

Hauser gave a fake hearty laugh. "We got a county sheriff over in Lake City. I'll send him there for now. Any volunteers to see to it?"

A chorus of men stepped up, all yelling they would handle the job. Hauser quickly chose three, then asked the men at the table if that suited them. When everyone agreed, they led the quaking Barlow away.

Only the thunderous look on Hauser's face kept him silent.

"Now, I owe you gents all free drinks and a chance to win back some money. The sky's the limit from here on, but first, everything in Barlow's afternoon winnings'll be divided even between you. That seem fair?" Hauser waited as they all took their seats again. Rhys's pistol had magically vanished during the confusion.

Hauser was no fool. But he was a very good player. He sized up the drifter, reassessed his skills, and noted his bankroll. Perhaps the afternoon was redeemable after all.

They played for another half hour. By then Laughton had lost his share of Barlow's money plus all of his own. "I need some credit, Emmet. You know I'm good for it."

Hauser looked at the sallow-faced rich kid with contempt. Drunk, spoiled, and pig stupid to boot. "Can't rightly do that, Sanders. You know what you're already into me for?" He waved away the boy's flustered assurances and said, "Your daddy may own th' bank, but he don't cotton to your spendin' his money faster 'n he takes it in."

Humiliated and half sick from too much warm beer, Sanders lurched to his feet. Emmet Hauser was mean, and everyone in town gave him a wide berth. He looked into the flat yellow eyes and backed awkwardly from the table. "Rest assured, sir," he said in parting, "that I shall repay every cent I owe you."

"I apologize for that young fool, gents. His pa'd be right unhappy if I took any more of his markers. Stoddard don't fancy owin' money to a Democrat." Hauser's remarks drew several snickers from around the room, then the game resumed and the onlookers returned to their own amusements.

All but Ginger. Too distracted to continue dealing, she signaled Barney to come take her table, then walked over to the high-stakes game. Within the hour, it became apparent that the contest was between Emmet and the pretty stranger. Bridges and Courtney dropped out during the next several hands. The pile of banknotes in front of the younger man grew as her boss's shrank.

She studied him openly, but, intent on the game, he seemed not to notice. His thick curly hair glowed a burnished sun-streaked brown. Ginger itched to touch the enticing curls just brushing the collar of his shirt. He had shed his winter coat and wore a black suit jacket and white shirt, a bit travel-stained but well tailored to fit his imposing body. His dark blue eyes watched each card dealt, then shifted to each recipient's face for an instant before moving on to the next. He had arresting eyes, with thick shaggy brows slashed above them and heavy lashes to shield their expression from the casual viewer. Ginger Vogel was no novice at games of chance, having grown up in a string of saloons from Kansas to Colorado. The young gambler was good. Suddenly she had an intuition, and her knuckles whitened on the back of the chair she was gripping.

"I'll see your two hundred and raise two hundred more," Hauser said, shoving his cash into the center of the table.

Although his speech was deliberate and his motions slow, Ginger knew he was angry. He'd lost over three thousand dollars, and the evening was young.

The game was seven card stud and Rhys, having two spades in the hole and three more showing, saw the raise. His flush was king high, and the saloon owner showed only the promise of a possible straight, far more likely the simple pair of jacks showing with another pair buried. The Welshman watched, studying the other man's nervous habits: the way he rubbed the bridge of his nose, the way he drummed his blunt, heavy fingers on the hole cards, each movement revealing whether or not Emmet had a good hand.

When the last card was dealt, Rhys calculated that the wily old shark had a straight buried. What could he milk it for? The past several hours he'd observed the older man's anger held in check. Hauser took a cut from Barlow's cheating: Rhys was as certain of that as he was of his own king-high flush. And now that the old man's shill had been caught, Hauser was out for blood.

Rhys looked around the room. An ugly set of deer antlers and some shabby Indian shields hung from one wall. The molting bird squawked again, then subsided. And that rather fetching red-headed faro dealer looked as if she wanted him for dinner. He grinned to himself. Maybe he'd have her for dessert—after he cleaned out the crooked Hauser. "I'll see your five hundred and raise a thousand."

The crowd around the table had grown steadily all evening. Now the room became deathly silent. Hauser had indeed filled his king-high straight and he was short, both of temper and money. "I'll see your thousand and raise another."

"Done," Rhys said without hesitation, tossing another thousand into the pot. "Call."

Hauser slid his king, queen, jack, ten, nine into sequence, throwing away the useless second jack.

Rhys peeled up his three hole cards, all of them spades, one to spare for the winning flush when combined with the cards showing. He silently raked in the pile of money, then looked at the big man and let his instincts guide him. Now he knew what his first investment in Starlight would be. It was his turn to deal. "One last hand. A chance for you to get even, Hauser. Five card stud, last card down."

Emmet had no more cash, having sent Ginger to the office safe for the last of his money an hour ago. "My credit's good. You vouch for me, Able?"

"I reckon, 's long's I don't have ta pay up fer ya," the miner said with a chuckle.

Rhys sat shuffling the cards calmly. "I'll take a note for your saloon. First card, the bar stock—second card, the fixtures—third card, the furniture—then the service of the ladies upstairs for the fourth. Last card, you wager the whole shooting match." He never ruffled a card as he shuffled.

Hauser could feel dozens of pairs of eyes on him. What in the hell had he fallen into? He was flat broke if he lost, but the foreigner's luck couldn't hold. He'd beaten the younger man in several hands earlier. He was due again. He couldn't lose face. "Deal the cards."

Side bets on who would win the Beer Palace were placed around the room. Ginger Vogel made several herself, having ample assets with which to wager. The first card was dealt. Hauser looked at his ten of spades and smiled. "Reckon my bar stock's worth, say, two thousand," he said with a rumbling chuckle.

Rhys looked at his deuce, nodded, and shoved two thousand onto the table. Then he dealt the second card, a six for Hauser, another deuce for him. The gaudy, tarnished chandeliers, scarred old pine bar, wall mirrors, and even the parrot were bet, matched by Rhys with another two thousand.

The third card brought Hauser a second six and Rhys a nine of clubs. This time his matching bet for the furniture, including "six prime brass beds upstairs," was a whopping three thousand. Rhys felt elated. He dealt the fourth card, a seven for him and a nine for Hauser.

"Damnation, ole man Hauser's done saved his whores," one man chortled. Ginger glared at the offender, a miner with a cowlick, who quickly nodded an embarrassed apology toward her. She and her girls were worth the five thousand Hauser asked.

Rhys shoved the money out calmly. The St. Christopher's medal around his neck, given him by Sister Frances Rose, seemed to scorch his chest hair as he dealt the final hole cards.

"I got me a pair of sixes showin' ta your deuces. I reckon that oughta reclaim my saloon and the rest of your table stakes there." Hauser eyed the remaining cash at Rhys's elbow. In a five card stud game he was a sure-fire winner with a solid pair.

Rhys smiled. "Not much chance of winning, Hauser. Not unless your pair of sixes have pearl handles, or you have a third one buried," he said as he flipped his hole card over. The third deuce!

The big beefy face mottled red in incredulity as Hauser looked at the cards. It simply was not possible! What had he done? Lost everything, the saloon, the bordello, five years' work in one night!

Ginger sauntered over to her ex-boss and said with quiet relish, "I'll get the papers, Emmet."

As she turned toward the stairs, Hauser considered his options. The foreigner was a drifter with no kin hereabouts. Of course he had a hideout gun, but it was a child's toy compared to the .44 rimfire Colt that Emmet had holstered inside his jacket.

As if reading Hauser's mind, Rhys said, "Don't be a fool, man. You lost fair."

"Yeah, Emmet. The stranger beat you, 'n' I know he didn't palm no cards," Bridges said. Several others chimed in as the heavy man slowly stood up. Before he could decide what to do, Ginger was back with the deed and a pen.

"You're all witnesses. From now on, gentlemen, me 'n' my girls 'n' this here place belong to—" she shoved the paper in front of Hauser and looked at the stranger.

"Rhys Davies, at your service, ma'am," he said, at last returning her wink.

Chapter Four

Charles Everett had the world by the tail on a downhill slope in the San Juans. Slapping the reins across his matched white horses, he leaned back on the soft leather seat cushion and studied the profile of his lovely companion. The team started off smartly, but the perfectly sprung new phaeton rode smooth as satin. "Well, Victoria, what do you think of it?" he asked with a hint of offended pride in his voice. His fiancée had seemed preoccupied ever since he'd called for her at her parents' home.

"Oh, the rig is really handsome, Charles. So are the horses. Your law practice must be doing very well for you to afford such an expensive new toy," she replied, rewarding him with a dazzling smile.

"Just wait until we get outside town. I'll show you how well this new toy handles," he said, stung by her amused tone that hinted of condescension. Always so unruffled, his Victoria. Of course, that was one of the reasons he wanted to marry her. Her prim elegance combined with her father's political power would make him the most influential man in Starlight, someday in all of Colorado. Charles Everett had ambitions that would take him from Denver to Washington. Being married to a granddaughter of the illustrious Lodge family would certainly enhance his chances of success.

When Victoria continued her serene observation of the streets, now muddy from last night's spring rains, he felt his annoyance growing. "Penny for your thoughts, my dear?"

Her eyes sparkled aqua beneath her thick dark blonde lashes. "Just thinking of all the details for Mother's tea tomorrow. I have quite a lot to do yet, Charles. This impromptu surprise is delightful, but we really can't be gone too long." She straightened her heavy lavender twill skirts. The small two-seater placed her in far too close proximity to Charles for propriety's sake.

"I do wish it were our engagement party you were planning, Victoria, instead of a mere political reception." He sighed and snapped the reins again as they cleared the edge of town. The road widened before them on a slow uphill grade, with the grandeur of the San Juans spread all around them.

"This *mere* political reception, Charles, will place the Laughton stamp of sponsorship on your candidacy for the state legislature, so I scarcely think it insignificant."

"Of course, darling. You will make a splendid governor's wife one day, you know that."

"First I'll have to be a wife, and we've already discussed the need to wait, Charles." Victoria hoped the note of uncertainty in her voice did not sound as evident to him as it did to her. Charles would be the perfect husband, she reassured herself. Wealthy, successful, handsome, from a fine family—even her mother approved of him. Her father and her financé had numerous business dealings together and were both active in Republican politics. Her engagement to Charles would be a match made in heaven. Still, the thought of what she must endure as a wife, even a gentleman's wife, filled her with dread. Just riding in the small open carriage made her uncomfortable.

Always considerate of a lady's sensibilities, Charles held his leg clear of Victoria's skirts lest he upset her by brushing against her thigh on the seat of the bouncing phaeton. He mulled over how to get her to officially announce their engagement. She had held him—and his ambitions—at bay for nearly six months now. "When I win the election this fall, I'll be preparing to leave for Denver, Victoria. We really could have a lovely festive wedding over the Christmas holidays." He waited a beat, then looked at her as the carriage moved along at a pace as brisk as the spring wind.

Victoria adjusted the tiny feathered hat atop her head and smoothed the tulle veiling that protected her hair from the breeze. "I do suppose that would be opportune, Charles," she said slowly. Then, wanting to change the subject, she asked, "Have you read that scurrilous editorial in the *Plain Speaker* about how no working men should ever vote for a Republican?"

Charles gave a gloating, superior smile. "I scarcely think that the riffraff who agree with that Irishman will carry the day. All the best sorts, every decent sober man in Starlight will vote for me, especially with your father's backing. But I do wish Sanders wouldn't work at cross purposes with us," he added irritably. Victoria's irresponsible brother could yet undermine all his plans.

Always defensive of her younger brother, Victoria felt her cheeks flame. "He's only a nineteen-year-old boy, Charles, easily led. If you win your seat in the legislature, you can see to it that all the saloons are closed forever."

Realizing that Victoria would always defend the weakling, Charles changed tack. He pulled a newspaper from beneath the leather seat and handed it to her. "You're quite right, my dear. You read Manion's stupid editorial last week. Just peruse this advertisement he ran yesterday!"

Victoria took the page from him and read the bold center-column announcement on the front page, beside an article discussing how Emmet Hauser's old saloon was under new management, completely refurbished and sporting a new name: The Naked Truth, Rhys Davies, proprietor. The ad boasted that the opulent pleasure palace planned "to grow rich by beggaring the men of Starlight, creating widows and orphans, inciting good citizens to riot and mayhem, and endangering public welfare. We will send your good citizens to the poor farms and the gallows! All beer and whiskey on the house for the first twenty-four hours after we open."

Her eyes grew large as saucers while she read, then blazed with fury as she crumpled the pages, smearing her white gloves with ink. "The nerve of the man! And I suppose every low element in town flocked to this Mr. Davies' grand opening?"

"I'm afraid so, my dear. The alarming thing is that it isn't only the miners and stockmen who are going to his den of filth. He's made Hauser's shabby old place over. I hear that it's garish but plush. Many wealthy men in the community have been seen entering its doors. Yesterday at the grand opening there was a near riot."

"And to think the mayor offered that trashy gambler a job as our sheriff." Victoria sniffed.

Charles avoided upsetting Victoria by mentioning that Sanders had been involved in the riot. She could be every bit as waspish as his departed mother. Indeed, his fiancée's behavior could even rival that of his odious sister-in-law, Laura. Tory had been cosseted and spoiled every bit as badly as her damned brother, but she was a fetching piece of fluff. He must impress her from the start of their marriage with the fact that he was head of the household. God forbid they should ever have a marriage such as his brother had endured with Laura! Jacob had actually sought his wife's political advice and even remained faithful to the old battle axe! Poor devil was better off dead, he consoled himself, then turned to Victoria once more. "Let me show you what this new team can do with such a splendidly engineered conveyance," he said, whipping the horses into a fast trot.

Victoria looked ahead at the narrow wooden bridge across the Uncompahgre River. They had climbed several hundred feet in elevation since leaving the small valley where Starlight nestled. The San Juan Mountains, after a long and bitter winter, had poured melted snow into all the winding streams, flooding them. The rushing water roared, licking and snapping at the rotted wooden underpinnings of the rickety bridge. "Charles, I don't think you'd better take the phaeton across that bridge," she cautioned.

"Nonsense. This rig is especially light, and well designed just for these narrow mountain roads. That's why I paid so handsomely for it. Surely you don't mistrust my driving, darling?" Without waiting for her reply, he sped up the horses.

Creaking and groaning, the bridge accepted the weight of the whites, whose hoofbeats were muffled by the noise of the water beneath them. Suddenly the horse on the right balked as icy water splashed up through the planking. Its teammate then shied as well. Charles gave the reins a sharp slap and added the inducement of a crack from his smart new driver's whip. He owned and raced fast horses as a hobby and had always fancied himself the best horseman in the county, but his skills seemed to desert him now. With the whip snapping above their heads and the water roaring beneath their feet, the terrified whites panicked and reared, causing the light phaeton to tip sharply to the right.

Victoria felt her hat rip free of its pins and reached up to grasp it just as the carriage lurched. Losing purchase with her right hand, she tumbled from the seat and out the side of the rig, her legs hopelessly tangled in her heavy twill skirt and petticoats. Before she could even scream, she hit the hard, knotty surface of the bridge's rail with her hip. The pain was agonizing but blurred as she continued her descent over the edge of the bridge into the roaring waters below. The icy impact tore a piercing scream from her throat; then there was silence as she sank beneath the surface of the turbulent water.

Victoria flailed helplessly in the freezing current, bobbing to the surface long enough to cry for help again, then being quickly sucked down. Her clothes, heavy protection against the brisk spring wind, weighed her down like an anchor. She felt her hair tangle about her head, blinding her as it was whipped by the churning water. Even if ladies had been permitted to learn how to swim, she could not have used such a skill encumbered as she was. The snow-fed water quickly numbed her, stiffening her limbs and stifling her desperate cries. *So this is what it's like to die.*

Suddenly her frozen body collided with something hard and warm. Still blinded and semiconscious, she clung to a human form. "Charles?" she croaked as a strong arm molded her to the length of a male body. He held her fast with one arm and began to rip her heavy jacket and skirts free with the other. She struggled in reflex as the current swirled around them.

"Hold still, dammit! I can't fight you and the river, too," a voice shouted angrily over the roar of water. It was not Charles. She quieted after being freed of the deadly weight of her suit, buoyant in the embrace of the yet unseen rescuer, who commanded, "Now wrap your arms about my neck. There's a love. Watch you don't let go in the current. I'll need both arms free to get us to shore."

He was braced against a rock jutting out in the middle of the river. As she disorientedly pushed the mass of sodden gold hair from her face, Tory could see that the man was a complete stranger, but the fear of death left no room for modesty. She obeyed him, and he pushed off from the meager protection of the rocks. As she clung like a leech, he swam with sure, powerful strokes.

Tory could feel the muscles in his shoulders and back bunching as he labored toward shore. When he reached the shallows, he scooped her shivering body up in his arms and carried her to the moss-covered bank.

Rhys had been riding back to Starlight after looking over a small ranch he had won at the Naked Truth when he heard her scream. Spurring Blackjack around the bend of the road, he had seen the fancy little rig in the middle of the bridge. While a man struggled to regain control of his team, a woman bobbed up and down in the churning waters.

He had leaped from Blackjack and yanked off his jacket and boots, then dived into the river after her. The rocks had been their salvation. Now, laboring for breath, he staggered up the bank and sank to his knees to examine the woman whose life he had just saved.

The sight that greeted his eyes set his pulses to racing anew. She was the most exquisite creature he had ever seen. Her long blonde hair was darkened to gold by the water and hung like a sheet of shimmering silk. Her body, shivering and clinging to his, was nearly revealed through a gauzy white shirtwaist and sheer pantalettes. She was slim but perfectly formed with high pointed breasts and a tiny waist. One fragile wrist was draped across his biceps as she held weakly to his arm. Her face looked pale from cold and fright, yet as her thick golden lashes opened, he beheld eyes the color of a lake he'd seen on his travels up in Idaho—not blue but not quite green, rather clear bright turquoise.

Victoria wrinkled her small straight nose and felt a most unladylike twitching. Holding tighter to her rescuer, she turned her head against a furry expanse of bare chest and sneezed, then coughed and sputtered as he sat her gently on the bank. Supporting her with one arm, he slapped her carefully between her slim shoulder blades. More water came up. She was freezing and waterlogged. Her hair felt like a cape made of icicles clinging to her back. As she came to her senses, she remembered the fall into the river and being stripped of her clothes by a stranger. Heavens above! Small wonder she was freezing—she was almost naked in his embrace. Before she could work up her courage to look at her deliverer's face, he spoke.

"I'd offer you my jacket, but I left it quite a ways upstream by my horse, which, unfortunately, is across the river. No help for it, miss. We'll just have to walk back . . . and hope your companion has his team under control by then," he added darkly. "Now watch you don't fall," he said solicitously as her knees buckled when she stood up.

His hands were cold from the water, yet far warmer than hers as he held her fast. "You've saved my life, sir. I'm most grateful," Victoria managed to rasp out between her chattering teeth as she finally raised her head to face him. His voice was low and musical with a faint trace of an accent difficult to identify. Whoever he was, he was astonishingly handsome, even soaked in icy river water. His eyes were a piercing dark blue that mesmerized her. A strong, clean jaw and prominent straight nose added to the aura of masculine beauty, but nothing could compare to the smile, as dazzlingly white as snow on the Rockies' highest peaks. His lips were sculpted just to smile, and he had dimples in his tanned cheeks! His hair was thick and curly, some shade of sun-bleached brown, she could not tell exactly as it was soaking wet. Suddenly embarrassed to be caught staring, she shook her head to clear it. He reached out and steadied her.

The smile evaporated into an expression of concern. "You're freezing and too weak to walk." He scooped her up in his arms effortlessly. "The sooner you're back to the bridge so I can wrap you in my saddle blanket, the better." When his stockinged feet came in contact with the sharp rocks along the twisting path of the river, he swore beneath his breath in sudden reflex, then immediately apologized.

Victoria merely nodded her understanding, a bit shocked at the language but too dazed to be really offended. Anyway, how could she be offended by someone who had just saved her life? Especially someone so attractive. He was a big man, tall and lean, with a rangy yet graceful stride that quickly ate up the distance back to the bridge. Tory gave herself a mental shake, shocked now, not at him but at herself. She was practically naked in his arms after a near brush with death, and all she had thought of was how he looked! And how he felt, carrying her as if she weighed no more than an aspen leaf on a spring breeze. And where was Charles? Had he, too, fallen into the deadly river?

Then Victoria remembered her rescuer's words about her companion struggling with his horses. Poor Charles could be dead and she was alone in the wilderness with a complete stranger! Before she could muster her scattered thoughts to inquire his name, she heard a halloo. Charles stood beside his phaeton, his clothes dry and unwrinkled. He hadn't even lost his hat! He rushed toward them and immediately reached out for Victoria, who felt an inexplicable and unsettling reluctance to give up the warm, hard body of her rescuer for the embrace of her fiancé.

"Victoria, you're half naked! What the devil's happened?" Charles demanded, his face twisted in shocked embarrassment.

"Take off your coat, you jackass, and put it about the lady," the stranger commanded. "She's nearly drowned and frozen, all thanks to you."

"Now see here, you ruffian—"

"I said, take off that thick warm coat, or I'll do it for you," Rhys repeated, his voice as steely as his facial expression. He could feel the woman quaking

71

with chill while this dolt argued propriety!

When Charles began to strip off his coat, Rhys relaxed. Victoria could feel the tension uncoil as he gently stood her on her feet, holding her protectively in his embrace, sheltering her from the cold spring wind with his big body. Caught between the two men in such a state of dishabille, she wanted nothing more than to become invisible. Victoria tried to cover her breasts with her arms, then realized belatedly that her undergarments clung in equal translucence to her lower limbs! She turned her back on Charles in mortification, only to stare point blank at the hairy, tanned chest of her rescuer. His shirt had been nearly torn off by the current and hung open. Mercifully, Charles draped his jacket about her then and possessively pulled her from the stranger's embrace. She felt her cheeks, white with cold, pinken as the two men exchanged words.

"Did you have to rip all her clothing off in the river?" Charles asked with a hiss of jealousy in his voice. She could tell he disliked the stranger. Did he know him?

"I could scarcely manage to swim with the lady if she carried double her weight in petticoats, now could I? I see you've rescued your carriage and team," the stranger added sarcastically as Charles drew her toward the conveyance.

"It took me quite a while to calm them and get off the bridge. By then you and Victoria had both disappeared around the bend in the river," Charles replied with a hint of defensiveness supplanting his earlier affronted dignity.

"We do thank you for your most timely aid," Victoria interjected as they reached the carriage. She could see he was nearly as cold as she, with his curly hair plastered to his head and a pair of expensive trousers molded to his long legs. "I fear you need your jacket, too," she said with a tremulous smile, looking across the river to where he had left his horse and clothes. Attempting to defuse the most awkward and antagonistic situation, she added in inquiry, "To whom do I owe my life, Mr.—?"

"Davies, Rhys Davies," he replied with another of those heart-stopping smiles.

Victoria's heart nearly did stop, so tightly was it lodged in her throat. "You're the saloon owner," she croaked in accusation, drawing Charles's jacket tightly about her like a shield. She nearly tripped over her fiancé, backing away from her bare-chested champion.

"I told you he looked like a ruffian. The owner of the Naked Truth," Charles sneered as his disdainful glare swept Davies' water-soaked, torn clothing and stockinged feet. "How fitting."

Rhys ignored him and looked Victoria up and down in thorough appraisal. "Yes, isn't it," he echoed innocently, then gave her a wink and a salute. "I'll see you in town, Miss Victoria—that is, if this gentleman can manage to return you safely and not overturn his dandy new toy again," he added as Charles quickly assisted her into the phaeton.

Everett wasted no time whipping the horses into a brisk trot headed back toward Starlight as Davies crossed the bridge to where his gear was strewn and the big black waited.

"Thank heavens he left his gun across the river," Charles said with a shudder.

Victoria felt the most overpowering urge to look back, but she fought it valiantly and focused on her fiancé's strained face instead. Rhys Davies's words about the carriage, Charles's "new toy," echoed her own earlier. She was furious with both of them—

Charles for his reckless foolishness that had nearly killed her, and Rhys Davies for . . . her thoughts tumbled over one another in jumbled confusion. Never had a man affected her *that* way! She refused to dwell on it a moment longer. Even as the chill wind whipped at her thin wet undergarments, she felt a strange heat flame through her body.

Then the thundering of the big black's hoofbeats caught up with them. Rhys pulled alongside the phaeton and thrust a rolled-up saddle blanket at Tory. "Wrap up in this until you reach town. I'd hate to have all my trouble be in vain if you take pneumonia, or, worse yet, be seen by half of Starlight in your underwear, fetching as it is!" With that he galloped ahead of them.

Victoria huddled against the leather seat and wrapped the warm, dry blanket around herself, unable to tear her eyes from the retreating figure of the horseman on the horizon. *I hope he catches pneumonia himself!*

"Did you get it?" The voice was thin with fright, yet oddly laced with petulance. Ella Hauser opened the door to her small cabin and let the light halo her long, brown hair. She was a short girl, sturdy and voluptuously built, but her face was pinched and marred by a perpetual frown.

"I got what I could," Sanders said as he slipped past her into the cabin's meager protection against the evening chill. "Is Emmet here?" he asked nervously.

"You know he never stays home at nights, Sandy. He's out swillin' beer with that pack of trash at the Forty Rod." Ella put one plump, reddened hand on his coat sleeve and reached out with the other for the envelope he carried.

Grudgingly he handed it to her and watched her tear it open and count the money.

"Only two thousand! You coulda brung more. I got me this young'un ta take care of now, Sandy—*your* baby," she added for emphasis, placing his hand on her slightly rounded belly.

"I thought you knew this fellow in Denver City who could get rid of it," Sanders said angrily. "I risked a lot taking that much money. You can go away with it and start over in Denver."

"But I don't wanna do it that way. Oh, Sandy, I still don't see why you 'n' me can't get married," she said, wrapping her arms about his waist.

Sanders could smell the odor of greasy fried pork in Ella's hair. *Fat, coarse sow*, he thought angrily. Why had he ever thought her attractive? Sighing, he pulled from her embrace and escorted her to one of the two cane chairs sitting by a splintering table in one corner of the room. In another corner stood her bed, into which he had been enticed on more than one drunken evening. "You know we can never marry, Ella. My parents would cut me off without a cent. You're a saloon owner's niece."

"Haw!" She snorted. "Uncle Emmet used to own a saloon. Now alls he does is drink in 'em. I got no one but you, Sandy." She hesitated coyly, letting her coarse hair fall over one eye.

Sanders used to think she was sexy and pretty. Now he only saw a dumpy pregnant girl with a pock-marked face and a mop of unwashed hair. She had been his first woman—and he supposed he was her first man. At least she had cried and carried on like he was last winter, but then he'd caught Sally Marsh's eye at the Gaiety and a whole new world had opened up for him. As the son of a banker, he found himself much sought after by the "ladies of the line." Of course, indulging his new appetite meant skimming a bit off the till at the bank, but it was worth it.

Then Ella had come to him in tears a month ago, saying she was expecting his baby. Now he looked at her with distaste clearly etched on his thin pale face. "Sit down, Ella. You have over two thousand dollars there."

Ella sensed the change in him, and anger welled up inside her. Her uncle had warned her about making eyes at the rich boy, but he was handsome and educated. She realized now that all Sanders wanted was to use her body to slake his lust. And Uncle Emmet was furious, with her in a family way and no man to support her.

"Uncle Emmet'll kill you, Sandy, if'n you don't do right by me. I gotta live when I get ta Denver, 'n' them special doctors Uncle Emmet knows, they cost a lot of money. He told me—"

"He's using you to wring more money from me because he's lost his damned saloon. I can't take more than this at one time without being caught . . . and then where would you be with me in jail?" Lord, if Ella began to blabber her tale about town and his mother found out!

The thought made him break out in a fine sweat. He could see Hedda's cold, aristocratic face staring at him with utter contempt. And if his father knew he had been embezzling money for the past six months, he would set his son adrift without a penny.

He scanned the rude cabin with its rough plank floor and dilapidated furniture, the sagging cornhusk mattress and grease-coated iron cook stove. The room stank of poverty. Poverty was cheap whiskey and starchy cornbread. Wealth was fine Madeira and rare roast beef . . . and the inventive, laughing women who lived at the uptown bordellos, not this dumpy, whiny girl.

She glared at him with fierce yellow eyes and a stubborn set to her jaw, reminding him uncomfortably of Emmet Hauser. "I'll get you more money, Ella girl. Only give me enough time. I'll see you're taken care of, you have the word of a Laughton on it."

Chapter Five

"I heard the new owner is a real gorgeous stud," Lizzie Custus said, adjusting her brassy yellow sausage curls.

"You better keep clear of him. I hear Miss Ginger has a claim staked out for herself and *she* handles his girls for him," another satin-clad whore replied, batting her kohled lashes at a patron across the bar.

"Well, I knew him back in Denver when he dealt for Mr. Drago. We worked together for a while. He had a real thing going with this fancy actress, but she was older 'n him. He was just a kid then, but you're right, Liz, gorgeous, even for a kid! Haven't seen him in five years."

All three applicants ceased their chatter and stood almost at attention when Ginger Vogel swished halfway down the richly carpeted stairs. Holding her green satin skirt between well-manicured fingers, she motioned for the three women to follow her back upstairs. Ginger's bright carrot hair was unaided by bleach or die, a vivid natural hue whose authenticity was attested to by a generous sprinkling of pale freckles across her nose and cheekbones. Once inside the office at the top of the stairs, she looked each of the women over with level, wide-set green eyes. Miss Ginger was young for a madam, but quite imposing.

"Blackie Drago vouches for you. Says you was healthy, had your own teeth, and didn't drink. Also that you looked good. Mr. Davies is running a classy place here and he don't want no cheap blowsy whores." She nodded at each, all apparently passing inspection. "You get your own room, your meals—'n' damn good ones they are. But I don't wanna see you outgrow your clothes, so don't overeat neither. We buy your dresses for workin'. Cash pay's half what you take from the customers. Any questions?"

"You dock us for our dresses if a feller tears one?" Mavis asked.

"Don't make a habit of it 'n' I won't. But I run a good-time house, not a dressmaker's shop." She looked at Carmelita Sanchez, the petite brunette. "You got a burr under your blanket, honey?"

"What if a man gets . . . rough? Mr. Drago had a bouncer."

Ginger's face split in a wide grin.

"Ben Grange is wide as that door 'n' he's got him a twelve-gauge sawed-off shotgun with a fourteen-inch barrel that could knock down a ten span of mules. You'll be all right. I understand you knew Mr. Davies in Denver. That so?" Her eyes narrowed imperceptibly.

"Yes. I had just come to work there and he was a

dealer—very young, but a natural player." Carmelita colored in spite of her dusky complexion. "He had eyes only for la Senorita Goldstock, never for any of Blackie's girls."

"Good. House rule number one. Be honest with your split and don't hold out on me. Two. Never let me see you drink. Three. Make eyes at Rhys Davies 'n' I'll personally skin you so slick you'll look like a newborn possum. Got all that?" At their affirmative nods, Ginger said, "I'll show you your rooms. Get unpacked 'n' head downstairs. We never close down, but now I got enough girls to work shifts. Business has picked up real good since Rhys took over."

As she sat in the office listening to the sound of glasses clinking across the bird's-eye maple bar downstairs, Ginger thought of how her life had been turned upside down since the Welshman entered it. Rhys, handsome, charming, laughing Rhys, her boss and her lover. Never in all the years since she had run away from an abusive father in the West Virginia coal mine country had she imagined finding a man like Rhys. Most had been like Emmet. Oh, a few had been kinder, but all the other good-looking ones were conceited, one-way high-graders, out for themselves. Just when she thought she had become immune to a dazzling smile and a smooth line of talk, the charmer had won the saloon from Hauser.

She ran one large well-shaped hand over a new velvet chair. It was plush and thick, the most expensive that Loring's Freight Emporium in Denver had to offer. She and Rhys had taken a stage as far as Silverton, then ridden General Palmer's fancy new railroad all the way to Denver, just to buy all new fixings for the Naked Truth: furniture, wallpaper, carpets, and even crystal chandeliers. He'd let her pick all the decorations for the girls' rooms and select mirrors, paintings, even shiny brass cuspidors for the saloon. The shabby former Beer Palace was now the classiest and busiest barroom and fancy house in Starlight. Ginger was in charge of things when Rhys was away. Emmet had never trusted anyone, least of all her, especially after she'd begun finding excuses not to bed with him. But all that was behind her now.

She closed her eyes and replayed that first night after Rhys had sent Emmet packing. He'd taken her into this very office, musty and shoddy then, filled with jumbled papers and overflowing ashtrays.

"You want to work for me? I'll run things different than Hauser," he had stated, resting his hands on the battered old chair behind the desk.

"You mean you won't hire crooked dealers like Ricky? I never cheated for Emmet. I just dealt faro, straight. I want you to know that. Me 'n' my girls, we never cheat customers er roll drunks. We don't take no beatin' er funny stuff from 'em neither," she had stated with a trace of belligerence in her voice as she faced him across the big desk. Lordy, he was too good to be true!

Rhys had walked around the desk, taken her hand in his, and raised it to his lips in a bone-melting kiss. "Agreed. I have plans for this place, big plans, and I need your help—Ginger? Is that your name, love?"

She had been lost then, looking into those fathomless blue eyes, feeling his big, warm hands holding hers. "My real name is Virginia Louella Vogel, but any handle with 'virgin' in it don't fit no more, so Ginger it is," she had replied with sass and delight in her voice.

A loud crash of breaking glass and swearing brought Ginger out of her reverie and back to the present. "Damnation, who's breaking up my fancy new fixtures," she muttered as she swished toward the door. By the time she had reached the top of the stairs and assessed the scene from the balcony overlooking the main floor of the saloon, near chaos reigned. Ben Grange caught her signal from the corner of his eye and reached beneath the bar for his twelve-gauge. He let go with one blast aimed at the floor behind the bar, where it would do the least material damage. The deafening blast stopped the fight quickly.

Taking advantage of the moment's lull, Ginger yelled, "Damn you to hell, Wylie!" Her voice carried like a whiplash. "Get lickered up somewhere else. This is a high-class place now."

Tomato Nose Wylie Wilcox straightened up and swayed to and fro, keeping a precarious balance by holding on to the edge of the polished bar with one hand. Long, stringy, dark hair of uncertain color hung across one eye, partially obscuring a thin face. His bulbous red nose was well on its way to incandescence as he lifted a full bottle of phlegm-cutter whiskey to his lips and gargled down half its contents before turning to face the wrathful madam. Wiping the back of a frayed shirt sleeve, crisp with filth, across his mouth, he belched and said, "Now, Miz Ginger, I ain't broke nothin much. Jist fell agin a stack o' glasses Ben wuz polishin' up. I'll pay fer 'em. I ain't thet drunk neither." His unfocused eyes and weaving body belied the last statement.

The old miner was a regular whenever he came to town. Once the best hard-rock miner in southwest

Colorado, he had dug his way to three fortunes and lost all three mines to drink. "How in hell are you gonna pay for that bottle of Forty Rod, much less them glasses?" Ginger demanded.

"I been doin' a leetle diggin' up north a ways. Got me a poke." He shoved a small leather pouch across the gleaming surface of the bar top. Ben opened it and dumped out some black sand flecked with grayish silver.

"That's low-grade silver and lead. You'd need a ton or two of it smelted down ta pay for damages," Ben said in disgust.

"Look agin." The tall, skinny man seemed to sober appreciably as he smeared the sticky sand across the bar and fished out several small jagged pieces of yellowish metal. "Ain't no Gregory Gulch, but it'll pay fer yer damn glasses," he said pugnaciously.

"Where'd you get this?" a man dressed in expensive clothes asked casually.

Wilcox snorted. "Like as I'm gonna tell yew. Alls I will say is it's a fer piece from here 'n' it's slim pickin's if yew don't know whut yore doin—which none of yew fancy gents hereabouts do," he added, turning his back on the sputtering questioner.

Rhys, who had overheard most of the altercation and its aftermath, was pleased with how Ginger and Ben had handled it. But he was also freezing wet and dying for a hot bath and a hearty meal. He stepped into the room from where he had been observing at the back door.

Ginger took one look at him and rushed to his side. "God-a-mighty, what happened to you, sugar?" Without waiting for a reply, she turned to the woman nearest her. "Lizzie, get Rufus to heat water for a bath and send for some hot food." Turning to

Ben, she commanded, "Bring up a bottle of the best brandy to Rhys' room."

With an amused smile twitching on his lips, Rhys watched her order everyone about. Yes, he had made the right choice for his second-in-command here. There were other compensations, too. Suddenly a slender, fine-boned figure with pale golden hair and delicate features flashed in his mind. Bemused, he let Ginger lead him upstairs and help him peel off his sodden clothes as he stood in the center of his big bedroom.

The private apartment was decorated in dark masculine colors and textures, all leather and stained oak furniture with dark blue draperies and carpets. The bed was a big, wide four-poster that handily accommodated him and any woman of his choice. To date, that had been only Ginger. He had not been interested in any other . . . until this morning.

Ginger noticed his preoccupation as he undressed. He was uncommunicative about how he had come to be soaking wet, only saying he'd gone for an unexpected swim in the Uncompahgre.

After the ebony giant Rufus poured two enormous buckets of water into the big brass tub in the corner of the bedroom, Rhys slipped beneath the steamy water and laid his head back against the rim. Ginger studied his striking profile for a moment, then asked hesitantly, "Can I massage your neck, darlin'? You seem . . . tense." She was afraid to pry any further. Rhys Davies was a man with a mysterious past that he kept well guarded. To date she knew only the barest facts about the long trail that had brought him from the coal mines of Wales to the silver mines of Starlight.

At first it seemed he would not answer her request, but then he nodded absently in her direction, saying,

"Ginger, come, love. I need the warm, soft hand of a woman."

She knelt by the edge of the tub, heedless of her luscious new satin gown, and began to knead his neck and shoulder muscles as he rested his arms on the sides of the big custom-made tub. "You're stiff as starch and frozen solid," she murmured as she worked. Irresistibly, her hand tousled the damp ringlets across his brow, and then she combed her fingers through his thick hair, massaging his scalp while she enjoyed the view of his long, muscular body half submerged in the water.

Small droplets splashed onto the thick brown hair of his chest, then trickled down to disappear beneath the steaming vapors. Her fingertips followed the trail as she leaned over his shoulder, pressing her ample cleavage against his cheek. Feeling the faint scratch of whiskers against her tender skin, she gave a contented moan and let her lips brush his temple. Her hot tongue flicked inside his ear and she bit his lobe playfully. Ginger looked down at his lower body, then chuckled wickedly. "Lordy, you're still stiff as starch, but it ain't from cold no more!"

Rhys felt curiously restless and filled with energy for a man who had spent the preceding morning in an icy mountain river, the afternoon making lusty love to his mistress, and the evening gambling. "I ought to be sleeping till Sunday," he muttered ruefully to himself as he walked down the street. In fact, he had tossed and turned most of the night, having recurrent dreams, some about ugly things from the past, others about quite different things full of promise for the future.

Freshly bathed, shaved, and turned out in an elegant new blue suit the tailor had just delivered,

Rhys was a man with a mission, one he could scarcely discuss with Ginger or anyone at the Naked Truth.

He had to learn the identity of the enchantress with the pale gold hair and aqua eyes—the breathtaking nymph he had rescued from the water: Victoria. Obviously she and her stuffy companion knew who he was. Turnabout was fair play. The logical place to begin was the local newspaper. As he neared the office, he could see that the glass-windowed front was covered with grit. The interior looked little more promising as he shoved open the door, which stood partially ajar. The acrid smells of linseed oil, printer's ink, and years of accumulated dirt greeted his nostrils.

Every conceivable space in the room was filled with cluttered piles of yellowed newspapers, books with spines bent open, and stacks of handwritten copy. Balled-up wads of paper littered the floor. A small, reedy man sat with his feet propped on top of an overflowing desk in the corner, furiously scribbling away on a tablet. One of his shoe soles had a hole in it. The reporter was so intent on his writing, he seemed not to notice the intrusion. But before Rhys could clear his throat and address the scribe, the man negligently waved a hand in his direction and spoke as he continued to write.

"Clear off a chair and have a seat, Davies. I'll be with you in a minute." As the visitor did so, the little Irishman finished his story with a flourish of his pencil and a hearty chuckle. "That damn fool mine owner in Silverton who's spending a fortune to endow their city park just carped about the cost of a half dozen Venetian gondolas the Council bought for the lake. 'Why buy six of 'em? says he. 'Buy two and let 'em breed. By summer you'll have all you need!" The little man stood up, shaking his head. "Beaumont's a jackass, but Silverton has no monopoly on those. Plenty in Starlight as well."

"You know my name, I assume you're Michael Manion," Rhys said as the editor extended an ink-stained hand to shake his.

"That I am, but call me Mike. I sent my apprentice Virgil to cover the story of your grand opening. I was out of town on business. Sorry I missed it. But I did stop by upon my return, just to see the fair lady on the back wall. Female pulchritude brought to sublime heights," he added with a sigh.

Rhys smiled. "The painting came all the way from Denver."

"The model came all the way from heaven—or perhaps the other direction."

"I bought it at auction at Loring's freight office. It's been quite a draw at the saloon."

"The ad you placed in my newspaper was quite a draw as well. You're a man after my own heart, Rhys Davies. I do believe we share a bit of Celtic blood?"

Rhys laughed. "I'm Welsh, not Irish, but I was raised by a fierce old lady, Sister Frances Rose O'Hanlon. There was a bully boy at the orphanage named Manion—Evan Manion. Any kinfolk of yours back in New York?"

Mike's thin face split in an elfin grin and his brown eyes danced with infectious mirth as he scratched his head consideringly. "Was he a big strapping fellow?"

"That he was."

"Then for sure he was no kin of mine," Manion replied, gesturing to his wiry body, encased in rumpled pants and a yellowed cotton shirt liberally smudged with ink. "At five feet four inches, I'm the tallest Manion in my whole family's history. What is it that brings you to the *Plain Speaker* this fine morning, Rhys?" He gestured back to where a well-used casebox of type leaned against the wall next to a very old Washington Hand Press. "Might I hope for more advertising? My typesetter will be in as soon as he sobers up. Work is the curse of the drinking class, you know."

"Since drinking is part of my work, I hope your employee spends his off hours in the Naked Truth. What I've come for today is not advertising, but information."

Manion's shrewd brown eyes appraised Rhys. "What do you want to know?"

"Not what. Who." Rhys paused, gathering his wits to frame a description of his spitting water sprite. "I'm looking for a woman—a lady. A real lady."

Mike chuckled. "Out West, who isn't, boyo?"

"No, this is one very specific lady. I met her yesterday, a ways north of town. She reads your newspaper and knew my name, so she can't live far away. About so high"—he gestured to his shoulder—"slim, with pale gold hair and eyes the color of sea foam. First name is Victoria."

"Waxing so poetic, it must be love. Forget her. Victoria Elizabeth Laughton's already bespoken. Charles Everett has her all but signed up for matrimony."

"Tall, thick-set sort, with dark hair and a terminally pompous air?" Rhys asked gloomily.

"A Republican if ever I saw one," Mike replied solemnly. "His future father-in-law's even worse. Owns the largest bank in Starlight. Married into old Eastern money years back. Victoria's mother is a Massachusetts Lodge. Being from a New York orphanage, you may not know what that means—"

"Sister Frances Rose encouraged me to read a book or two. I've kept up, Mike," Rhys replied, half defensively. "I know who the Lodges are. So, her father's the bank owner, Stoddard Laughton. I met him last month—the very day I arrived in town. He offered me a job." Rhys grinned. "I'll be back with more advertising next week, Mike." He turned to leave, whistling jauntily.

Victoria Elizabeth Laughton. The name fit her perfectly. So intent was he on picturing his vision that he nearly collided with the short, plump woman who was entering the office. Steadying the well-dressed matron with her cherubic round face, he apologized profusely, doffing his hat with his best courtly flourish. "I am so very sorry, ma'am. I was woolgathering. Did I hurt you?"

She chuckled. "Scarcely, sir. You didn't even touch me, and I am built to withstand a shock or two, as Michael here can well attest," she added, turning to greet the little Irishman.

"Aren't you ashamed to be seen in public with the likes of me, Laura Everett?" Mike asked mischievously, ushering her inside the dank office.

"No more of your charming blather, Michael. I have here a notice for my garden club's monthly meeting." She thrust a paper at him and then turned back to Rhys. "And who is this perfectly charming rogue?"

"You'll be shocked," the editor whispered. "He's an even lower sort than I."

"I don't tend toward vapors," she replied as her dancing blue eyes appraised the expensively garbed stranger.

"Rhys Davies, ma'am. I'm afraid Mike is right. I own a saloon."

"And you think I resemble a Temperance crusader?" she replied with a smile lifting little puffs at the edges of her mouth. Surprising Rhys, she thrust out her immaculately gloved hand and said. "I am Laura Everett. Jacob's widow," she added with pride.

"And Charles Everett's sister-in-law," Mike added with a wry grin.

"Please don't hold my brother-in-law against me, Mr. Davies," she said.

"I would never subject a lady to such an indignity," Rhys replied, raising her hand with a flourish for a light salute.

Laura Everett laughed heartily and her chubby body bounced with mirth, from the gray ringlets on her head down to the hemline of her striped bombazine dress. "I like you already, Mr. Davies, and I take it you've met my brother-in-law Charles?"

"His aspirations to be an expert horseman exceed his abilities, I'm afraid. His phaeton overturned on the Uncompahgre Bridge. He lost control of his team while he and Victoria Laughton were out driving."

Laura gasped. "So that's what happened! Hedda was in a royal snit when Charles brought Tory home soaking wet, wrapped in a blanket. I'm afraid it did little good for her reputation," she added regretfully.

"It should've done a lot worse for his—the damn fool could have cost her her life. She was nearly drowned, and he was dry as tinder when it was all over." Reddening, Rhys quickly added, "I apologize for my language, Mrs. Everett."

She waved her hand dismissively. "Phoo! I can well imagine who rescued Tory from the river. That was your blanket she was sporting, was it not, Mr. Davies?"

"Yes, ma'am, it was. And I intend to get it back," he said with a wink. Tipping his hat politely, he bid her and Manion good day and departed.

Laura's eyes crinkled at the corners and she pursed her lips in consideration. "Perhaps I can be of assistance to Mr. Davies, Michael," she said. "Just you tell me all you know about that handsome rascal. Other than the obvious. I can already see he's smitten with Tory."

Mike's eyes rolled heavenward. "Mither of Our Lord, deliver us," he mumbled in a thick Irish brogue. "A Welsh saloon keeper and the banker's daughter, beset with a proper Republican match-maker."

Laura Everett sniffed. "I'm proud to be Republican, you rapscallion Democrat. At least I'm not Temperance, else I'd never consider your Mr. Davies for Tory."

"Little likely it is her parents will," Mike replied.

"He does have a way about him, though. And I heard how he acquitted himself in that frightful shooting last month. Stoddard offered to make him sheriff, you know."

Manion's jaw dropped. "No foolin'? So that's what he meant when he said Laughton offered him a job. I guess once he won the saloon and stirred up all the ruckus with his grand opening, that pompous old windbag hushed up the offer real fast."

"I dare say yes. But I like young Davies' sense of humor. Did you write that outrageous advertisement for him?" She paused and affixed him with a stern schoolmarm look. "Be honest, Michael."

"No. Although it was a piece worthy of me if I do say so myself. As to Rhys Davies' background, I don't know much. He's been a real mystery ever since he arrived in Starlight."

"But he saved Tory's life, didn't he?" she asked.

He scratched his chin and looked at her guilelessly. "Now why is it, Laura Everett, that my Irish intuition suddenly tells me you know more about this situation than I do?"

Her pudgy little hand reached out and clasped his thin arm with surprising strength, guiding him to the only two cleared chairs in the crowded room. "I shall unburden myself to you in strictest confidence, Michael, and you shall return the favor by doing some investigating for me."

Chapter Six

Tory opened her eyes, then squeezed them shut against the bright morning sunlight. She simply could not face another day like yesterday. But the instant her eyes closed, she was back in that icy river—with *him*, reliving the whole frightening, fascinating experience. All night she had tossed on her bed, pounding her pillows and trying to block Rhys Davies from her mind.

Hedda Laughton had been furious, when Charles brought Victoria home, soaked to the skin and wrapped in that odious gambler's blanket. Her daughter had been pulled from a river, nearly nude, then paraded into town wrapped up like some Ute squaw. Such a spectacle was simply too outrageous to be borne! Numb with cold and humiliation, Victoria endured her mother's clipped denunciation, then let Bessie assist her into a steamy hot tub.

As she had soaked, a bit of righteous anger pulsed through her veins, defrosting her blood. Mama was more concerned with her reputation than her life! Hurt had welled up in her along with the anger, but she could not seem to focus either emotion on her beautiful, perfect mother. Instead she fumed at Charles—and at *him*. Tory could not stay angry with her fiancé, who had been so solicitous of her on the way back to town. The accident had been Charles's fault, but he was terribly contrite. He had defended her to her mother, taking all the blame on himself, as any gentleman would.

That disreputable Rhys Davies was certainly no gentleman! He was the reason for all the furor, ripping off her clothing and carrying her naked in his arms. She had awakened at least a hundred times that night, always with his handsome face mocking her and her memories of their shocking physical intimacy tormenting her. No lady should ever feel such things, far less dream of them over and over again! How dare he invade her mind in such an immoral, disgusting way? But somehow Tory sensed that a man like Rhys Davies would dare a great deal.

Slapping the covers back furiously, she sat up in bed, willing herself to stop thinking of him. He was trash, totally outside the social circles in which she traveled. "I'll never even lay eyes on him again. Why let this upset me?" she muttered as she slipped from bed, wincing as her bruised hip gave a sharp stab of pain. Tory shoved her feet into a pair of fleece-lined slippers and belted a heavy satin robe around her slender waist. Every inch of her body hurt! "I'm lucky to be alive," she said through gritted teeth as she splashed cold water over her face, ignoring the pain.

The physical discomforts of her brush with disaster were endurable. The mental anguish of disgracing her family was quite another issue. On the surface, the events of the accident left her blameless, but her inner turmoil over Rhys Davies left her guilt-ridden and more than a bit confused. She rang for Bessie to dress her hair and began to prepare for the ordeal of facing her parents over breakfast. *The sooner I get this past me, the better I'll feel.*

Tory paused in the hallway next to the dining room, inspecting her appearance in a large oval mirror. A pale face with immaculately coifed pale gold hair stared back at her. Her turquoise eyes looked enormous and seemed to betray her innermost secrets. She shuddered, then began to walk resolutely to the dining room. Her hand froze on the porcelain doorknob when she overheard the conversation within.

"That odious Davies person is the cause of this whole mess," Hedda said waspishly. "Don't talk to me about his financial successes. He'll never be a part of our circle. He's merely a cheap card player."

Stoddard snorted. "That cheap card player owns not only the most prosperous saloon and fancy house in Starlight, but he's acquired a dozen other substantial properties with the proceeds from it."

"No doubt by cheating the poor sodden fools who frequent such disreputable places," Hedda sniffed.

"Be that as it may, he's becoming a man to reckon with in this town, thick as thieves with that scoundrel Manion and his Democrat newspaper. They swing a good block of votes."

"Surely not as many as Charles," Hedda replied with a start in her voice. "I know he'll be our next state senator."

"All you care about is Tory being the govenor's wife some day," Stoddard replied dismissively.

Tory stood still like a guilty child, unwilling to enter the room while they discussed her, yet afraid that one of the servants would catch her eavesdropping. Swallowing hard, she opened the door with a flourish and entered just as Hedda said, "Have you spoken to Sanders yet? Oh, Victoria, good morning. Have you seen your brother about? You're both tardy for breakfast."

"When has that ever bothered your son, madam?" Stoddard asked sourly of Hedda, nodding perfunctorily to his daughter as she slid into her seat. "Sanders was probably in Davies' place or some such last night, carousing."

"Let's not discuss such matters now, Stoddard," Hedda interrupted with steel beneath the level tone of her voice.

He harrumphed but said no more as the cook entered with a large tray laden with covered silver platters.

Tory had always felt compelled to defend her younger brother's shortcomings to her parents. In this case, it also served to deflect their ire away from her escapade. She took a forkful of the fluffy eggs Tess had served her and chewed slowly until the cook finished her task and left the room. "Sanders was up late last night reading, Papa. He stopped by my room carrying a volume of Tennyson."

"Just what a banker should read! Romantic rubbish," Stoddard replied in disgust. "Mark me, young lady, he had better be on time for work this morning and no mistake. Charles and I have to discuss several important deals including a mining property he recently acquired. I want your brother there to learn something practical."

"There is more to a gentleman's education than reading bank ledgers, Stoddard," Hedda said patronizingly.

Always on edge when her parents sparred, Tory attempted to excuse herself before the battle was joined in earnest. Stoddard's stern countenance turned toward her. "Finish your meal, Tory. I have some things to discuss with you, too." He paused as she sank reluctantly back in her chair. "Exactly how did you come to be wrapped in a blanket, looking like a drowned cat deposited on our doorstep? Charles was most evasive about the whole thing."

"Nonsense," Hedda interrupted. "He took full responsibility for the carriage accident."

"That doesn't explain the way Tory returned to town."

"I was washed downstream, Papa. I would've drowned when the phaeton went out of control and I fell into the water. But Mr. D—that gambler dived in after me and pulled me ashore. I was soaked with icy water. He . . . he just offered me a blanket to keep me from freezing."

His eyes were like gray agate as he replied, "You neglected to mention that somewhere along the way you managed to lose all your clothing from beneath that blanket. At least that's what I overheard the servants gossiping about last night after your mother trundled you off to bed."

Tears welled up in her eyes and Tory fought them back, hating to use such a girlish trick, even if she was hurt by his accusation. "He ripped my skirt and jacket off in the water so he could swim to shore without the weight of them dragging us both down. Believe me, no one could have been less happy about the whole situation than I!" she added angrily.

Obviously Charles's noble defense in front of Hedda had not carried over when he explained things to her father.

Seeing her distress and fearing an outpouring of female tears, Stoddard realized how useless it was to pursue the topic. "Just see you take more care in the future. After all," he said, looking over at Hedda, "we can't have a breath of scandal touch the future governor's wife, now can we?"

After the dreadful ordeal of breakfast, Tory was in no mood to encounter Sanders's green face two hours later. So, their father had been right. Sander had left the house to go carousing after he put in his solicitous appearance at her room last evening. She watched him walk stealthily from the stable toward a side door as she stood at the bay window in the library. Tennyson, indeed!

She sighed. Sanders was too much the dreamer to ever be a banker or any kind of success in the harsh world of builders and doers that flourished in the boisterous new state of Colorado. Rhys Davies obviously fit right in—at least as far as crass material successes went. She gave herself yet another mental shake for thinking of the blackguard and returned to her perusal of Goody's latest fashions. It was a bridal issue. With some trepidation she inspected the concoctions of white silks and lace. She would have to set a date with Charles soon.

A timid knock on the library door caused her to look up. "Yes, come in," she called out.

Ralph the butler stood in the doorway. The old man said uncertainly, "Miss Tory, you have . . . that is, since Mrs. Laughton is out, I can't ask her . . . he is most insistent."

"Who is? Whatever are you carrying on about, Ralph?"

"Guess I make uptown folks nervous, Miss Tory, even the classy servants," a familiar low voice answered. Rhys Davies shouldered his way past the indignant butler. His flat-crowned hat was in one hand, and he made a flourish of greeting with it, turning loose that slashingly wicked smile on her once more.

She shot to her feet. The impudence of the ruffian! "What are you doing here uninvited, Mr. Davies?" she asked in her best imitation of Hedda's chilly inflections.

"Why, Miss Tory, I've come to collect what belongs to me," Rhys replied innocently. "We won't be needing an audience. There's a good fellow," he said to Ralph, fairly shoving the sputtering elderly butler from the room as he handed him his hat.

"How dare you dismiss my servants! It's highly improper for you to be here, Mr. Davies. I realize I owe you a debt, but you are presuming a great deal more."

"Is that any way to speak to the poor sod who dragged you from an icy grave at great risk to his own person?" he asked in mock hurt, all the while walking nearer, like a big tomcat stalking a hypnotized robin.

"I repeat, what do you want, Mr. Davies?" she asked, backing around the heavy leather chair as she spoke.

His grin was predatory. "I don't think you'd really like me to tell you that, at least not here . . . not yet, Miss Tory." His words mocked her as he continued his advance. "I came here to retrieve my loan to you—the blanket? I see you do recall the blanket," he added with a low chuckle as she reached for the bell pull near the big window.

He was too quick for her and grasped her slim wrist gently but firmly, pulling her away from deliverance and into his arms. Tory fought for breath as fear and fury warred within her. "I shall scream down the house if you don't unhand me this instant!"

He shook his head reprovingly. "And add to the scandal already brewing? I don't think so. I'll just collect my loan and be on my way . . . but first"— he paused and studied her face as she pressed her small hands ineffectually against the hardness of his chest. "I'm a businessman, Miss Tory, and a good businessman always collects interest on a loan."

She could smell leather and shaving soap, feel the steady thud of his heart as he drew her closer. She knew he was going to kiss her, and short of creating a humiliating uproar, she was powerless to stop him. Her bruised hip ached abominably, but she refused to give him the satisfaction of crying out in pain.

"You are a cad to take such advantage of a lady," she said coldly, trying to turn her head.

One large hand held her head immobilized and then gently tilted it up to face him. "I never laid claim to being a gentleman, love. Mayhap you could teach me someday. But not just now." With that his mouth, warm and firm, brushed hers, then ever so softly his lips settled on hers, caressing and probing in the most intimate manner. His tongue slid out and traced the tight seam between her lips.

Tory held herself rigidly still, but her body sent off all sorts of wildly clamoring alarms. Instinctively she knew that if she thrashed or twisted, he would only tighten his embrace. She fought for breath and finally opened her mouth in an involuntary gasp of outrage. His tongue danced inside, fleetingly ringing the sensitive interior of her lips, then retreated before she had the pressence of mind to bite down on it.

As if reading her mind, he shook his head, then released her. "Now, the blanket, love."

"I am *not* your love, you insufferable, immoral, egotistical . . ." She sputtered, trembling with wrath, utterly drained of expletives. When she raised her hand to slap him, he easily caught her wrist and caressed the racing pulse in it.

"Tut, tut, love. A lady always controls her temper— or so Sister Frances Rose used to tell the girls in our school."

"You never went to school, you, you foreign ruf- fian!" she retorted, yanking her hand free. "I doubt that you can even read—at least in English," she added spitefully. Tory was rewarded by a look of sudden hurt that flashed across his handsome face.

Rhys quickly replaced it with another cheeky grin. "Oh, I can read all right. Here lately property deeds have become my specialty. Ask your fiancé, Charles."

Remembering her father's breakfast talk about Davies buying land and businesses in Starlight, she grew curious, then defensive. "Charles and I certainly do not discuss business matters," she replied haughtily as she slid around him, pray- ing that her sore limbs would not betray her. Her quaking legs held as she marched to the library door.

He said softly, "A pity you and Charles have so little to talk about. You think to marry that fool?"

She started to retort, then caught herself and turned to face him, saying in withering dismissal, "Ralph will escort you to the kitchen, where Tess, our cook, will return your blanket. Good day, Mr. Davies."

Watching him saunter across the room with a graceful long-legged stride, she forced steel into her spine and walked briskly into the hall, where she called for Ralph. The old man materialized immediately and nodded at her terse instructions, eyeing Rhys with obvious distaste and equally obvious apprehension. Very carefully he handed Davies his hat.

Rhys took it absently, all the while looking at Victoria's face. Her cheeks flamed with anger and some other equally primitive emotion. "Good day, Miss Tory," he said softly.

"Good-bye, Mr. Davies," she replied firmly, slamming the library door in his face.

Tory stood at the front window watching him walk down the stone path to where his big black stallion waited. He paused for a moment and held the blanket up to his face, inhaling her fragrance, soaked into its damp woolly surface. She felt a sudden stab of heat stain her cheeks and move through her body. Quickly dropping the lace curtain closed, she turned away as he resumed walking toward his horse. Tory felt like an intruder, watching an intimate tableau, yet one in which she was oddly an integral part.

What does he want? She feared to answer her own question.

The sounds of tinny music echoed across the deserted alley behind the Forty Rod Saloon. Sanders Laughton shivered in spite of the three stiff drinks with which he had fortified himself before agreeing to meet Emmet Hauser. Nervously he looked over his shoulder, but the big man's shadow did not appear in the alley. He was late, probably drunk inside. Sanders would never have agreed to see Ella's vicious uncle, but she had hinted that if he refused, Emmet might just present himself at Stoddard Laughton's bank. He shuddered.

"You 'fraid 'o me, boy? You oughta be," a low growling voice spoke from the darkness between two buildings. Then Hauser emerged into the dim misty moonlight, towering over the slight youth.

"You asked to see me, Emmet. What do you want? I told Ella—"

"Forget what you told Ella!" Hauser interrupted. "Now I'm tellin' you. She's increasin' real fast. Got no more time for your game-playing. You come up with enough money to get her that doctor in Denver or I go to your daddy. Or mebbe better yet, your mama," he added slyly.

Sanders sagged against the building, then gathered his wits and forced himself to look at the leering face etched harshly in the half-light. "You tell my parents and we'll all go down, Hauser. They'll disinherit me and have you and Ella run out of town. You'll never get another cent."

"I ain't got much playin' it your way so far. You got more excuses 'n a deacon with his hand caught in the collection plate." He grabbed Laughton's coat lapels and yanked him away from the building, lifting him off the ground until the expensive tailoring began to rip.

"Let me go, for God's sake!" Sanders stumbled back, smoothing his ruined suit coat ineffectually. The smell of Hauser's rotted teeth and unwashed body made him dizzy with nausea. "I told you, as soon as my father finishes the books for the month I'll get you the money—probably the first of the week."

"That's about all the time Ella's got herself. I want at least five thousand now, mind you. We gotta live

in Denver, 'n' I hear it gets real expensive up there."
He grinned and gave Sanders a hearty slap between
the shoulder blades.

Laughton nearly fell over from the blow, but steadied himself in time to watch Hauser shamble down
the alley toward the back door of another saloon. He
ran his fingers through his hair in frustration, then
reached for the silver hip flask he always carried
these days. He took a long, satisfying pull on it and
began to walk in the opposite direction, mulling over
his options.

The youth had precious few. Hauser and Ella
would bleed him dry, demanding money on a
regular basis until someone caught his carefully
covered embezzlements. He considered denying all
involvement with Ella, but immediately abandoned
that idea. At least two of her spiteful women friends
had seen them go into the Hauser cabin on numerous
occasions. She could produce enough witnesses to
create a ghastly scandal if it came to that—and Ella
Hauser was every bit as vindictive as her uncle. She
would do it if he did not pay up.

He also needed money for his own vices, chief
of which over the past months had become alcohol. He had been so upset over Ella and Emmet's
threats that he had failed miserably to perform at
the bordello the last several times. Humiliated, he
now avoided the ladies of the line and frequented
saloons. If only he could confess his plight to Tory.
If only there were some way he could get her to
take the blame for him as she had when they were
children. He ruminated. No chance there. His prim,
perfect sister would be so aghast at his fall from
grace, she would probably break her neck running to
their parents—to help him, of course, he thought
snidely.

"God, I hate you, Tory! I hate you, too, Mama, Papa! I hate you all," he sobbed, pounding the wall of the building until his fists bristled with splinters.

Chapter Seven

Laura Everett did not consider herself a vindictive woman, merely one with a strong sense of justice. She also deemed herself a damn good judge of character. That was precisely what brought her to Mike Manion's office on a sunny morning in late June. She was ready to right an old wrong. And Rhys Davies was her means of doing it. If along the way she could also serve as a matchmaker, well, so much the better. Humming softly, she smiled at passersby as she walked briskly down Main Street toward the *Plain Speaker*.

Inside the office, Rhys sat on a rickety chair, curiously eyeing his small birdlike companion as the latter scribbled frantically on a last-minute editorial. The Washington Hand Press in the back clanked and squeaked as Virgil turned out the first pages of today's edition.

Rhys once more scanned the firm no-nonsense

script of Laura Everett's note. Why in the devil did the sister-in-law of Tory's fiancé want to see him? His thoughts turned from the Everetts to Tory: Tory with her flaming cheeks betraying passion beneath that perfect ladylike exterior. He wanted to be the one to unleash it. No, he amended the thought with an arrogant grin, he *would* be the one. Certainly that prissy Charles never could. Everett would be the type to let her hold him at bay with her prim sensibilities. Then he would sneak off to a bordello to ease himself with a whore.

Of course, a man didn't trifle with a lady like Victoria Laughton outside the bounds of marriage. Rhys balked at the enormity of the concept. What had he heard that English m'lord in New York call it— "leg-shackling"? Well, if he was going to be bound to her, she would damn well be bound to him just as completely.

Maybe Laura Everett could help. With all his growing wealth, he still was not considered socially acceptable by the better sorts in Starlight. Oh, they had to come to him for their carnal amusements, usually on the sly, and they even did business in real estate and livestock with him. A few, turned down at the local banks, borrowed money from him—at higher rates because of the risk. But if he planned to settle down and build the life of his boyhood dreams, he had to become respectable. That meant in time even selling the Naked Truth. Maybe he would work out a deal with Ginger enabling her to buy it over a period of years. He owed her that.

His thoughts were interrupted by a light tap on the glass-paned door. As he stood up, Laura Everett entered with a broad smile lighting her round, friendly face. Mike continued his furious scratching, only waving in her general direction and muttering about his deadline.

In the manner of a longtime, very tolerant friend, she ignored his lapse in manners. "It's a good thing I didn't come to see you, Michael, else I'd haul you bodily from that chair and perish your deadline! No doubt some foolish Democrat diatribe, anyway." With that good-natured dismissal, she turned to Rhys and offered her plump lace-gloved hand for a firm shake. "Good morning, Mr. Davies. I do so appreciate your meeting me here, on more or less neutral territory, so to speak."

Rhys smiled as he shook her hand and then dusted off the best of Mike's battered oak chairs. "I could scarcely expect a lady such as you to meet me at my place of business, but this is hardly all that much more respectable," he said, waiting for a rebuttal from Manion.

"Watch it, Welshman," Mike retorted without missing a stroke of his pencil. "You're dealing with the two social arbiters of Starlight. One from the right side of the tracks and the other from the wrong side—on which you quite clearly happen to reside."

Laura chuckled. "That is true, at least for now, but I do believe you have possibilities, Mr. Davies. As to this incorrigible Irishman here, he aspires only to write his inflammatory editorials and incite foolish voters so they buy his newspapers."

"*You* buy my newspapers," Manion replied absently.

Laura sniffed as she sat down, motioning Rhys to do the same. "I'm not foolish, nor have the men of this benighted state seen fit to allow me to vote. But that is beside the point."

"Er, just what is the point, Mrs. Everett?" Rhys

studied her twinkling blue eyes, still puzzled by her request to meet him.

"The young are always impatient and straightforward. But I like straightforwardness in a man, Mr. Davies, and that is precisely why I detest my brother-in-law. The man is a thief," she said baldly, then sat back awaiting Rhys's reaction.

"She's quite right, you know. I saw the documentation," Mike said, then returned to his work.

"Then why isn't he in jail?" Rhys asked. Inscrutable when playing cards, his face now openly showed amazement.

"Why, indeed. He is Jacob's baby brother. Think of the scandal if I were to go to a federal marshal with such accusations. I did put a stop to his 'borrowing' from my assets after Jacob passed on." She snorted in contempt. "The arrogant young fool thought I'd never notice the loss of thousands of dollars as long as he doled out an allowance to me."

A grin creased Rhys's face. "I take it you are a very astute pupil when it comes to financial matters."

"A widow with a thief as her next of kin has to be! Now I handle my own money matters. Possessing such a keen nose for news, our mutual friend here"—she nodded to Mike, "has been a great deal of help to me over the past few years—with several land purchases and sales."

"She means mining speculations," Manion said, finally stopping his pencil and looking up, his eyes bright with newly awakened interest.

"There is no story in this for you, Michael, at least not yet," Laura scolded. Then her eyes crinkled at the corners as she chuckled. "Do you recall that, er, property up by the Uncompahgre River Charles bought last year?"

"That played-out silver mine near Mear's toll road?

Now, that was a real steal for Charlie boy!" Manion elaborated for Rhys. "He thought it held a fortune in silver and needed only enough capital investment to make it profitable."

"I wonder where he got that idea?" Laura said innocently. Manion merely grinned and shrugged, then waited for her to continue. "I have several friends from Denver who just might have some good news for Charles—if we were to share it with him. However, on the other hand . . ."

"You think the mine is worth something?" Rhys asked.

"Let's just say Charles has little background in mining and even less patience. When it failed to yield enough with minimal investment, he quickly dismissed the failure and covered it up saying he had paid so little for it that he could wait for a more opportune time to develop it." She paused and fixed shrewd blue eyes on Rhys. "You're from Wales. I understand you worked in the mines there."

His face was guarded as he replied, "Yes, coal mines. But the stink is the same either way. So is the danger. I'll not be going below ground ever again."

"No need to. Charles never did. Of course, Charles never knew if a mining engineer was fabricating a story for him either. He's rather short of cash now and needs funds for his political aspirations."

Manion's eyes lit with understanding. "You can't offer for the mine without getting his suspicions up. You need a partner in the venture."

"I'll want to verify your information about this mine, Mrs. Everett," Rhys said cautiously.

"I think one of your best customers, a Mr. Wilcox, will be able to furnish you with all the verification you'll need. If you can keep the poor wretch sober long enough."

"Tomato Nose Wylie Wilcox?" Rhys asked incredulously.

"He was the best hard-rock miner in Colorado before the whiskey got him," the Irishman said. "Dry him out and set him to work. If there's silver in that mine, he'll smell it out."

Rhys turned back to Laura Everett. "Say I decide to buy the mine. Why would you choose me, of all people, for a partner? Surely you know more respectable men who'd love to best Charles."

"Perhaps. But Charles hasn't half the dislike for any of them he has for you. He'll leap at the bait. Anyway, after you purchase the mine, I'll be introducing you into the very best social circles, Mr. Davies, even if you remain a Democrat!" With that startling pronouncement she stood up and stretched out her hand. "Do we have a deal?"

Rhys shook hands with her, saying, "If Wilcox can satisfy me, I'll go halves with you. As to the other . . ." He hesitated, groping for words. "You'd sponsor me in Starlight society?"

"Only if your intentions toward Victoria Laughton are honorable, you young rascal!" With both men silently gaping, she swept briskly from the office.

Manion looked at Davies's face and detected a tinge of color in the Welshman's cheeks. "Well, I'll be damned," he muttered in amazement.

The Fourth of July in Starlight, Colorado—population two thousand, five hundred and one—was celebrated with sufficient sartorial splendor, culinary magnificence, and elocutionary pomp to rival any silver city in the Rockies, Denver included. Men sweated in starched collars while ladies fanned themselves. Citizens from infancy to infirmity were dressed in their Sunday best for the festivities.

The city park was crowded to overflowing with picnickers feasting on every delicacy attainable, from golden fried chicken to imported oysters. All the saloons' bars were polished and strung with red, white, and blue bunting and groaning beneath bowls of hard-boiled eggs and baskets of pretzels. Beer and whiskey flowed freely. So did the oratory.

Waiting impatiently, Charles Everett stood next to the speaker's podium on a platform erected in the center of the park. Bereft of trees to provide shade, the bunting draped wooden structure soaked up the merciless sunlight. Charles appreciated Stoddard Laughton's sponsorship in his bid for the state senate, but he detested all this plebeian pressing of the flesh, making speeches to small town yahoos and shaking their sweaty hands. He also detested the endless droning of his future father-in-law's introduction. He would be soaked with sweat before he even began his presentation!

He must make a good impression with several members of the Republican Party from Denver who were present to evaluate him. The state legislature was only his entree to the governor's mansion, thence to the United States Senate and national politics. He would take Victoria to Washington. What a perfect senator's wife she would make. Even a cabinet officer's wife.

Just then Laughton gave way with a grand flourish, and a ripple of applause filled the air. Charles took the speaker's podium, thanking Laughton, the mayor, and all the visiting dignitaries. After a brief exchange of smiles with his beautiful lady, seated in the front row of the assembly, he focused on his text and began to speak.

Tory fought the urge to wriggle on the wooden

chair. It was beastly uncomfortable, but better than standing as most of the crowd had to do. Hedda sat next to her, beaming, not a hair out of place on her silver-blonde head as she listened raptly to Charles. Her mother never perspired or fidgeted or did anything the least bit unladylike. Right now Tory wanted nothing more than to kick off her slippers, peel down her stockings, and go wading in the icy clear waters of the creek that raced along the edge of the park. Sighing, she forced the atrocious thought from her mind and attempted to forget the heat as Charles's staid, dignified delivery continued. He addressed the issues of political corruption and immorality, the encroachments of destructive sheepmen onto good cattle-grazing lands, the need for restrictions on the use of alcohol and an end to the shame brought on by the ladies of the line who corrupted the streets of Starlight.

"Do you think he'll ever stop? Should I offer a rebuttal before he closes down the Naked Truth?" Rhys asked Mike. Stifling a yawn, he leaned against a large white oak to the right of the platform where the two had repaired to seek relief from the press of the crowd and the heat of the day.

Manion guffawed loudly. "Do you have political as well as social and economic aspirations, boyo? We could use us a few more solid Democrats behind President Cleveland. 'Tis fearful lonely he must be in Washington these days." The little Irishman lay stretched out in comfort on the grassy knoll as a slight breeze ruffled his unruly hair.

"I have enough to occupy me these days without going into politics, Mike," Rhys replied as his eyes scoured the crowd, fastening on Tory's sculpted profile. She was perfection itself in a pale pink muslin dress. Daintily she smoothed the crisp gathers of her skirt, then fanned herself. Even from his vantage point, Rhys could see the flush of color in her porcelain cheeks. She must be roasting in all those clothes. At once thoughts of stripping away her gown, petticoats, corset, and chemise rose in his mind. If that pale delicate body looked so good frozen in river water, what would it look like when warmed by passion? His erotic ruminations were interrupted by his companion's question.

"How is the mining venture coming? You've not mentioned it in weeks."

A hint of a smile twitched on Davies's lips but did not reach his dark blue eyes. "Wilcox took a while to sober up. The mine has checked out rather well, but the would-be senator's finances haven't. It seems he has rather badly overextended himself on this campaign."

"And on this speech," Manion added, rolling up to lean back on his elbows. "Think I'll liven up things a bit. If you don't want your lady's ire, you'd best be on your way," he added with a devilish wink.

Rhys shrugged in indifference. Everyone, including Tory, knew he detested Everett.

"Beer's gettin' warm while you blather on up there, Charlie boy," Manion called out, projecting his voice with surprising clarity.

Everett shuffled his speech papers in irritation without looking up the hill to acknowledge the heckler. A small ripple of laughter echoed about the crowd, which had already begun to thin. "A typical response from one of Starlight's leading debauched drinkers masquerading as a newspaper editor," Everett replied acidly, returning to his text, only to be interrupted once more.

"Then consider all these poor sober folks about you, just hankering for a cool draught of lemonade,"

Manion called out, still stretched out indolently on the hillside.

From the back of the crowd another voice chimed in, "Yeah, Charlie, remember 'Lemonade Lucy'!" At the mention of former President Hayes's wife, a series of muffled guffaws could be heard around the park.

"Yes, you might even lose the vote of those men who supported John St. John on the Prohibition ticket. I heard he got nearly as many votes as the Republican Blaine!" Mike called out.

"Since it appears our good editor's intellect is as weary as his frail body, I shall bring my remarks on this historic day to a speedy conclusion," Everett said with all the dignity he could muster. He was rewarded with polite applause from the handful of seated dignitaries, but Manion's voice cut through their attempts to rally behind the orator.

"Ah, Charlie, me boy, I can lie up here for as long as you can lie down there, rest assured."

At that sally the crowd began to whoop and yell. Stoddard Laughton gave an agitated signal for the band to strike up a rousing Sousa march before the place erupted into a full-scale riot.

Charles furiously crumpled the remainder of his twenty-page speech in his haste to stuff it into his coat pocket. Narrowing his eyes on the little Irishman who had incited the debacle, he watched the big Welsh saloon keeper pull Manion to his feet with a hearty laugh. A tight smile replaced Everett's scowl as he considered Davies and the mine deal. "We'll just see who's laughing at who when you find out you've bought a worthless hole in the ground," he muttered to himself as he stalked off the platform.

Rhys observed Tory's placating gestures to the irate candidate. *She's soothing him like a moth-*

er would a pouting, spoiled child, he thought in vexation. Still, he continued to stare at the beautiful woman, ignoring Manion and the jocular men who had walked up to congratulate him. Rhys stood apart from their levity, deep in thought.

Charles's bitter anger rubbed Tory's heat-frayed nerves raw as she attempted to assure him that all the sensible men of property in attendance would certainly vote for him while the rowdies would be too drunk in their saloons to even find the ballot box.

When Hedda and Stoddard joined them, Charles turned his frustrations from his fiancée to his prospective in-laws. Tory let the threads of their conversation slip away as she rubbed her temples, feeling inexplicably that someone was staring at her. She looked up to where that vile little editor had disrupted the festivities, and her pale eyes met burning blue ones.

The big Welshman stood with his hat pushed rakishly to the back of his head, revealing sweat-dampened curling brown hair. A wide smile insinuated itself across his insolent face as he leaned negligently against the rough bark of the white oak. He wore no jacket, and his white linen shirt clung indecently to the hard, hairy chest she remembered so well. When he touched one hand to the brim of his hat in a mock salute, she finally had the presence of mind to tear her mortified gaze free of his hypnotic spell.

The nerve of that . . . that . . . foreigner! "If you will excuse me, Mother, Father, Charles, I must get some fresh air before the press of the crowd overwhelms me," Tory said breathlessly as she saw Senator Collins and several other important Republican guests moving through the celebrants toward Stoddard and Charles.

Hedda remonstrated with her daughter. "A lady never rushes off without an escort, Victoria."

"I'll find Sanders, Mother. He was here just before the speeches began," she replied, slipping into the crowd before Hedda could stop her.

In truth, even if she had not felt a desperate need to escape Rhys Davies's mocking smile, she did need to locate her brother. When last she saw him he had been well on his way to overindulging once more. If Sanders disgraced himself publicly again, their father might take drastic measures.

Something was troubling her young brother. He had grown increasingly quiet and morose over the past weeks, spending long hours at the bank and locking himself in his room alone at night to drink himself stuporous. Only two mornings ago she had heard mother and son in a sotto voce argument with decidedly ugly overtones. Sanders had been too ill from drink to go to work, and Hedda had made chilling threats that brought the youth quickly to heel.

A large miner clad in a sweaty, odoriferous flannel shirt bumped into her, then apologized as she pushed carefully through the crowd. Would the Welshman smell like that? He had obviously been perspiring. Without conscious volition her mind instantly conjured up the picture of that nearly transparent linen shirt and the hard muscles beneath its flimsy covering. *Disgraceful!* her conscience cried out. But another part of her mind said he would smell much different than the unwashed miner. She shook her head to clear it, once again massaging her temples as she leaned against the side of a crude wooden plank table at the edge of the park. Thank heavens the crowd had thinned.

117

A small boy bouncing a ball came skipping by her while a woman in a calico dress yelled for him to return and finish his gooseberry pie. Sighing, Tory knew she had to skirt around the park to where Tom Kitzler and several other wealthy young men had been drinking with Sanders. Prying him away from Tom might prove tedious, but she must at least attempt it. *My penance.* The thought popped into her mind. Tory raised her wilting pink skirts to avoid a scampering yellow cur chasing after the boy and his ball, then squared her shoulders and walked purposefully toward the west end of the park.

Sanders saw the wavering vision of his sister materialize at one end of the park. Then Ella Hauser appeared from the opposite direction. He wobbled to his feet amid cheers from Tom and Donald. He must stop Ella from accosting Tory and saying Lord only knew what!

"Well, there she is, Miss Royal Highness herself," Ella said spitefully, "come to rescue her poor drunk sot of a brother."

"We got business with him first, girlie." Emmet Hauser's deep voice elicited a gasp of surprise from Tory. His big dirty hand pulled at her arm. He had emerged from the shadows of a large fir tree, following his niece into the clearing.

"See here, Mr. Hauser, there's no need to involve my sister—"

Sanders's slurred words were cut short by Ella. "So now it's Mr. Hauser. Ain't we got formal, Sandy."

"Let me go, you filthy ruffian," Victoria said with as much strength as she could muster. Her heart was pounding with fright. Tom Kitzler and Donald Tolley were both far too drunk to protect her, as was Sanders. What did that nasty little niece of the saloon keeper mean, calling her brother so familiarly?

Ella pushed past Tory and began to whisper furiously to Sanders, practically dragging him into the bushes as his companions jeered and hooted.

"Let 'em talk. They got things to be settled," Emmet said, tightening his hold on Tory's arm.

His breath was fetid with sour beer and hard boiled eggs. She turned her head away from his face and pushed angrily at his chest. Beneath the thick padding of fat lay iron-hard muscle that yielded nothing. Tory grew frightened as he leaned down and pressed his mouth against her temple, inhaling her fragrance.

"Release me this instant!" she whispered furiously.

"I'd do as the lady says," a low, steely voice interrupted. Rhys Davies walked slowly into the clearing and stopped in front of Hauser. His posture was decidedly menacing as one hand rested firmly on the butt of his Colt Peacemaker while the other took Tory's arm from Hauser's unwelcome grasp.

When Hauser released her, she was pulled against Rhys's side and held fast. His heart was slamming in his chest and every muscle in his body quivered with fury, as if someone had just trespassed on his personal property. He shoved her behind him, daring the mountainous Hauser to make a move. Emmet took a step forward, then stopped short.

"It'd be my pleasure to kill you," Rhys said in a low, cold voice.

Hauser's yellow eyes narrowed in consideration. Then he replied, "I got no quarrel with you, ner her. Come on, Ella. That there boy's too drunk to talk now anyways. Leave him be." Hauser turned and walked quickly over to his niece and Sanders, who were engaged in a furious whispered argument. Just as Emmet reached them, Ella gave Sanders a sharp slap that sent the weaving youth reeling to the ground, then turned and fled with her uncle shambling behind her.

Tory's stunned reaction to the violence was broken when she saw her brother strike his head on a rock. She broke free of Rhys's protective hold and raced to kneel beside Sanders.

Rhys watched her frantically call her brother's name and dab at the cut on his head. Then he quickly strode to the stream and wet his best linen handkerchief. Returning, he knelt beside her. "Here, let's use this to stop the bleeding." He pressed the snowy linen to the wound and then examined it with a practiced eye. "It isn't too bad. Just a little knock, but he'll have a right royal headache in the morning." He began to bind up the cut by tieing the handkerchief about Sanders's head.

"He's still unconscious." Victoria fretted as she tried to rouse Sanders.

"He's dead drunk, love. Not to worry. He'll wake up all too soon, first afraid he'll die, then afraid he won't." With that he hoisted the youth's body up effortlessly and stood him on very unsteady legs. Wrapping one of Sanders's arms across his broad shoulders, Rhys half-walked, half-dragged the semiconscious youth toward Main Street.

"Where are you taking him?" Tory cried, dogging his footsteps.

Rhys turned with the boy dangling like a sleeping puppy and said with a smile, "To my saloon. Come along with you, love."

Chapter Eight

"To . . . to that sinkhole of depravity? You can't mean it. I must take him home."

Rhys looked her up and down like a father inspecting a half-bright child. "Your brother is covered with blood. So are you. I would suspect arriving at your house in this condition might send a few tongues to wagging if we walked. There's a buggy in back of my place. We can take the back streets and slip him in the servants' quarters—that is, if you can rely on your servants." He waited a beat, then shifted the boy's weight. "Make up your mind, love. Your dear brother isn't getting any lighter as we stand here arguing."

She bit back a frosty retort at his presumptuous familiarity. Like it or not, she was at his mercy. Any of her parents' friends could happen on the scene at any moment. Shuddering at the possible scandal, she took Sanders's other arm and they walked quickly into the cover of the trees. By the time they reached the Naked Truth's livery barn, Victoria was a nervous wreck. The saloon, like all others up and down Main Street, was filled with raucous drunken men and those awful women. But everyone seemed so intent on celebrating they failed to notice the two fugitives dragging a drunken companion through the back alleys. Rhys moved with amazing speed and catlike stealth in spite of his burden.

"You seem to have had a good deal of practice at this, Mr. Davies," Tory gasped out as Rhys propped Sanders's moaning form against the stable wall. The interior was dim and smelled of fresh hay and horses.

He flashed her a grin. "I've been pitched into a few back alleys in my day, if that's what you're asking."

"In Denver?" Why did she care!

"Denver, St. Louis. Even New York—the real mean alleys are there, believe me," he added grimly as he began to hitch up a big bay gelding to a smart little carriage. The newly built livery housed three carriages of various styles and over a dozen fine horses, including the magnificent black she'd first seen at the river.

The look on his face when he mentioned New York was haunted. Oddly, Victoria felt his long-buried pain touch her. What kind of a childhood could an immigrant boy from Wales have had? In spite of herself, some perverse curiosity bested her sense of decorum. She pried, "How old were you when your family came from Wales to New York?"

His hands tightened on the harness for an instant, then he replied in a flat voice. "I had no family. They all died back in the old country. I was fourteen."

"How awful," she blurted out, unable to imagine her life not surrounded by her family, or the security of growing up in her sumptuous home.

"I survived," he replied. "America's the land of opportunity. Even a Welsh boy who couldn't speak an English sentence can become a man of property."

Recalling her taunts to him about being able to read English, she reddened in mortification. "Obviously you've achieved a great deal, Mr. Davies," she said primly.

"I don't have everything I want . . . yet," he replied softly as he walked toward her.

Tory stood in the darkness, frozen, as he approached her. Just as he reached out for her, a bright shaft of light blinded her. The door swung open with the loud creek of new wood.

"What the hell's goin' on?"

Tory stared at a carrot-haired woman dressed in a shockingly low-cut gown of red, white, and blue stripes. The redhead blinked as she held a six-shooter in front of her. As soon as she recognized Rhys in the dim interior, she lowered the gun. Tory could feel the whore's cat-green eyes narrow spitefully as she inspected her rival's wrinkled, filthy muslin gown and tangled hair.

"There's been a little accident, Ginger," Rhys said smoothly. "I'm helping the lady get her injured brother home. Be a love and check to make sure the coast is clear, will you?"

Ginger sensed the protective way Rhys stood next to the fancy uptown girl, and she was having none of it. She swished closer to inspect the shambles of the blonde's clothing and hairdo. As her hard eyes appraised Tory, she ran her hand down the gleaming satin stripes of her own gown. "Whadaya think? Red, white, and blue for the Fourth. I had it made up special," she purred.

"How very . . . patriotic," Tory replied, half appalled, half curious. She had never been this close to a "lady of the line" before. She supposed the woman was attractive in a brassy, voluptuous way.

Rhys's expression hardened when Ginger reached out to place her hand possessively on his arm. She quickly withdrew it and said tartly, "I heard a commotion in the stable and thought I'd save you from a horsethief. My mistake!"

As she stomped out and slammed the door, Sanders groaned loudly.

"Will she spread gossip?" Tory asked, her throat tight with dread. She knew that lots of the leading men of Starlight frequented Rhys's exclusive premises.

"Not if she expects to live out the week," he replied grimly, cursing the rotten luck that had brought Ginger to the stables amid all the pandemonium of the Fourth of July.

Tory's eyes widened at his curt dismissal of the woman. Judging from her jealousy and his power over her, she must be his mistress. She watched Rhys heft Sanders like a sack of grain and toss him onto the buggy seat, where the semiconscious man began to slide.

"Get in and anchor him so he doesn't fall while I open the back door to the alley," Rhys said, placing his large hands about her waist and lifting her into the buggy. Sanders was muttering something about a stomach ache as she held his head back against the soft leather of the seat. Thank God the bleeding had stopped.

Rhys opened the door, checked the alley, and then leaped into the left side to drive. Since he had draped her brother against the far right panel, she was forced to sit between them, sandwiched tightly next to the

Welshman's broad shoulder and hard thigh. She could feel his muscles ripple as he flicked the reins and the gelding took off at a smart trot.

They took the back streets, skirting far outside town, then cutting up a deserted alley for the rear of the Laughton mansion.

"All the servants should be off for the day," Tory said half to herself as she struggled with her increasingly restless charge, who was beginning to complain about his belly hurting.

Rhys recognized the signs and reined in the bay. They were at the rear of a big frame house with an elaborate formal garden. No one seemed to be stirring.

"Why are you stopping at the Throckmorton place?"

"Because we'll never make it to your house," Rhys explained as he rounded the buggy and helped a stumbling, gurgling Sanders toward some elaborate topiary.

Tory swallowed her own bile in mortification when the unmistakable sounds of retching assaulted her ears. *Mercy! What should I do now?*

As if in answer to her quandary, Rhys called from behind the hedge, "I could use some help. Do you have an extra kerchief or some such to clean him up with? I'm fresh out of linens."

She dug quickly into her reticule and extracted two small lace squares. Not much, but it would have to do. When she rounded the topiary hedge she gasped in horror. "Mrs. Throckmorton's prize roses! She always wins the blue ribbon in Starlight's garden show."

"Well, she won't this year," Rhys said philosophically, inspecting the noisome mess withering the scarlet blooms like acid. He watched her as she wiped

Sanders's face. "Do you grow roses, perchance?"

"Laura Everett does." A small smile unwillingly lifted the corners of her mouth. "Maybe she'll win for once. I never did like Mrs. Throckmorton anyway," she added puckishly as she helped her brother stumble unsteadily to his feet.

"She ushta yell 'n' send her shtableman after ush," Sanders mumbled to Tory. "When we'd climb in her pre-preshus flower beds."

"And I used to hide you and Tom Kitzler under the bed in my room," Tory said with asperity. Once after Mrs. Throckmorton had come storming over to report to Hedda, Tory had been caught with the culprits. Her punishment had been far worse than Sanders's. Girls were never to engage in such boyish high jinks.

By the time they helped her brother back into the carriage and completed the drive up the alley to the Laughton house, Sanders was snoring again. Since the bleeding had stopped and Rhys knew for certain that the contents of his stomach had been emptied, he slung the youth carelessly over his shoulder and had Tory lead the way through the aspens and privet hedges to the servants' stairs.

The house was silent as a tomb. Sounds of Sanders snoring echoed down the long, narrow hallway that stretched from the second-floor landing to the heavy walnut doors of their bedrooms.

"In here," Tory commanded as she opened the door to an ornately furnished room.

Although the decor was heavy and dark, it didn't have the feel of a man's living quarters. Too many vases and too much bric-a-brac. Sanders was a collector of expensive junk in Rhys's estimation. He dumped his burden across the bed as Tory wrung her hands, then rushed to the dry sink where she wetted down a towel. As he watched her bathe the boy's pasty face, he asked quietly, "Have you always covered up for his weakness?"

Her head shot up. "Sanders isn't weak! Just a bit confused. He's only nineteen."

"At nineteen I was riding shotgun on a stagecoach between St. Joe and Council Bluffs," Rhys shot back.

Tory read the disgust on his face as he looked down at Sanders. Cold anger welled up in her. Holding her head high, she tilted it haughtily just as Hedda did when she delivered a setdown. "I scarcely think emulating the deprivations of your childhood would benefit my brother."

Rhys took the wet towel from her hand and threw it carelessly on the thick wool carpet. "The poor boy's passed out cold. Best let him sleep it off," he said. Then his eyes fastened hungrily on her pale face with its enormous turquoise eyes. "You could use some help yourself." He inspected her blood-smeared, dusty dishevelment. "When will your parents return? You wouldn't want to frighten them, love."

"Once and for all, I am *not* your love, Mr. Davies. I thank you for your timely assistance, but you really must leave now. It isn't proper for—"

Rhys reached out and snatched her hand before she could withdraw it, then pulled her into the hallway. "All the servants have holiday, right? Which room is yours, love? I think you'll be needing a lady's maid unless you plan on cutting that outfit from your body with a kitchen knife."

She gasped at the indelicacy of his suggestion. Then when he began opening doors, searching each room, the seriousness of her situation dawned on her. The servants *were* gone. Mama and Papa would be several hours yet. Sanders was unconscious. She was alone with this ruffian, who had already taken shockingly improper advantage of her!

Opening the door at the far end of the hall, he clucked in recognition. "This has to be yours. All frilly and bright. Not cold and cluttered like your mother's. How long has your father let her sleep separate from him?" he asked as he pulled her through the door and into his embrace.

Tory stiffened in outrage. "How dare you even voice such an unmentionable question!" She struggled ineffectually in his arms.

"That long, eh? Pity. A husband and wife should always share a bed."

"I'm sure you're an expert at sharing beds, judging from that jealous strumpet in the stable!"

He laughed softly. "Now who's jealous, Tory?" He could feel her heart pounding furiously as he held her pressed closely to his chest. She turned her head away to avoid the kiss she knew was coming. He raised one hand and caught it in her hair, forcing her to face him.

Night blue eyes locked with pale aqua ones as he lowered his mouth. But instead of kissing her, he nuzzled her ear and whispered, "Lace-covered buttons always were the worst ones."

Tory could feel his fingers deftly unfastening the long row of tiny buttons that ran down the back of her dress. Before she could break free he had the gown half undone. It fell from her shoulders as she backed away from him. Rhys stood between her and the door. She was trembling uncontrollably as her eyes scanned the room. The window was half open.

"You'd break that lovely neck, Tory. It's a long drop to the ground," he said as he offered her his hand, palm up. "Just turn about like a good girl and let me unlace you. Then—"

"Then you'll throw me on the floor and ravish me! Do you actually think I'll cooperate with your mad scheme?" she shrieked.

He shushed her like a parent would a child. "If I wanted to 'ravish' you, Tory, I wouldn't need to unlace your corset to accomplish it, believe me." He was rewarded by the crimson staining her cheeks. "I'll just untie the laces so you can disrobe after I leave. You have my word on it."

"The word of a gambler and rake," she spat scornfully, edging for the window.

He cut her off and she backed toward the bed. Then realizing the tactical error of that move, she lunged for her dressing table and grabbed her large silver hairbrush with one hand while holding up her dress with the other. She threw the heavy missile and he ducked. Piece by piece she began clearing off the dresser as he drew closer and closer, miraculously ducking most of her toilette articles. Finally a bottle of expensive perfume her aunt Helene had sent from Paris found the mark. It first shattered against the bedpost, then splashed his upper body with essence of violets.

Rhys swore as the sickly sweet liquid drenched his shirt front. He made one last giant stride and grabbed her, pulling her onto the bed with him. As he sat on the edge of her silk coverlet, he threw her across his lap and ripped loose the laces of her corset in exasperation. She wriggled and screamed as her delectable little rump bounced enticingly before his eyes. Without thinking, he gave her a sharp smack, then a second.

The spanking stung even through layers of skirts and petticoats. "You miserable, despicable, vile—"

He gave her a third and final whump, then dumped her onto the bed. Staring down at her, he brushed ineffectually at the violet perfume stains. "Your parents should've administered that sort of punishment to you and your sorry brother a lot more often. Good day, love."

Tory resisted the urge to hurl another bottle at him when he paused in the doorway and clucked at the mess. "Watch you don't cut your feet on the broken glass. I hope you can explain all this to your poor maid when she comes back from holiday."

As he whistled jauntily down the hall, Tory flopped back on the bed, exhausted and frightened. Never in her life had she made such a spectacle of herself. Or lost her temper that way. But that man could turn a saint into a snarling bobcat! Then she remembered his shirt soaked with violet perfume. Victoria's musical laughter filled the empty room. "Just explain *that* to your red-headed whore, Rhys Davies!"

Sanders rolled over in bed and pulled a soft goose down pillow over his throbbing skull, whispering harshly, "Go away, Ralph. I won't be going to work today. Tell my father I am most indisposed."

"Most indisposed, indeed, young man!" Hedda Laughton's icy voice cut through his sleepy hangover like a Bowie knife through cornmeal mush. "You turn over in that bed and face me."

Sanders groaned and uncovered his head, then sullenly sat up in bed, resting his arms across his knees. He knew better than to open his mouth.

"Look at you, sleeping in your clothes—the same ones you wore to the celebration yesterday. And brawling again," she added, looking at the dried blood on his head. "It isn't bad enough you disgraced us by becoming inebriated at a political function where so many of your father's influential friends were present, but you had to worry us half to death as well, dragging your sister back home with you. You ruined Victoria's day as well as your father's and mine!"

He felt the rage boil up in him, churning in his already sick gut. He ruined his precious, perfect sister's day, did he? What did she have to worry about besides which gown to wear tomorrow? He had Emmet Hauser threatening to beat him senseless! He rubbed the scabbed cut on his head and cursed. Ella hadn't done a bad job unassisted by her uncle!

"You should see the doctor about that awful-looking wound, Sanders," Hedda continued. "Of course, that would only add to the scandal. Dr. Runcie is such a gossip! Your father has gone to Mayor Johnson's home for a political meeting. Make yourself presentable and go to the bank. One of the Laughton men should be there today. You owe it to your family's good name."

After Hedda left the room, Sanders struggled to the washbasin and splashed cool water on his face. What should he do? As he shaved with unsteady hands, cutting himself twice, he recalled last evening. Tory had brought clean water in and tried to cajole him into eating some supper. She had also questioned him about Ella and old man Hauser. Just what he needed—to have her interfering, trying to save him from himself! If she found out about his getting Ella pregnant . . . For a moment his mind closed down. Then Hedda's words echoed in it: "Your father has gone to Mayor Johnson's home for a political meeting." Those tedious affairs lasted almost as long as the speeches. Stoddard would be absent from the bank all day. Sanders could get more money for

Emmet if he made up another phony mortgage.

Suddenly he dropped the razor with an oath as he nicked himself again. What was the use? Hauser would bleed him dry . . . unless . . . He was heartily sick of his mother's icy criticism, his father's yelling rages, his sister's cloying solicitude, and Ella's fat, ugly face. Why not leave them all in his dust?

He stared into the mirror, trying to gauge whether he had the nerve. Bloodshot eyes stared back at him from a sickly greenish face. The cut and bruise on his forehead was scabbed over and purplish. His was the face of a desperate man. Lips thinned grimly, he began the parody of a smile. The Union National Bank of Starlight was about to have the largest withdrawal made in its twenty-five-year history. Picturing Ella's pudgy pockmarked face when she heard he had vanished, he smiled broadly. By the time he had completed his toilette and dressed, he was whistling. He even stopped on his way out to wish his beloved sister a good morning.

"So, Charles has sold you the mine. I trust you are satisfied that the property was worth the price?" As Rhys nodded, Laura Everett poured tea into an impossibly fragile china cup, added sugar and cream, and handed it to him. She watched him hold it awkwardly and take a sip, then said, "I'm happy you've finally accepted my standing invitation for tea." She paused a beat and tasted her own tea with lemon. Over the past weeks she and the likable young rogue had formed both a business partnership and an unconventional friendship. "It's time to introduce you to Starlight society. I think the end of July should give us ample time to plan a gala, don't you?"

Rhys carefully set the cup down. He shifted in the stiff-backed chair, but Laura Everett's patient blue eyes calmed his nerves. He cleared his throat. "You may become a social pariah if you sponsor me, Laura. Maybe it's best if we're just silent partners in the mine."

"What's brought on this loss of that boundless Welsh confidence? Couldn't be one small blonde girl with blue-green eyes, could it?"

Rhys put his head in his hands, then ran his fingers through his hair. "Did she tell you? Or her mother, worse yet?"

Laura chuckled. "Both Hedda and her daughter are mum indeed when any sort of scandal impinges on their family. I did hear a few rumors about Sanders being drunk again at the Fourth of July celebration in the park."

Rhys groaned. "Did anyone mention Tory?"

Laura set her cup down and raised her eyebrows. "So, you and Tory did have another set-to. I take it Sanders was involved. No, no one connected you or Tory with her brother's problem. Tell me about it," she coaxed sympathetically.

He shrugged helplessly. "Every time I come near her it ends in disaster, Laura. I've never made so many mistakes with a woman before. Of course, she's a lady," he added glumly as if that explained everything.

"And you feel socially inferior?" she asked gently.

With a shaky laugh, Rhys replied, "Well, I'm no gentleman, Tory and I agree on that!" He stood up, stuffed his hands in his pockets, and began to pace. "I *am* socially inferior, Laura. You're the only lady who's ever been my friend."

"Believe me, you'll acquire lots more," she said drily. "As to becoming a gentleman, most of it's pure veneer, especially out West. A lot of money and a little training will do the trick. You've already done quite well in the money department. I can tutor you about social etiquette." Laura had noted the painfully careful way Rhys handled the fragile china cup and saucer. "You haven't broken anything yet—that gives you a head start over eighty percent of the men in southwest Colorado."

She elicited a relaxed laugh from him as she motioned for him to follow her from the elegantly appointed sitting room down a thickly carpeted hallway into an enormous formal dining room. The gleaming mahogany table was a good twenty feet long with a huge crystal epergnes sitting in the center, filled with magnificent red roses and flanked by heavy silver candelabra. One single place was set at the table. An ornate Haviland dinner plate was flanked by more flatware, bowls, and glasses than Rhys had ever seen in his life.

"It takes all this just to eat one dinner? With this many spoons and forks and a dozen miners we could dig a mine shaft."

Laura laughed and replied, "When you arrived I instructed my butler to prepare this so you could practice. I rather anticipated you'd not seen the table setting for a formal dinner party—and Hedda Laughton is a stickler for formality."

"She's raised her daughter to be one, too," he replied with a sigh.

"Sit down and let us begin with the appetizer course. Basically you use the utensils from the outside, working your way in."

Rhys sat gingerly on the brocade cushion of the elegantly carved mahogany chair and faced the bewildering array of dishes and utensils. "I feel like Alfred Packer facing Judge Gerry," he said grimly.

At his reference to the infamous cannibalism trial then going on in Lake City, Laura could not resist retorting, "You don't know what's on the menu yet!"

Rhys was a fast study, as a traveling thespian manager had told him when he had done a brief stint of acting. After they moved from appetizers through dessert to coffee and port, he looked up at her and said, "This is a lot easier than learning to deal blackjack. I think I can manage not to disgrace myself."

"My butler and maid will serve each person through all seven courses. You can watch what the others around you do and simply follow suit. I'll seat you and Tory near the end of the table so you can watch how it goes first."

"You're pairing me with Tory?" he asked as he stood up. Perplexity was plainly written on his face. "I understand about the mining deal and your wanting to get even with Charles. But why me for Tory?"

"Several reasons." As she rose, Rhys carefully pulled back her chair, then followed her leisurely stroll back to the parlor. "Most obviously I do not favor Charles as the right husband for Victoria. He wants her family's name and political influence, and I want to thwart him. Moreover, Victoria would be unhappy with him and she deserves a chance for better. She's not like her mother. Oh, there is a superficial physical resemblance. Hedda was the reigning beauty of her day just as Tory is now, but beauty is not everything—else I'd never have snared Jacob Everett," she added as a rueful aside.

"You dislike Hedda Laughton?"

"Let us just say I find her manipulative. Between her and Stoddard they've turned poor Sanders into a wastrel and drunkard, but at least he's defied their wishes."

"And Tory never does?" Rhys supplied. "I know she's taken the blame and shielded her brother from punishment since they were children."

"Far too much so. But if Sanders carries enjoyment of life to excess, Tory is just the opposite. She's so painfully correct, so obedient to Stoddard and Hedda's every wish . . ."

"You mean she's laced too tightly into her corset of propriety. You think I should cut the strings?" Rhys said with a hesitant smile twitching his lips.

Laura laughed and nodded. "Aptly put, Rhys. You're a breath of fresh air for this stale, corrupt little town, and for Tory, too."

"I represent everything she hates, Laura. That remark about the corset wasn't just a metaphor," Rhys said as his face turned grim once more.

"Pray tell me about your latest battle with Victoria," she said as she poured him a small goblet of whiskey from a crystal decanter on a side table in the parlor.

He tossed it down in one gulp. "This is a long, complicated story. It really began at the river."

"When you saved her from drowning? I already know about that." She gave him a refill.

"You don't know about how I reclaimed my blanket the next day . . ." Fortified with two shots of smooth Kentucky bourbon, he told the whole tale of the stolen kiss when he retrieved the blanket to the confrontation with Hauser where he rescued Victoria and Sanders. By the time he reached the part about Mrs. Throckmorton's roses, Laura's laughter began a slow burble.

Seeing he was not shocking her with vulgarity, he proceeded onward with a slightly edited version of the scene in her bedroom that culminated with his ruined shirt, her unlaced corset, and the wreckage of the room. "So I turned her bottom up and spanked her," he finished on a note of dejection.

136

Laura's eyes widened in amazement, then she doubled over with laughter. "You spanked her," she echoed in delighted incredulity.

"I fail to see what's so funny. As you said, Sanders was spoiled by his parents. So was Tory."

"Did you tell her that?" Laura asked, still hiccuping.

"Yes. I'm afraid so. When I first met her I thought she was attracted to me—"

"As most women have always been?" Laura interjected.

He smiled sheepishly. "Most women of my acquaintance have scarce been ladies, Laura. I thought I could shake some sense into her by outraging her delicate sensibilities—calling her pet names, teasing her, even stealing kisses. But I ended up with two choices yesterday afternoon—rape her or spank her! Some courtship!"

"Oh, I think the courtship is going along beautifully. Tory never loses her temper. Don't you see— you're chipping away the protective shell of ice that Hedda's built around her. All we need do is see to it that the two of you continue to be thrown together, figuratively speaking." She cocked an eyebrow at him and gave a devilish wink. "And perhaps literally speaking as well."

He digested that, and a slow smile lit his face. "Then I guess I'd better practice with my utensils, hadn't I?"

Laura laughed. "And let us not forget your ice pick."

Chapter Nine

Rhys sat at the big oak table in the kitchen of the Naked Truth, sipping a cup of Kelly's strong black coffee, awaiting breakfast. The big Irishman always served fried eggs, potatoes, and bacon, all hashed up in his greasy iron skillet. The food was not elegant, but it filled the hole in a man's stomach. Before meeting Laura Everett, Rhys had never thought much about the plain, substantial fare that his employees and customers wolfed down.

He watched Kelly dump a greasy, starchy mass of yellow and brown onto his plate, then stabbed into it as if expecting it to fight back.

"The potatoes are hard," he groused as a chunk bounced stubbornly away from his fork.

"'N' the eggs? Might they not be to his lordship's likin' either?" the burly, black-haired giant asked, already knowing the answer.

Rhys arched a brow and raised his fork to shake

it at the irreverent cook. A fatty piece of bacon slithered down the tines and flopped against his fingers. "Ginger can cook better than this, you slovenly Mick. The eggs are burned dry."

"Then why not ask Miss Ginger ta cook yer food?"

"Yeah, why not?" the lady herself replied as she entered the sunny kitchen, wiping sleep from her eyes. Ginger sank onto a big oak chair, and her paisley silk robe slithered open below shapely knees. She crossed her legs, unconcerned with her nakedness beneath the scant cover of the wrapper, and gratefully took a cup of bitter black coffee from the cook. "For all the time you spend around here nowadays, cooking for you wouldn't be much work, Rhys."

He stabbed at the rubbery potatoes and fished out a few smaller chunks that were edible. "If this is going to be a concerted attack on me, let's get everyone in on it. Wake up the rest of the girls, call in Rufus and Ben." Rhys knew he sounded guilty. He'd left running the saloon to Ginger more and more lately as his other business interests broadened. "If you need extra help, Ginger, hire anyone. You're in charge. In fact, I've been thinking . . ." He hesitated, deciding not to discuss selling her the saloon in front of anyone, especially the crotchety old cook who treated her like a surrogate daughter.

Ginger looked at Rhys measuringly, waiting for him to finish his sentence, almost afraid of what he might say. When he let it drop, she said, "You and that fancy Mrs. Everett are pretty thick these days. Real democratic of her to rub elbows with you."

Rhys laughed. "She's still a Republican." Then he asked, "You can't be jealous of Laura. She's old enough to be my mother."

"I heard tell 'bout a fancy party next week at her

house. All the swells in town are invited. Why do you care about them kind of folks, Rhys?"

His eyes darkened to what she called poker blue, expressionless, fathomless. "That's under the heading of business, love. You run the Naked Truth. Let me worry about the rest."

Sensing the need for the two of them to be left in private, Kelly made a big production of hefting a sack of potato peels and other garbage and headed out the back door to dispose of it.

Ginger put her hand on his forearm and caressed it through the expensive white lawn shirt. She could feel the angry tension in his body. "You been sleeping alone all week, darlin'. Is it somethin' I did? I—I'll stay outta your way with them rich folks. I didn't mean to get nosy."

He could sense the entreaty in her voice. She let her robe gap open and her large, ripe breasts gleamed enticingly, snuggled in their silken wrappings. He felt the old familiar stirring of desire and swore beneath his breath as he took her hand in both of his and raised it to his lips. "I'm sorry, love. I didn't mean to hurt you." *I don't want to hurt you, but I'm afraid I will.*

She smiled tremulously. "You got a real important meeting or something this morning, darlin'? If not—"

"Hot damn 'n' boilin' brimstones, I gotta see th' boss man!" a loud voice boomed from out front, accompanied by pounding on the saloon door. Rhys heard Rufus open it and usher in Tomato Nose Wylie Wilcox. "Give me a drink whilst yew fetch 'em. We got us some celebratin' ta do, yessiree."

Planting a quick kiss on Ginger's open lips, Rhys stood up and said, "The odds aren't bad that Wylie's struck a vein of silver in that mine I bought from

Charles Everett." As he strode down the hall toward the big barroom, he was torn by ambivalence about his mistress. He was glad of the reprieve, yet his body ached with sexual hunger. With a vow to deal later with that problem, he greeted Wilcox.

"No need to get slop-pail drunk before I'm even in the room, Wylie," he said as the big miner upended a bottle of whiskey.

"Pretty fair phlegm cutter. This place useta serve real swill."

Rhys smiled. "It still does . . . for some customers. You got into the good stock. This better mean we have a silver strike to celebrate."

Wylie stood up straight. Paunch and all, he was as imposing as his formidable proboscis when he asserted himself. "How's a vein a foot wide sound ta yew? Goes clean to China. Yew kin hire them yeller miners ta start diggin' where they come from 'n' meet us betwixt!"

Laura Everett would be pleased.

Charles Everett and Stoddard Laughton were not pleased. The evening of Laura's dinner party, they sipped drinks in Laughton's study as they waited for Hedda and Tory.

"You were foolish to sell that mine to Davies so precipitously, Charles," Stoddard said tersely, tossing down the remainder of his bourbon in one gulp.

Everett's fingers tightened on his glass. "It was scarcely precipitous. When I bought that mine for a pittance, I had an engineer investigate it. The so-called expert assured me it would produce a profit. But two crews dug for three months and got nothing but traces in tons of black sand."

Laughton fumed sourly. "Well, your miners obviously didn't dig in the right direction." He'd been counting on a rich son-in-law to bail him out of his present predicament. "That damned old drunk Wilcox has made a fool out of you and a rich man out of Davies."

Charles's face darkened an angry red. "No need to get testy with me, Stoddard, because Davies is doing more lending than your bank these days. I've been hearing some rather nasty rumors about your solvency. No truth to that, I presume." When Laughton did not meet his gaze, he voiced another question. "By the way, I understand Sanders has gone back East." At least the worthless sot would be out from underfoot, no longer distracting Tory and embarrassing the whole family.

Stoddard fought to steady his voice, then answered calmly, "Yes, he's visiting his grandparents in Massachusetts." Hearing the light chatter of his wife and daughter, he quickly changed the subject. "Well, here come the ladies, beautiful as always."

"Just so," Charles echoed as his eyes inspected Victoria's superb pale turquoise gown of watered silk, impeccably cut to flatter her slim figure and match the strange sea-foam color of her eyes. Her hair was styled in a smooth bouffant chignon on top of her head. He took her arm and said, "You look lovely, my dear." The perfect wife for a man with boundless political aspirations. Of course, he still needed Stoddard's backing, both with the party and with money. He devoutly hoped the rumors about the bank were untrue.

Hedda beamed on her child and Charles. "What a marvelous couple you make. Do let us go, Stoddard. Laura makes such a fuss when we're late."

"I hate these dinners at Laura's. She's far too unconventional for a properly bred female," her husband groused as they left the study.

"Be that as it may, she's still the social arbiter of Starlight, even if she and Charles don't get on all that well. If he can tolerate her, so can you, Stoddard." Hedda's voice was steely.

"Who will be there?" Charles asked, mentally ticking off all the important politicians he wanted to impress. His pesky sister-in-law had her uses.

Hedda replied, "All the people who count in Starlight society, I'm certain."

Their carriage pulled up in front of Laura's two-story white frame house, encircled by wide porches liberally trimmed in gingerbread latticework. The yard was already filled with other carriages, all of them as opulently appointed as Laughton's.

"I can't understand why Laura clings to this shoddy relic of a house. It's frightfully old-fashioned—and frame, for pity's sake, when all the best houses are brick with mansard roofs and wrought-iron trim," Hedda said as Stoddard helped her from the carriage.

"Mama, you know Laura's sentimental about the house because Jacob built it for her when she was his bride," Tory said.

Charles pulled a sour face. "It's scarcely because she can't afford better."

Just as he took Tory's hand, she glanced over at the big black brute tied to the rail by the side of the house. *It couldn't be Blackjack!* But such a magnificent stallion stood out among the other horses like a brilliant cut diamond atop a pile of dirty broken glass.

When they entered the house, Tory's worst fears were confirmed. There *he* stood in the middle of the big arched doorway to Laura's parlor, seeming to fill the room with his vitality and that dangerous, masculine aura of the forbidden. Rhys flashed her a blinding smile.

She felt Charles's hand tighten possessively on her arm as he muttered, "Who let that ruffian in here?"

"I'm sure he didn't just wander in off the street," Stoddard said grimly.

"Whatever has gotten into Laura Everett?" Hedda murmured, seething but hiding it as she smiled serenely at several female acquaintances.

Tory was speechless. Here was her nemesis, the villain who had repeatedly humiliated her, laid hands on her so intimately, and then *spanked* her! He stood surrounded by drooling women— even Mrs. Soames and that idiotic old gossip Esther Smitherton. Lissette Johnson, hoydenish flirt that she was, batted her eyelashes at the big Welshman and giggled at some offhand comment he made. After a brief but thorough inspection of Tory, Rhys turned back to his companions, ignoring her!

"I suppose some women would find him attractive in an uncouth sort of fashion," Hedda said as she appraised him dismissively.

Her daughter was unable to ignore him so easily. Rhys's beautifully tailored suit of dark blue wool was cut in the height of fashion, as was the snowy linen shirt with heavy gold cuff links adorning it. His satin vest and tie were a deep maroon that blended handsomely with the suit.

"Money can buy expensive clothes, but the cut of the man is never disguised by mere tailoring," Stoddard stated pompously as he attempted to smooth his vest, which was straining against its buttons.

"Victoria, are you unwell?" Charles asked when her silence finally became apparent.

Before she could answer, or make a complete fool of herself by continuing to stare at those broad shoulders and that devastating smile, Laura descended on them with welcoming hugs. Mayor Johnson and his wife accompanied their hostess.

After cursory greetings were exchanged, Will Johnson said, "Quite a change in that Davies' fortune since we offered him a job as marshal, eh, Stoddard? Now he can buy and sell half of Starlight 'n' he don't even have to carry a gun."

"I'm certain a chap like Davies always carries a gun," Charles said acidly. "His sort has too many enemies to risk going unarmed."

"Well, if he's good enough to be in business with Laura here, he's good enough company," Will replied jovially.

"My Lissie is quite taken with him and he with her," Thelma Johnson gushed. Ignoring the mayor and his wife, Charles focused on Laura. Making a glib excuse to the others, he ushered her down the hall to a deserted corner near the kitchen. "What's this about your being in business with that saloon keeper?"

"Tut, Charles. Don't be such a poor loser. You sold the mine, silver and all, to Rhys and me. You should've hired Mr. Wilcox to investigate its value for you."

"He doesn't happen to frequent my club," Charles replied snidely. God, he hated Jacob's widow! She had been the one behind that upstart. "You will go to any length to exact revenge, won't you?"

"Merely simple justice, Charles," she said with a light rap of her fan on his wrist. Smiling, she swished past him and returned to the crowded front parlor to announce dinner.

Vellum place cards sat by the diners' plates, their elegant calligraphy announcing who was to be partnered by whom. Smiling smugly, Rhys made his way to the end of the table after proclaiming his disappointment to Lissie Johnson for not being seated by her side. He could well imagine the reaction of the lady who was to share dinner conversation with him.

As Laura ushered guests hither and yon in her no-nonsense motherly fashion, Tory scanned the place cards. She was not seated by Charles. Suddenly she glanced across the crowded dining room and met the gleam in Rhys Davies's indigo eyes. *Laura wouldn't dare!* At his gesture toward the seat next to him, her heart sank. The unprincipled rogue had taken in the gullible widow.

Rhys watched dismay, mortification, and anger flash across Tory's beautiful face. Then that impeccable breeding won out and she walked around the long table toward him, head held regally high, facial expression serene and cool. She allowed Rhys to seat her with a soft murmur of thanks.

Struggling for calm, Victoria stared at the gleaming sea of crystal, sterling, and china. She forced herself to concentrate on the magnificent floral centerpieces that lined the long table. Discreetly she looked across to see John Swaggert and Sibyl March take their seats. Although wheezy and boring, John was a dear friend of her father. Sibyl was a young widow and a member of the Starlight Garden Club. At least Sibyl would have someone with whom to converse.

Whatever had possessed Laura to do this? Doubtless, the slum-bred ruffian didn't know a salad fork from a Bowie knife. Surreptitiously she observed as the waiters served the first course, smoked oysters on a bed of crushed ice. Rhys chose the tiny three-tined cocktail fork and ate the slippery little hors d'oeuvre with consummate ease. Picking up his long-stemmed crystal wineglass, he raised it in a mock salute to her and sipped the delicate French Vouvray.

"I even know enough not to drink the consommé from the bowl, Tory," he whispered intimately to her as he replaced his glass.

Realizing that he had intuited her thoughts, she felt her cheeks tinge with rosy heat. "If you do not let me dine in peace, I shall speak to Laura about your outrageous behavior," she whispered between sips of wine.

His eyes widened innocently. "Oh, no need to bother, love. She already knows about the shambles you made of your bedroom and how I was forced to administer corporal punishment. She found it quite amusing, in fact."

A sliver of the smooth oyster lodged in her throat. Reaching for her glass, she almost tipped it, then clutched it securely and took a slightly unladylike draught. "I will thank you to lower your voice. Even better, don't speak to me at all!"

Charles, seated well up the table, could not hear the exchange between Tory and Davies above the amiable chatter around him, but he observed the intimate way the big Welshman saluted her with his wineglass and the answering color in Tory's cheeks. As the waiters cleared the first course and brought on the next, Charles decided to give the boorish interloper a good set-down, his meddlesome sister-in-law be damned. "I understand you're a friend of Mr. Manion, Mr. Davies. Tell me, do you agree with his political leanings?"

Rhys looked up, a hint of a smile tugging at his lips. "If you mean, am I a Democrat, I fear to answer yes in this room filled with Republicans."

"Now that you've become a man of property, perhaps you'll shift your political alignments," Willaby

Johnson said as a ripple of laughter traveled up and down the table.

"Yes, Mr. Davies, I hear that new silver mine is the richest strike in Colorado history," Lissie Johnson cooed.

"I think you very kindly overstate the case, Miss Johnson, but I did get an excellent deal when I bought the mine from Mr. Everett," Rhys countered.

Charles Everett's face darkened in mortification at the unwelcome turn in the conversation. Then Laura added to the laughter provoked by Rhys's remark. "Yes, Charles. I believe you bought the mine a year ago, then concluded it was quite worthless."

"It would seem even the best mining engineers can make mistakes," Charles replied defensively.

"Maybe you should've hired old Tomato Nose Wylie Wilcox," Laura suggested.

As chuckling around the table subsided, Lissie Johnson again fixed Rhys with her large doe eyes and asked, "Have you chosen a name for the mine, Mr. Davies?"

"As a matter of fact I have," he said as his glance swept up and down the table before coming to rest on Victoria's delicate face. "The Lady Victory." He was rewarded as her carefully schooled expression of indifference shifted to alarm before he completed the word *Victory*. Her cheeks flamed, for she knew he meant the name to signify her. How many others around the room would guess?

"Speaking of victory, I think a toast is in order to the impending election of Charles Everett to the Colorado State Senate," Stoddard said, breaking the strange spell that seemed to be building between his daughter and that accursed gambler.

"Here, here!" Will Johnson added, followed by a

chorus of others, even though not everyone was as enthusiastic as the mayor and the banker.

Laura raised her glass dutifully, but after sipping, she asked a question. "Do you really believe that Charles's election is a forgone conclusion, Stoddard? After all, this is southwest Colorado. The Democrats have a formidable candidate in Sam Benson."

"He's a sheepman," Charles said, as if that made him the equivalent of pond scum. Indeed, for most of Colorado's monied classes—bankers and cattlemen—sheepmen were worse than pond scum.

"Your very doubts about my winning, dear sister-in-law, seem to imply you give credence to the opinions expressed by that odious Mike Manion."

"Most Democrats, whether they're sheepmen or not, are foreigners, just as Mr. Manion is," Hedda Laughton said primly. Her quiet voice cut through the murmured conversation about the long table. She daintily sliced a strip of beef swimming in bernaise sauce and ate a small bite as the silence thickened.

"Foreigners like my friend Mike Manion and me, Mrs. Laughton, may be poor benighted Democrats, but we'll likely place a man in the governor's mansion next year."

"Alva Adams is a radical upstart and a common political manipulator," Stoddard Laughton said belligerently.

Rhys smiled. "I've not read a lot of American history, mind, but wasn't that how Andrew Jackson was described by his adversaries?"

"Here, here!" Laura said with a laugh, defusing the increasingly heated debate. "Your point, Mr. Davies, is well taken. A number of our illustrious presidents have been Democrats. I think we should forgo arguing politics any further, however."

Charles, seething at Rhys's attentions to Victoria, was in no mood to let the debate end with the Welshman having the last word.

"Your *friend*"— he stressed the word scornfully—"Mr. Manion, displays questionable taste in headlining the sensational details of that grisly Packer trial. Could it be that he does so because the paragon handling the case, Judge Gerry, is a Democrat?"

Laura was about to censure Charles when Rhys raised his napkin and dabbed at his lips, motioning her to let him handle the slur. His eyes were alight with glee when he said, ""Whether or not details from the trial of a Republican cannibal by a Democratic judge are fit to print, they are without doubt unfit dinner-table conversation in the presence of ladies." He turned to Victoria and smiled guilelessly, then looked back at her fiancé. "As to Mike being my friend, he is and I'm proud to own him. I won't say his newspaper is always impartial in its coverage, but his readers know for certain where he stands on any issue."

"Well said, Mr. Davies, well said!" John Swaggert spoke up, surprising Tory so much she almost dropped her fork.

Rhys looked enormously pleased with himself as he polished off the last bite of his meat. As various conversations about the table picked up once again, he leaned over to Tory and whispered, "Six courses down, two to go. How am I doing so far?"

Noting with disgust the rapt way Lissie Johnson and Earline Hawkins were watching the handsome Welshman, she smiled sweetly. "Your repartee at dinner is quite adequate. You've even been rehearsed in table etiquette. A pity knowing *which* fork to choose doesn't compensate for not knowing *how* to use it." She glanced smugly at the cuff of his starched white shirt, which obviously had been dredged through the bernaise sauce. Victoria felt like shouting in triumph as her antagonist flushed slightly.

Swearing silently, Rhys unobtrusively wiped his napkin over the heavy gold cuff link and squeezed the excess of moisture from the limp cuff edges. "One for the lady," he said, regaining his aplomb. "Let's see if I can get through dessert and brandy without running up an even larger laundry bill. If I do, may I claim a reward from my charming dinner partner?"

"Certainly not!" she replied through gritted teeth. When the flaky-crusted blackberry pie with hand-turned ice cream was served, she shoved it about on her plate, praying for the meal to end.

Finally Laura stood up, signaling for the ladies to leave the gentlemen to their brandy and cigars. Tory almost overturned her wineglass in her haste to escape. Never in her life had a man made her so wretchedly uncomfortable. No, make that miserable. No, furious! As Rhys pulled back her chair, she could feel his warm breath on her neck, stirring tiny loose tendrils of hair that tickled her nape. She wanted to run from the room.

Rhys watched her walk away from the table after an icy "Thank you" for his courtesy. The cool little filly would make a first-rate poker player, he mused.

The evening progressed from dreadful to nightmarish for Tory. She was trapped in the parlor with Lissette, Earline, and several older women, who should have had better taste, all of whom were singing Rhys Davies's praises. How handsome! How witty! How charming! Tory was the butt of sly looks and subtle questions as to why she'd been partnered with Starlight's most eligible bachelor.

By the time Charles and the other men rejoined them, Tory's head was pounding. Fearful of even seeing Rhys, she rushed to Charles for consolation. "Please, I have a frightful headache. Can we step outside for a moment? I need some fresh air."

"Whatever you say, my dear," Charles replied stiffly. He was still smarting from his set-down at dinner.

They walked onto the wide veranda with its elaborate scroll-worked banisters and posts. The lattice screens were thick with wisteria. Soft shafts of moonlight peeked through the vines, dappling them with silver. Since the porch stretched all the way to the rear of the house, Charles strolled away from the babble of conversation and laughter. At first Tory was grateful for the quiet and the cool, crisp air. Then Charles's words ended her brief respite.

"You and that trashy gambler seemed quite the charming couple at dinner. I would hardly have suspected my sister-in-law was such a matchmaker."

Tory froze in disbelief. "You actually think I was flirting with that . . . that uncouth, ill-bred gunman?"

"Well, he was certainly flirting with you," Charles replied indignantly.

Perhaps if her nerves had not been so frayed by Davies she might have found some humor in Charles's absurd jealousy, or at the least been flattered by it. But Tory was too rattled to respond with anything but anger. She stiffened and slipped her hand from his arm. "This conversation is worsening my headache. You provoked Laura and that Welshman with your jibes. Please don't think to vent your spleen on me because of your faux pas."

He sucked in his breath. Never had his proper, cool fiancée been so outspoken. Before he could reconsider his folly, he said, "Since I appear to be such a buffoon in your eyes, mayhap that saloon keeper will serve as your escort for the duration of the evening as well! Let him see you home." With a curt bow he stalked down the steps and headed across the yard. His house was only six blocks down the street. Feeling secure that Stoddard and Hedda would see their daughter safely chaperoned, he would walk home.

For a moment Tory considered calling him back, but his unfair accusations had truly angered her. Best to let him stew a day or two. He would come around and apologize for his behavior.

"The strain of the political campaign must be getting under his skin," Rhys said as he materialized from the back hall door.

Tory gasped in surprise, then her expression hardened. "Eavesdropping, Mr. Davies? How in character, as is your doing it from the servants' quarters," she said, gesturing to the door that he stood in. It led to the kitchen.

"That's where you think I'll always belong, isn't it?"

She shrugged and stepped away from his advance. "You may have money now, but you'll always be a gunman and a gambler beneath the facade. You may deceive Laura, but not me."

The moonlight turned her pale blonde hair to spun silver magic. He wanted to bury his hands in the fragrant silken curls and loosen them to fall about her shoulders like a perfumed mantle. Sensing her wariness, he moved slowly, letting a rueful grin flash as he held out his right hand. "You were right about my needing to go to the kitchen. The cook soaked my cuff clean of that damned gravy. See?" Before she could snatch away her hand he'd grasped it and

153

pressed her slim cool fingers about the damp cuff, but he made no further move to draw her closer.

Tory could feel his sinewy wrist through the linen shirt. His hands were warm and large, the well-manicured hands of a gentleman—or a card shark! The two figures stood frozen in the moonlight, staring into each other's eyes.

She was afraid of the tension sizzling between them like summer lightning. He was afraid to speak and break the spell. His words always provoked her, yet he could sense the power his touch held over her.

"Someday, Victory, some day, you'll see the truth." The words were spoken so softly she barely heard them. Then he slid his hands away and vanished back through the kitchen door.

"Victory," she murmured beneath her breath. So, the Lady Victory was named for her, she mused as she stroked her hands together absently, still feeling the tingling heat. Like a sleepwalker, she retraced her steps around the veranda to the parlor door and reentered the bright gaslit interior.

She did not see Stoddard Laughton standing in the shadows with a calculating expression on his face.

Chapter Ten

"This is entirely too much, young lady. First your brother takes off without the simple courtesy of a fare-thee-well, headed for heaven only knows where—then you quarrel with Charles on the very brink of your engagement announcement. I won't have it, do you understand me? I simply won't have it!" Hedda Laughton paced furiously across the Turkish carpet of her private sitting room where she had summoned her recalcitrant daughter. The hour was late and they had just returned from Laura's dinner party, minus Charles.

Tory rubbed her head and sighed. "Could we discuss this tomorrow, Mama? Charles was jealous of that horrid Rhys Davies—as if I could help Laura's abominable seating plans. He'll come around in a day or two. He always does." Her voice sounded curiously flat and emotionless to her own ears. *As if I don't care if I ever see Charles again!*

The thought disturbed her even more than Hedda's cold, clipped lecture. Her mother never really lost her temper, never raised her voice. Of course her withering icy anger could slice to the bone when she merely whispered. Tonight Hedda's mortification over Charles's desertion focused on Tory and that silly fight. *This whole mess is Rhys Davies's fault!* She would not be the subject of her mother's wrath and Charles would not have behaved so stupidly if that saloon keeper had not been Laura Everett's guest.

Finally, realizing her daughter was barely attending her, Hedda sighed and said in a conciliatory tone, "Perhaps you're right. Everyone is exhausted and overwrought. What a taxing evening, having to endure that vulgar foreigner. I can scarcely credit Laura's sanity some days, foisting him on you as a dinner partner."

"Charles was jealous." The words seemed to slip out unintentionally.

Hedda's eyes narrowed and she tapped her fingers against her folded arms in agitation. "How absurd! Jealous of that riffraff? Not that some of those foolish twits like Lissette and her friends didn't demean themselves, flirting with him."

"He is handsome in an unpolished way, I suppose," Tory said, trying to sort out her own very confused feelings.

Her mother stiffened in horror. "Surely you aren't serious!"

"I didn't mean *I* found him attractive," Tory replied hastily. "I was merely speculating as to why Laura invited him and why so many women who should have better sense seem dazzled by him. I'm sure his ill-gotten wealth helps," she added with feigned indifference.

"Let's not discuss that distasteful man any further. I'll expect you to have luncheon with me at Mrs. Drayton's tomorrow. It's been a long and distressing evening. Get some rest now." Hedda dismissed her daughter.

After retiring to her room, Tory sat before her mirror and brushed her hair until she felt a trance-like weariness ease the tension coiled inside her. Yet when she slipped between the sheets and closed her eyes, sleep eluded her. Large warm hands held her body fast while deep blue eyes pierced her soul. She pounded her pillows and muttered some most unladylike expletives. Her night was filled with troubling dreams.

"'Damn you, Alfred Packer! You Republican son-of-a-bitch! There was only seven Democrats in Hinsdale County 'n' you had to go 'n' eat five of 'em! I sentence you hang by the neck until dead, dead, dead!'" Mike Manion quit reading to mop his eyes. Still convulsed with laughter, he tossed the copy of the *Plain Speaker* onto his already well littered desk and said, "Judge Gerry was in fine form at the trial. He's an illiterate old curmudgeon, but at least he's *our* illiterate old curmudgeon."

Rhys chuckled along with his friend, then couldn't resist saying, "Still it seems they're gaining on us. One Republican cannibal in exchange for five Democratic prospectors." He shrugged. "Besides, I heard rumors Packer's lawyer's going to appeal the death sentence."

Manion had recovered his poise by this time and said half seriously, "I'm going to Lake City today to get the story first hand. It wouldn't be all bad if they did drag this into a new trial. By damn, I haven't sold this many newspapers since you tangled with

Phil the Cannibal last spring. You've come quite a way since then, boyo."

A smile played around Rhys's lips as he recalled the conversation at Laura's party the preceding week. "I still choose my own friends, Mike. That's one of the advantages of having enough money."

"Or enough nerve," Mike replied. "Somehow I can't picture you kowtowing to anyone."

"But there are people I plan to impress, Mike. That's why I stopped by this morning—not that your story on the Packer trial wasn't amusing."

"Amusing, is it? And that's all? It was brilliant!" When Rhys pulled an elegant gold watch from his pocket and checked the time with mock impatience, Manion calmed down and said, "All right, what is it you need to know?"

"I want to build a house. Just a modest place, mind. Say three stories of good solid stone with gas lighting, central heating, hot and cold running water." He paused with a twinkle in his eyes. "Maybe a ballroom. For sure a formal rose garden."

Mike's face was incredulous. "I knew the silver was pouring out of that mountain, but you must have a gold mine on the side! Why such a mansion? You'll put even the Laughtons to shame."

"That's exactly the idea. Not to mention that monstrosity Charles Everett's built on the east side of town. I've chosen a splendid site a bit outside Starlight, with a stand of pines on the southwestern slope as a backdrop. I've hired the best stonemasons and carpenters in the area. But I need one man to oversee the whole project. Who built the Laughtons' place?"

Manion scratched his head. "The best man did build Stoddard Laughton's house, but that was over fifteen years ago. He moved to San Francisco, last I heard. A big German named Klaus Kruger."

"If Kruger built their house so grand, he can build one even better for me," Rhys said thoughtfully. "I'll get in touch with Blackie Drago. He'll be able to locate the fellow if he's still this side of the grave."

Manion grimaced. "If half of what I hear about Denver's underworld boss is true, Drago can locate anyone this side or the *other* side of the grave—providing, of course, it's the hot side." He studied Rhys with his shrewd brown eyes. "You keep holding on to your past associations, but you have plans that will put you in high society. Think you'll like the thin air once you get there, boyo?"

"It all depends," Rhys replied enigmatically.

Manion sighed. "It all depends on Tory Laughton is what you mean."

"There is no other way out. Don't you think I haven't looked at every conceivable alternative? I know how unthinkable it—"

"You know! You couldn't possibly know how a lady would feel being sold like some saloon whore." Hedda stared at Stoddard. Her wintry aqua eyes were almost white with glacial fury. "You won't sell your own daughter to that . . . that foreigner, that low-class, crude, boorish saloon keeper."

Stoddard resumed his agitated pacing in the face of his wife's frozen wrath. If she screamed and cried he'd feel better. Anything but that unshakable ice-cold facade. She even carried it to bed with her, even twenty-two years ago when he first married her. He steeled himself to deal with her. Hands on the massive walnut desk in his office, he stared into those burning, freezing eyes and said, "Either Tory marries Davies for his money or we are bankrupt. You won't even have enough left to buy a railroad ticket back to Boston after the bank examiners get through. You can't outrun the disgrace your son's created. Blame Sanders, not me, for the disaster we're facing."

She waved that bit of logic aside with a swift swish of one white hand. "So now that Sanders has ruined *your* precious bank, he's *my* son. Where were you this past year while he was supposed to be learning how to run the institution, not destroy it? Surely Charles can make you a loan or something."

"I've already talked to Charles. Davies and that damnable widow of Jacob's have virtually ruined him. He's been forced to sell off most of his properties just to finance his campaign. And now even the election seems in doubt. Charles can't help us, Hedda. We need a small fortune, and we need it within the week or the bank will be closed."

Hedda wrung her hands. Then she stopped and smoothed them down the trim sides of her dove-gray silk skirt. "What makes you think Davies has such money?"

Stoddard gave a hoarse, bitter laugh. "Don't you ever read anything but garden news and fashion magazines? Davies has the biggest saloon, the richest silver mine, and two of the most prosperous cattle ranches in southwest Colorado. He's building a palace south of town—a palace for a bride."

"A vulgar display of his newly acquired riches," she sniffed coldly. "You could never trust a man of his low character to keep his word—that is, if he would even consider marrying Victoria." She shuddered.

"Oh, he'll consider it, all right," Stoddard said grimly. "He's been after her like a stag in rut, pursuing her with Laura's connivance. I even caught them that night of the dinner party at her place. They were alone on the porch, and she wasn't exactly fighting off his advances," he added, knowing that that thrust would horrify his frigid wife.

"That's obscene. Tory abhors the man," Hedda protested even as her mind flashed back over the past months. Since that initial encounter with Davies when he had rescued her from the river, Tory had been acting strangely. Surely . . . no, it couldn't be.

Seeing Hedda turn the matter over in her mind, Stoddard pressed his advantage. "Unlike her brother, Victoria will do what we tell her. When we explain the alternative, she'll accept it well enough."

Stoddard paused by the front door of the Naked Truth, loath to enter its cool, dark interior. The sun was shining with a cheering brilliance that ill suited his mood. Damn, it was scarce nine a.m. and he was sweating, no way for a businessman to bluff an opponent—especially one as shrewd and dangerous as Rhys Davies. He should have insisted that the meeting be on neutral territory, but the damnable gambler had outflanked him by sending an answering note: "Be at the Naked Truth at nine tomorrow or I don't talk business." Rhys Davies's arrogance was galling. He was, as old Jake Everett used to say, a man who could strut while sitting down.

Stoddard had worried about the tone of the note a great deal. He had sent a simple request for a business meeting, no specifics given. Did Davies know that his bank was in trouble? Again he cursed the land speculations with Charles that had gone sour, his losses in backing the railroad, all the other capital ventures that had failed, leaving him desperately vulnerable to Sanders's treachery.

Stoddard took a deep breath and entered the wide doors of the saloon. For such an early hour, the bar was doing a brisk business. There had been a time when he would have feared what his presence in such a place would do to his reputation, but now so many of his friends and associates frequented the establishment, it was almost respectable, or at least winked at by Starlight's better sorts.

The long, handsomely carved bird's-eye maple bar gleamed like satin. The much-touted painting of a voluptuous and skillfully posed nude woman filled one wall. Its gold-leaf frame measured twelve feet by five feet, dimensions almost as impressive as those of the nude. All of Hauser's shabby fixtures and cheap furniture had been replaced, and a few more novel embellishments added. Diamond-dust mirrors and crystal chandeliers gleamed grandly. Hauser's ratty old parrot had been supplanted by half a dozen exotic birds, fanning their rainbow tails in gilded cages. A seemingly endless tank full of iridescent orange and green fish stood along one wall, and on a large table near the bar sat paper, envelopes, and ink pens with the admonition: "Write your dear old mother back home."

Snorting in disgust, Laughton searched for Davies, who was nowhere in the room. *The Welsh bastard, he's going to make me ask for him like some damn supplicant!*

Rhys stood at the top of the wide walnut stairs, hidden in shadows, observing Laughton's fury. Rhys had heard rumors of the bank's troubles. He knew that Laughton had called in a lot of notes recently. Rhys himself had made a tidy profit from renegotiating some of those loans for higher interest. Laughton's other business ventures had fared poorly, too. Surely he could not expect the lowly saloon keeper to bail him out? The Welshman smiled grimly and returned to his private quarters.

When Stoddard Laughton entered a few moments later, Rhys was seated behind a big oak desk, eating a hearty breakfast of flapjacks and scrambled eggs. Casually wiping his mouth with a snowy linen napkin, he indicated a chair in front of the desk. "Have a seat, Stoddard." He pushed the plate aside and reached across the desk for a beautifully inlaid teak humidor. Opening it, he said, "Cigar?"

The expensive fragrance of the tobacco enticed Stoddard. "Thank you, yes," he replied stiffly.

On cue, the big black servant named Rufus walked in from a side door. After lighting both men's cigars, he picked up the remains of Rhys's breakfast and departed silently.

Rhys leaned back in his leather-cushioned chair and took a long, sweet drag on the cigar. Studying the man across from him with his expressionless gambler's mask, he waited.

Laughton puffed and fought the urge to fidget. He was used to being on the other side of the desk. Finally, clearing his throat, he asked, "Are you certain we're alone? What I have to say is most private."

Rhys's eyes darkened imperceptibly. "We're alone, Laughton. You wanted to talk business. Talk."

This had seemed so reasonable a solution to his dilemma when he first had conceived the plan. After the battle yesterday with Hedda, it had become increasingly unpalatable and difficult to present. He harrumphed and swallowed his pride for the opening announcement. "I need a loan. My investments over the short term have been . . . unlucky. The bank needs a sizable infusion of capital until I can recover."

"Your bank will close within the week. Somehow I don't see your investments, long or short term, being sufficient to save you from bankruptcy." Rhys watched the older man blanch and clasp the cigar between his teeth. *So, I'm right on target!* "I doubt you have sufficient collateral for me to advance you a loan the size you'll be needing."

Now Laughton's face took on a crafty smile. "Ah, but I think I do, Davies. You want to enter respectable society—"

"I already have. Laura Everett's seen to that," Rhys interrupted. Then examining his nails idly, he asked, "Speaking of the Everetts, why not ask your future son-in-law for some help?"

"You know Charles is in financial difficulties himself," Stoddard replied stiffly. "And he won't be my son-in-law now that he's let you and Laura ruin him!"

Rhys raised his eyebrows. "Really? How fortunate for Tory," he added insolently. Was the old goat going to offer what he suspected? Rhys sat back and waited with apparent calm, but his heart slammed in his chest like a miner's steam drill.

"Let's forgo the niceties, Davies. You're saloon spawn, a no-name foreigner. You want a lady for a wife, to buy you respectability, help you climb socially." His beefy face hardened in cynicism. "I married a Boston Lodge because I wanted the same thing. Men marry for advantage the same as women. The institution is purely pragmatic. I had sufficient wealth for Hedda's parents. She had a pedigree I coveted."

"And Charles? He had political potential, but now without money to back it, he's out of the running?" Rhys asked, already knowing the answer.

"Yes, Charles is no longer suitable for Victoria, but let's forget him. You covet something, too. And I don't just mean Victoria. You want acceptance, every immigrant's dream. My daughter is your ticket to advancement in business, and, who knows?" He gestured expansively with the cigar. "Maybe someday your entree to politics."

"Right now I'm not the least bit interested in elective office," Rhys said coolly.

"But you do want to join the ranks of Colorado's business elite. You're building a mansion on that hill—a mansion for a fine lady, not the likes of Ginger Vogel. No respectable woman will ever marry you—"

"Unless her father is desperate enough for my money?" Rhys supplied quietly. "Let's do drop the 'niceties,' Laughton. We despise each other, yet you're sitting in my office, smoking my cigars, asking me for money. Then you give me a lecture on the politics of marriage. Where exactly is all this leading an ignorant, unpedigreed nobody like me?"

"Damn you, I've watched you with my daughter and I've heard stories about how you sought her out after that incident at the river. You want her. You want Victoria!"

"And the price for your daughter's virtue is how much?" Rhys asked coldly. A sickening wave of nausea was churning in his gut. He still could not believe that Laughton would do it.

"One hundred thousand immediately. Then your bond underwriting the bank. Of course you'll have to do this before the marriage."

Rhys felt a bizarre combination of triumph and disgust. "What makes you think I'd marry her? You only said that I wanted her." He had the satisfaction of watching the older man crumple and turn ashen before he relented. Leaning forward in his chair, he sighed and said, "Hell, yes, I'll marry her—if she'll have me."

Laughton recovered quickly with a cynical laugh of triumph. "Of course she'll marry you. Victoria is a sensible girl. She'll do as I tell her."

Rhys laughed hollowly. "I'm the saloon spawn and you're the gentleman, yet you're selling me your daughter in exchange for a bank." He paused. "You have your deal, Laughton."

"Good. We don't have to like one another to do business. In fact, it has been my experience that most in-laws roundly detest each other. I'll have the documents drawn up and sent to you tomorrow." Stoddard rose to leave.

"Tell me, are you going to have your attorney Charles Everett handle the paper work for you?"

Rhys's question froze him for an instant, then he replied, "Like me, Charles is a realist when faced with unpleasant alternatives." Without another word Laughton turned to the door.

Rhys's parting words rang in his ears, "Everett must be even more broke than you."

After his prospective father-in-law had left, Rhys sat in silence for a moment. Had he made the right decision? How would Tory react? He had assumed it would take months of arduous wooing to win her away from that fop Everett. In truth, Rhys had never been sure he *could* win her, but he had never let himself dwell on the odds, which he knew were lousy. Then this, dropped in his lap. How could he turn down Laughton's offer?

Once we're married, I'll make her happy. Then why did a niggling sense of uneasiness hover over him so relentlessly? He felt as if he'd just foreclosed on Sister Frances Rose's orphanage. Dammit! Stoddard Laughton had made him the most incredible proposition he had ever heard. He didn't know whether to laugh, cry, or get drunk.

As if in answer to his dilemma, Ginger walked in from the bedroom and set a bottle and two glasses in front of him. She wore the yellow satin kimono he'd bought her in Denver last month when he'd gone up to order materials for his house. Tossing her unruly carrot curls back over her shoulder, she took a seat in the masculine room, feeling at home with the heavy, dark furnishings. It was Rhys's place now, filled with his presence, his scent. He had made Hauser's old saloon into a palace. What did he need with more? What did he need with *her?*

She poured two drinks neat and handed him one, then swallowed the smooth bourbon for courage. "You ain't goin' to do it . . . are you?"

One look at his face convinced her of the futility of her question. "Yer a fool, Rhys Davies. She ain't our kind. She'll hate you for forcin' this."

He smiled sadly and tossed off the drink, then leaned back in his chair. "Maybe, maybe not. It's sort of like winning this place, Ginger. It dropped into my hands, unplanned. One thing led to another. . . . I always wanted to go respectable one day, have a family."

"And you think this ice princess will make your dreams come true?" she scoffed, hiding her pain beneath a facade of sarcasm. "She'll freeze you out of her bed."

Finally Rhys smiled. Recalling the way Tory had trembled against him at the river, responded to his kiss, held his hand at Laura's party, he felt a surge of elation. She did not know passion, not yet. But he would teach her, his lady. *She will love me!*

Chapter Eleven

"I hate him!" Tory choked out in a hoarse whisper. "You can't mean to do this. It's utterly . . . barbaric!" She looked like a lost waif, swallowed up by the velvet sofa on which her father had solicitously insisted she be seated before he spoke with her. A good thing it was, too, for Tory knew that her knees would have buckled at the announcement he had made. Her face was chalky but for two bright spots on her cheeks.

Stoddard stood across the room from her, with Hedda seated in the chair before him. They were united against her in this. "You must understand, my dear, what would happen to you, as well as your mother and me, if you don't marry Rhys Davies," Stoddard said patiently.

"But . . . I'm engaged to Charles," she echoed with a hollow voice, still numbed by shock.

"Charles is nearly as destitute as are we. Davies has all but ruined his land speculations and duped

him out of a fortune in silver with Laura's connivance. Anyway, your engagement was never formally
announced, so it won't create that much of a stir,"
her father placated.

"Not nearly so much as the announcement of my
engagement to a saloon owner will, I'll warrant,"
Tory replied as the red splotches on her cheeks
enlarged. She trembled with hurt and fury, tightly
held in by a lifetime of conditioning. "Surely, Mama,
your family could help," she pleaded, turning to
Hedda.

"They would take us in, of course, if the bank and
our house were foreclosed," Hedda said stiffly. "But
there simply is no time for me to make any kind of
arrangements . . ." Her voice faded. Then she cleared
her throat and resumed, "After all that's happened to
Stoddard's bank and other holdings, your grandpapa
would never consider pouring his reserves into a venture so far from home. We'll be disgraced and destitute, cast like paupers on the charity of my father. He
would take us in, but think, Victoria, think of how we
would live, the ridicule, the humiliation. The scandal
would follow us all the way back to Boston."

"You mean the scandal would follow you, don't
you, Mama?" Tory said as she rose on wobbly legs,
fighting back the tears. "This way, I'm the only one
who has to endure humiliation. Our family home
will remain as intact as Papa's bank. I'm the only
one who is compromised."

"You prattle all you want about family honor and
your humiliation, young lady. Just understand one
thing: it was your brother who brought us to this
pass. If he hadn't cleaned out every cent in the bank
when he vanished, we wouldn't be here discussing
these disagreeable options. One child has betrayed
the parents who lavished so much on him. Will you

do the same?" Stoddard's eyes narrowed.

"But you're selling me to a virtual stranger, a gambler." Recalling Rhys's fierce, hard embraces and the unseemly temper he had provoked in her, she felt her heart thud. Turning to her mother, she pleaded, "Rhys Davies is not a gentleman."

Hedda flinched imperceptibly, but Stoddard deserted his place behind her chair and confronted his surprisingly recalcitrant daughter in the center of the ornate parlor. "He may be no gentleman, but women flock to him. Virtually all the unmarried females in town have been batting their lashes at him."

"Well, I don't share their bad taste," she said waspishly.

"No? He brought you back to Charles with scarcely a stitch of clothes on your body after that debacle at the river. Esther Smitherton saw him leave this house on July Fourth after he stayed here unchaperoned a damn long time."

"Esther Smitherton is an incorrigible gossip!"

"What about that touching little scene on Laura's veranda? That was not just gossip. I witnessed it," he said triumphantly.

Tory's eyes dilated. What had this ruffian done? Her own father thought she was infatuated with him. She shook her head in denial. "No, no, it wasn't at all as it seemed. Charles and I had just quarreled. I was—"

"You were making sheep's eyes at the rogue and holding his hands, that's what you were doing," Stoddard interrupted hotly.

"So, because I allowed him to hold my hand for a couple of minutes, I'm pledged to him for life!"

Hedda finally rose. Things were not going smoothly at all. She hated it when plans went awry. Stoddard never could handle a difficult situation without her assistance. Gliding over to her daughter, she said in a clipped voice, "Do you want Sanders to go to prison?" At Tory's gasp of denial, she continued, "If you refuse Rhys Davies, the bank examiners will discover he embezzled the funds—not only our money but hundreds of other people's as well, Victoria. Your own brother will be a wanted man." She held her breath.

Tory crumpled back onto the settee like a puppet with its strings suddenly cut. "What choice do you leave me? Tell Mr. Davies I shall be honored to be his wife," she said woodenly.

Tory inspected herself in the mirror for the hundredth time. Her face was pale, her eyes smudged with dark rings from the sleepless night she had just spent. But the numb, black despair that had left her spent and exhausted was now giving way to other emotions—bitterness, betrayal, and above all else, a bright burning anger.

Davies had manipulated her, Charles had deserted her, her brother had betrayed her, and her parents had sold her. Never in her life had she felt so utterly bereft and alone. Yet that very isolation had fueled her fury as she tossed and turned through the endless night. Acting the spoiled and spiteful child in front of the Welsh barbarian would avail her nothing. If she offended him enough, he might well call off the marriage, but the results of that eventuality had been made brutally clear to her yesterday. She would suffer ostracism, disgrace, penury, and the unbearable guilt of knowing she was responsible for Sanders's imprisonment.

Tory knew her brother. His weakness would make him easy prey to the hardened criminals and brutal guards in a penitentiary. He might even take his life in fright and despair. *So I am the one who will sink into despair in his place.* Her head snapped up and she squared her shoulders. No! Rhys Davies and all his machinations would not defeat her. Had she not promised herself that in the early hours of the morning?

"I will play the gracious, dutiful fiancée, act out his social fantasy, do what I must to survive," she whispered in her empty bedroom. Bessie had helped her dress for her first official meeting with her new fiancé. She had chosen a soft mauve suit of light-weight linen. The fact that it flattered her pale gold hair and turned her aqua eyes a smoky blue gray had been only a superficial consideration. Mauve was also a color for mourning.

Patting her smoothly coifed pompadour, she gave herself a final inspection and fluffed the frilly white lace at her throat. Delicate. Understated. Ladylike. Quite the opposite of that hennaed whore at his infamous saloon. As soon as the comparison flashed into her mind she squelched it, vowing never to think of that sordid place or the unimaginable things that went on in Ginger's bordello.

Her mother had always assured her that when ladies married it was different. Yet she was marrying a man who was no gentleman. His searing, sensuous touch and the inexplicable feelings he engendered in her made her tremble. She walked toward the door in response to Ralph's gentle tapping. Mr. Davies awaited her in the parlor.

Rhys paced across the thick floral carpet in the Laughton parlor, as nervous as a schoolboy. Mercifully, Hedda and Stoddard were gone for the morning. They had made the arrangements and spoken to their daughter. She knew he was taking her to view the construction of his house south of town.

What would he say to her? She to him, now that everything had been settled? He forced himself to calm down and remain standing near the leaded-glass window. As he stared unseeing at the immaculately trimmed lawn outside, he wondered if this whole thing wasn't a fiasco. What if Ginger was right? What if she did hate him, if the chasm between them was too great to breach? The marriage would become a frigid farce. What if Stoddard's cynical assessment was right? Did he only want a lady to symbolize his success? Assure his social position? Then he heard the heavy door slide open on its oiled hinges. Victoria glided in, officially announced by the family butler, who then withdrew.

All his bitter self-doubts and misgivings fled when he looked at her porcelain perfection. He couldn't remember Tara Thomas's face, or even the faces of the elegant rich ladies in New York in whose homes he had worked, but surely none of them could compare to the beauty before him. She was a lady. Soon she would be *his* lady.

He sketched a bow and strode across the room to take her cold fingers in his warm hands. When he kissed her hand chastely, she didn't flinch or draw back. Taking that for a good sign, he said, "Good morning, Tory. You look exceptionally beautiful, love."

Rhys's smile was heart-stopping, and she hated him for it. His clothes had doubtless been chosen with care, an impeccably tailored lightweight tan wool suit, and a sheer white lawn shirt that contrasted with his sun-darkened face. The simple brown string tie and polished brown leather boots gave him the air of a prosperous rancher. The only jarring note was his fondness for expensive jewelry. Schooling herself not to betray her emotions, Victoria felt the electricity of his lips as they brushed her hands. Raising his head, he said with a twinkle in his eyes, "Well, do I pass inspection?"

She felt her cheeks heat up but said coolly, "Your tailor gets high marks, not so your jeweler. The gold watch and chain are a bit much, especially combined with the diamond stickpin and the sapphire ring. You look like a riverboat gambler."

"Really? Maybe because I once was one." His eyes dared her to say more.

"I suspected some such," she said almost beneath her breath.

He reached for his hat on the table, then decided to postpone plans for their outing until they had some things settled. Fixing her with a level dark blue stare, he took a calming breath, then cupped his hands over her shoulders and forced her to look at him. He could feel a slight tremor beginning in her now.

"Tory, you know I didn't go to your father. He came to me," he said gently.

"But you didn't turn him down—or offer to help without this marriage." The minute the words escaped her lips she feared she had been too blunt, but how was she to respond? "You must forgive my candor, Mr. Davies, but my finishing-school teachers never taught me how to handle an unheard-of situation such as this."

He reached over and tilted her delicate chin with one hand so she had to meet his eyes. "Yes, I suppose you never imagined such a sudden, unwelcome engagement. Do you still think yourself in love with Everett?" His eyes searched hers.

She shrugged helplessly, honestly puzzled. "I—I

don't know. We were well suited."

He laughed softly. "And we're not, obviously. Maybe that's why I took your father's offer. I had planned to court you, Tory. You know that. But you were so near to marrying that jackass." When her eyes flashed angrily, he apologized. "I'm sorry—for my language, not for the fact that Charles Everett is what he is. He's wrong for you, Tory."

"And you are right?" The question seemed to ask itself before she could squelch it.

"I think so. No. I know so," he added forcefully. "Charles is a weakling. He was given everything from birth, and all he's done is squander it. Now that your family has lost its money and can't help his political aspirations, he's left you."

"That's not fair! You're twisting things. He . . . he just couldn't help my father and you can." His words wounded her, for she did indeed feel that Charles had bowed out of her life without really attempting to fight for her.

"He doesn't love you, Tory. And you don't love him. You as good as admitted it earlier."

"And I suppose you do love me," she scoffed, too angry to guard her tongue.

"Maybe no more than you love me," he answered enigmatically. "We're attracted to each other—no, love, don't try to deny it," he added when she gasped in indignation. "You need protection for your family, and I need a wife, a lady, to preside over the home I'm building. I have grand plans, Tory, and you're part of them."

Tory bit back her angry retort. How dare he imply, just because he'd mauled her on a couple of occasions, that she was actually attracted to him! She changed the subject to one less emotionally charged. "Let's go see that gargantuan mansion I've heard such rumors about, Mr. Davies."

He swept up his hat and took her arm, guiding her to the parlor door. "Call me Rhys, Tory. I think, under the circumstances, it's quite proper, don't you?" He watched her blush as he opened the door. When she made no reply, he paused in the hallway and pulled her hand from around his arm, raising it to his lips again. "Say it, Tory. Say my name," he commanded softly.

"As you wish, Rhys," she complied, hating the foreign sound of his name almost as much as she hated his power over her.

As he assisted her gallantly into his carriage, Tory recalled July Fourth and their last ride together with a drunken Sanders. Remembering the hideous aftermath of that afternoon, she maintained a frosty silence.

Rhys whipped up the team smartly and smiled lazily. "A beautiful day to plan a wedding, Tory. Where do you want the ceremony—in church, or at our new house? You choose."

She wanted to cry out that she had been given no choices at all—what matter where the deed was done? Biting her tongue, she asked, "Would the Episcopal Church be permissible?"

He shrugged. "Why not?"

"You once mentioned something about being raised by nuns. I assumed all Democrats were Catholic," she replied dismissively.

He laughed. "You say the words Catholic and Democrat as if they were social diseases. As to my run-in with the good sisters, well, I'm afraid it was too late to save my soul. I was fourteen when they had me baptized. Any church is fine with me, love. There, you see how easy I am to get on with?" he asked genially.

"You are still a Democrat," she replied tartly.

"You want everything your way, woman?" he teased. "Maybe if I go into railroads I'll have to change my politics, but mind, I haven't decided on that yet."

She studied his cleanly chiseled profile as he drove. "Railroads? Soon you'll be running for governor."

He looked at her. "Would that please you? Charles is a politician, or fancies himself one."

She bristled. "Charles is in the running for the Senate. I have every confidence he'll make a fine senator. But to answer your question, no. I never cared for all the crowds, for being on display the way a politician's wife would have to be."

He considered for a moment, then leaned over and whispered teasingly, "Is that only because you might end up a Democratic politician's wife?"

She sniffed but didn't deign to give a reply. "Let's discuss churches, not politics."

"Ah, more accord. All right. Would you fancy having the bishop come from Denver to marry us?"

Her head swiveled in spite of herself. "You know the Episcopal bishop?" she asked with obvious disbelief.

"Let's just say he's a friend of some old friends in Denver. I think I can arrange it while we're up there shopping for your trousseau." He paused, then could not resist adding, "I've heard rumors, though, that he's a Democrat."

This time she only smiled. "Nonsense."

They rode through the streets of Starlight between the elegant rows of houses built by the rich, some of whom were merchants, some mine owners, a few stockmen who preferred town life to living in the wilds of the San Juans' grazing valleys. After Rhys had driven his posh black carriage a mile or two south from the edge of town, she could see their destination. The house, half-finished, sat high on the slope of a hill about a quarter mile away.

Tory had heard rumors about it for weeks. A palace, some said. A fairy-tale castle, Lissette Johnson gushed as she speculated on who would be the lucky woman to preside as its mistress. Walled in misery as she was, Tory still could not resist squinting a bit to see the much-fabled mansion.

And a mansion it was, built of the magnificent pink-and-rust-toned sandstone native to the state. The stones were cut in big squares, giving the structure a massive, almost forbidding appearance. It was three stories high with an enormous arched porch stretching across the front. On the left side was a tower topped by a battlement, and on the opposite end was another smaller turret with a steeple. The stained-glass windows were huge and arched, opening to the bright Colorado skies. In spite of the looming bulk of the house, it would never be dark inside.

It looked like a medieval castle, right down to the stone dragons guarding the steps. As Rhys handed her down from the carriage, he said with a flourish, "Welcome to Dragon's Lair, love." He paused uncertainly then, watching her crane her neck to take in the mammoth proportions of the house. "Well, what do you think?"

Tory was speechless. Regaining her voice, she echoed, "Dragon's Lair?"

"Welsh dragons. When the architects showed me drawings of a stone mansion, I couldn't resist. Richmond himself would've been proud of them." When she still made no reply, he added patiently, "Richmond was Henry VII, the first Tudor monarch whose standard was—"

"A red dragon," she interrupted with asperity. "I have read some history Mr.—Rhys," she amended. In fact, when Hedda had caught her poring over Sanders's textbooks as a young girl, her mother had been aghast and quickly supplied her with illustrated fashion books and magazines. Ladies did not read history or the scandalous poetry of men like Byron and Keats.

He raised his eyebrows in surprise at her knowledge. "Score one for the lady. You still haven't answered my question about the house. Do you like it?"

"I'm overwhelmed," she murmured honestly. The place was overbearing and ostentatious, but since so many of the homes of Colorado's wealthy men were every bit as bad, Tory had grown used to garish displays of wealth. She still preferred Laura Everett's simple white gingerbread frame house to the brick mansion her parents had built. But at least its mansard roof and wrought-iron grillwork were the norm in Starlight. This was—she grasped for a word—medieval.

"Let me show you the exterior first. I have a few surprises out back."

What, she wondered. A bear pit? Or were workers digging a moat and building a drawbridge? He took her arm, but before they had strolled but a few steps, a giant of a man with thinning blondish gray hair and a blunt, sour face came shambling toward them.

Feeling her stiffen at Klaus's approach, Rhys greeted the obviously distraught man. "Good day to you, Herr Kruger. Tory, may I present Herr Klaus Kruger, my master builder. Herr Kruger, this is Miss Victoria Laughton, my fiancée."

Tory nodded uneasily, but the German's face split

into a wide grin, erasing his earlier scowl. He bowed formally with surprising grace for such a big man and said, "It is my greatest honor, beautiful lady, to meet Herr Davies' future bride. Always he is out here rushing the men, ever anxious to complete the house for you."

Feeling that Kruger was revealing too much of his vulnerability, Rhys interrupted, "Is there some problem, Klaus?"

"Ya. The man who delivered the glass for the solarium broke one sheet. He says he will not pay for it."

"Was it packed improperly?" Kruger shook his head no. Rhys replied, "The ride from town to here isn't that far, nor that rough. He shouldn't have broken it."

"This I was telling him when you arrived," Klaus said. Just then a tall, surly-looking teamster carrying the badge of his profession, a coiled blacksnake, sauntered around the side of the house. He wore greasy buckskins and a wicked-looking knife strapped at his waist. His shaggy hair was matted with filth. He paused to take a last chaw from his plug and then spit a blob of noisome brownish sludge onto the ground.

"You Davies?" the muleskinner called out with a slur in his voice. He was decidedly antagonistic and had obviously been drinking.

"I'm Davies. You work for Loring Freighting?" Rhys asked easily.

"Yup. 'N' I ain't payin' fer thet damn stupid-ass bent-up glass bein' broke neither."

"Wrong on both counts. When I tell Cass Loring you're drunk on the job, you won't work for her any longer. And she'll dock your pay for the glass. Now apologize to the lady for your language and get out of here," Rhys commanded.

"Damn if I will, you rich son of a bitch," he swore, reaching for his whip.

Knowing what a skilled muleskinner could do with his blacksnake, Rhys wasted no time in closing the space between them. Fortunately the distance was short and the man's reflexes slowed by liquor. Rhys grabbed the whip before his adversary could uncoil it. Using the heavy rawhide like a club, he swung it against the teamster's skull, knocking him to the ground with a ringing whump. When the downed man pulled his evilly gleaming knife from its sheath, Tory gasped.

Rhys didn't hesitate. With blurring speed his booted foot connected with the knife-wielding fist, sending the blade arcing through the air. It landed with a clatter near Kruger's feet. Tory jumped back, but the German picked it up, grinning as Rhys reached down and hauled the drunk up by his filthy buckskin shirt. Holding his foe with one hand, Rhys smashed his fist into the muleskinner's jaw. His head snapped back in a whip-like motion, then lolled sideways as he crumpled into unconsciousness.

Rhys dropped him and said to Klaus, "Dispose of this problem, if you please."

"I was going to handle him, Herr Davies. Only not so gentle as you," the German replied with a smile which Rhys returned.

"Oh, and Klaus, send word to Denver about the situation. Cass'll handle it from there."

The German dragged the tall, lanky man off with no more effort than Tory would have expended hoisting a feather pillow. Rhys turned to her after wiping his hands on a beautifully monogrammed linen handkerchief. His hair was scarcely mussed but for that one unruly lock that persisted in falling

181

over his forehead. "Shall we continue our tour?"

"Are you always so calm after a man tries to whip and then stab you?" Her heart was still hammering. "You actually enjoyed that violence, didn't you?" she accused.

His eyes rounded innocently as he took her arm with solicitude. "You were afraid for me, Tory. How touching."

She gritted her teeth but said nothing as they circled the house, wending their way through scattered shadows cast by whispering aspens and shaggy evergreens. The site was magnificent, and the builders had obviously been instructed not to cut the surrounding trees and mar the natural beauty. If Tory had been rendered speechless by the front of the house, the back left her equally so, but this time it was with pure delight.

Rhys sensed her surprise and pleasure but could see she was trying to conceal it. "Do you like it, love?"

"I haven't seen a solarium since I left school in St. Louis," she said, trying to remain cool and unimpressed.

The big cast-iron bands curving out from the southern side of the house were partially filled with frosted glass. Several of the remaining panels of specially curved glass lay in the grass. One was broken in several jagged pieces.

"When it's complete, the solarium will be thirty feet long and fifteen feet wide. It adjoins the rear sitting room to maximize the southern exposure. You can import all sorts of hothouse plants—anything as beautiful as you—orchids from Hawaii, protea from South Africa—"

"I really prefer our native Colorado flowers, blue columbine, mariposa lilies, and lupine," she replied, disliking the comparison between herself and hot-house plants.

"How loyal of you, Tory. Patriotic even. You may grow your Colorado wildflowers all winter long," he countered. "We will sit in the solarium and watch them bloom at Christmas with snow glistening outside. The house will have central heat."

"Some of the best houses in town already have it. Papa was going to convert our house next year, but I've never felt it was that important," she said lightly as they walked toward a big fountain in the center of the yard.

"I've added a few fireplaces, too. I love a crackling blaze on an icy day." He could also envision the two of them luxuriating on the huge hearth in the master bedroom. Tory's hair would glow with incandescent gold reflected from the leaping flames, her skin would be like hot white silk beneath his fingers as he caressed her. He shook away the erotic reverie as they passed the fountain, heading toward the large stable at the rear of the property.

"I heard you had purchased several racers. Are you competing with Charles, Rhys?" she asked when they turned from the stable to the house.

"I just may, at that. I've bested him in cattle deals and silver mines, why not a horse race?" He shrugged casually, knowing he was nettling her. "I could wear your colors," he said as he opened the front door for her.

"Like a maiden from *Ivanhoe* or some other absurd medieval romance? After seeing this place, I think you have read too many such tales."

"And you not enough," he said, then made a grand flourish. "This is the front foyer. I see it with a six-foot drop crystal chandelier, don't you? I want you to do all the interior decorating, Tory. Choose the furniture, the wallpaper, draperies, everything. The carpenters will be done within the month. You can order everything you want from Lorings in Denver. They're the largest import house and freight haulers in the state."

"You mentioned a woman named Loring to that awful teamster. Does she own the company?" Tory looked at the gleaming oak floors and intricately carved mahogany staircase, spiraling upward to dizzying heights.

"Yes, Cass and her husband Steve run it together, but he's been into railroads with his friend William Jackson Palmer in recent years. Cass handles the muleskinners. Always did," he said with a grin, recalling those outrageous stories about a sixteen-year-old girl who wielded a whip and swore with the best of her men.

"A female who runs a freight business?" Tory asked. Her tone made it clear that she considered no woman so engaged to be a lady.

Rhys supposed that Cass was not a lady in the strictest sense. She was just Cass, Blackie Drago's friend and his friend, too. Letting the matter drop, he gave Victoria a tour of the enormous round parlor on the first floor of the tower, the formal dining room, the ballroom, his office, the library, several smaller sitting rooms, and then the kitchens.

"It's so big, it's like a maze," she said as they approached the winding staircase to the second floor. Workmen swarmed around them like drones, each busy with his task, all under the watchful eyes of Klaus Kruger.

"You'll have all the servants you need—cooks, maids, butler. I'll leave the staff plans up to you for the indoor help."

His hand on her elbow as they climbed the stairs

was proprietary, perfectly proper for an engaged couple, yet it annoyed her. When she gazed down the long hallway, big walnut and mahogany doors lined it.

"You must have kept lumberyards employed from Minnesota to Africa," she said tartly. This much wealth meant a great deal of power, a lesson learned from a lifetime with Stoddard Laughton.

Rhys opened the first door and showed her a lovely room with an enchanting view of the San Juans. Their footfalls echoed on the deserted second floor's tongue-and-groove surface. Unlike the first floor, the upper stories had been completed by the carpenters. They were alone as he said, "I thought of this as a child's room. Not the nursery, of course. That will adjoin our bedroom."

Our bedroom. His words hung in the air. Every man expects a male heir. Hadn't her mother told her that incontrovertible fact? She felt her knees weaken, her pulse race. *I'll have to let him do terrible things to me, just as Mama said.*

Rhys could feel the fear radiate from her. Whenever they'd been alone before, she'd acted angry, tense, superior, even outraged, but never truly afraid. Puzzled, he tried to remember what he had said to upset her as he guided her down the hall. "These rooms on the southern side will be for family, those across the hall for guests." Then it hit him. Bedrooms for children—the children he hoped they would one day have. "This is the nursery, Tory," he said in a low, neutral voice as he ushered her into a small, beautifully appointed room with intricately carved woodwork.

A second door opened from it to another room. Guiding her toward it, he said, "This is the master bedroom."

185

Shirl Henke

She looked through the narrow door frame into an enormous room filled with windows on two sides. Against the far inside wall was a huge fireplace. "This is your room? Where is mine?"

He frowned. "I already told you. This is the master suite. It's ours, adjacent to the nursery, but still private."

"Proper gentlemen always allow their wives to have separate bedrooms," she parroted woodenly. Her parents had never shared their sleeping arrangements.

He swallowed a crude expletive and said coolly, "I'm not a proper gentleman, Tory. My wife will sleep with me."

Chapter Twelve

Tory sat glaring out the train window as the small Denver and Rio Grande passenger car wended its way through the mountains toward the capital. Denver! The promise of the beautiful city almost made her forget the sooty discomfort of riding on a train in the August heat. Perhaps if it weren't for the infuriating man sitting next to her she would have been better able to endure the billowing smoke from the train's engine.

Rhys looked at his mutinous bride-to-be, watching her surreptitiously twist the two-carat diamond engagement ring beneath the glove on her dainty finger. She remained angry with him for a variety of transgressions. Insisting they would sleep in the same bedroom had been heinous enough. Later he'd had the temerity to say aloud that she would have to get pregnant in order to have children. Gentlemen, he had been frostily informed, never discussed things so indelicately with their wives, much less their fiancées.

He hoped the trip to Denver with Stoddard and Hedda would help mend matters. So far her mother's frigid disdain and Stoddard's sour resignation seemed only to reinforce Tory's negative feelings about their upcoming marriage.

But what woman did not love to shop? Tory and Hedda were to select her trousseau and all the furnishings for Dragon's Lair. Considering the price tag of such an excursion, it should have delighted his fiancée, but it obviously did not. He ignored her chilly expression and silently teased her with his eyes, knowing she was keenly aware of his intent.

Stoddard watched the interchange between his daughter and Davies. Hedda detested him so much she was barely being civil. Announcing the engagement last week had all but killed her, in spite of his presentation to Tory of a ring worth a fortune. Hedda took out all the contempt and disgust she felt for the Welshman on her husband. Laughton hoped this trip would change matters.

Stoddard knew his son's dissolute ways and had hired detectives immediately upon discovering the embezzlement. One lead was in Denver. If he could get his hands on the boy and his money before Sanders spent it or lost it, he could redeem his bank and send the arrogant gambler back to his saloon where he belonged.

He looked out on the spectacular scenery flowing past the coach windows. There had been a light dusting of snow last evening, not an unusual occurrence for August in the high elevations that General Palmer's narrow-gauge rails dared to travel. It would be melted away in the Indian-summer warmth by midday. The aspens rustling in the breeze would soon turn to gold. That grand old sentinel of the state, Pike's Peak, glistened in the distance. Jagged red and gold mountains rose all around the precariously cut rails that hugged the hills in a tortuous switchback embrace. Spruce and pines, made spiky by winter winds, jutted at the train with hungry green branches as it sped by. Preoccupied with financial and family problems, Stoddard saw nothing of the beauty surrounding him.

Rhys did. The awe-inspiring grandeur of the Rockies, the sheer size and diversity of Colorado's landscape, always left him breathless, even after living in the state for over five years. He'd traveled a lot since leaving Sister Frances Rose's orphanage in New York, following the Mississippi from St. Louis to New Orleans. Then he'd he moved on west to Galveston and north across the vast panorama of Texas. He had even seen the much-fabled Pacific and dealt faro in a posh San Francisco casino, but always the mountains drew him back. *This is where I want to build my life.* He looked from the vista outside to the woman seated next to him. She was the one with whom he would share the rest of his life. Tory was everything she should be—beautiful, well-bred, innocent, yet intelligent, even spirited when he could get her loose from Hedda's corset strings. She was everything except in love with him. He decided that must change in time and looked out the window to enjoy the view.

After a moment he gave Hedda a cheeky grin and watched her wince, then turned his attention back to Tory. "We really should set a date, love, don't you agree? After all, the engagement is official now."

Tory looked from Hedda back to Rhys, but before she could reply, Stoddard intervened. "Plenty of time for that after we get things settled in Denver—all the clothes and household folderol bought, that is," he amended hastily.

"Lorings have an enormous emporium. They stock as much merchandise as most top New York import houses. I don't think selecting the furnishings will be any problem," Rhys said, still fixing his eyes on Tory. "Of course, there is the matter of the trousseau . . ." He let his words trail off suggestively just for the pleasure of watching her blush.

Tory could well imagine his lascivious thoughts about see-through lingerie and sheer silk stockings. Her lips twitched in spite of her embarrassment as she considered buying half a dozen high-necked, red-flannel nightrails, complete with long johns. *But he'd delight in peeling them off you*, an insidious voice whispered inside her mind. She blushed again.

"I think we should plan for December," Hedda said coolly. "That should provide ample time for preparations. The holidays are such a festive time for a wedding, after all," she added with sweet sarcasm.

"Let's wait and see how long it'll take to have the goods delivered," Rhys replied, daring her to say more.

Flavia Goldstock stood transfixed behind a potted palm in the lobby of the American House. She had just come from a delightful luncheon with Blackie when four soot-stained train travelers approached the front desk. The two women were expensively dressed and attractive. She dismissed them with scarcely a glance, fixing her attention on the men— Stoddard Laughton and Rhys! Rhys was back in Denver, five years older and looking handsome as sin, not to mention very prosperous.

She smiled impudently behind her blue lace gloves at the thought that two of her former lovers were obviously business acquaintances. Stoddard was getting paunchy, but then he'd been no prize when she knew him in Starlight either. The surprise was Rhys, who only a few years ago had been a green boy following her about like a worshipful puppy dog. Even then he had been an eager pupil and she a skilled teacher. But he had been virtually penniless.

Inspecting the cut of his suit with a practiced eye, Flavia noticed the ruby stick pin gleaming from his silk cravat. She was an expert at carat weights. Even his boots were custom made. Yes, he had decidedly come up in the world. But what was his connection to stuffy old Stoddard? She shifted her attention back to the women. One was older—Laughton's wife, the bitch who had blackmailed the old fool into dropping her without a cent. Of course, that had been a blessing in disguise since it brought her to Denver for the first time. The younger female was a replica of her mother—pretty enough, Flavia supposed, if a man's taste ran to delicate blondes with ice water in their veins.

Her eyes narrowed speculatively when Rhys finished at the desk and strode back to the plush upholstered settee where the two blondes sat demurely. He solicitously took the girl's hand and drew her up, oozing that devilish Welsh charm that Flavia had found so irresistible. "So that's the way the wind blows," she murmured, checking Tory's hand for a ring. Even at long distance, the large diamond winked back at her. For snobs like the Laughtons to let someone of Rhys's background into the family, he must be very rich indeed!

Flavia Goldstock, actress, was not now nor ever had been a sentimental woman, else she would have ended up at the mercy of men such as

Emmet Hauser. But she did bask in male adulation. Once, Rhys had supplied that in abundance. So had Stoddard. Her lips curved into a silky smile as she impulsively formed a plan that would revenge her against the Laughtons and at the same time reacquaint her with Rhys.

She glided from behind the giant potted plant just as the foursome began to stroll toward the hotel stairs. They were on a collision course. "Why, hello, Rhys. It *is* Rhys Davies, isn't it? What has it been— four, no don't tell me, five years?" She reached out one soft white hand, gloves removed, expensive rings winking, and let him engulf it in his.

"Miss Goldstock, what an unexpected pleasure," Rhys replied as he gave her hand a perfunctory salute. *What an unexpected disaster.* He smiled his damndest and turned to the Laughtons to make introductions. At least Flavia was dressed like a lady in an elegant dark blue suit.

"May I present my fiancée"—he stressed the word but saw the imp dancing in Flavia's dark eyes and knew it was useless—"Miss Victoria Laughton. Tory, this is an old friend, Flavia Goldstock."

Tory had watched the beautiful brunette approach with disbelief. *Her!* That actress Papa had been involved with so many years ago. And so had Rhys, obviously. She nodded woodenly but did not smile, not even daring to look at her mother.

"This gentleman—"

"Ah, Stoddard, how are you?" Flavia interrupted. "And Mrs. Laughton, of course, a great pleasure." Flavia inclined her head coquettishly with just the right theatrical nuance of condescension to Hedda. "Your husband and I were acquainted back in Starlight some years ago when my troupe toured there. He was always a patron of the arts."

At that moment, Rhys would gladly have traded places with Tomato Nose Wylie Wilcox at the bottom of the deepest shaft in the Lady Victory.

Stoddard gave a strangled cough and shifted his weight, while Hedda simply stared in frosty disdain. Reluctant to let her moment in the spotlight pass so quickly, Flavia delivered what she thought would be her exit line. "I do hope you'll stop by to visit old friends while you're in Denver, Rhys. Blackie Drago would so love to see you." That received everyone's attention. The infamous Denver underworld chief was known the length and breadth of the Rockies.

Rhys gave up all pretense at propriety and grinned at her sharkishly, daring her to do her worst. "Perhaps I will pay a call on him. Is he by any chance a patron of the arts, too?" He couldn't resist watching Stoddard's starched shirt wilt.

"Of course, darling. I'm in production right now—at the Opera House. You simply must attend a show while you're in town."

Hedda's spine stiffened and the outraged woman actually seemed to grow inches taller. She said witheringly, "My husband and I are not patrons of the musical stage. We find it far too vulgar and not at all appropriate for gently reared young ladies such as my daughter. Now, if you will excuse—"

"Oh, Mrs. Laughton, I assure you I do not play musicals. I perform drama, Shakespeare. Tonight's production should be of particular interest to you . . ." She paused for effect and with flawless timing turned to Rhys and Stoddard. "Perhaps the gentlemen would find it even more instructive—*The Taming of the Shrew*. Good day." She swept away, silk skirts swishing and lustrous ebony curls bouncing as she made her exit.

When she passed Victoria, she had the audacity to wink! Tory fought the urge to reach up into that elaborate coiffure and loosen a few pins. Perhaps loosen a few teeth, too! Horror-struck by her own vulgar and obviously jealous reaction, she turned to face Rhys with her cheeks afire.

Stoddard, for once bereft of pomposity, stuttered as he said, "I do think . . . that is, my wife and daughter are quite in need of rest, Rhys. I'll see them to their rooms."

Rhys looked at Tory and read her emotions with a mixture of amusement and alarm. She was jealous, a good sign, but she was also hurt. It was bad enough that his own past relationship with Flavia and connections with Blackie had come to light, but worse that Laughton had fallen in thrall to the actress, too. Hedda was seething, and Tory looked shocked and disillusioned by her father's infidelity.

"I'll see that the bell captain brings up the luggage directly, Stoddard." He turned to Tory and gave her a beautiful, lopsided smile. "Until dinner tonight, love?"

"Perhaps you'd rather see Miss Goldstock's *instructive* play than dine with us," Tory said tartly.

Rhys shrugged and said, "I've already seen Miss Goldstock play, Tory. I'm no longer interested." Before she could react, he snatched up her hand and kissed it with firm, warm lips. "Tonight."

Hedda's eyes bored into him like crystalline daggers, but she said nothing as Stoddard awkwardly ushered the two women toward the stairs.

After seeing to the stowing of the luggage, Rhys decided to pay a call on Blackie Drago at his saloon. The Bucket of Blood had not changed a great deal in the past months since he had left Denver. Still plush and raucous, it shared many features with the Naked

Truth, including furnishings ordered from Lorings. One thing had changed—the return to Denver of Flavia Goldstock.

He strode up to the bar, greeting old friends and customers. The big bald-headed bartender gave him a toothsome smile. "Well, Rhys. A lot's happened since you quit dealin' here and headed out with your stake. Looks like it paid off for you. Boss man's upstairs. He'll pour ya better 'n what I got here."

"Thanks, Odd Job." He took the long flight of steep stairs to Blackie's private apartment in brisk strides and knocked on the heavy walnut door.

"Come in," Drago called out. Engrossed in tallying last night's profits, he did not look up but barked, "Well? What is it yer wantin'? Speak up."

"I see your rascally old Irish disposition hasn't improved any."

"Rhys!" The older man's head snapped up. His dark eyes gleamed with delight as he took in his young protégé's appearance. "Travel-stained a bit, but right prosperous. What's brought you back to Denver? It's not a loan you're needin', I know that."

They shook hands heartily, and Rhys pulled up a chair next to the big desk filled with account books and clutter. "I'm here to escort my fiancée to Loring's. She's decorating our new house in Starlight—and buying her wedding trousseau."

Blackie's eyes widened and he slapped his knee. "Wedding, eh? I heard about your winnin' a saloon, even strikin' silver. You're for sure going straight now, boyo. Who's the lucky lady?"

"She is a lady, Blackie, fine as they come. Victoria Laughton. Of course, I could wish for better in-laws, but . . ." He shrugged philosophically.

"Couldn't every man who's foolish enough to be the marryin' kind?" Blackie said with a chuckle.

"You just hop off one of the general's smokers?" he asked, looking at Rhys's sooty clothes.

"Yes. We just checked into the American House."

"Odd. I must've missed you by minutes. I just had lunch in their dining room." Remembering Rhys's old infatuation with Flavia, he volunteered no more, but waited guardedly.

"I know. Your luncheon date accidentally encountered me—and the Laughtons in the lobby."

Blackie winced. "The very divil gets in her now 'n' then."

"She knows Laughton from Starlight," Rhys said.

"So, the puddin's really thickenin'," Drago replied with a sigh.

"When did she come back to Denver? I thought her San Francisco millionaire was keeping her happy," Rhys said cynically.

Blackie shrugged. "She always had grease paint for blood. Got bored livin' in one place, I guess. Or bored with him. She had quite a tourin' company of actors. Traveled everywhere between the coast and the Mississippi over the last five years. She came back to Denver just a few weeks after you'd left."

"Why'd you take her on? You know what she is," Rhys said quietly.

Blackie smiled cynically now. "Oh, I know what she is, right enough. That's why it works out so well. Neither of us has any illusions."

Rhys scoffed. "She's an actress, Blackie. She creates illusions. Don't let her hurt you."

Drago chuckled gently with the tolerance of age. "She got to you, boyo, I know. Bein' dry behind the ears now, you've learned your lesson. If you can figure it out in twenty-seven years, think I can't be doin' the same after sixty-five? Did she, ah, insinuate a reunion?"

Rhys looked distinctly uncomfortable. "Not directly. I think she wanted to spite Stoddard and Hedda
more than anything, but . . . hell, Blackie, I don't
know what she might do."

"But you do know what you'll be doin'. I'd bet this
saloon it won't be the likes of Flavia Goldstock you'll
be doin' it with either!"

Rhys laughed and then sobered. "No, I can resist
Flavia's charms easily enough now."

"Because of this lady you're to marry?"

"Not the way you mean it, alas," Rhys said with
a sigh. The prospect of celibacy until December
loomed bleakly before him.

Blackie poured some excellent brandy to console
his young friend as they caught up on the past
months and reminisced about bygone years.

Tory tossed fitfully, then gave up her futile
attempts to sleep. This whole trip had changed
from a much-anticipated dream into a dreadful
nightmare. To think her own papa and that . . . that
womanizer she was being forced to marry were both
involved with the Goldstock hussy. *How humiliating
for Mama! How much more humiliating for you*, that
inner voice chided. That was the most terrible part
of all. She had been jealous of the beautiful, sophis-
ticated woman! At first Tory denied it, but as she
had sat next to Rhys at dinner that evening, fending
off his teasing charm, she finally admitted the truth.
Rhys had had an affair with the actress, a woman
many years his senior, a woman who still found him
attractive. Did he find Flavia equally attractive?

Rhys lay across the wide bed in his hotel room
with a drink balanced on his bare chest, staring at
the ceiling. One dim gaslight flickered on the far wall
and the bright Colorado moon filtered through the

curtain. Dinner had been a disaster. Hedda's veneer of politeness was near to cracking, and Tory was jealous and angry over Flavia. Laura would think the jealousy a good omen, no doubt. If only he could have his fiancée alone here in Denver, away from her parents. He sighed. Propriety wouldn't allow it any more than Tory herself would. If she were the kind of woman who would come to him now, she would not be the lady of his dreams. *You can't have it both ways, old sod.* If only it weren't going to be so damn long until the wedding. He took a last swallow of the drink and decided he'd put it to Cass in no uncertain terms: the fastest delivery on every item, no matter what the freight cost!

Still, realistically, there was no way he could expect to have the house completed before the end of September. He had made a promise of sorts not to touch another woman since he and Tory had become engaged. Ginger had been openly disbelieving at first, then went into a royal snit when he gently fended off her advances over the past several weeks. How long could he hold out?

A soft rap sounded on the door. It was well past midnight and the exclusive hotel was quiet as a tomb. No one should be about. Being a betting man, Rhys knew the odds on whom he would find when he opened the door. He rose with an oath, drained his glass, and strode barefoot across the carpet to yank the door open.

Flavia licked her lips as she inspected his nearly naked torso. "My, my, you may have matured, darling, but some things never change," she purred, gliding through the doorway and reaching her beringed fingers to embed them in his chest hair. Her cool palm gently pushed him back as she discreetly closed the door behind her.

"What's changed, Flavia darling, is my financial status. When you left Denver five years ago, I was an impoverished dealer in Blackie's place. Now that I'm a man of means, you're back. Scarce a surprise, love." His voice was cool, but her perfume evoked memories that remained surprisingly warm.

She leaned against him, allowing him an excellent view of her generous cleavage while her hands stroked his bare back and shoulders. "I have missed you, Rhys, whether or not you believe it. I had to leave you then. It was a matter of survival. I hoped in time you'd understand . . ." She punctuated her speech with light kisses and nips to his chest and shoulder, working her way up to his face.

"Oh, I understand well enough—now. Then I was devastated. But youth is resilient. I recovered." He began to unfasten her busy hands from around his neck.

She resisted, rubbing her lower body against his tantalizingly. "I want you, Rhys. Your little virgin sleeps across the hall, her maidenhead still intact, I'd bet."

"You'd win. But I want her—and I'm willing to marry her to get what I want." His voice was implacable now.

"She'll never know about tonight," Flavia whispered pettishly, still clinging.

"Were I you, love, I would go back to Blackie before he finds out what a fool you've been."

She gave a scornful laugh to hide her fury over his rejection. "Surely you aren't afraid of an old man? He and I have an understanding, Rhys." Once more a cunning hand reached out.

Once more he intercepted it. "I'm not afraid of Blackie, but he's my friend and I never betray a trust."

"Or a fiancée?" she asked with dawning understanding. "You're actually in love with that virginal little ice princess. More fool you, Rhys. She'll freeze these off," she said, lowering her hand and cupping him before he could stop her. She was rewarded with his involuntary response and chuckled knowingly. "You'll be looking for me or someone like me within a week of your wedding, you randy stud."

He cursed silently as he grasped her hands and began to back her toward the door. "I'll take my chances with Tory, Flavia. After all, I am a gambler, remember?"

She shrugged in defeat, loosening his hold on her hands. Reaching for the doorknob, she opened it, then paused. "One kiss good-bye, Rhys. For old times' sake?"

Tory paced in her room, then poured herself a glass of cool water from the pitcher beside her bed. A muffled noise distracted her. Was it from Rhys's room? No, probably her mother's room next door. Hedda had been most upset at dinner. Tory hoped she was not ill. She and Papa always took separate rooms and he was a sound sleeper. Perhaps she should see if Mama was all right. Slipping on a silk wrapper, Tory grabbed her room key and eased open the door. Surely no one would be stirring to see her in this disreputable state of dishabille. She had barely put one foot over the door sill when movement and color down the hall caught her eye. Rhys's door was open. He was standing partially in the hallway, nearly naked, passionately embracing that actress!

Repelled and fascinated at the same time, she watched Flavia fuse her body against his, opening her mouth to exchange a hot, lascivious kiss.

Remembering that day at the river, she again looked upon his bare upper body. The muscles in his arms flexed as he held his paramour. That curly lock of hair danced on his forehead as he bent over Flavia, lost in the kiss.

Tory bit down on her fist to keep from sobbing, then quietly slipped back inside and slid the door silently closed. Tears scalded her cheeks as she leaned against the door, shivering in pain so raw, so new, that it terrified her. She had known what kind of man he was. Her mother had warned her about his type. Why should she be upset or surprised at his ruttish behavior? Hedda had taught her to be grateful if her husband sought out his carnal pleasures elsewhere and left her in peace. Then why did she feel so betrayed, so agonizingly hurt?

Chapter Thirteen

Loring Freighting and its warehouses alone took up a city block, not counting the corrals filled with mules, oxen, and horses stabled behind the front office. Early on their second day in Denver, Rhys escorted Tory and Hedda to meet Cass Loring and select furnishings for Dragon's Lair. Stoddard went about some errand of his own in the bustling capital city.

Hedda was, as usual, disdainful and self-possessed, but Tory was very quiet and tense. Rhys dismissed her subdued behavior as bridal nerves, hoping the fun of lavish spending at Loring's would improve her disposition. They entered the front office where half a dozen clerks worked at desks piled high with invoices. Greeting one youth named Chester, Rhys was received with a wide grin and told, "Miz Cass is out back seein' ta a special order."

Rhys escorted them through the labyrinth of offices to a gargantuan warehouse at the end of a cluttered hall. Turning into it, he wended his way through boxes, bales, and barrels, leading the two women to an open loading dock in the rear. At its far end an adolescent girl dressed outrageously in boy's denims and a baggy plaid shirt was tallying sacks of wheat as a muleskinner carried them by. A small boy collided with her, nearly toppling her into the heavily bearded man.

"Damnblast you, Billy, I'll skin your ass with my blacksnake if you don't git!" she yelled after the culprit as he raced into the arms of a striking woman coming up the outside stairs.

"Kylie, I've warned you about that swearing, young woman!" the lady said with biting authority in her well-modulated voice. She and the girl shared the same pale copper hair and gold eyes, but the older woman was dressed in a respectable tan skirt and white blouse.

"I've heard *you* say a lot worse, Mom," the girl replied, glaring at the tan-haired boy. "Billy's driving me crazy while I'm the one doing the work."

"I swear at my mules—and that only on the road. Using such language on your brother is not acceptable. What would your father say if he heard you?"

"Probably that he'd make her stay home from the picnic on Saturday if she doesn't behave," interrupted a low male voice. A tall, slim man with straight tan hair and the chiseled features of one born to privilege approached them. Taking the squirming boy from his mother, he said, "And you, young man, will lose your picnic privileges, too, if you keep tormenting Kylie."

"I see nothing ever changes around here." Rhys walked toward the striking couple and their children. Hedda's face was tinged with scorn and Tory was in shock over the girl's appearance and language. Both stood at the warehouse door while Rhys exchanged hearty greetings with his friends. Turning to his fiancée and her mother, he walked toward them saying, "I have some very special ladies I want you to meet." He winked at Kylie, who stared up at him like an adoring puppy, then added, "Best behavior now, promise, love?"

"I promise, Rhys," she breathed as she looked suspiciously at the two elegantly dressed women.

"This is my future bride, Miss Victoria Laughton, and her mother, Mrs. Hedda Laughton." Turning to his friends, he said, "Ladies, please meet Steve and Cass Loring, owners of this little place—oh, yes, and two of their three offspring, Kylie and Billy."

Cass moved forward gracefully to greet the stand-offish visitors while Steve doffed his elegant flat-crowned brown hat.

"Rhys has always been full of surprises, but this takes first place! I am so pleased to meet you both, Mrs. Laughton, Miss Laughton," the redhead said.

Coming up behind his wife, Steve bowed formally. "I am truly enchanted with this young rascal's good fortune, ladies." With a touch of gray at his temples and his faultlessly cut brown suit, he looked the epitome of a cultured Eastern gentleman. Hedda thawed a bit and gave him a wintry smile. Tory felt overwhelmed as the two children joined them and everyone asked questions at once about Rhys's surprise engagement.

Taking charge, Cass instructed the children to return to their chores. "You'll get to visit with Rhys later, I'm certain," she added in firm dismissal. Cass had not failed to note the wariness of Rhys's fiancée and future mother-in-law. "Please do come inside.

We have a shiny new office where we can talk in peace."

"I've brought Tory and Mrs. Laughton to order all the furniture, wallpaper, and carpets for the house I'm building in Starlight."

"I have a feeling a lot has happened since you won that saloon," Steve said with an arched brow. His cool golden gaze took in the younger man's expensive clothes. "A house in Starlight, huh?"

"I heard some rumors from Blackie about a big new silver strike in the San Juans," Cass said excitedly.

Hedda's eyebrows went up at the Loring woman's casual mention of the infamous Blackie Drago. "Perhaps you had better make your selections without me, my dear Victoria. I feel the most frightful headache coming on. I trust I shall see you both at the hotel this evening?" She cocked her head at Tory, who simply nodded, feeling deserted and angry, but unable to voice her protest. She, too, wanted to flee Rhys's friends.

"Perhaps I should go with you, Mama?"

"I'm sure your mother will be fine with a bit of rest. I'll have my driver take her back to the hotel," Rhys said with evident relish.

"Why don't we let Cass and Victoria discuss decorating?" Steve offered. "After we see Mrs. Laughton safely to the carriage, I have a couple of prime horses I think you'll appreciate, Rhys." He executed an elegant bow to Tory, gave Cass a light but oddly intimate kiss on the cheek, and then gallantly offered his arm to Hedda.

As they retraced their steps toward the front of the building, the men argued over race horses. Hedda's head was erect, her walk stiff and regal. She never glanced back at Tory.

Cass guided her guest into a large, handsomely appointed office and offered her a seat. Tory felt swallowed up by the big leather chair, but leaning back, she found it quite comfortable. Unclasping her reticule, she took out the floor plans for Dragon's Lair that Rhys had given her and said, "I have quite a few items to order, Mrs. Lor—"

"Your mother detests Rhys, doesn't she? And, please, call me Cass." Her clear amber eyes measured the delicate but strained face of her young charge.

Tory felt her face heat with embarrassment. "You're very direct, Mrs.—Cass. I suppose Mama's feelings are rather apparent, but then this won't be an ordinary marriage."

Cass laughed softly and leaned back on the edge of her big oak desk. "There's no such animal as an ordinary marriage. Judging from the way Rhys acts, he's the one who pursued you."

Tory sat up. "That is the usual manner of things."

"Not always. I railroaded Steve into marrying me with the threat of a hanging, but that's another story," Cass said dismissively as Tory's eyes widened. "You are in love with Rhys." Her matter-of-factness left Tory short of breath.

"I am not—" she stammered to a halt, aghast at the intimate turn the conversation was taking. "That is, my feelings for Rhys Davies have no bearing on our marriage."

She looked so forlorn, yet fierce, like a small fluffy kitten pursued by a large bulldog. *Or perhaps a Welsh terrier?* Cass mused whimsically. "One's feelings always have a bearing on marriage, believe me." Seeing Tory stiffen, Cass changed tack. "Just remember, if you ever need a friend—or want to talk to someone who's known Rhys since he was a kid, well, I'm a sympathetic listener. Now, let's see that list." Scanning the lengthy order and the floor plans, Cass let out a low whistle of amazement. "We'll be here all day and then some, selecting all these furnishings. Rhys really did strike it rich."

"Yes, you could say so," Tory replied with a hint of bitterness in her voice. Damn the ruthless gambler for the day he ever set foot in Starlight and turned her world upside down!

They spent the day poring over catalogues and climbing through warehouse rooms full of furniture, crystal, and chandeliers. They examined rolls of wallpaper, even the latest in kitchen stoves. As the day wore on, an idea began to form in the back of Tory's mind. Cass had flipped through several sections of a catalogue filled with pictures of gaudy flocked wallpapers, grotesquely carved four-poster beds, and all manner of absolutely indecent statuary.

"This is the kind of stuff Blackie orders for his place," Cass said with a chuckle. "You wouldn't be interested in these selections."

Then Tory spied a naked Cupid perched suggestively on the edge of a claw-footed porcelain bathtub shoved into one corner of the warehouse. She did not blink. She knew how she would accomplish her plan.

Later that evening, after dinner in the hotel's elegant dining room, Tory excused herself from her fiancé, her parents, and the Lorings, whom Rhys had invited as his guests. Pleading sheer exhaustion, she practically fled to her room. But once there, she made a detailed list of bedroom furnishings. Having seen Rhys's signature on various legal documents in past weeks, she practiced copying it over and over. When she was finally satisfied with her forgery, she signed the order list. "If I post it the day we leave, that should allow plenty of time for this shipment for

207

Ginger's place to arrive in Starlight."

There would be a problem when the wagons headed to the Naked Truth, but she would figure out a way to divert them once she was home. Their cargo was really destined for the Dragon's Lair, a special wedding gift from her to her bridegroom.

"I don't like it, Steve. The girl acts so unhappy. And that ice bag of a mother!" Cass brushed her waist-length hair as she watched her husband peel off his formal clothes.

Steve chuckled. Knowing the expression in her amber eyes, he looked forward to bed. "Stoddard Laughton's a stuffed shirt and his wife's rather cold, but Tory is exactly the kind of woman Rhys always wanted, Cassie. A lady with a pedigree. Now he's rich enough to afford her."

Cass put down her brush and said thoughtfully, "She's in love with him, Steve, that's the strangest part of all. Oh, not that he couldn't charm birds out of trees, but that she's denying her own feelings. I'm sure of it. He must've forced the marriage somehow . . ."

"And she resents him for it?" he replied, walking over to stroke her burnished hair. "We can't help them, Cassie. I know dinner tonight was a disaster, but we tried to be entertaining guests. The Laughtons are simply snobs."

"Poor Rhys. I only hope he knows what he's in for." She leaned back against his chest as he bent down and put his arms around her.

"No man knows what he's in for when he gets married. Let him take his lumps like the rest of us poor devils," he murmured into her neck, nibbling kisses.

Her squeal of outrage was lost as he swept her into

his arms and carried her to the handsome walnut bed in the center of the room

Tory stood in the midst of chaos. Teamsters unloaded velvet sofas, soft leather chairs, and massive mahogany tables. She directed them where to place each piece, while conducting an ongoing inspection of the work of the paper-hangers and the men installing the enormous six-foot crystal chandelier in the foyer. Within a week it would all be done. Well, almost all. Her secret special order had not come yet, but she had bribed the agent at the freight station outrageously, saying it was her surprise for her husband. He would forward it from the saloon to the house, no questions asked.

Rhys stopped by periodically, checking with her on the progress of her new domain, delighted with the seeming enthusiasm she exhibited at decorating Dragon's Lair. All the furnishings reflected her elegant good taste, from the off-white damask wallpaper in the ballroom to the lacy cobweb-edged curtains billowing from ceiling to floor in the parlors. Hand-painted tile fireplace screens depicting fox hunts and bucolic country scenes complemented the inlaid cherrywood fireplaces. A stately grandfather clock chimed softly from Rhys's office, the only room for which he helped her select furnishings—bold, masculine leather chairs and a sofa flanked a big roll-top desk.

"Put the gold settee in the front parlor, Louis," she instructed a teamster hoisting an exquisite piece of cherrywood and velvet as if it weighed no more than feather ticking. Following her direction, he headed toward the designated room. Tory followed so she could decide exactly where she wanted it placed. She massaged her temples after Louis had left to get the rest of the parlor furniture from the wagon.

"Tired, love?" The low, intimate caress of Rhys's voice reached her just as he placed his hands on her shoulders and began massaging her delicate collarbone and neck.

Tory fought the urge to lean into his solid strength. "It's late. I didn't expect you this afternoon." She could not break the hypnotic spell of his hands and hated herself for it.

He leaned down and kissed her neck lightly as he kneaded. "How could I stay away?"

That galvanized her into putting some distance between them. "Please, Rhys. The servants. It isn't proper."

He sighed. "When we're alone it isn't proper either, Tory. You always find some excuse to avoid my touch . . . and it isn't because you dislike it, either."

"A gentleman never says such a thing to a lady!" The truth hurt. Avoiding being caught alone with him in the past weeks had been increasingly difficult. Rhys was oh so clever at stealing kisses, touches, caresses, when no one was looking.

"You're a lady, Tory, and I do respect that, whether you believe it or not," he said patiently, fighting down the waves of frustration. "I didn't mean to frighten you, love. It's just that . . ." He walked toward the open window and stared out in hopeless misery. How did you explain to your gently reared fiancée that you were randy as a longhorn ram in rutting season? "You're jumpy as a cat every time I come near you. It isn't natural, Tory."

She stiffened angrily, hating the way he seemed to see through her. "There is nothing 'natural' about our relationship, Rhys. You knew that from the beginning."

"But you made a bagain. Since our trip to Denver

last month, you seem to regret it—more than you did before. Why?" His midnight eyes studied her keenly.

"Let's just say I found your choice of friends enlightening."

"I assume you mean Flavia. She's part of the past, Tory. Forget her."

Will you forget her, Rhys? "Actresses, underworld cutthroats, female freighters. Certainly I found it disconcerting. So did my parents. Mama—"

"Your darling mama," he interrupted with a hint of steel in his voice, "found Steve Loring to be quite the gentleman. Why, he's even a Republican! None of you had to endure dinner with Blackie—who I might add is also a good friend to Steve as well as Cass. How is it, do you suppose, that a fine Philadelphia aristocrat like Steve has withstood fifteen years of marriage to a 'female freighter'?"

"I'm certain I don't know. A pity she doesn't have a sister waiting in the wings for you." She slipped past him and headed into the ballroom where two paper-hangers were hard at work. Over her shoulder she said, "Maybe you should wait a couple more years for Kylie. I'm sure you'd suit."

Remembering the sassy fifteen-year-old cussing Billy on the freight dock, Rhys had to laugh in spite of his aggravation. "I'm not a cradle robber, and just because I admire Cass and want you to become friends with her doesn't mean I'd want to marry a woman like her. I chose you, Tory." He caught up with her by the big newel post at the foot of the curving staircase and swept her around with one arm. "Show me the upstairs. I haven't seen it yet."

"No . . . that is, nothing much has been done yet. The wallpaper isn't hung and the carpet hasn't been laid in the guest rooms," she temporized.

"What about our bedroom suite?" he asked, daring her to resume her old prim arguments.

She placed her palms against his chest and shoved to put a decent distance between their bodies, thinking fast. "Nothing is set up in the master suite either. I, uh, ordered some especially expensive pieces. Cass had to send back East for them."

His eyes lit up. "I can't wait to see the bed," he said with a devilish grin. He was rewarded with a blush.

Tory smiled thinly and forced herself to meet his teasing eyes. "The suite is my special project, Rhys. Since I must share it with you, I want it to be decorated perfectly. I promise it will be ready before the wedding, but, please"—she paused and searched his dark blue eyes entreatingly with her pale aqua ones—"let it be my surprise, won't you?"

He felt the pressure of her palms ease and drew her closer once more. "Just as long as it's ready for our wedding night, love," he said huskily. Stealing a quick look about the chaotic foyer, he whisked her out the wide front door onto the spacious porch. Her silk blouse with its frilly ruffles was molded deliciously to her soft curves in a demure, lady-like way.

He crushed her against him and his mouth descended for a swift, electrifying kiss. Startled, she opened her lips and felt his hot tongue barely brush hers, then retreat so quickly that she was not sure if she had imagined it. "On second thought, it doesn't matter if the suite is done or not," he whispered raggedly. "We can use a guest room if we have to! Wouldn't that be one to tell our children, Tory!"

With that he was off, taking the wide stone steps in swift long-legged strides. He did not see the cool smile that barely curled her lips as she watched him

swing up on Blackjack. *Just wait, Rhys Davies . . .*
Just you wait.

"The bishop's here—all the way from Denver!"
A drunken miner came ambling into the Naked
Truth. "When Rhys Davies ties th' knot, he does it
right enough," he said as the hubbub around him
increased.

Someone ordered a round of drinks to toast the
popular saloon owner's health and wedded bliss.
Glasses and tin pails in hand, miners, cowboys, and
store clerks poured out onto the sidewalk, rubbing
elbows with nattily dressed businessmen and ranch
owners. Everyone wanted to see the Episcopal bishop of Colorado, come so far into the hinterlands just
to perform the marriage of Starlight's new favorite son.

This was a newsworthy event. Mike Manion, pen
in hand, wended his way through the crowd to get
an interview. Muttering beneath his breath that the
fool cleric wasn't due in Starlight until tomorrow,
he shook his head to clear it from the effects of too
much celebrating. Although given the circumstances
of Rhys and Tory Laughton's marriage, he had not
been truly certain whether he was celebrating or
mourning.

Tomato Nose Wylie Wilcox, having deserted his
post at the mine to attend the upcoming festivities,
was at the head of the impromptu welcoming
committee. Weaving left to right like an aspen
in a thunderstorm, he swept his hat off with a
grand flourish in front of the dignified man in the
small black buggy. "Greetin's, honored reveren'. I'm
right pleased ta meetcha. Whut with yew comin' all
this way ta save them poor souls from th' evils o'
drink."

213

Bishop Grey, a reed-slim little man with a no-nonsense manner, stepped from the carriage and took a whiff of Wylie. "You, sir, are drunk yourself," he pronounced.

"Right, I am at thet, but doncha know, yore reverence, when a real live bishop comes all the ways ta th' San Juans ta marry my boss 'n' his lady, well, a feller jist hasta celebrate!"

"I suppose so," the cleric replied gravely as the crowd roared hearty approval. Looking about the street crowded with boisterous men, Bishop Grey could see no room for his buggy to pass through the throng.

A dapper little man wearing a bowler hat and carrying a pen and paper made his way toward the bishop. "Your reverence, Bishop Grey? My name's Mike Manion, publisher of the *Plain Speaker*. In return for a few brief words, I'll clear a path for you."

"If you could also be so kind as to direct me to Rhys Davies' house?"

Manion turned beet red. "Er, the groom resides in that establishment," he said, pointing back to the Naked Truth, "but a man of the cloth such as yourself couldn't be expected to meet him in there, now, could you?"

The older man's eyes danced. "It would tend to breed scandal, Mr. Manion."

"How about directing you to the bride's home?" Mike ventured.

"A far better plan, I vow. Lead on, sir, lead on."

Rhys stood at the upstairs window watching the scene below. It was unseasonably warm and the men's voices carried through the opened glass. He took a sip of brandy and watched Mike Manion whisk the bishop away. Tomorrow he would be married . . . and tomorrow night? He almost groaned aloud thinking about it. His weeks of celibacy might prove his undoing.

She's a lady. I can't just pounce on her, especially not the first night. Rhys had never had a virgin in his life. So many women over the years, but none of them innocent, none of them really *his.* He amended that with a guilty sigh. Ginger Vogel was certainly no innocent, but she had come to love him. He still remembered their lusty tumbles in bed with great fondness. He had hated hurting her when he became engaged to Tory and broke off their relationship. One time after he returned from Denver last month, he'd gotten drunk and let his guard down. No, he amended that with a chuckle. Ginger had very skillfully gotten him drunk, then seduced him.

What to do about Ginger? He no longer needed the saloon. The Lady Victory and his land ventures had made him a millionaire—now he even owned a bank! He had considered selling her the Naked Truth for weeks, but every time he tried to broach the subject and explain how she could pay him off with profits over the next several years, she simply got a pugnacious expression on her face and said tightly that she wouldn't take his charity.

"So, you're really gonna do it? Fancy preacher from Denver 'n' all. Wasn't any of the locals good enough for them Laughtons?" Ginger stood in the doorway, her cat's eyes decidedly cloudy with tears. Until this very last day, she had hoped he would come to his senses. Each time he returned from an outing with Tory Laughton he seemed frustrated and grim. Each time Ginger tried to soothe and entice him. Now she looked accusingly at the expensive white silk shirt and black wool suit hanging in the open armoire. "Well," she sighed bitterly, "you'll make one hell of a great-looking groom."

He walked toward her and reached out to wipe her tears away with the pads of his thumbs. Gently he said, "Thank you for the compliment, but no, the bishop was my suggestion, not the Laughtons."

She muttered a solid Anglo-Saxon expletive. "You sure are goin' uptown, aincha?" Some of her old gamin bravado had returned as she swished past him to the marble-topped table where the brandy decanter stood. Pouring herself a drink, she refilled his and handed it to him. Raising her glass, she clinked it against his and said, "Don't let her hurt you, Rhys."

"Ginger, you're one of a kind, you know that? A very special woman. I need your help with this place. Hell, I can't keep running it now. I need you to take over when I'm gone." He paused a beat.

"I ain't gonna take it from you," she said stubbornly, then grinned crookedly. "But since you need help, I'll run it for you. A favor fer a friend."

He watched her walk slowly from the room, saucy hips swaying in her scanty red silk wrapper. *Don't let her hurt you, Rhys.* He swore and turned back to the window.

"Oh, my, this one is delicious," Laura Everett cooed as she held up a filmy pale pink nightrail made of the most delicate lace.

Tory smiled in spite of herself. "You only say that because you bought the indecent thing for me." She added hastily, "But it is lovely, just a bit, well . . . you can see right through it."

Laura put the gown back on the bed amid the piles of wedding clothes they were packing. "I won't see through it. Rhys will." She watched the bright red flush creep up Tory's face. "My dear, has your mother had a discussion with you?" she asked shrewdly.

"Certainly, Laura. I'll get by. All women do, I suppose," she said, anxious to drop the subject.

"Exactly as I thought. Duty, forbearance, and all that rot, that's what Hedda told you, isn't it?" Laura had come over with her special gift for the bride as a pretext to talk with her.

"It's a wife's duty to provide her husband with a male heir. That's a plain fact, not 'rot' at all. Now, please, can we leave off the distasteful subject? I know what I must do," Tory added in a misery of embarrassment, balling up several fine linen undergarments and stuffing them in a trunk. "Where is that Bessie? She's supposed to be doing this while I supervise," she said crossly.

Laura stood up and walked around the bed to where Tory stood and took the younger woman in her arms, something she feared Hedda seldom if ever did. "Victoria, my dear, I fear you don't have the vaguest idea of what you *should* do, or feel. I am going to be very blunt, young lady, so take a seat and let us have a little talk about wedding nights."

Tory loved Laura Everett as she would a beloved aunt or even, if she were totally honest, like the warm and demonstrative mother she did not have in Hedda Laughton. Dutifully, she sat down beside Laura on the bed, ignoring strewn clothing, boxes, and trunks.

"The first time your husband makes love to you, there may be a slight bit of discomfort—very little if he goes slowly and is careful penetrating your maidenhead," Laura began as matter-of-factly as she could. "Has your mother mentioned bodily functions at all to you?" One look at Tory's wide-eyed incredulity gave her the answer to that question. "I suspected as much," she said drily. "Well, now, let's begin at the beginning . . ."

By the time she had completed her disquisition, Tory's eyes were about to pop from their sockets. "And . . . and you actually *enjoyed* that with Jacob?" Her voice broke into a girlish squeak.

Laura smiled wistfully. "More than you can now imagine, my dear, but soon I think you'll understand—if you give yourself a chance. My greatest sorrow was that Jacob and I were not able to have children, but we had each other for thirty-three years. Love between a husband and wife is a joy in every sense of the word, Tory, not a duty—unless you make it so."

Tory struggled to integrate Laura's viewpoint with her mother's. It seemed frightfully disloyal to her parents to compare their sterile marriage to the loving one of the Everetts. "But . . . but Jacob was a gentleman, considerate and refined. Rhys is . . ." She searched for a word which would not offend Laura, whom she knew had taken the viper to her bosom.

"Rhys is a rogue and a rascal," Laura completed the sentence for her. "He may lack polish, but not brains or charm. He is devilishly handsome, and I don't doubt has had a deal of practice with women."

Tory felt the bitter sting of those words. "Yes, a very great deal of practice—but those women weren't ladies," she said with as much dignity as she could muster.

"But you are a lady. That is one reason why Rhys is smitten with you. He's marrying *you*, Victoria, not Ginger Vogel!" Tory's eyes were set with a cold aqua light and her jaw had a rebellious tilt that Laura recognized all too well. "Give him a chance—give yourself a chance, my dear. I know you are attracted to him as he is to you." She raised her hand soothingly. "Now, don't deny it. I have eyes. Follow your heart. I promise that even if you don't believe you love Rhys, after tomorrow night you'll like him well enough!" she added drily.

Tory swallowed in mortification. Laura was right about the unfathomable, damnable attraction she felt whenever that cad came near her. But Laura was wrong, oh so wrong, to believe that Rhys loved her. He had two whores at his beck and call—Ginger Vogel in Starlight and that odious actress in Denver. *I'll only be his ornament, a fancy possession to parade in front of respectable people.*

Love, indeed! At that moment, all Victoria Elizabeth Laughton wanted was revenge.

Chapter Fourteen

Standing in the middle of the master suite the evening before her wedding, Tory was no longer so sure about her plan for revenge. The walls and furnishings seemed to close in on her. The huge room's high ceiling was hung with two seraglio-style red swag lamps, their gas lights flickering on the red velvet flocked wallpaper. A big brass cupid perched on the backboard of the large bed, able to observe whatever went on in its luxuriant depths . . . and perhaps whisper lewd suggestions. The bed was ringed with a translucent curtain of multicolored glass beads that tinkled and glistened at the slightest movement. God, would he use one of the ropes of beads to strangle her? She shivered and turned away from the bed.

The rest of the room offered no solace. A large statue of Pan playing his flute sat in the open space before the large front window, winking obscenely at her. Huge mirrors with gargoyles carved around the gilt frames filled the walls. Even the carpets added to her sense of suffocation. They were made of exotic skins from leopards and tigers, complete with snarling heads and flexed claws.

When she had seen the bizarre items separately and selected them in a childishly jealous snit, they had seemed the perfect way to show Rhys Davies what she thought of his boorish pretensions to refinement. He had flaunted his wealth and bought a wife as an ornament; she had retaliated by making their honeymoon chamber as much of a travesty as their marriage. But now, seeing it completely assembled the night before she was to be bound into his charge for the rest of her life . . . Tory was repelled by her own pettiness. And she was frightened. Fleetingly she considered trying to remove some of the furnishings. Two specially paid workmen had spent the whole day assembling the heavy pieces. She could not undo what she had gone to such pains to create.

"He'll be my husband. He can do anything he wants to me and I'll have no recourse." She heard the words echo, muted in the big cluttered room. Perhaps he would beat her—or turn her out in disgrace. Then her sacrifice for Sanders and her family honor would be for naught. No, Rhys Davies was too proud and stubborn to publicly admit defeat. The gambler wanted a lady. He had made his bargain, even knowing how she felt about him. Tory squared her shoulders and walked to the door. The gilded brass gargoyle on the doorknob made a sepulchral click as she opened and closed it. Never looking back, she walked resolutely down the wide stairs to her waiting carriage.

* * *

Rhys stood at the front of the church watching the vision in white silk and lace glide toward him. Tory's face was obscured by yards of sheer white tulle. He could read nothing of her expression but noted the way she clung to her father's arm as he escorted her slowly down the aisle. The ornate church was filled to capacity with flowers and people. All the elite of Starlight and environs were seated in the front pews. Many of his friends from the less reputable and less church-going side of town crowded the rear. Ginger was not among them, but Lizzie Custus and Carmelita Sanchez sat in one corner, demurely gowned and veiled for the solemn occasion.

Tory watched him through downcast eyes as her fate drew inexorably nearer. Laura was right about one thing. He looked splendid. The sun streaming in from the stained-glass windows above the altar gilded his curly brown hair with gold and russet highlights. She felt those keen blue eyes measuring her, searching her deepest thoughts. *Does he want my soul as well as my body?*

His large, warm hand reached out for her small, cold one. He squeezed her fingers reassuringly as he took her arm and assisted her in kneeling before Bishop Grey. Rhys could feel her trembling as the priest began the long, elaborate wedding rite. He covertly studied her delicate profile and caught her glancing up to meet his eyes. She quickly turned away with lashes lowered.

Rhys spoke his vows in a deep, resonant voice that echoed melodically over the assembly. Tory repeated hers in a whisper-soft voice, as if reciting them by rote, without emotion. When it came time for him to place the heavy gold band on her finger next to the extravagant engagement diamond, he expected her to flinch or hold back. Tory surprised him and placed her slim, elegant hand into his. He slid the ring onto her finger while his other hand stroked the pulse in her wrist. He smiled faintly when it leaped in response to his touch.

When the final blessing was bestowed and they were bid to stand, Tory did not think her knees would support her if Rhys removed his firm grip on her elbow. Taking her arm proprietarially, he escorted her back up the long aisle. She held her head high, heeding neither the envious expressions of flighty belles like Lissette Johnson nor the veiled disapproval of many leading citizens.

Rhys, too, sensed the widely divergent feelings rippling across the assembly. He would have found it amusing but for the pallor and trembling of his bride. About halfway up the aisle he felt her hesitate and misstep, then quickly recover as they passed Charles Everett. Rhys gave the arrogant fool a curt nod of dismissal as he swept Tory forward to the church door.

The reception was lavish, held at the Laughton mansion, paid for with Davies's money. He had left the details to Hedda and Tory. Fresh flowers rioted in a profusion of colors everywhere. Crystal glasses bubbled with French champagne and tables groaned beneath the weight of roast beef, glazed English pheasants, smoked oysters, and broiled mountain trout. One whole table was filled with nothing but ice cream molded in fantastical shapes. An orchestra played a lilting waltz as elegantly dressed men and women ate, drank, and quietly speculated about this most unlikely pairing in Colorado's history. Not since Leadville silver baron Haw Tabor and divorced musicale actress Baby Doe had married—he without benefit of divorcing his previous spouse—had there been such a matrimonial furor in Colorado.

Friends of the Laughtons, bankers and cattlemen, sipped champagne and daintily ate chilled pheasant. Rhys's hearty companions, saloon folk and sheepmen, toasted the marriage with libations of beer and whiskey while swallowing whole platters of oysters on the half shell. The overflowing house was segregated into enemy camps, but Laura Everett moved gracefully from one group to another, oiling the waters with her considerable charm. She was aided in her endeavors by the Loring clan.

As a leading Republican with close business connections to his Civil War commander, General William Jackson Palmer, Steve Loring could move with ease in any circle. Cass was vivacious and elegant in a beige silk gown that perfectly complemented her unusual coloring. If a few gossips whispered that she had a scandalous reputation, running her own freighting company, no one dared say it aloud. Even the tomboy Kylie had been metamorphosed into a lovely young woman in a stylishly demure pale green dress. Rhys had promised to dance with her at the reception, and even the antics of her two younger brothers could not diminish her delight.

Hedda and Stoddard stood dutifully in the receiving line next to their new son-in-law, accepting congratulations, well-meant and hypocritical, with forced smiles and stiff nods. Rhys nearly choked when Mike Manion gallantly kissed Hedda's hand, his Irish blarney slathering out in that thick brogue he could turn off and on at will.

"Be watchin' the likes of that rascally Welshman you've cloaked with respectability, ma'am. He may be pretendin' a leanin' toward the Republican party, but only until the next election."

Stoddard harrumphed fiercely and Hedda pulled her hand back as if snake-bit. Undaunted, Mike turned to Rhys and Tory. "Well, you've gone 'n' done it, bucko. Married the most beautiful lady west of the Mississippi."

"Have you ever been east of the Mississippi, Mr. Manion?" Hedda asked with acid condescension.

The little Irishman scratched his head. "Countin' me last two trips to New York or just the sivin I made to Europe, ma'am?" he asked guilelessly.

"Met Queen Victoria and presented her with a copy of the *Plain Speaker*, or so he says," Rhys chimed in with a wink.

"That I did, lad. A bit long of jowl, but not bad for a *Sassenach*, that queen. But you're more beautiful than any queen or princess in all Europe," he whispered to Tory.

"Be off with you, Irish scoundrel, trying to charm my bride," Rhys said good naturedly as Manion shook his hand and headed for a group of German miners hefting beer steins. "Never mind Mike. He's a good friend, Tory, and he likes you."

"Somehow I doubt that, Rhys," Tory whispered as the Wiltons, wealthy ranchers from Ouray, moved up to give their felicitations.

By the time they sat down to eat, Tory's nerves were jumbled and her stomach a twisted knot. She shoved a slice of pink beef back and forth across her plate. Rhys handed her a glass of bubbly golden champagne and then raised his own to hers in a toast.

"To my beautiful wife, Victoria Davies." His deep blue eyes held her aqua ones in thrall.

She raised her glass and looked at his handsome smiling face through thick golden lashes. "To your triumph, Mr. Davies," she whispered back and took a sip of champagne. It tasted bitter as persimmons to her.

After dinner, the worried groom wasted no time getting Laura Everett alone. "How much longer do we have to be on display, Laura? Tory's as white as her gown and nervous as a treed cat," Rhys said quietly as they watched the bride across the room talking in subdued tones with several of her parents' older friends. "She hasn't eaten a bite and I can't get her to drink more than a few swallows of champagne."

Laura smiled serenely. "Probably just as well, else she'd fall asleep on you all too soon. I'll get the orchestra to start playing again so you can quickly get on with that bridal dance nonsense. Oh, don't forget your promise to Kylie Loring. She's a lovely child. While you're dancing with her, I'll get Hedda dancing with poor bereft Charles. Then I can steer Tory toward the rear door. You can make a discreet exit from the side and meet us with the buggy out back."

"You are a love, and if I weren't a married man, I'd make you an indecent proposition," he said, giving her a swift kiss on the cheek.

"Are you certain no one will follow?" Tory asked, nervously looking over her shoulder toward the receding town, whose lights were winking on in the twilight. "Some of your ruffian friends from the ranch were talking about a shivaree." She shuddered, dreading the upcoming scene when he saw the bedroom, not wanting her humiliation compounded by a crowd of raucous, catcalling drunks surrounding the house.

"Don't worry, love. I left strict orders. No one will disturb us tonight. We'll be alone. The cook, maids, and butler won't even set foot upstairs until morning."

"Then how will I . . ." She stopped, and her cheeks blazed in the cool fall air.

"Ah, I see you recall the last time I unlaced you. This time it'll be different, Victoria. I promise not to spank you."

Don't make promises you may not keep, Rhys, she thought in misery.

When they pulled up in front of Dragon's Lair, a stablehand took the carriage away, a knowing smirk on his youthful face. "I am a passably good ladies' maid," Rhys said teasingly as he swept her into his arms at the front door of the looming fortress.

"Yes, you've had lots of practice undressing women, haven't you, Rhys?" She felt her anger rise at his casual remark and decided to use it to fortify herself.

He only chuckled as he carried her past the stone dragons on the front steps. "There's a love, now, watch your veil." He turned sideways to edge her billowing gown and headdress through the open door into the entry hall. The front door had been left open by a servant who would doubtless come to close it after they were upstairs.

"Mrs. Craighton left some wine and a light supper in the rear parlor . . . or we can send for food later if you'd prefer." He set her down beneath the blazing splendor of the drop chandelier's hundreds of crystal prisms.

Tory felt like a felon facing the gallows. Why postpone the inevitable? She had thrown down the gauntlet when she decorated the master suite. There was nothing for it but to have done with the confrontation. "First you had best see my little surprise. Then you may want a drink," she replied with more bravado than she felt.

With a puzzled smile he reached for her, intending to carry her up the steps. When she shook her head and backed up a step, he taunted, "You aren't afraid of me, are you, Mrs. Davies?"

"No! No," she modulated her voice, "I am not, *Mr.* Davies." With that she lifted her full silk skirts daintily and turned toward the wide arc of stairs.

"Lay on, Macduff," he said with a flourish.

Hearing the old Shakespearean line, she stiffened for an instant and said, "Something Miss Goldstock taught you?"

"*Macbeth*, act 5, scene 8," he replied noncommittally, following her up the steps. Surely she wasn't still jealous of Flavia! But he did expect bridal nerves. In fact, he had carefully thought out everything for their wedding night.

Laura had cautioned him about the delicate sensibilities of a proper young lady raised under the strictures of Hedda Laughton's prim New England hand. He would lower the lights, allow for her maidenly modesty and proceed very slowly. Nothing exotic or fancy at first. It would take time to show Tory her own passion, to awaken her. Being a gambler, Rhys was a patient man when circumstances called for patience. Victoria was a virgin, his first and only lady, and he would treasure her.

He watched the long tendrils of golden hair bouncing beneath her veil as she climbed the steps. Regal as a princess was his wife, but also angry as a scalded cat. Again doubts about the forced marriage assailed him. Resolutely he quashed them, assuring himself that he was far better suited to her than Charles Everett or any other weakling her parents would have chosen.

When she reached their bedroom suite, Tory's courage began to fail her. Rhys's warm breath on her neck as he eased her veil away and planted a soft kiss at her nape galvanized her into action. She must show him the room before this seduction went any further. Turning the handle, she shoved the massive walnut door open.

Without even a glance at the interior, he scooped her up and stepped inside. Tory squealed in surprise and kicked ineffectually, but he walked into the center of the room without relinquishing his hold. She could feel his whole body tense as he looked around, but his facial expression remained unreadable, devoid of all visible emotion. Yet as he slowly lowered her to her feet, she could feel the leashed fury coiled in his body. He molded her closely against his broad chest, holding one iron-hard arm around her slim waist.

He shook his head in disbelief. "Your special surprise for me?" He gestured around him. "Very inventive, Tory. A lot more inventive than kind. Ginger wouldn't use this junk in her bordello, you know that?"

"My experience with bordellos being somewhat more limited than yours, I had to improvise," she said tartly.

"So that's how you see our marriage? You're going to whore for your precious family? For the money? Well, darling, you sure do charge a handsome price. If I live to be seventy, I figure it'll cost me about a thousand each time I take you."

She slapped him in pure reflex, stunned at his crudity. "How dare you—"

"I'll dare a lot, Tory, darling. I'll make you beg . . ." He let her go then, let her back away from him, trembling with fear.

229

Shirl Henke

"This is a farce, Rhys. You don't want me there." She gestured to the bead-tasseled bed. "You want a hostess, an ornament, something to show off to your new business associates."

Now his face took on a new expression, the slow, killing smile of a predator. "No chance of that, darling. I want you there, now. If this decor reflects how soiled you feel by marrying me, you'll just have to act the part—soiled dove. You, the whore. Me, the whoremaster."

He slid off his suit jacket, tossing it over the leering Pan. Then he unfastened his heavy ruby cufflinks and unbuttoned his brocade vest, which he shrugged off and tossed atop the jacket. His silk cravat floated to the floor after he removed the ruby stickpin. He removed the shirt studs, revealing that hard, furry chest, then threw the fistful of expensive jewelry at the maw of one tiger's-head rug. The bright rubies bounced like angry sparks. Tory came out of her petrified trance. Throat choked with fear, she knew that pleading was useless. She bolted for the door, but he was on her in three steps just as she tripped on a ponderous tiger's paw. He swung her up against his bare chest and walked to the bed where he tossed her through the twinkling beads onto a pile of soft velvet pillows.

"We'll probably stain them," he said crudely, then shrugged and continued his methodical strip.

Tory could hear the rustle of his silk shirt, shoes, and hose being discarded. He sat on the edge of the bed, shoving the annoying beads back to get a better look at the beautiful, heartless bitch he had married. His virginal wife, eyes tightly closed, face turned away from him, lay ready to "submit" to a bestial rape. He could see the tears trapped beneath her thick golden lashes, but she refused to cry openly. Stiff upper lip, Boston Brahmin to the last, he thought bitterly.

"The lamps were lit when we came in. How many people saw this miniature bordello, Tory? Should we give a home tour, hmm?" He was rewarded when her eyes flew open.

"No one but the two workmen from Denver saw anything! They're gone. Even the teamsters who delivered the furnishings didn't uncrate anything."

He smiled like a shark. "You were actually worried about the scandal of this furniture—after lowering yourself to marry me? Will wonders never cease, Tory?" he reproved cynically.

"You will do what you want. Have done, Mr. Davies. I'm tired of being mouse to your cat," she said with resignation, then felt the bed shake with his soft laughter.

"So," he said as one warm hand trailed down her throat and circled the curve of her breast, "You think I plan to leap on you and brutalize you, *Mrs.* Davies, and you'll just close your eyes and think of England—or whatever it is spoiled little virgins in America think of." He reached up and loosened her headpiece. The silk and pearl tiara's long sheer veil lay beneath her. He rolled her over and pulled it free, then tossed it to float like gossamer to the foot of the big bed.

"I've always loved your hair, Tory, you know that? So soft and fragrant, like flower petals in moonlight," he murmured as he unpinned the curls on top of her head and let them spill across the pillows. He ran his fingers through the shiny mass, massaging her sensitive scalp. It tingled from the heavy headdress's biting combs. His touch was soft, his words sharp. "I said I'd make you beg. I didn't mean I'd rape you or

231

beat you. I mean to make love to you . . . until you cry out for more."

She shook her head in furious denial, but his fingers tightened on her scalp and his mouth descended slowly. He held her immobilized with one hand while his lips brushed her temples and cheeks, then his tongue teased and licked her throat, blazing a trail to her trembling mouth. "I see you remember," he whispered as she opened her mouth to cry out. His tongue invaded, softly as a thief in the night, scalding velvet that danced and twined with hers, then glided over her small white teeth and departed.

He raised up and studied her flushed face, framed by the disarrayed masses of pale gold hair. Silently he cursed her delicate, unique beauty. At the same time he gloried in it, for she belonged to him. He turned and reached for one slim ankle, buried in the billowy cascade of silk and lace. She kicked in reflex, but his large hand easily encircled the fragile bones until she quieted.

He pulled off her satin slipper, then repeated the process with the other foot. He paused, appearing to debate.

"Should I undress you from the inside out . . . or begin with the gown?" He ran a questing hand up her silk-clad leg, caressing her calf.

"You are despicable, crude, vulgar, disgusting . . ." She struggled for more pejoratives until he once more pulled her to a sitting position on the bed.

The buttons were looped all the way down her back, but he was a very good ladies' maid, as he had boasted. His skillful gambler's hands, whose deft fingers could flip cards faster than the eye could follow, unlooped buttons with equal ease. He caressed the delicate vertebrae in her back through her corset, then quickly began to unlace it.

Feeling the cool air on her back, Tory panicked. Soon he would have her completely naked! She tried to push him away, but he quickly peeled the gown from her shoulders, imprisoning her arms, baring her breasts as the unlaced corset slid lower until the sheer lace chemise revealed everything.

Well, almost everything, he amended to himself as he stroked one small upthrust coral bud, then the other. She could not stifle the small gasp of dismay that escaped her lips. He cupped a small perfect breast in each hand, hefting them tenderly.

Such raw intimacy took her breath away, paralyzing her. He lifted her hand, stroked the racing pulse at her wrist, and then unlooped the white silk buttons. After repeating the process with the other wrist, he slid the sleeves free of her arms with one satiny swish. Her arms automatically came up to shield her breasts.

As she hugged herself, he pushed her down and rolled her over onto her face. Caught in the tangle of her skirts, she was hopelessly ensnared, kicking and making muffled cries with equal ineffectualness. Rhys began to unfasten the tapes to her petticoats and complete the unlacing of her corset. "You're so slim you don't need this silly thing," he said as he pulled the whalebone and lace contraption free and tossed it onto the floor with a thunk. The bead curtain rattled its approval.

She turned her head, coughed, and then hissed at him, "All ladies wear corsets!"

He rolled her onto her back once more and smiled coldly. "Well, whores don't, and from now on you won't wear one either. I'm the only man who'll put his hands on you, Tory . . . ever again." To make good his claim, he softly caressed her arms, then moved across to her breasts. She gasped as his deft fingertips caught the hard point of one nipple thrusting errantly between the shield of her arms.

Tory looked up into his face. His eyes were darkened with passion, his lips grimly set. No more the roguish charmer or teasing suitor, he was coldly angry and at the same time lustfully aroused. He meant to take her virginity, not in the way a gentleman would treat his bride, but the way a man took a whore, the way he no doubt took that horrid Goldstock woman. Swallowing to gather her courage beneath his harsh inspection, she whispered, "Please, not this way . . . don't—"

"Don't what, Tory? Don't claim my husbandly rights? You knew when you agreed to marry me that a wife had to allow her husband to make love to her. Even Hedda must've told you that!" he added scornfully.

"Yes, she did . . . but not this way, not in anger—"

"You ask me to respect your delicate sensibilities after you set the scene like this?" he lashed back, swinging one arm out to rattle the beaded bed curtains. "You've made your feelings for me very clear, Tory . . . or what you *think* your feelings are. Maybe I can show you that you were wrong," he added cryptically.

With that he reached for the loosened gown and petticoats bunched about her waist and yanked the whole pile of fluff down her hips and legs. He tossed it over the cupid perched atop the backboard. "No one but me gets to watch," he said with a hint of a smile, but his eyes were still cold as he studied her slim, nearly naked body. She lay breathless, clad only in silk stockings, sheer lace pantalets, and a chemise.

"Better at the river when the fabric was soaking wet, clinging to your skin. But then you were cold . . . you're shivering now, love. Cold again?" he asked in mock solicitude. "Let me warm you. I assure you, I'm hot as a furnace."

He rolled full length beside her on the bed and pulled her tightly against him with one arm. The other was free to roam up and down her body. Her hands, trapped between them, pressed palms out against the hard surface of his chest. He did not exaggerate; his skin was on fire and the heat transmitted to her. She closed her eyes, drowning in terrifying new sensations. His mention of that day at the river seemed to conjure up all sorts of memories of the two of them, nearly naked, clinging together breathlessly, much as they did now.

But now they were lying in a bed and he was touching her with his hands and mouth, touching her in places where no one had ever touched her. Her breasts ached and her heart thudded. Rhys's hard thighs rubbed insinuatingly against her lower body as he held her buttocks with one splayed hand. His lips sent a wet trail of kisses from her ear, down her throat, then back up to slowly brush her eyelashes, nose, lips. Oh, yes, she remembered what he could do with his mouth just as he reached her lips, then his teeth nibbled delicately, patiently. He willed her to open for him. She resisted until his hand roamed across her hip, insinuating itself between their bodies until he found her breast and stroked it.

Convulsively she arched against his caress, and her lips opened at the same time. He invaded in swift darting forays, withdrawing, then plunging in again until she was faint. Before she realized what

235

he was doing, he rolled up over her, pressing her into the soft mattress with his body stretched full length over hers. He deepened the kiss, then slowed it.

A feeling of lethargy began to steal over her as he continued kissing her, doing nothing more, but oh so very much, using only his very persuasive mouth. She could feel the steady thrum of his heart, the heady warmth of his body. He supported his weight mostly on his elbows lest he crush her. It was intimate, comfortable, almost comforting, not the savage invasion she first feared. Finally he murmured softly against her mouth, "Put your arms around me, Tory," then resumed the drugging kiss. She amazed herself by complying and felt the hard muscles in his back flex as he repositioned himself over her.

Slowly, ever so slowly, his left knee inched its way up between her legs, parting them. Then one roving hand slid over her hipbone and caressed the mound of silky curls at the juncture of her thighs. He could feel her stiffen for an instant, then, when he let his palm cup her and held still, she again gave herself up to the kiss. He moved his hand lower, massaging through the sheer silky undergarment until she moved her hips instinctively.

Tory ached. The tightness that had begun with her breasts now perversely spread lower, down her belly to that shameful place where Rhys was working some kind of shocking, unbelievable magic. It felt good, yet she ached. A moan escaped from deep in her throat, vibrating against his mouth.

Slowly he broke the kiss, moving lower, grazing her breasts with his lips until the nipples hardened and tingled. He took one hard nub between his teeth softly, teasing it through the thin silk. She arched as he moved from one to the other, repeating the love nip, suckling. Then he raised his head and straightened his arms. "Now you're wet at both ends, almost like you were at the river."

A smile that did not reach his eyes slashed across his lips as he rolled away from her and glided off the bed. He stood up and began to unbutton his pants. In a haze of need, Tory was bewildered by the exquisite assault he'd made on her senses. His words did not register, only the loss of his heat. She watched mesmerized as he shed the last of his clothes beyond the shadowy glitter of the curtain.

When he shoved the beads aside and placed one bare knee on the bed, she finally broke free of the trance. Laura had told her about that *thing*, but she had not adequately conveyed how large it was! Instinctively her legs clamped together and her hands covered the place of entry. Then his words sunk in. She was wet! The sheer silk was sticking to her body. Gasping, she looked at her breasts, which he had wet with his mouth. Small, taut rosy points thrust through the chemise as if it were invisible. She tried to remember the fine points of Laura's explanation. Nothing registered but her own wanton shame.

Rhys chuckled. "You hurt, don't you, Tory love? Now you know a wee bit about how I've felt all these past months. But I'm going to be kind. I'll ease the ache."

When she tried to roll away in mortification, he quickly caught her and slipped the ribbon on her chemise, pulling it open. The tie on her pantalets gave way even more easily. He slid them over her hips with practiced ease, then pulled her up into his embrace and slid the chemise from her arms. She did not protest. The gossamer-thin undergarments hid little, and the wet spots were an indictment against her betraying body.

I'll make you beg. His earlier words flashed into her brain. She was beginning to understand what he meant.

Chapter Fifteen

After laying his wife back against the velvet coverlet, Rhys looked down at her naked beauty. "Like silk, cream, pure fresh snow," he breathed as his fingers stroked softly across her belly. She arched against the warmth of his caress but turned her head away from his possessive perusal.

"You want me to get on with it, don't you, Tory love?" he taunted. His hand negligently grazed her breasts, then cupped her chin and turned her face to him. "Open your eyes . . . or are you afraid to look at me?"

Her eyes snapped open, blazing silvery aqua defiance. The defiance turned to alarm when he took one slim wrist and guided her palm to his hard belly, then moved it lower, following the tan arrow of body hair in its descent to his straining shaft. He closed her fingers around it and let her feel the pulsing hardness of his desire, clenching his teeth to keep from betraying how close he was to losing control. She tried to pull away. He laughed and held her hand prisoner for another stroke, then released it in the nick of time.

He rolled down beside her and let his hard tumescence probe her soft, silky little belly as he tangled his hand in her hair and brought her forward for another languorous kiss.

Tory could not resist his embrace no matter how loudly her mind cried out she do so. He was right. She did want him to consummate the marriage. She hurt, damn him! She ached. Body overrode willpower and she resumed embracing him, clinging tightly, her hips rocking with his as he drew her ever so slowly into his sensuous web.

He left her mouth, trailing his lips lower to her throat, then to her breasts, suckling, licking, tormenting with such exquisite tenderness that she arched and moaned. When he found the wet aching place between her legs, she made no effort to deny him access as he stroked, then stopped, stroked, then stopped. He waited for her to move against him, urge him to continue. She did. He obliged, almost bringing her to release. Then he stopped again.

Tory moaned and writhed against him. By now Rhys was sweating. The strain of holding himself back was taking a toll, but he focused on the humiliation she had inflicted upon him, on the fierce anger he felt. Still, it was not going to be enough if he did not bend her to his will quickly.

When she moaned again, he whispered, "What do you want, Tory love?"

"Please . . ." her words choked off as shame flooded her.

"Please what, Tory?" he asked ruthlessly.

Tory felt the bitter sting of tears burn her eyelids but squeezed them closed. Why was he doing this? He did not even want her, not really, not the way he wanted Flavia. He was just punishing an errant wife, breaking her. She refused to answer the taunt.

He guided his hardened shaft to brush against her wetness, then withdrew it. Could she feel the tension about to snap inside him? His body felt as brittle as spun glass. He waited, unable to breathe.

Tory was totally unaware of the effect she was having on him. All she could think of, could feel, was the effect he was having on her. "Please, make love to me," she choked out, hating herself, unable to stop the words.

"Say it again, Tory . . . and say my name," he commanded softly as he once more grazed her mound. "Say my name."

"Rhys . . ." She arched against him and dug her nails into his shoulders. "Please, Rhys, please make love to me."

He took a deep, shuddering breath and poised at the opening of her warm, wet body. *Go slow, go slow*, his mind screamed at his body. He must not hurt her, must not end it quickly, no matter how great his need. Ever so gently he eased into her until he could feel the tightness of resistance. He stopped and moved in a lazy, circular motion that elicited a moan from her. "Hold on, love. Hold tight," he murmured against her throat as he met her desperately arching body with one swift, short thrust that carried him through the barrier. He could feel her stiffen with pain. Rhys held very still inside her, cradling her in his arms, kissing her throat and murmuring love words in her ear, trying desperately to reassure her, while at the same time struggling not to spill himself in the hot, tight wonder of her body.

Tory felt the sting that Laura had warned her about, but it was the least of her discomfort. She felt an ache, a knot of coiled tension deep inside that was driving her wild with the need for release. She could feel the heat of his hardened shaft as it stretched and filled her, poised at the brink of her womb, unmoving. His kisses and soft words of reassurance only added to her blinding animal passion. She arched and bucked, whether to dislodge him or urge him to plunge deeper, she did not know. Pure instinct drove her.

Feeling her desperation match his own, Rhys held her down against the soft bed and began to move, trying with single-minded concentration to keep control. He stroked slowly, languorously, then gradually increased the tempo as he felt her respond. "Tell me, love, tell me when . . . you'll know, I promise, you'll know," he gasped out as he continued the exquisite rhythm.

Her mind ceased to function, but her body told him what he needed to know when the crescendo began. She cried aloud, a jagged wail of pure physical bliss that transcended mere words. He could feel the amazing strength of her silky little sheath as it convulsed around him, driving him over the edge to share that brilliantly colored world of ecstasy. Everything shattered as he spilled himself deep inside her, giving himself over to this all-encompassing joining, like no other he had ever known.

"Victory, my beautiful wife, my Victory," he whispered hoarsely as he collapsed on top of her.

Tory felt as if she had drowned and come back to life. The aftershocks of her climax still gently ebbed and flowed, growing weaker ever so gradually. She became aware of Rhys's sweat-soaked body weighing her down, of his words of endearment—*Victory*.

His Victory. Like the silver mine named for her, she was his prize, his trophy, very literally his victory. He had kept his word and made her beg! Just as she regained enough strength to push him away, he rolled off of her, carrying her with him as he lay on his back, molding her tightly to his side. He yanked the coverlet up over them without releasing her.

Rhys was exhausted after holding back his release for so long. Indeed, the weeks of celibacy had cost him dearly, seeing the object of his desire daily, touching her, teasing her, playing the waiting game that culminated in their protracted contest of wills in bed. He had bent her to him, made her want him, then given her the satisfaction that revealed her passion. All his anger over what she had done to their bedroom, her cruel words, his own arrogant revenge, everything simply evaporated after their lovemaking. He had her lying naked in his arms and he would never let her go. With that thought in mind, Rhys quickly drifted into a deep sleep.

Not so Tory. She lay welded to his side, her body physically satiated and spent, her mind crying out with pain and humiliation. If only she could retreat to her own bedroom, but he had long ago made it clear how he felt about civilized conjugal arrangements.

He stirred in his sleep, and she could not resist looking at him. The multicolored beaded bed curtain cast flickering shadows from the lamps, making his sun-darkened skin appear even more coppery. Thick burnished hair curled against the nape of his neck and that errant lock fell across his forehead. With those mocking blue eyes closed, she fought an overpowering urge to run her fingers through his hair—and lost. It was coarse and springy and damp with sweat, yet he smelled clean, a vitally male smell but not at all the sour, unwashed odor she associated with lower-class men. He was wonderfully handsome, damn him! And so arrogantly skillful as a lover. *Why not? He's had so much practice,* her mind taunted cruelly.

She dragged her eyes from his satanic beauty and looked around the room. It was truly awful. Guilt assailed her. She had made a bargain, understanding the harsh consequences if she did not redeem her family. Whatever he had done, he had not deserved this. But he had exacted his revenge. Her mother had hinted at degradation and unpleasantness associated with the marriage bed. Laura had spelled out great beauty and intense pleasure, but Laura's description was valid only if husband and wife were in love. Her mother had been correct about the feeling of degradation that suffocated her—but not because she had been physically hurt or abused. Quite the contrary, she had reveled in pagan, wanton need, physical pleasure so intense it robbed her of her will. Unlike Laura and Jacob, she and Rhys did not love; they lusted.

Trapped. I'm tangled in his sensual web for as long as he chooses to keep me ensnared. How long would that be? Tory wondered. Until she grew fat and ugly with child? Until he tired of her and returned to his other women? Hedda had felt such desertion a blessing, no matter the reason. Tory cringed in mortified confusion. Did she want Rhys to leave her, or did she want him to love her?

When his arm tightened around her waist and his warm breath caressed her throat, she finally ceased her fruitless pondering and gave in to sleep.

Rhys awakened just after dawn to the soft tickle of violet-scented hair against his face. Silky strands of pale gold danced across the bridge of his nose with each breath he took. He reached up and took them between his fingers, marveling at the glowing softness. Tory's hair was spread like a silken skein across his body and over the pillows. She nestled alongside him, a tiny, porcelain, perfect figure. His wife.

Recalling her passion last night, he found its intensity difficult to reconcile with this demure female. Then memories surfaced of everything that had preceded the wildly abandoned loving. He looked about the room. It was even gaudier in the harsh light of day. Did she really despise him this much? Then he recalled his arrogant cruelty, the things he had said in retaliation, the humiliating things he had done to her and made her do and say.

His fingertips laid the silky curls back across the pillow, then lingered on her cheek and glided over to caress her soft pink lips. He could feel his desire rising and resisted the urge to pull her into his arms and plunge into her. Would she turn from him in disgust? He had ignited her passion last night, but that sort of seductive battle could not sustain a marriage. Perhaps they could begin over again. For now, he would reaffirm his pledge to go slowly. He disentangled himself very gently from her arms and the silken coils of her hair, then slid from the bed. When he replaced the covers over her, he could see faint smears of blood on them and on himself. She would be virginally sore and in need of a bath.

He padded silently into the bathroom and turned on the spigot above the large marble tub. "Let's see if this water-heating system really works," he muttered to himself. It did. After testing the water temperature, he returned to the bedroom and retrieved the valises the butler had left sitting outside the door. Taking a robe from his valise, he donned it, then rummaged through her bags until he found a silky peignoir, which he laid at the foot of the bed.

Tory awoke slowly, drugged and disoriented from her first night of passion. She was cold in spite of the heavy covers. Rhys was gone. She reached out to where he had lain beside her, then sat up and looked around the room. She could hear water running, then it stopped and her husband appeared in the doorway. He looked wonderful in a dark blue robe that hung casually open to reveal that hard chest with its sensuous patterns of burnished hair curling across it. Tory didn't realize she was staring until he spoke.

Giving her a blinding smile, he said, "Your bath awaits, love."

She sat mesmerized, clutching the bed covers up to her neck as he walked silently across the garish room toward her, the beautiful smile now erased. He looked somber. Angry? Remorseful? She could not tell.

Rhys reached for the lacy white robe and held it up for her. "The hot soak will make you feel better. I've ordered breakfast to be brought up later."

She eyed the robe warily. "That reveals more than it conceals."

"I saw all there is to see last night. Come now, up you go," he said, reaching for one hand and pulling her free of the concealing covers.

They had slept on top of the velvet bedspread, wrapped in its folds! She crimsoned in mortification as the memories all rushed back to her, but slid unprotesting from the bed. As she let him wrap the robe about her, she could see that the gold coverlet was smeared with her blood.

"I'm sorry I hurt you last night," he whispered, holding her back against his chest, inhaling the fragrance of her hair. "I don't just mean your virgin's blood. That part was unavoidable. As to the rest . . ." His words faded away.

"I'll send for the workmen and have this room stripped," she said softly as he released her. "I shouldn't have done this. I'm sorry, too."

She started to walk toward the bathroom door, but his words stopped her midway. "Sorry for the decorations? Or sorry you married me?" he asked simply.

"I'm not certain. Both, I think," she replied without looking at him."

"We were both wrong, Tory. Can't we begin again?" He held his breath, knowing he would never let her go but desperate for some word of assent from her. "We are married, love," he added softly. "Tory?"

Her spine straightened. "Victory," she said flatly. "Not Tory—not love—Victory! That's what you called me after you reduced me to . . . to . . ." Her voice broke and she tried to dash to the bathroom, but he caught up to her in a few swift strides.

His hands were gentle as he restrained her. "Don't be so certain of who won the victory over whom, love. And yes, you are my love, my lady, my wife. We could have something very special, very good, Tory, if you'd let us."

"For how long, Rhys? Until you tire of the game? Until I bore you and the charms of your other women beckon you?" The moment she said the words, she hated herself. *You don't want to know!*

"There are no other women, Tory," he said, while his hands glided up and down her arms.

She broke free of his caress and turned with fury blazing in her eyes. "No other women! I suppose I mistook you for my father in that Denver hotel with Flavia Goldstock draped all over your body," she said scornfully, beyond shame over her jealousy.

Incredulity stamped his face, then the expression gave way to anger. "How the hell did you—"

"My room was across the hall from yours, in case you don't recall. I thought I heard Mama call from across the hall and I opened my door."

"I didn't make love to her. She came to my room, but I sent her away, Tory. I only gave in to a good-bye kiss in the damn hallway," he added, half snarling in self-disgust. Of all the rotten luck!

Her face reflected patent disbelief. "That was a spectacular good-bye," she snapped, then tried to turn away from him.

Suddenly he chuckled in that old infuriating way and snatched her wrist, pulling her back to face him. "You were jealous. That's what triggered this little shopping spree, wasn't it?"

She shook her head in vehement denial, but the memory of her feeling of outraged betrayal would not go away. Already he had such power over her body. He would not have power over her mind, her spirit as well.

He held her in his arms, her face pressed against his bare chest, while he stroked the long, silken fall of hair spilling down her back. "Tory, Tory, love, this isn't the game for us. It was over with Flavia five years ago. There'll be no other women—only you. Give us a chance, love. Let me show you how good it can be. You're everything I ever dreamed of in a wife—a beautiful lady, bright, passionate—"

She flinched at the word and pulled away. "Passionate, yes. So you demonstrated. For your information, ladies are not supposed to exhibit that kind of behavior, so it appears you've been short-changed in a wife. I must be as much a whore as your other women!"

When she fled into the bathroom, he let her slam the door and turn the lock. Once he was certain she had entered the tub, he took the master key from his jacket pocket and inserted it in the lock, then swung the door open and leaned casually against the sash, watching her sink beneath the violet-scented water with a small gasp of dismay.

"Who filled you with such rubbish? Your frigid mother? You're not like her, Tory. You're a passionate woman, but that doesn't mean you're a whore. You're a lady. My lady. Forget your mother's warped ideas. Forget Flavia. Forget this room and what happened last night. We'll begin again." He paused and looked at the pearly sheen of her wet little body, then smiled seductively. "I promise you'll enjoy the rest of our honeymoon, love." With that, he turned and closed the door. When a crystal flagon of bath oil shattered against it, he sighed and said, "Old habits die hard, I see. Watch you don't cut your feet on the shards."

A moment later a pair of satin mules were quickly tossed in the door, landing with a plop alongside the tub. Tory muttered a shockingly unladylike oath and sank back into the water.

Late that afternoon, Mrs. Rhys Davies sat in the solarium letting the warm sunshine seep through the translucent glass and soothe her tense body. She leaned back on the silk-cushioned chair and stretched lazily. A few muscles, unused to exertions like last night's, protested. She sat up and resumed her perusal of the catalogue from Loring's. Already the workmen had come and carried out all the ghastly furnishings from the bedroom and were now stripping the red flocked wallpaper from the walls. She and Rhys would sleep in a guest bedroom until their suite could be redone tastefully.

She scribbled an order number for a large sofa in moss green damask, which would go well with the celery and white printed wallpaper. Her concentration was broken by a conversation echoing down the long hallway from the front foyer. Recognizing her mother's voice dismissing Zenia, the downstairs maid, Tory rose and set Loring's catalogue aside. She glanced nervously at her reflection in the hall mirror as she passed it on her way to greet Hedda. Did she look different? Changed in some way that betrayed her wanton behavior last night?

Hedda Laughton watched her daughter pause to smooth her coiffure, then walk regally down the hallway toward her with a nervous smile on her face. She gave Tory a light kiss on the cheek and then released her. "Good afternoon, Victoria. I saw Mr. Davies in town earlier and assumed you would welcome a visit before he returns," she murmured as she swept Tory into the front parlor and closed the door.

"Would you care for some tea, Mama? I think Mrs. Creighton, our cook, has baked a pound cake this morning."

Hedda waved her hand in rejection and walked to the mantel. Turning dramatically to face Tory, she cocked her head and said, "You seem nervous. Did he frighten you, child? Trust me, the worst is over now. If you are quite careful about how you handle it, you can keep him out of your bedroom most nights. I've always found headaches a good excuse. Of course, your monthly can come with great frequency and—"

"Mother, you're wasting this lesson on tactics," Tory interrupted. Her cheeks flamed at Hedda's cool listing of subterfuges she had doubtless used on Stoddard Laughton over the years. *Forget Flavia . . .*

There'll be no other women . . . only you. Did she dare to believe her husband's words? Did she want them to be true? She forced the disquieting questions aside and said, "I can't control Rhys Davies as you've controlled your husband. We share a bedroom. Rhys was quite adamant about that even before we were wed."

Hedda's lips thinned in distaste, then she walked over to Tory and held her cold hands. "My poor child. Why didn't you tell me? I could have had your father intercede. No gentleman subjects his wife to such an excess!"

Tory felt her temper rising. Strange, how often in recent months that had occurred. She was uncertain if she was upset because her mother disparaged Rhys or because Hedda was so willfully blind regarding the marriage arrangement itself. "You pointed out often enough that Rhys Davies was no gentleman, so it hardly signifies that he should not abide by social etiquette."

"If he expects to be received in polite society, he will conform," Hedda said implacably. Her voice was ice cold.

Tory raised one gold eyebrow and returned her mother's intimidating look. "Oh, and how do you expect to enforce this 'conformity'? Publish rules for bedding one's wife in Mr. Manion's newspaper?"

Hedda almost slapped her defiant daughter. Then, with a stricken look, she reached into her reticule and pulled out a lacy kerchief. She dabbed at her eyes and said, "You are behaving with unspeakable vulgarity, Victoria. How can you treat your own mother so? All I want is your happiness."

"My happiness? You and Papa forced this marriage, and I agreed to it to save our family. Now I shall have to abide by my husband's wishes. Let's not discuss this any further," Tory added with a flush of misery. If her mother knew only a fraction of what had transpired last night—it did not bear considering! She was too confused ever to discuss it with her. Perhaps in time she could talk with Laura. For now the emotions were too new, too painful.

Hedda put her hankie away and said briskly, "Very well. If that's how it's to be, I assume you'll find your own way to deal with Mr. Davies. I only wanted to advise you . . ." She hesitated. "I regret the necessity for this ghastly misalliance, Victoria. So does Charles."

"Charles?" Tory could not keep the incredulity from her voice. "I've not seen him since my engagement. Once the vaunted Laughton wealth evaporated, he vanished quickly enough."

"He's done no such thing. He truly cares for you. Why, only this morning he was at the bank with your father and expressed his concern for you."

Tory scoffed. "What was he doing, helping Papa count Rhys' money?" The moment she said the words, Tory regretted them. What was happening to her manners, her sensibilities?

Hedda's look became frosty. "You mistake his fine feelings. And those of your father, not to mention mine. Only think of this as a trial to be withstood, Victoria. You were always stronger than your brother. When we locate Sanders, we can put all this behind us."

Tory listened with disbelief. "Do you think reclaiming the stolen money from Sanders will negate my marriage? That Rhys will just let me go?"

Hedda avoided Tory's disconcertingly direct gaze and smoothed her skirts nervously, then changed the subject. "As you said, my dear, let's not dwell on unpleasant things. This house is quite grand in its ostentatious way. With a few minor modifications, it could be truly magnificent. Show me your decorating handiwork. I must see the dining room. We can plan a dinner party. Yes, that's just the thing, your first venture as a hostess." Hedda swept from the parlor with Tory following.

Would Rhys let her go if her family had the resources to reclaim her? Deep in her heart Tory knew he would not—not for all the wealth in Colorado. That certainly gave rise to emotions she did not wish to examine.

Chapter Sixteen

Tory sat at her dressing table nervously checking her appearance. She looked pale, she decided, and eyed the rouge pot dubiously. Ladies did not wear face paints. At least not so as to be detectable. She and several of her friends at Mrs. Jefferson's Academy had experimented with them and had become quite skilled. Upon returning home, she hid them from her mother. Now they sat openly in front of her. She reached for the rouge.

Within two weeks of the wedding night their new furnishings arrived from Loring's. She and Rhys were once more sleeping in their own bedroom. Each night they did much more than sleep, no matter whether in this room or any other. *If only I didn't . . . participate so wantonly*, she thought in misery. She tried to hide her response to his touch. True to his word, Rhys had begun again the second night, making no arrogant demands that she beg for release. He was slow, sensuous, and skillful. Far too skillful, damn him! She did not have to verbalize her need for him to know what she felt, what he made her feel. Her body simply overrode her mind.

Rhys stood in the doorway of his closet fastening shirt studs as he observed his wife fuss with her last-minute toilette. She was exquisite with her pale spun-gold hair piled in a soft, smoothly rounded chignon atop her head. Her profile was classically perfect, delicate but oddly strong. "The watered silk matches your eyes," he said in his husky voice. She turned like a startled fawn and her turquoise eyes appeared enormous.

Tory looked at him as he casually leaned one muscular shoulder against the door frame. His snowy linen shirt was half open, revealing a portion of his bronzed chest. With negligent slowness he fastened the studs, all the while feasting his eyes on her. She stood up and smoothed the slim, elegant lines of the aqua silk gown. It was cut daringly low, revealing a shocking amount of cleavage, which she noted Rhys inspecting. Heat infused her cheeks and spread downward.

He gave a low, seductive chuckle and said, "Watch your blushing, love. In that gown it's doubly attractive." He walked across the room with pantherish strides, pausing at his bureau drawer. "I'll make you a trade. I'll give you this to help cover a bit of that delectable skin if you fasten these damn studs for me." He produced a slim oblong velvet case and offered it to her. "Come on. It won't bite you . . . but I might," he added with a wolfish grin as she accepted the jewelry box.

Nestled inside was a silver filigree necklace and

earrings set with aquamarines. "Oh, they're exquisite," she breathed.

"My taste in jewelry's improving, hmm?"

He took the delicate necklace, reached around her slender throat, and deftly fastened the clasp at her nape. "The silver's from the Lady Victory. I had it made specially for you. The stones match your eyes, Victory," he whispered, brushing her throat with a feather-light kiss.

He watched her turn to her dressing mirror and fasten the teardrop earrings, then stood closely behind her and reached around to adjust the largest stone in the necklace so it nestled in the valley of her cleavage. "Lucky gem," he murmured as his fingers grazed her breast. He turned her to face him. "Now, does that merit help with these?" He held out the rest of his onyx shirt studs and cuff links.

"Thank you for the gifts, Rhys. They're truly lovely," she said softly as she began to fasten his shirt, covering up that disturbingly masculine chest. She could smell his shaving soap and a faint hint of expensive tobacco. Even his scent aroused her. She forced a teasing lightness in her voice and said, "For a man so deft with women's jewelry and clothing, you certainly seem maladroit at handling simple shirt studs."

His hands rested on her waist, then slid to her hips as he pulled her lower body against his. "That's because women's things are so much more entertaining. And undressing is much more fun than dressing." He watched her mouth make a disapproving moue that was surprisingly endearing, not at all the prissy, cold thinning that he so often saw on Hedda's lips. Tory tried to emulate her mother but failed, thank God. His wife thought that a great shortcoming, which bothered him. He had awakened her passion. Now if only he could erase her guilt. *Time and patience,* he sighed to himself.

She completed her task and he slid into his jacket. Belying his professed incompetence with the studs, he tied his tie faultlessly the first time. "Our guests await, Mrs. Davies," he said with a flourish, offering her his arm.

Tory caught sight of their reflection as they passed the pier looking glass in one corner of their suite. They did make a striking couple. In unrelieved black and white, his elegant dinner clothes emphasized his startling handsomeness. Now that she had weaned him away from garish jewelry, he looked like a man of rare good breeding as well as wealth. Next to his tall, tanned ruggedness, her slim delicacy was a perfect complement. *See what a lovely, expensive bauble you've bought, Rhys,* she thought sadly. "I assume all your friends will appear in proper attire, including Mr. Manion?" she asked with apprehension. The guest list had been a compromise.

"I won't promise Mike without an ink stain or two on his fingers, but not to worry, love. I won't let him touch you," he whispered in her ear with a chuckle.

"I'm certain the same goes double for Charles Everett," she replied sweetly, knowing that would rile him.

"I'm amazed the wretch had the nerve to accept our invitation. He'll secure damn few votes tonight."

"That's only because you've invited all your Democratic friends."

"They'll mind their manners, love. If *I* was teachable, anyone as clever as that little Irishman can figure out which fork to use."

"Hopefully he'll stick it in the pork roast, not Senator Gates," Tory replied.

"I'll watch him," Rhys said in mock seriousness.

"Just watch your French cuffs," she replied smugly.

He chuckled as they began to descend the wide staircase. Below in the grand ballroom a string sextet imported all the way from Denver was tuning up. Huge sprays of fresh flowers brightened each hallway and room, leaving their fragrance to blend with the heavenly smells wafting from the kitchen.

Tory smiled nervously at her father and several of his banking and mining friends, who were conferring in one corner of the huge ballroom. Just across from them Mike Manion was holding court for Laura Everett and half a dozen of her garden club ladies.

"And the preacher, after hearing the sentence, looked across the courtroom and said for all to hear, 'Hanging is the only thing that will make a man like Packer quit his cussedness'!" Mike finished off his tale, leaving the ladies convulsed with laughter.

Hedda, standing within earshot, raised her eyebrow disdainfully and turned toward Charity Soames, who whispered some disparaging remark.

The mix of people of the better sort and those from the wrong side of the tracks was volatile enough, even if this had not been southwest Colorado in an election year. To further complicate matters, the sensational Alfred Packer trial had ended disastrously. The convicted cannibal's attorneys were able to appeal to the State Supreme Court for a mistrial on technical grounds. Because the judge was a staunch Georgia Democrat and Packer's backers were Republicans, the rough-and-tumble politics of the Rockies had become even rockier. Everyone argued about the overturned conviction.

Rhys did business with miners, merchants, stockmen, and freighters. He was even investigating opportunities with the railroad, rumored to be laying narrow-gauge track on the way to Starlight. A spur line into town was a distinct possibility. Money cut across party lines, and Rhys played both sides. As hostess at their first social gathering, Tory was distinctly uneasy about how smoothly business in the ballroom would go.

Rhys kept her close to his side as they greeted arriving guests, proudly introducing her to awestruck mine owners and sheep ranchers. Although he knew most of the town's wealthy businessmen, he had not yet met Stoddard's friends from the capital. Tory made the introductions, amazed at how quickly he was accepted by these men from the citadels of power and wealth. Their wives, whom Tory had expected to be standoffish and cool like Hedda, mostly fell victim to Rhys's devilish charm. Senator Gates's dumpy little wife positively gushed over his every word.

Things were going smoothly and Tory began to relax a bit after checking with the cook on the progress of dinner. Just as she returned to the ballroom, Charles strode from the foyer into the glittering press of people. He was late, his hair and clothes slightly damp from the rain that had begun to fall in earnest only moments ago. His facial expression matched the weather as he scanned the room with a disgusted glance at Mike Manion and a sheep rancher named Rudolfo Vasquez. Then he saw Rhys and his cold, dark eyes narrowed.

Laura walked up to him and began to chat, but Tory knew it was up to her as hostess to soothe her father's protégé. She approached as Charles and

Rhys exchanged barely civil greetings.

Seeing the way the pompous young ass eyed Tory, Rhys could not resist taking her arm possessively and saying with a taunt in his voice, "Of course, you and *Mrs. Davies* don't require introductions, do you, Everett?"

"Good of you to invite me, Victoria," Charles addressed her, then turned offhandedly to Rhys. "I assume in view of my lifelong friendship with Victoria, you will allow me the familiarity of addressing her by her first name?"

Laura interjected, "The gathering is absolutely perfect, Tory. You've done a superb job." She watched the two men sizing each other up like two fighting cocks.

"Tory does a superb job with *everything* she undertakes," Rhys replied with pride. A devilish light glowed in his eyes as he looked from Laura to her brother-in-law, whose complexion had darkened with anger.

"Beastly business, this Packer mess," Senator Gates said as he and Stoddard strolled up to them. "Good evening, Charles, Mrs. Everett. Splendid party, Mrs. Davies," the paunchy old state senator said, bowing over Tory's hand. "My best wishes on your marriage."

"Thank you, Senator," Tory replied politely, grateful the old curmudgeon had decided not to question her abrupt shift in bridegrooms. Her gratitude proved premature.

"I can at least congratulate you, Everett, on the upcoming election. You're certain to win my seat in the race, even if you didn't win this fair lady's hand."

"Don't go betting all your cash on that, Senator," Mike Manion said, entering the conversation with a cocky grin. "Our candidate stands a better-than-even chance to take the seat on your retirement."

"You're a betting man, Davies," Gates said coolly. "Who do you favor?"

Rhys smiled broadly. "Mike here knows my politics and Stoddard knows my bank balance." He cast a meaningful glance at Laughton, who looked in discomfiture from the senator to his son-in-law. Then Rhys continued, "A Republican senator from our district would sew up the railroad deal with the Denver crowd and make me a pile of money . . . but in this case I may just have to sacrifice the money for my principles."

"You don't really comprehend the intricacies of Colorado politics, Davies, nor do you, Manion," Everett replied with a sneer. "Our state would be better served if you both returned to your barbarous Celtic homelands."

"Our state, boyo, would be better served by an Irish wolfhound than the likes of you," Manion replied in his thickest, most baiting brogue. "Small wonder you Republicans have to resort to devouring Democrats to stop our progress! Why don't you run Packer for the senate?"

Rhys laughed. "Civilized Coloradians and barbaric Celts, eh? I think you're wide of the mark, Charles. At least in Wales when a man's invited to dinner, he knows his name will appear on the guest list, not the menu."

"Gentlemen, gentlemen," Laura remonstrated, grabbing Senator Gates by one arm and Charles by the other, "Why don't the two of you plan election strategy, or whatever it is senators do." She quickly led them toward the refreshment table.

"I think it's time for dinner," Tory said to Rhys. Stoddard started to offer his arm to his daughter, but

Rhys smoothly tucked her slim wrist about his arm with ingratiating possessiveness. "Oh, in case you're wondering, Michael, Tory's serving crown roast of pork tonight—no Democrats."

"You are both awful," she whispered as they approached the dining room.

The dinner was lengthy and sumptuous and went smoothly, considering the antagonistic diversity of the guest list. Tory had planned the seating arrangements with great care.

Hedda toyed with a crystal glass of German Riesling, watching her daughter play the gracious hostess at one end of the table. At the other end, in the captain's chair, Rhys Davies laughed and talked expansively, but Hedda could tell each time his heated gaze passed in Victoria's direction. The little fool seemed to feel his eyes on her and always rewarded his obscenely scorching glances with flushed cheeks. Something was happening between them, something Hedda had never dreamed could occur when she had agreed to Stoddard's proposal for this hideous misalliance. She shuddered in revulsion. What would happen when—

Just then a loud noise came from the entry hall, followed by yelling and cursing. The butler and two maids followed Tomato Nose Wylie Wilcox into the dazzling light of the formal dining room. He was almost unrecognizable with mud smeared from head to foot. "Rhys, they's been a washout on th' road ta th' Lady. Half th' damn blasted mountain's done slud down 'n' buried ever'thin'!"

Davies stood up and tossed his snowy linen napkin onto his plate. "Any of the men hurt?"

"We wuz tryin' ta beat th' rain in with a big ore haul. Got us six twelve-span wagons loaded ta th' brim. Mules 'n' drivers all down. 'Bout ten or twelve miners hitched a ride with us 'n' they's in a turrible fix, too. We gotta dig 'em out!"

"I'll be right along, Wylie. Dr. Runcie?" Rhys said, looking down the long table at the physician.

"My bag's always in my carriage, Rhys." The silver-haired doctor excused himself as several other men volunteered to join the rescue mission.

"That road has to stay open," Able Courtney said. A wealthy mine owner, his own holdings were situated just off the same treacherous mountain road as Rhys's Lady Victory. "If it snows in the next week, we'll not get our silver down or the men out till spring."

"Silver will keep. The men won't," Manion snapped curtly.

Wilcox nodded. "We got us no time ta lose. Them men 'n' wagons er slippin down th' side of th' west slope. If'n this rain don't let up afore mornin', they's goners."

Rhys turned to James Allen and asked, "I assume you'll open up and extend me credit, Jim? We'll need shovels, pickaxes, ropes, buckets, blankets. Able, you're in charge of provisioning from Allen's store."

"Done. Let's go, Abel," the merchant replied. Within a few minutes most of the men in the room were dispatched on various tasks.

Rhys walked over to Tory and took her hands. "You'll have to play hostess without me, love. Have the older gentlemen see that all the ladies get home safely. I'm sorry your first dinner party had to end this way. It was great while it lasted," he added jauntily and pulled her into his embrace for a fulsome kiss.

Too stunned to resist the public display of affection, she melted against him. When he released her and started to leave, she called out, "Rhys, your clothes. Surely you aren't going to dig in the mud dressed like that?"

He shrugged and gave her a heart-stopping grin. "No time to change, Tory." He laughed and said, "Be a love and have my tailor make up new evening clothes for me while I'm gone." Then he turned and saw Charles sitting near Stoddard and Senator Gates. As the only young man left at the table, Everett was conspicuous. "You don't have a suit to spare, Charlie boy?" Rhys taunted, then left.

"I assumed those mine ruffians could handle the problem," Everett said to no one in particular, but he noted the disdain on Victoria's face.

"Look bad with the voters if you aren't in on this rescue mission, Charles," the senator said cynically.

Muttering ungraciously, Everett looked at Victoria and said, "Very well, I suppose they could use a hand."

"Just be careful crossing any bridges, Charles," Tory couldn't resist advising, ignoring a quelling look from her mother.

Dawn came, gray and grim as a funeral cortege. The rain finally stopped by mid-morning. Tory had slept a few hours after seeing all the remaining guests off and supervising the army of servants who cleaned up the mess from the lavish gala. Used to Rhys's body heat and embrace, she had tossed in their big cold bed until five a.m., then rose and dressed to wait for his return.

When no word came from the mountain by noon, she grew concerned. Then Laura arrived with a worried frown. "Still no word from Rhys?" she asked, shaking her wet wool cape and handing it to a maid.

"No," Tory replied, studying her friend's agitation.

"I was just at Dr. Runcie's office. His nurse has the infirmary prepared. Three injured men have already been brought in. Jacob once saw a man suffocated in a mud slide." She shuddered. "I only pray the rain's abatement may help in this case."

Tory blanched. "Those are Rhys's men and wagons. He'll be in the thick of any danger. I'm riding up there to see what's happened," she replied.

Laura's eyebrows arched. "For a woman who professed to despise her husband scant weeks ago, you seem to have changed your mind rather dramatically."

"I don't have to be in love with the man, Laura. He *is* my husband, and I owe him a certain allegiance." With that she dashed upstairs, calling for May to lay out a pair of sturdy boots and a heavy riding habit.

"Allegiance, is it?" Laura said with a satisfied smile.

Tory rode carefully on the mud-slick trail, grateful the rain had ended and that her placid gelding was sure-footed. It took her over an hour to reach the site. She could hear pickaxes thunking into the mud and debris, mules squealing, and men cursing before she rounded the curve on the narrow trail hacked up the mountain.

To her left lay a sickening drop-off, the ravine hundreds of feet below. The steep cliff side was broken by a few jagged outcrops of rocks and some pitifully wind-twisted scrub pines. It was desolate in the San Juans with winter coming on. Tory hugged the right side of the narrow wagon road and braced herself for what lay ahead. All too soon she saw the chaos. A giant reddish mass filled with boulders and uprooted trees had literally erased the narrow ledge of trail. For hundreds of feet ahead of her on a steep uphill grade a series of huge Murphy wagons were buried in mud. Some of the mules harnessed to them struggled and brayed frantically, but others, buried up to their bellies or even shoulders, were immobilized and silent. Injured teamsters, covered with mud, lay on the soft wet earth in front of the slide. Dr. Runcie tended them one by one. Workers with shovels and picks were digging through the deadly mud, searching for more survivors and attempting to free thrashing mules. Occasional shots rang out as badly injured animals were dispatched.

Tory scanned the hellish scene, looking for Rhys. Everyone was so covered with the reddish mud that it was nearly impossible to distinguish one man from another. Then she heard his voice, strong and commanding, calling for more workers over near the edge of the abyss. His evening clothes were ruined beyond redemption and muddy sweat ran in rivulets down his face as he shoveled furiously, trying to free a man nearly buried beneath rocks and debris. One large boulder pinned the teamster.

"Bring crowbars," he yelled. "We'll have to pry this rock off his leg. Doc, come watch us work so we don't do more damage moving him."

The elderly doctor, silver hair unrecognizable beneath a film of mud, brought his leather instrument bag to where Rhys waited with Mike Manion. Passing Charles, who stood leaning on a pickaxe, the doctor curtly commandeered his services. Reluctantly he followed the physician to the edge of the drop-off.

"Mike, you and Charles use those bars to lift the boulder. Doc, watch and yell if they're hurting the leg. I'll pull him free when they get the boulder up."

"I don't like this, Davies," Everett said. "The earth's soft and slippery. This whole section could give way if we move the rock."

Tory, having dismounted, struggled closer and overheard his words. In the frenetic activity, no one had noticed her. Her boots sunk in the mud and her skirts dragged, weighing her down with each slogging step. She could see the disgust in Rhys's eyes as he looked at Everett. Charles stepped back, then turned and saw Tory. Her look of disapproval galvanized him as her husband's contempt could not. Charles turned and snarled, "All right, let's get it done."

Tory could see that Rhys was kneeling precariously close to the slippery edge of the trail, ready to pull the injured man free. Charles and Mike stood to Rhys's right, behind the rock. He gave them the signal and they slid long steel shanks into the soft earth around the unconscious man, raising the big rock and tilting it toward the abyss.

"Now, the leg is free. Pull, Rhys," the physician cried, grabbing the patient's arms as Rhys reached beneath the teetering boulder to free the leg.

"Watch you don't let that rock fall on us," Rhys said to the two sweating, struggling men as the soft ground shifted.

Manion held fast as Davies freed the man's leg, but just as he and the doctor had the teamster clear, Charles began slipping. He panicked and dropped his pry bar, leaping backward with a curse. The little Irishman held on valiantly, but the sudden shifting of all the load onto his bar was more than he could withstand. The boulder lurched to the left, then tore away the edge of the trail and plunged downward, gouging huge clumps of earth, rocks, and trees as it bounced to the ravine floor. Mike, standing immediately behind the rock, was swept along with it as the whole section of the ledge evaporated beneath his feet.

"Grab him, Everett!" Rhys yelled as he leaped over the unconscious miner. Even if he had moved closer to the edge, it was unlikely that Charles could have undone what his panic had wrought. Rhys, who had been kneeling on the other side, could not reach his friend.

A scream ripped from Tory when she saw her husband teeter and slide over the edge, but the doctor's quick thinking saved him. Grabbing the steel shank Charles had dropped, he flattened himself in the mud and extended it for Rhys to grab hold of. Slowly and carefully, Rhys climbed back over the top onto firmer ground. For an instant their eyes met, hers filled with terror, his with amazement, but then he was calling for men with ropes and kneeling to peer over the edge of the drop.

"Mike, you Mickey son-of-a-bitch, don't you dare go 'n' die on me," he yelled, frantically scanning the sickening path the boulder had chewed down the mountain side.

A faint voice echoed up, "Would I be so inconsiderate of a fellow Democrat, Rhys, me lad?"

Manion hung about thirty feet below, precariously clutching onto a jagged splinter of rock with one hand while his other was wrapped around a twisted scrub pine. Either handhold could give way at any moment.

"Hang on! I'm coming down. You're damn lucky that boulder was in front and not behind you or you'd be shaking hands right now with Lucifer."

"Luck o' the Irish boyo, but I don't think you ought to press it coming down here—a mere Welshman doesn't share the charm. Drop me a rope." Just as he called up, the roots of the pine loosened more and he lost footing for a moment.

"And how would you let go to grab the rope before you fell?" Rhys yelled as he tied one end of the stout hemp around his waist and signaled the three burly men behind him to let out the slack.

Tory stood behind them, her teeth clamped on one small whitened fist as she watched her husband vanish over the edge of the trail. Lodged in her throat were words she could never speak, feelings she could never admit: *I love you, Rhys!*

The last thing Rhys saw before he scrambled below the trail was Tory's anguished face, her aqua eyes fastened on him. Did her concern reveal some deeper emotion? He had no time to contemplate it as he slipped and slid down toward Mike.

"Lord help us both if this rope breaks," he muttered.

"I've already called up the Holy Mother and all the saints, just in reserve, you understand," Mike grunted as Rhys reached him. Just then the pine's roots let go with a squishy whoosh and Mike's other hand bit into the splintering shale outcropping even tighter.

"Call on the reserves," Rhys gasped as he grabbed Mike around the waist with one arm, while the other arm and both feet braced against the side of the mountain. "Lucky for you you're not related to Evan Manion, else I'd have to let you drop, you skinny little Irishman. That other Mick outweighed me by at least three or four stone!"

"Right now, boyo, I'm wishin for both our sakes I wasn't the largest of the Pennsylvania Manions," Mike said as he clung to his rescuer with both arms. Rhys yelled up for the men to pull.

Tory could hear their conversation indistinctly as a whole group of men gathered to tug the rope and its human cargo back up the mountain. The sounds of loose rocks clattering down the cliff made her heart nearly stop. Once Rhys lost his footing and the rope gave a sharp lurch.

"Watch out so's it don't snap under the weight," Wilcox yelled. "Steady men, steady," He was nearest the edge and the one to reach out a hand for Rhys as he crested the top. Tory bit her clenched fist until she drew blood, willing herself not to cry out and distract the rescue effort.

Charles stood well back from the action, a detached observer of all the havoc he had created. Everyone was so absorbed by the drama they ignored him. As soon as Rhys shoved Mike to safety, he stepped away from the precipice and removed the frayed muddy rope from his waist. Tory remained rooted to the ground as relief washed over her. She felt an overwhelming impulse to run into his arms. Before she could gather her wits to act on it, he strode furiously toward Everett, who backed away.

"Now see here, Davies, it was an accident. I never knew that damned Mic—"

Rhys's fist connected squarely with his nose, sending blood flying as the lawyer fell backward into the mud, out cold.

"No one but me calls Manion a Mick, you cowardly bastard," Rhys ground out. Then he looked over at the cut and bruised little Irishman, who was limping toward them, followed by Dr. Runcie, Wylie Wilcox, and several other irate miners.

"Don't waste yer time on him, Doc," Wylie said. "Thet feller Rhys dragged out from 'neath th' rock's comin' round. His laig's busted up somethin' fierce."

270

Everyone dispersed to other tasks except for Rhys and Tory, who stood staring at each other across Charles Everett's unconscious body.

For the life of her, Tory could not utter a sound, but she stepped hesitantly near him, hungry to touch his muddy body and assure herself he really was safe. He stepped over Charles and closed the distance, sweeping her into his embrace.

"What the hell are you doing up here? Riding sidesaddle, all alone, you could've been hurt!" he rasped.

"You could've been killed," she accused, shoving him away.

"Sorry I've marked you, love," he whispered intimately as he surveyed the muddy hand prints on her shoulders and smears on her face. "Would you have cared if I'd met my end at the bottom of the canyon? You'd be a rich widow, Tory."

Her eyes widened in horror. "You fool! How could you say such a horrid thing?"

"Would you miss me, then?" His eyes danced and he looked roguishly handsome in spite of sweat and mud.

She ignored the question and said brusquely, "As long as I've come this far, I might as well help Dr. Runcie."

Bemused, he stood and watched her squish her way toward the row of blankets where the injured men had been brought.

His heart felt queerly light. She had ridden all the way up here alone, just to see if he was safe. The look on her face before they lowered him over the side told him what she might never openly admit. She had to care for him.

Just then Charles groaned and rolled over. Rhys frowned at the worthless bastard, then considered the possibility she had come after her ex-fiancé, not him. Surely not. Certainly after Everett's exhibition of cowardice she was done with him. Uncertainty warred with hopefulness as he rejoined the rescue operation.

Chapter Seventeen

Tory knelt by the injured miner and propped his head up so that he could drink from the canteen she held. His arm was broken, but Dr. Runcie seemed to think that the injury was one of the least serious among the victims. Several men had been crushed by the avalanche of mud and rocks, and many of the broken limbs were hideously mangled. Gritting her teeth, she continued her simple mission of mercy, dispensing water, while trying not to listen to the screams of pain.

"What on earth are you doing up here in this godforsaken mess? No lady should be exposed to this. I'll escort you safely to town," a recovered Charles pronounced, reaching down to pull Tory away from an injured teamster.

She slapped his hand away and rose unassisted, staring coldly at him. "I'm here to help the doctor and the injured, a task at which you've proven sadly

273

deficient, Mr. Everett. Feel free to return to town. I'll stand in your place."

Wylie Wilcox, walking nearby with a limping miner leaning on his arm for support, gave out a loud snicker. The injured man joined in and hobbled past. Charles's florid complexion turned dark with fury. "Your father and mother—"

"Are no longer my guardians, Charles. Nor are you. Please leave." She heard the doctor call and rushed off, eager to be quit of the pompous coward. The thought flashed through her mind that she had been fortunate indeed to have escaped marriage to him. Dr. Runcie and Wylie were kneeling on the ground, trying to restrain a man thrashing in agony. "I have to set a compound fracture before he can be put on a wagon and moved to town," the doc said wearily.

Tory's own exhaustion paled when she realized that this elderly man had been at work since the previous evening.

"What do you need me to do?" she asked levelly.

"Wylie'll hold him down and I'll pull the lower leg. You can hold here," he indicated the upper portion of the femur—"steadying the bone until I can realign both pieces and shove them together. It won't be pretty," he warned her.

She rubbed her palms on her skirts and said, "I can do it."

He looked at her and nodded. "Women usually end up having more sense than men when it comes to blood and pain." He showed her exactly how to feel the broken femur's position, then moved her hands to hold it. "*Now*, Wylie," he said, and the big miner virtually fell across the man's upper body and right leg, holding him down while the doctor quickly pulled on the broken leg just above the knee and twisted it into the upper portion.

Tory held on to the bunching muscles around the bone with every ounce of her strength. She could feel the pieces of bone grind as they made clean contact. Just then the man's muscles went slack.

"He's fainted, poor devil," Runcie said as he quickly poured more disinfectant over the open wound where the bone had protruded through the flesh, then began to splint the injury tightly. "Got damn little to work with up here. May have to redo this one when I can get him on my table tomorrow, but at least he won't be grinding up the edges of the femur while he bounces down the mountain," he said grimly.

Tory felt her bile rise, but forced it down and followed him to another man laid out on the ground. They knelt beside the delirious moaning teamster, and the physician made a quick, efficient examination, then sadly shook his head. "Lungs crushed and filling with blood," he whispered. "See if you can sit with him a few minutes. Shouldn't be long."

She nodded, fighting back tears. The youth looked to be Sanders's age. His face was contorted with agony and he was coughing up blood. She took her canteen and wiped his brow with cool water. "Rest easy, don't try to talk."

He held on to her hand for a moment, whispered something unintelligible, and was gone. Tory covered him with the blanket and stood up unsteadily. Upon hearing the doctor call, she turned and slogged through the mud toward him.

The afternoon soon passed into evening. While she worked, Tory's eyes kept searching for Rhys's tall figure amid the men digging and hauling. All the men, alive and dead, had been brought out of the slide and loaded into wagons. The mules that could be freed had been dragged clear, but the ore wagons would have to be dug out with a full work crew in the days following. One night of hell on the mountain was all any of the rescuers or rescued wanted to spend.

All her life Tory had been sheltered and cosseted by her parents. Hedda had never let her daughter see anything violent or painful. Once, she had asked her mother if she could assist Laura Everett when there had been a hotel fire and the infirmary was in need of extra help. Hedda had refused in horror. Looking down at her bedraggled, mud-and-blood-covered clothes, she grimaced, imagining what censure she would receive for this day's work.

As she stood rubbing her aching back, surveying the last of the clean-up, she felt a sense of amazement and of freedom. The doctor and many of the men had already complimented her efforts. But she suddenly realized that there was only one whose opinion mattered. Rhys seemed to materialize from nowhere, walking across the muddy road bed in long, graceful strides. In his arms he held a quivering bundle of mud with a madly thumping tail. The small pup let out an excited bark as Rhys stopped in front of her, holding the little wriggling offering awkwardly.

"He belonged to one of the men who was killed. You're to ride in the hospital wagon. I was wondering if you'd hold on to him until we get to town."

Tory stretched out her hand and scratched the animal's bewhiskered chin. She was rewarded with a slurping lick. Delight spread across her face, erasing the bone-weary exhaustion of a moment ago. "Oh, yes, of course, Rhys. I've always loved dogs."

He looked at her in puzzlement, knowing how indulged her childhood had been. "Didn't you ever have one?" he asked as she eagerly took the little raggy mess in her arms.

The puppy's furiously wagging tail sprayed them both with mud, but she only laughed and scratched his head. "Mama said they were too much bother and messed up a lady's clothes." She paused and looked up at him with the wistfulness of a little girl. "Could we keep him?"

His smile matched hers as he, too, scratched the pup's head. "I was hoping you'd ask. We have lots of room at Dragon's Lair for dogs—and children," he added with a grin.

Morning dawned bright, golden, and unseasonably warm after the past week of cold gloom. Weather at the end of September was always uncertain in the San Juans. Rhys awakened alone in their big bed. Stretching his aching muscles, he sat up on the edge of the bed, then rose and reached for his robe. As he slid it on he wondered where his wife had gone. He always awakened earlier than she.

They had come in last night mud-covered and exhausted. After quick baths and a light meal hurriedly put together by Mrs. Creighton, they had slipped into blessed oblivion. Rhys had been too bone-weary after thirty-six hours without sleep to even consider making love to Tory. When they had retired, she had reluctantly given the mud-soaked dog over to the old cook's care. Remembering how protective and excited Tory was about the pup, he smiled, sure of where he'd find her.

The scene that greeted him was an endearing surprise. When he neared the kitchen, he heard Tory's soft, rich chuckle, interspersed with sharp barks. She knelt on the floor in one corner next to a large copper wash bucket which had been converted into a bathtub for the small dog. Her hair was mussed and damp, and a bubble of suds clung to the tip of her nose as she scrubbed the splashing furball who was trying to climb out of the tub.

"No you don't, you stinker. Your fur's caked so solid with clay you look like a mud pie. Let's see what's beneath all this dirt." She turned to the cook, who was standing by with another large pail of clean water. "All right, rinse, but try not to drown him."

Mrs. Creighton, caught up in her prim young mistress's good humor, ignored the water soaking her usually immaculate kitchen floor and doused the wriggling pup. "Why he's near white," she said as Tory lifted him from the water and let him shake on wobbly legs that slipped from beneath him on the wet, slick tiles.

"He *is* white," Tory exclaimed in delight as she scooped him up in a thick, fluffy towel and began to dry him off. "When all this fur dries—"

"You'll need a bath," Rhys interrupted, bending down on one knee to kiss a soap bubble from her nose and drape an escaped curl back behind her ear. "Here, allow me," he said, taking the dog from her with one hand and helping her up with the other. He inspected the dog with mock severity as she straightened her rumpled dress and fussed with her tangled topknot, which had lost most of its pins.

"What shall we name you, hmm?" He rubbed the ball of white fluff in the towel, considering. "I haven't had a dog since I left St. Vincent's. Sister Frances Rose had a big brute, a black and white sheep dog. Oddly enough, the children called him Shep."

"I want this one to have a special name. Just give me time to think of one." She looked down at her dress and sighed. "I'd better change and fix my hair."

"Put on something comfortable for a buggy ride. I'm taking you and our unnamed companion on a picnic," Rhys said. "I'll have Mrs. Creighton fix the food. Go change. I'll watch this rascal." He stroked a floppy ear with one finger and was rewarded with an excited bark.

Tory cast nervous glances at her husband's profile as he drove the small carriage up a winding mountain road a good distance from town. The wind ruffled his curly hair and sent that rebellious lock falling onto his forehead. He wore an open-collared tan shirt and brown trousers, looking more like a ranch hand than Starlight's newest millionaire. Holding the reins in his relaxed hands, he let the horses trot at a leisurely pace, seeming to enjoy the sun on his face.

"It won't be long until the snow comes to stay," Tory said, trying not to think of how appealing he looked, or how she ached to reach out and brush that look of hair across his forehead.

He smiled and looked at her. "The place we're going is always warm," he said cryptically. "I discovered it on a trip up here in the spring. It's special. You'll see."

They rode for another half hour across a wide meadow between two peaks then, followed a barely discernible trail down a narrow path between sharp outcroppings of striated rock formations. Water bubbled up like liquid crystal, glistening silver in the noonday sun, following the twisting course between the rocks. The narrow stream spewed from underground and widened as they followed it into a small, secluded canyon. Its steep, smooth sides were punctuated by the lush late summer greenness of spring-fed evergreens. A tall stand of aspens rustled their golden leaves beside the stream, which filled a series of bubbling pools in the center of the canyon.

Tory let out a breathless gasp of surprise at the beauty of the place. "It's enchanting," she said as he helped her from the small buggy. The dog jumped down and ran around their feet, barking furiously. "I think he likes it, too."

"It's almost as beautiful as you . . . but not quite," he said quietly, looking intently into her eyes. "Why did you ride up to that mud slide yesterday, Tory?"

"I was afraid something had happened . . . I thought I could help," she added, breaking his hypnotic hold on her by turning away and following the bounding pup toward the largest pool.

Rhys reached in the buggy for their picnic basket and blanket stowed beneath the seat. "I knew it wouldn't be that easy," he muttered to himself with a sigh. Then, watching her inspect the bubbling water, he smiled and strode up behind her. He placed his load on the ground and knelt to pluck a Shasta daisy and tuck it behind her ear. "Test the water," he whispered.

Tory knelt with a puzzled look on her face as the dog raced around the edge of the pool, splashing and yipping in obvious delight. She put her hand in the silvery water, expecting it to be icy cold as the mountain streams in the San Juans always were, then yanked it back in surprise. "It's hot!"

"Not too hot—just nicely warmed." His husky voice was filled with sensuous promise as he spread the blanket beside the pool. The sun sparkled on the water, casting reflections on his face as he spoke. "This is a natural hot spring. I've seen a few others up north outside Denver, but never around here."

"Then no one knows this place exists?" she asked in wonder, looking at the grandeur of the sheer gray-and-tan-striped rocks that stretched around them toward the azure dome of sky.

"Several folks know—the man I bought the land from, for one. You see, I had plans for this place, even then." With a disarming smile that only made her more nervous, he sat down on the blanket and patted a spot beside him for her.

"I'll unpack the lunch," she replied, setting the basket strategically between them. He chuckled and watched her place the feast Mrs. Creighton had prepared on the blanket. Fried chicken, sliced ham, crusty sourdough bread, a small crock of dark spicy apple butter, and a larger one of canned peaches.

She dutifully filled a plate and handed it to him, then poured the sparkling white wine he had uncorked into two glasses and gave him one. He watched her sip her wine and take a few hesitant bites of ham, then shove a succulent golden peach about her plate. Polishing off a drumstick, he tossed several bits of meat and bread to the dog, then set the plate and bones back inside the hamper. After wiping his hands on a napkin, Rhys leaned back on his elbows. He knew she could sense his eyes on her even though she refused to meet them. "I won't devour you, Victoria. I'm not Al Packer." He waited a beat, then continued. "I asked you a question earlier. You didn't really answer it."

"What do you want me to say, Rhys?" She, too, tossed her leftovers to the dog and placed the plate in the hamper for safekeeping.

He lay back and stared at the sky, crossing his arms over his broad chest with deceptive casualness. "I know we got off to a bad start with the marriage, Tory. Our wedding night wasn't exactly what either of us had planned. I've tried to make amends for what I said and did—no, that's not really true. I'm not sorry for what I did—only the way I did it. I wanted to show you your own passion, gently, slowly at first, not by taunting you and . . ." He sighed, watching her stiffen with angry mortification.

"Making me beg," she whispered, hating the words. "You've done as much every night since."

He sat up abruptly. "Now, that's a bloody lie! I've made love to you and you've responded. That's no shame to either of us, Tory, but you seem to think it is. You deny your feelings, even try to hide them from me. Why?"

She turned away and looked out over the dancing water, too mortified to speak.

"I'll tell you why," he persisted. "You're afraid you might be beginning to care for such a totally unsuitable ruffian, a man who's not the gentleman of your girlhood fantasies."

"You're right about one thing. You're not Prince Charming—and I'm not in love with you any more than you're in love with me," she added defensively.

He reached over and took her chin in his hand, tipping it toward him. "So, that's it, is it now, love. You think I don't love you?"

"Don't be absurd," she snapped, breaking free of his hold. "I'm a trophy to you, a prize possession to be flaunted in silks and jewels, your entree to my father's world."

A surge of anger swept over him. "I already had an entree to your father's world—money," he said flatly.

"With which you bought me," she replied with tears of fury clogging her throat.

He reached out to her, then stopped, his hand clenched impotently. Then he dropped it to his side. "Tory, maybe I did buy you . . . or at least I took advantage of your father's offer, but I didn't do it to have a hostess for social occasions. You're not a trophy to me—you're my wife. God help me, I love you. Maybe I always did, from that first moment I held you in the freezing water of that river." He did not touch her but willed her to turn to him. Didn't she understand what he had just risked by speaking to her so openly?

She began hesitantly, still not daring to face him, "If you love me as a gentleman loves his wife, you wouldn't still ask me to . . ." her voice broke. "You would allow me my own bedroom and respect my privacy, not expect me to spend every night in your arms." Her whole body felt on fire with embarrassment.

"You don't say that because you hate it—I know you've had the same pleasure I have. You can't hide your physical responses from me, Tory. Why do you keep trying? Because I'm beneath you? Is that it?" He steeled himself to hear her say the words, to deliver the stinging verbal slap, but she did not. Instead her shoulders shook with silent, shuddering sobs.

Instantly he reached out and took her in his arms, holding her and murmuring low endearments, feeling her pain, bewildered at its cause. "What is it, love? Talk to me," he crooned.

"Women . . . ladies don't feel that way," she hiccuped against his shoulder. "I shouldn't—I'm not supposed to want . . . Mama said it's a wife's duty to give her husband children, but—" She felt his body go tense and his hands still their gentle caressing.

"I should've known Hedda Laughton put that garbage in your head! Tory, love, forget duty, forget when we're together like this that you're a lady"—he raised one hand to still her protest. "You are a lady and I love you for it, but you're also a woman, beautiful, desirable, flesh and blood, capable of giving and receiving pleasure." He felt her tremble, and his own body answered as he shuddered with need. His hands stroked the curve of her breast and his heart slammed in his chest. He kissed her throat, then let his lips roam higher, up her tear-stained cheeks to her thick golden lashes. He kissed her eyelids, the tip of her nose, then moved irresistibly to her lips. When he closed over them, she gave a sob of surrender and opened to him, returning the caress as her hands clawed at his shoulders.

Slowly, he lowered her to the blanket and began to unbutton her frilly pink blouse, reaching inside to stroke her breasts through the sheer silk camisole. When she arched at his touch, he pulled the blouse all the way open and began to slide it from her arms, all the while continuing to rain kisses over her face and throat, down onto her breasts.

"We'll talk later," he rasped out, then began to unfasten her skirts.

"This is why you brought me here, isn't it?" she whispered between kisses, too breathless to be convincingly accusing.

"Let's just say I don't ever want you to drown," he murmured cryptically as he continued undressing her with amazing skill and speed. "I'm going to teach you to swim, love."

"But . . . but I thought . . ." She sputtered into stunned silence as he removed her skirt and petticoats and began to slip off her shoes and stockings.

"That, too, Tory, that, too," he replied as he pressed her against the blanket and kissed her into breathless acquiescence. Seemingly satisfied with her bemused reaction, he sat up and quickly pulled off his boots and hose, slid his shirt off, and peeled down the tight wool pants. He could sense her eyes on him, but when he looked at her, she quickly averted her flushed face. "You're cold. The water is warm, but first . . ." He paused and slipped the hooks on her chemise, then untied the lace of her pantalets. Gently, he peeled the last of her sheer undergarments from her body and then offered his hand. "Come with me," he whispered in a passion-roughened voice.

Tory was unable to resist, as she raised her trembling hand and let his larger one engulf it, pulling her to her feet. They were both stark naked, in the middle of the day, outdoors. She should have been scandalized, but the sun felt paganly glorious on her bare skin. Rhys's upper body, bronzed by long hours under its merciless rays, contrasted starkly with her milky paleness. Her breasts pressed in the crisp mat of hair on his chest as he embraced her, then picked her up and carried her, unprotesting, into the bubbling pool.

"Hold on tight, love." He scarcely needed to make the admonition as the warm water rushed around her, plastering her long hair to her back. She felt the pull of the current and the alien tingling of hot mineral salts on her bare flesh. Both frightened and intrigued, Tory let him carry her deep into the center of the pool. When he released his grip on her and began to float on his back, she held her arms firmly about his neck and stretched out in the water, using his body like a raft to buoy her up.

"I feel so strange," she murmured, shaking her hair out of her face. Lying on top of him, she could feel every muscle in his body, all water-slicked, moving gracefully with the whirling currents in the hot spring. The erotic friction of her breasts rubbing against his furry chest caused her nipples to harden and his shaft pressed insistently between her thighs. These were the same sensations she felt each time they lay together, only subtly altered and heightened in the water.

His lips curved in a smile as he felt her respond. "Do you like this, love?"

"I . . . I don't know," she whispered.

His arms made a lazy backstroke, propelling them through the water, then one hand came around to glide over her back and down the wet, silky curve of her buttock, eliciting a gasp of surprise from her. Instinctively her legs stiffened and her thighs tightened around his phallus, imprisoning it for a moment.

The force of her response pushed him beneath the surface. Rhys's feet found the bottom of the pool and he stood up in the chin-high water laughing and choking. "Love, what a terrible wife you are!" His voice mimicked Mike Manion's. "Ta be drownin' your poor lovin' husband and in such a devilish manner, saints preserve me!"

Victoria, her floating body still stretched out on the water's surface and her arms still clinging to his neck, giggled, joining in the unexpected fun. "The saints is it? Sure and the saints would have little to do with the likes of you, Rhys Davies. If you're to be preserved, it'll have to be the devil's work, for he always takes care of his own!"

An amazed Rhys threw back his head and laughed. "Ah, girl, I love you," he choked out and planted an exuberant kiss on her smiling lips. But what had begun as a spontaneous act of affection quickly became one of passion. After several moments, Rhys pulled back and whispered, "Come to me, darling." He pulled her body under the surface and molded it to his. "Now wrap your legs around my waist." As she obeyed, he began to stroke her back and buttocks. "Kiss me, Tory," he coaxed as he continued the slick, slow movements, using his whole body to rub and excite hers.

She held her arms fast about his neck but did not raise her head to comply. Gently he tugged on her hair, pulling it down her back until she raised her face and their eyes locked. With a ragged sob she obeyed, tightening her arms to lever her body higher on his until their lips again met and fused.

After the long, exploratory kiss that tasted of salt water, he murmured against her lips, "This is much better than our first encounter in the water." With that his arm gripped her waist firmly to his side as he turned to glide them into the shallows. When her feet touched bottom he slowly eased her free so she could gain purchase on the soft, mossy surface. Rhys stretched out in the pool, partially submerged in less than a foot of water. He pulled her down to lie beside him, softly disentangling her hair from around her throat and face, then lifting the water-darkened golden masses behind her back.

"First things first," he whispered as he kissed her with fierce yet oddly gentle possessiveness, molding her to him as they twined arms and legs in a tight embrace. "Hold me," he commanded, guiding her hand between them to grasp his shaft and stroke its water-slicked length. His hand left hers and reached to caress her mound of silky curls, then deeper until he elicited a moan from her. He stopped until she writhed silently. He caressed again, ever so delicately over the wet hot flesh, then stopped, feeling her hips buck. Rhys rolled on his back and raised her by her hips, impaling her.

Water splashed in frothy turbulence about them as he arched up into her, showing her with his hands on her hips how to ride him. Once she began to follow his languorous rhythm, he pulled her head down to kiss her as their passion built to exquisite new heights, lured on by the soft, hot promise of the lapping water. Tory felt her whole body growing hotter and hotter, yet all the fire centered low in her belly, moving to where he joined with her so intimately. He raised and lowered her on his velvety hardness, arching up into her for the deepest, most incredible penetration. It should have hurt—or at least caused her acute embarrassment, riding atop him in such a wanton fashion, but it did neither. She could not think, only feel, and move faster and faster.

Now, after all the nights in Rhys's arms, she knew what the goal was, and she eagerly sought it. When the final splendor burst on her, she raised up, feeling his hands sliding over her waist to cup her breasts, lifting them to the blazing sun like some barbaric pagan offering. She arched and cried out in climax, flinging her head back until her heavy gilded hair swept over his thighs.

Rhys looked up at her golden perfection and spent himself in a blinding surge of ecstasy that seemed to go on for infinity. Slowly they both returned to reality. He could feel her skin beaded with fine goosebumps as the breeze licked at the droplets of water, evaporating them. Tenderly he pulled her back into the water and rolled her to lie on the soft mossy bottom, facing him. He kissed her nose and held her protectively in his arms. "I really do love you, Tory," he whispered against her cheek. And he waited for her reply.

Chapter Eighteen

Victoria felt the words lodged in her throat. Her chest tightened and she could not breathe for fear she would blurt out, *I love you Rhys Davies, gambler, foreigner, slum ruffian, whoremaster of the town's leading bordello*. She could not own up to that shameful truth, nor even trust his declaration. He used her body against her in such wanton, unnatural ways. He kept other women. Tory knew in that heart-wrenching moment that while she might love him she could never dare trust him. Her husband had far too much power over her already.

She could feel him waiting expectantly and was afraid of arousing his anger. Whenever she scorned him he retaliated with biting sarcasm about her family's financial situation and her own base response to his touch. "Rhys, I—"

Her hoarse whisper was cut short by a series of high-pitched frantic barks as the pup bounded around the water's edge in pursuit of something in the grass. "A snake!" Tory cried, unable to see what kind, terrified it was poisonous. The dog caught it and began biting it and throwing it into the mud on the bank of a smaller pool that spilled off into a natural rock quarry.

"It's a damn garter snake," Rhys muttered in disgust. Nevertheless, he released her and shoved off into the deeper water with a few swift, sure strokes, crossing the pool and wading out near the muddy fracas.

Self-conscious about her nakedness and chilled by the cool breeze, Tory edged the pool and reached the blanket. She snatched a length of towel from the large hamper and wrapped it around herself, then raced toward the battle.

Rhys knelt, holding the little mud-spattered furball by the scruff of the neck while prying its jaws open to release the snake with his other hand.

"Be careful! What if it's poisonous?" she called out, picking her way across the squishy mud near the lower pool.

"It's harmless, played to death anyway, by Fang here," he replied, tossing the dead reptile into the weeds and shoving the muddy dog at her. When she reached out to take him, her towel slid down to lodge around her hips. The pup, mud and all, snuggled against her breasts, liberally smearing her with the goo. Rhys could not resist a smile. "Lucky dog, he knows where to go for his reward."

He stood beside her, completely unconscious of his nakedness, scratching the pup's ears, watching him smudge more mud across her breasts with his thumping tail. Rhys's hands strayed from the dog to her skin, tracing patterns in the mud with his fingertips. Tory felt her nipples hardening at his touch. She reached to rescue the towel, which was sliding precariously low on her hips, only to have the dog leap from her arms, leaving a muddy trail down her belly. "Ooh, you rascal. You've coated me," she scolded as the pup darted about her feet.

"You both need a bath," he said with a chuckle. "Looks like you'll spend most of your time washing muck off him. He seems to have an affinity for the stuff."

She pulled up the towel, then realized how useless her efforts were. "Give him to me. We'll bathe together," she said, then gasped as an inspiration struck her. "Mudpie! That's it," she exclaimed. "I'll call you my very own Mudpie." She hugged the squirming pup like a child with a Christmas toy.

Rhys's lips quirked in a disbelieving grin. "You don't seem the type who spent her childhood making mudpies."

"Maybe I wanted to but wasn't allowed. Boys get to do all sorts of things girls aren't permitted. Sanders used to go swim in the creek with his friends, but I . . ." She stopped, realizing how much she was revealing and how intently he was taking it all in.

"Your brother got too much freedom—you didn't get nearly enough, Tory."

"There you go, attacking my family again. I don't want to discuss them," she said defensively.

He shrugged in acquiescence, accepting the fact that it was too soon for her to shift her loyalty from the Laughtons to him. Changing the subject, he said, "I promised to teach you to swim. I'd wager that Mudpie here can keep his whiskers above water. You game to help me teach your mistress?" he asked the dog in mock earnestness. "It'll mean getting clean again."

Mudpie gave a sharp bark, and Tory and Rhys

both laughed. Accidentally her hand brushed his when they scratched the pup's ears. Their eyes met for an instant, but then she self-consciously turned away, saying, "All right. Let's try swimming. Promise not to let me drown?" she asked the dog as she waded gingerly into the big pool's clean bubbling water.

Rhys followed close behind and whisked her towel away. She still held the dog, but sank up to her neck, kneeling beneath the water for protection from his scorching gaze. "How does one swim?" she asked nervously.

As if in answer, the little dog took off, paddling around her, barking and splashing furiously. She blinked back the droplets of water from her eyes and tried to emulate his four-legged churning. Although it served him easily enough, Tory sank like a rock and came up spluttering to meet amused blue eyes.

"It takes timing and a bit of practice. Let me show you." Rhys glided across the pool with a few clean strokes.

Tory watched the water shine on his rippling shoulders and back. Then, angrily dragging herself away from the carnal fascination he held for her, she tried to use the long, bold arm strokes he used. The attempt was even more disastrous than her doggie paddle. This time she went under head first with feet thrashing above the surface.

Strong familiar hands pulled her up and held her afloat as she coughed and spluttered. "I must have lead in my bones—or Mama was right. Perhaps ladies aren't supposed to swim."

"Here, let's try again." He stretched his arms out on top of the water and instructed her to lie across them. "Now kick with your legs while you cut through the water with your arms—in sync. Feel the rhythm?

Smaller, shorter strokes. Cup your hands slightly. That's the way."

He coaxed and cajoled, drilled and scolded while Mudpie cavorted in circles, splashing them both. Slowly Tory began to propel herself through the water, breathing in and out in time with her arm and leg movements while he instructed her and supported her weight. Then, suddenly, she realized she was moving unassisted. She was actually afloat on her own and Rhys was several yards behind her! She turned, trying to copy the way he was treading water so as to show him her triumph. That was a grave mistake. Once more she sank, but this time she was able to surface unassisted and resume her propulsion through the water. However, such concentrated thrashing was exhausting and her limbs began to feel like leaden weights.

Rhys watched with considerable admiration as she doggedly persevered. For a city girl, gently bred and unused to hard work or exercise, she was amazingly resilient, making up with willpower what she lacked in strength and skill. He swam with effortless grace over to her and swept her arms around his neck,. "Hold on while I ferry you back to shore. I think you've had enough practice for one day. So has your charge." Mudpie sat on the bank, sunning himself contentedly in a small swale of brackish mud.

"Oh, you miserable wretch!" she fumed as she let her husband's strong sure strokes carry them quickly to shallow water. "He'll have the whole buggy ruined before we get home."

"You dress and pack the picnic up and I'll clean him off. Then you can hold on to him until I'm dressed. But I bet we won't make it back to Dragon's Lair before he's into something again."

Tory watched Rhys dunk the little dog and then

towel him clean, grateful her husband was otherwise occupied while she donned her clothes. Nervously she considered his declaration of love—a love he wanted her to confess as well. *I can't love him!* her mind cried in panic. *You can't deny him!* her soul answered in pain. But she held her peace.

"Whatever are you doing, digging in the dirt like a common gardener? Your husband does pay a gardener, doesn't he?" Hedda Laughton stood poised with her parasol stabbing the rich black loam accusingly, looking down on her daughter, who knelt in a flower bed behind the house.

Tory stood up, brushing off her hands and nervously smiling at her mother. "We have several yardmen, but I always wanted to help with the flowers. Mr. Batby, the head gardener, showed me how to plant the tulip bulbs."

Hedda's lips thinned as she listened to her daughter's explanation. Dressed faultlessly in a pale cream-colored walking suit, she had not a hair out of place. Once, Victoria would have mirrored her elegance. "Marriage to that saloon keeper seems to be affecting you adversely, my dear. Don't let his vulgar tendencies influence you to follow his lead, please," she added with a softening smile that did not quite reach her pale eyes. "I heard the most distressing news yesterday about your riding up to that mud slide where all those dreadful men were injured. Alone!"

"You and Rhys agree on something, Mama. He was worried about me, too." *He was afraid I'd be hurt. You're only afraid I'll sully the Laughton name.*

Hedda sniffed disdainfully and ground the sharp point of her parasol in the dirt. "That is doubtless all Rhys Davies and I shall ever agree upon," she said coldly.

Before Tory could reply, a small raggy bundle came barreling across the yard and flew into the soft loose earth of the tulip bed, sending clumps of sand and mud flying everywhere.

Hedda's pristine skirt was liberally splattered with dirt as she poked her parasol furiously toward the yipping pup to fend him away. "What is that . . . that creature?"

"Mama, meet Mudpie. I, er, acquired him while I assisted Dr. Runcie at the mud slide," she said, kneeling once again to scoop up the little tornado.

"You know I don't approve of pets. I thought you shared my sentiments. Look at the mess it's made!"

"Bessie can clean the dress, I'm certain, Mama," Tory soothed. She considered uneasily that not so long ago she would have reacted in a similar fashion. "Let's go inside and I'll have Mrs. Creighton make us some tea."

One slim silvery brow arched as Hedda looked at the muddy little dog.

"Oh, I'll put Mudpie in the kitchen so he can't track over the carpets. Why don't you wait for me in my parlor—by the solarium?"

After depositing the dog in the housekeeper's care, Tory rushed upstairs to repair the damage to her person. She looked a fright. Shrugging, she scrubbed her hands, brushed her hair free of tangles, and then changed into a simple dark green day dress. Her cheeks were rosy from her exertion and from the sun. Six, no, seven, small freckles marred the bridge of her nose. She made a mental note to wear a bonnet tomorrow when she finished the gardening.

Hedda was holding a book in her hands when Tory walked into the parlor. "Shall I pour, Mama?" she asked as she sat down beside the tray on the oval table by the settee.

"Where did this come from?" Hedda shoved the heavy volume of Gibbon's *Decline and Fall of the Roman Empire* into her daughter's face, then dropped it as if it were another muddy pup.

"Rhys gave it to me . . . as a gift. I always loved history—"

"History is full of violence and iniquitous deeds better left unknown by young ladies. I always forbade you to read such things," she chided, sipping her tea experimentally as if checking for poison.

Some imp pricked Tory. "Did you know Mr. Gibbon credits Christianity with the demise of the Roman Empire?"

Hedda almost dropped her cup and saucer. "Really, Victoria! You sound like some bluestocking. Gentlemen do not approve of such ideas coming from a lady."

"But I'm not married to a gentleman, as you've often stated," Tory replied flatly.

"Well, Charles would never—"

"Charles Everett is a miserable coward. He nearly killed an unconscious teamster, Dr. Runcie, and Rhys. He would've killed Mike Manion if my husband hadn't risked his life to climb down the mountain and save him." Tory could still see Charles flinging his pry bar away and running as the side of the mountain evaporated in a rumbling mass. She swallowed a taste of bile and took a deep breath.

Hedda watched her daughter's reaction. "One would think you value that trashy little Irishman more than a lifelong friend. Charles Everett is a fine man, and I'll hear nothing against him."

"Then let's change the subject, since you find my opinion of Charles as distasteful as my reading habits."

"Let's do. I assume you've had no word from your

brother?" At the sad shake of Tory's head, Hedda said, almost accusatorily, "He used to always confide in you, ever since you were children."

"Things have changed, Mama."

"Yes, they certainly have. Charles, who you're so willing to castigate, has initiated a search for him. Very discreetly, you understand. Your father learned Sanders arrived in Denver within a week of leaving Starlight."

"How did he find out?"

"When we were in Denver shopping before the wedding—he went to that horrid Drago person who knows everything that goes on in the city. Sanders arrived but just as quickly vanished. Charles has an agent of some sort trying to trace him." She paused, then added with a meaningful arch of her brow, "Didn't your husband work for Mr. Drago at one time?"

Tory felt the thrust. "Yes, he was a faro dealer in the Bucket of Blood off and on for five years before he came to Starlight. You and Papa knew his past associations when you affianced me to him. Why bring it up now?"

"You're the one casting aspersions on Charles and defending your saloon owner, my dear. Oh, I hear he still goes into that vile place every morning. He could be more discreet." Hedda sniffed in reproof, watching her daughter's reaction.

"He goes there quite openly because he owns the place and has to count the night's profits. Being discreet would imply he was using the services of those women, which he isn't." The minute she said it, Tory could have dropped through the floor in embarrassment. She sounded possessive and even proud of her husband's fidelity. Whatever made her say such a thing—especially considering that she

Shirl Henke

was not at all certain about the nature of Rhys's relationship with Ginger Vogel.

Hedda gave her a pitying look, bringing to both their minds that earlier talk about Rhys's insistence on sharing a bedroom with her. Tory looked down into her teacup, feeling confused and miserable.

"You are young and see life unclearly, Victoria. In time, you'll understand a great many things." Hedda's eyes glowed as she stood up and ran her fingers across the lacquered keys of the mahogany piano standing next to the window. "This house is really splendid," she mused aloud. "Please play for me. Something soothing. It's been a trying day."

Dutifully Tory took a seat at the elegant upright and began to play a Mozart andante

While Tory hid her feelings from her mother, Rhys confessed his to his friend. Laura Everett watched him pace up and down across her parlor floor. "Light someplace before you wear out my new carpet, Rhys," she said dryly as she held out a drink in one plump little hand.

Gratefully he accepted it. "A bit early in the day for it, but welcome. Thank you, Laura." He took a sip and then sat on a delicate cabriole chair, resting his arms on his knees. He hunched over the glass, which he twisted nervously in his hands.

"You won't find the answers to your problems in there, Rhys. Talk to me."

He looked up with a wistful smile. "I don't know where to begin . . . or if I should begin." He paused and considered.

"Afraid you'll shock my sensibilities?" she asked with a gleam of humor.

He sighed and launched into an edited version of their wedding night, describing the bedroom decor and his reaction to it and concluding with his discovery that Tory had seen Flavia in his room in Denver. "So you see, I think she was jealous and ordered those awful furnishings to lash out at me, but I've tried making amends, Laura. I apologized for, er . . . well, for the things I said and the way I made love to her that first night." He felt his face actually heat with embarrassment, but Laura remained solemn and unperturbed, nodding in sympathy. "She said she was sorry for the room and has redecorated it. Ever since, I've tried to be a good husband, Laura. I've bought her jewelry, given her complete control of the staff at Dragon's Lair, suffered through boring teas, even been polite to my mother-in-law."

"No mean feat, that," Laura muttered beneath her breath, drawing a rueful half-laugh from her troubled young friend. "And to reward all your labors, Tory still shuns physical relations with you?" she asked baldly.

Rhys's eyes widened and he nearly dropped the whiskey glass on the carpet.

"Now I've offended *your* sensibilities," she said unrepentantly. "Tory's upbringing was rather inhibiting, even by the usual standards for a well-bred young lady, you see."

"I know about her mother's warped ideas," he said quietly.

"Then you must be patient. You must not take her . . . reluctance as a slight against you, Rhys. It's not that you're a gambler or a foreigner. I'd even discount the rather unorthodox circumstances of the arranged marriage. Tory would be terribly cool with any man at first."

He combed his fingers through his hair and looked at Laura in rueful perplexity. Then sighing, he said, "You've misunderstood what I was trying so awkwardly to say, I'm afraid. Tory isn't cold. She's incredibly . . ." his voice failed him. He polished off the whiskey and said, "She responds very well every time we make love. Then, afterwards, she withdraws—as if she's guilty for feeling what she does with a man who's so beneath her class," he finished angrily.

"She's guilty all right, Rhys, guilty because she loves you and desires you—feelings her mother has taught her to disavow. If you've surmounted the barriers of her maidenly modesty so effectively, then that's the only answer. I always thought in time she'd succumb to your charms. It would seem it's happened even more quickly than I suspected."

"Don't count on it," he said bitterly. "She doesn't love me."

"Have you told her you love her?" Laura asked gently.

"Yes." The admission was wracked from him as if he were confessing a great crime. "I told her— gave her that weapon over me. The lady declined comment on it and changed the subject."

Laura could feel the pain in his voice. "She loves you, Rhys Davies. I've known Tory since she was in pigtails. She's not like her mother. But she needs you to shake her loose from her mother's apron strings. To help convince her of your sincerity, you might consider pandering to a few of her sensibilities." She smiled and said, "She was jealous of Flavia, and Flavia's all the way in Denver. How do you suppose she feels about Ginger, who you see every day?"

He threw up his hands. "You make it sound as if I was—that is, as if we were—oh hell, Laura, Ginger runs the saloon and fancy house for me. It's business, nothing more."

"You're making a lot of money from the Lady Victory, your investments in land and livestock, even your share of Stoddard's bank. Do you really need the Naked Truth any more?"

He sighed. "I thought of selling it ever since our engagement was announced, but Ginger doesn't want to accept it even if I sell to her with years to pay back the loan. And I won't sell her out. She's my friend, Laura."

"If she's really your friend and you explain your reason for quitting the business, don't you think she'll agree to a deal?" Laura searched his face, now open and vulnerable.

He looked dubious, then hopeful. "I suppose I can get Ginger to agree—if I explain why I need to sell. Do you honestly think Tory will care?"

"Isn't it worth the risk, Rhys? Take a gamble and see."

Sanders Laughton looked up and down the street nervously. No one was about except for a few snoring drunks passed out on the saloon's front porch across the street. He pulled his hat down to cover his face, hunched his back against the chilly fall wind, and stepped out into the Cheyenne back street. Only a few more days hiding and then he would be safe. His father's men were after him, he was certain, but he had outsmarted Stoddard, outsmarted them all, especially that wretched Emmet Hauser and his sniveling niece. He had transferred most of the money to an account in San Francisco after eluding the men who had traced him in Denver. Then he'd taken the Denver Pacific train to Cheyenne and laid low for several months. His father and Emmet would expect him to head to San Francisco or even St. Louis right away. Although he was sure Hauser would quick-

Shirl Henke

ly abandon the chase, Stoddard might not. Even
bankrupt, his father was a stubborn man with some
resources still available to him.

Sanders thought of all that money sitting in a San
Francisco bank, just waiting for him. He had only
kept a few thousand here in Cheyenne for pocket
expenses while he evaded pursuers. Once he was
certain no surprises awaited him in California, he
would board a Union Pacific train west and never
set foot in the Rocky Mountains again.

Pulling his coat collar up, he walked quickly out
of the doorway of the cheap boarding house, headed
on foot to a small, quiet saloon. Everyone would
expect a spoiled rich boy to be living high on his
daddy's money, but he'd been far too clever for that.
He congratulated himself for thinking of this hidey
hole and the shabby disguise. His only consolation
during his short-term deprivation had been alcohol.
Each night he went to a different bar and got foxed.
Since it was so cold, with the air hinting of snow,
he decided to make this a short walk.

Rounding the corner, Sanders spied the weather-
beaten old saloon's welcoming sign. Just as he
stepped off the sidewalk between two buildings,
intent on his goal, a pair of strong arms grabbed
him and hauled him into the thickening darkness
of the alley.

"Don't make no fuss 'n' I won't break your neck,"
a terrifyingly familiar voice growled.

"Emmet!" Sanders croaked, going limp in the
giant's bear hug.

"Yeah. Emmet who's been followin' you for weeks.
Found out you'd left Denver 'n' figgered you'd take
the Union Pacific to Cheyenne. Lost you for a piece
after that." He paused and turned the pasty-faced
youth around, shoving him against the splintering

302

wall of the building. "But you 'n' me know your weakness, don't we, Sandy boy? You may of given up on women but you still need your daily dose of phlegm cutter. I just kept checkin' every saloon. Started with them expensive ones 'n' worked my way down. Now I gotcha."

"We can work a deal, Emmet. I have all my father's money—"

Hauser's eyes hardened and he slammed the thin boy against the wall again. "Yeah, you got all that money, 'n' me 'n' Ella, we're livin' like trash. She's too far gone for that doc in Denver now, Sandy boy. I reckon you just might have to marry her." Hauser's smile was cruel, as if he were toying with his prey.

Sanders swallowed his revulsion and worked up his courage. He must keep his head! "If I marry her, who's to say she'll keep you on, Emmet? Let's leave her out of this. You and me can split the money." His hands shook, and his tongue filled his mouth like a piece of wet felt. God he needed a drink! "What do you say we go inside and talk this over, Emmet?"

Hauser shrugged in false good nature. "Couldn't hurt. You got a thirst, Sandy boy? I'll buy us a bottle, but don't go gettin' no ideas. I can outdrink you the best day you ever lived. We'll settle up right enough— or you'll be sorry. Real sorry."

"Kill me and you'll never get your hands on the money," Laughton blurted out. "I've put it in a safe place. Only my signature can release it from that bank."

"Is that so, now? Well, let's have us that drink and see what we can work out."

Chapter Nineteen

All the votes had been counted. The press at the *Plain Speaker* was straining to put out enough copies of the news that Sam Benson had defeated Charles Everett for the Colorado Senate. Gleefully Mike Manion rubbed his hands before picking up a banner-headline front page announcing the news. His clothes, always rumpled and ink-stained, looked even worse than usual. He had spent the night sitting outside the locked room at the courthouse in Lake City while the votes were tallied, then had ridden furiously back to Starlight.

The *Plain Speaker*'s first edition beat the new Republican newspaper, *Herald of Truth*, to the streets by nearly two hours. Virgil was running the second edition as Mike drank silty coffee from a chipped granite mug. Between gulps he chortled. "This is better than the Packer trial. God, what a seller. I thought Sam would beat that ass Everett, but I never dreamed it would be by a landslide."

"I see you're enjoying the triumph—and the newspaper sales. Did you write that piece on horseback to beat the *Herald* to the streets?" Rhys sauntered across the cluttered floor and sat on the edge of Mike's overflowing desk, shoving open his thick wool greatcoat.

"Part as I rode, the rest as Virgil set the type for the headlines. Not a bad job if I do say so. This calls for a celebration! We should have a real gala shindig down at the Naked Truth." He paused, and a sheepish look came over his face. "Er, that might prove awkward, though, what with your in-laws being so thick with Everett. However, I do imagine Laura's glad to see this particular Republican go down to defeat." He paused, then asked casually, "How's Tory taking the news?"

Rhys shrugged. "Charles is the least of my worries with Tory. She's scarcely heartbroken over his political misfortunes. Stoddard is upset though. He backed Everett to the hilt, and this is a real embarrassment with his Denver cronies." He pondered a moment. "I suppose a party would be a good idea. I'll have Ginger whip up some plans and set a date. Think our triumphant senator-elect would come to town for it if you asked him to be guest of honor?"

Mike grinned and looked at Rhys with a measuring eye. "Might you want to talk business with him—railroad business?"

"I might at that. Pass the word along and get back to me." He winked at Manion and pulled his coat closed against the icy blast of cold wind whipping outside the door.

Mike quickly went to work, scribbling a note to

the new senator. The next day, word of Benson's delighted acceptance arrived and the party was on. Every voter in Starlight was invited to the Naked Truth to celebrate the election. Of course, the staunch Republicans and better sorts in town would not accept, but every sheepman, hard-rock miner, cowhand, and store clerk for miles around waited with eager glee to shake the hand of their champion. Even though denied the vote, Ginger's girls were just as eager to join in the hoopla.

If the denizens on the wrong side of the tracks were delirious with joy, the Laughtons were cast into gloom. "Ruined, that's what I am—ruined! That imbecile has wrecked my credibility with the party in Denver. I'll never be able to show my face after the way he let that shirt-sleeve, rabble-rousing lout defeat him!" Stoddard gulped a swallow of coffee and fought the urge to throw the delicate china cup across the room. Crumpled copies of both the *Speaker* and the *Herald* lay on the parlor floor at his feet.

Hedda stood up and walked over to her red-faced husband, placing a cool, placating hand on his arm. "It's scarcely Charles's fault all that saloon riffraff can vote and defeat the better candidate. The worst part is that horrid debacle your son-in-law is throwing to rub salt in our wounds—in his nasty saloon."

Laughton laughed harshly, without mirth. "He's *my* son-in-law, madam, when he does something unacceptable, *your* son-in-law when he pays the bills for all those fancy teas and parties you and Victoria throw."

Hedda's frosty gaze went from Stoddard to their daughter, who sat white-faced and silent across the room. "You might try exerting some civilizing influence on him, Victoria. This is truly mortifying."

"I can try, Mama," she replied, knowing how fruitless such an attempt would be. "But I doubt he'll listen to me. I really stopped by to ask if you had any word about my brother. Last week when I ran into Charles, he mentioned that Sanders had been seen in Denver."

Hedda sat down on the sofa, suddenly deflated. Her worried eyes moved to Stoddard.

He cleared his throat and replied, "No, nothing definite. He seems to have departed Denver, taking all my money. We're left to deal with the wreckage he's wrought. You'd best forget your wastrel brother and concentrate on placating that husband of yours."

Tory felt her stomach knot. "You care more about your money than your own son!" The words burst from her.

Stoddard's face blanched and he, too, sat down, but before he could retort, Hedda said, "That is monstrously untrue, Victoria!"

Regaining his voice, Stoddard added, "You, above everyone, should feel the price this family's paid for Sanders reprehensible actions."

Tory sobbed. "I'm sorry. I didn't mean what I said." She bowed her head, unable to meet the censure in her parents' eyes. Stoddard had aged years in months, losing weight and growing haggard and nervous. Charles's defeat was just one more burden for him to bear.

"Perhaps you might be able to get your husband to cancel this awful saloon gala," Hedda suggested in soothing tones.

Tory looked up and saw the resolution in Hedda's eyes. Odd, as Stoddard grew more frail, his wife seemed to draw greater strength from some inner source. Tory vowed once more to emulate her mother. "Yes, Mama, I'll talk with Rhys. The party is a horrid idea."

"The party is a wonderful idea," Rhys said flatly. "I'm holding it at the saloon in deference to you. God forbid any more Democrats should darken the doorstep of Dragon's Lair, even if one is a state senator."

"This is all Mike's idea, isn't it?" Tory stood in the solarium, looking as fragile as the wildflowers blooming profusely in defiance of the cold mountain climate outdoors.

"Mike suggested it, but I backed him. I want to discuss railroad right-of-ways with the new senator. Be reasonable, Tory. This is business. Or are you worried about poor Charles's offended sensibilities? I saw you engaged in earnest conversation with him the other day." The minute he cast out the jealous accusation, Rhys felt himself redden. Damn, did he have to keep showing her his vulnerability?

Tory's temper rose. She felt suffocated, trapped between the unreasonable demands of her parents and those of her husband. "For your information, I was asking Charles about Sanders. He's been trying to help Papa locate my brother."

"Forget that weakling. Sanders is probably back East living high on the money he stole from all the depositors in his father's bank."

Her eyes filled with tears and she dashed them back furiously, struggling to keep the cool control that Hedda always seemed to have in reserve. "You don't care about me or my family—only your grubby wealth!"

"My grubby wealth provides this modest shelter."

He gestured sarcastically about the solarium and elaborate parlor behind it. "Every Staffordshire teacup, everything you own comes from what I scratched and scrambled to earn, Tory. I'm only sorry I have such a lamentable pedigree to sully the precious Laughton name!" With that he stalked from the room.

Tory watched his long legs carry him through the parlor into the hall where he vanished from sight. She hated him. She loved him—no, she quickly amended that unbearable idea. But the alternative was every bit as awful. If she did not love him, then she lusted after him, as wantonly as any saloon whore. Arguments notwithstanding, with bitter certainly she knew that very night she would melt in his arms in their big warm bed.

"The nerve of that pompous ass! Election fraud! Vote-early-and-often may work in Denver, but not in southwest Colorado. Benson won his seat fair and square." Mike fumed and paced as he read the scathing indictment on the front page of the *Herald*, alleging that the Democrats had paid drunken cowhands and miners to use assumed names and to cast hundreds of illegal ballots.

"Write a rebuttal. You can easily verify the election results and check the voter lists." Rhys shrugged as he sipped his beer in the saloon. Mike had stormed in brandishing the *Herald* moments before while Rhys had been mulling over Tory's angry pleas and his jealous accusations.

"Yes, that I can." Suddenly he snapped his fingers. "When the matter's put to rest once and for all, along with Charlie boy's political aspirations, we can celebrate with a real tail-twister." He began to jot down a list of names—Charles Everett, Willoby Johnson,

Stoddard Laughton, Daniel Rumsfeld, Benjamin Gates—all the local and regional Republican Party's luminaries, pillars of their respective communities.

"Just what the hell are you planning in that deviously clever little Mick mind of yours?" Rhys asked as he scanned the page.

Manion murmured low in his ear, looking about the saloon, careful to let no one else overhear his little "surprise."

Rhys roared and slapped his thigh. "This is just what I need to take my mind off—well, never mind, it's just what I need. I'll even donate the livestock."

Although it was only four in the afternoon, the party in honor of Senator Benson was in full swing at the Naked Truth Saloon. Days were short with the brutal onslaught of winter, and everyone wanted to get a jump on the night's festivities—even if the guest of honor was not scheduled to arrive for another hour.

Signs went up in barber shops, diners, hardware, and dry goods stores: "Closed." Everyone was celebrating the new senator's election. The crowd spilled out of doors in spite of the blustery cold, but luck favored the festivities with clear sunshine. Men bundled in woolly coats shambled down the streets, and teamsters hunched against the wind on their wagons, urging their horses or mules onward with cracking whips. Garishly clad ladies of the line, their bright finery mostly concealed beneath winter coats and boots, joined in the celebration, soliciting customers on the crowded sidewalks. Everyone on Main Street seemed to be on their way to where the whiskey flowed and music played, even a goodly number of nominal Republicans. In the wilds of Colorado, partisanship took a back seat to pleasure.

In the open door of the Naked Truth, Mike and Rhys stood expectantly. "Did you send the notes to his honor the mayor and Charlie boy?" Mike asked, his brown eyes dancing with excitement.

Rhys gave a low chuckle and replied, "My new secretary was rather taken aback when I had him write notes to Starlight's leading citizens, each one signed by the other." He looked across the street. "There's the mayor now."

"He's checking the crowd for Charles. Ah, there. He's rounding the corner in his fancy rig. If only those fool muleskinners aren't too drunk to tell time," he added worriedly.

As if in response to his remark, a rumbling sound reverberated from the far end of the street, growing steadily louder over the raucous noise of the celebration.

"Stampede! It's a herd of Gawd-damn mules," one burly miner bellowed over the din.

Whores squealed in dismay and scurried to the safety of their saloons. Teamsters pulled their wagons quickly to the sides of the wide, muddy street. Stockmen, miners and townsmen leaped up onto the wooden boardwalks as suddenly several dozen mules burst into the melee. Like a hoard of furies, they kicked with sharp hooves and snapped with yellow teeth, braying in protest at the congestion that impeded their dash down Main Street.

Soon catcalls and laughter drowned out the donkey serenade. "Lookee at them asses!"

"Got th' names o' other asses on em!"

"Seems fittin' if'n ya ask me."

"Son-of-a-bitch—Everett's is a lantern-jawed sucker."

"Nothin' as ugly as Johnson's, ner thet scraggedly plug o' ole Senator Gates!"

311

Rhys and Mike stood poker-faced on the sidewalk, surrounded by hooting men and women, all doubled up with laughter as they read the names inscribed with bright red paint on the shaved rumps of the mules. Charles and every one of his political backers had their own namesake.

A group of men had surrounded Everett's carriage and were chortling as they read the roll call, much to the consternation of the defeated candidate. Mayor Johnson glowered at anyone who even looked at him as he shoved his way into a back alley and vanished. Here and there a few staunch allies of the beleaguered leading citizens shouted out their indignation at such vulgarity, but they were drowned out in the press of the crowd.

Rhys watched Charles point an accusing finger at him and Manion. The hapless attorney then turned his rig around and escaped the revelry.

"He knows we're behind it," Rhys said with a grim smile.

"A foregone conclusion where I'm concerned. As to you, well, I guess it's guilt by association," Mike said cheerfully. Then he sobered. "How do you think Tory'll feel about our makin' fools out of Everett and his backers?"

"We didn't make them fools. They already accomplished that all by themselves. Your story yesterday dispelled Charles's absurd election fraud charges once and for all." He paused and considered his wife's reaction. "I guess I'll just have to go home and see if Tory's sense of humor is as good as I'd hoped."

"Ah, here comes the guest of honor." Mike slapped Rhys on the back and urged him to wade into the crowd toward Senator-elect Benson.

By the time he had talked with Sam in his private offices above the Naked Truth and then put in an obligatory appearance at the revelry downstairs, Rhys was ready to go home. It was nearly eleven, and Tory would doubtless have heard about the high jinks with the mules.

At least the discussions with the new senator had gone smoothly, he consoled himself as he pulled Blackjack up in front of Dragon's Lair. He handed the reins to a waiting stable boy and trudged up the wide stone stairs. The foyer was silent as he removed his hat and coat and handed them to the butler, Fuller.

"Mrs. Davies has retired for the evening, sir," the graying little man said stiffly.

Tory had hired Fuller on Hedda's recommendation. Rhys thought he walked like he had a hickory cane jammed up his rump and possessed a disposition to match. He nodded to the butler and began to climb the winding stairs to their bedroom.

Tory was far from retired. Perhaps retreated was a more apt word. She simply did not know how to face her husband, whom she was certain had been a major contributor to the afternoon's debacle. She had taken a long, leisurely bath to calm her nerves and now sat at her dressing table brushing her hair. She debated trying to feign sleep when Rhys arrived, then decided it would be useless. She always betrayed the ploy when he merely touched her and sent her breathing out of control. Of course, it would be hours yet before that drunken debauch was over. Perhaps Rhys would simply pass out across their big bed—or not return home at all. He might stay at the Naked Truth with Ginger Vogel. Oddly enough, that idea bothered her more than the image of him snoring until morning. The brush halted in mid stroke, then resumed slowly as she pondered.

Rhys stood in the doorway silently observing her bedtime toilette. His chest tightened as he considered how much he loved her. *You're a fool, Davies.* Aloud he said quietly, "I didn't expect you'd still be awake, love."

Tory nearly dropped the brush when she heard that familiar whiskey voice. "I couldn't sleep," she said tightly.

"I gather you've heard about the festivities in town?" he said as he began to undress with far more nonchalance than he felt.

"I'm amazed you'd leave all the revelry so early," she replied, finally working up her courage to turn and face him. He had pulled off his boots, rolled up his shirt sleeves, and unfastened the studs, an intimacy that he knew disturbed her.

"I had my talk with the senator. No reason to stay with the drinkers. I have better at home," he said cheerfully as he padded barefoot to the cabinet next to the fireplace. Reaching inside, he extracted a bottle of fine aged brandy and poured it into a snifter.

Tory watched the play of muscles in his broad back as he knelt at the cabinet. She resented how he made her feel and looked away angrily.

"Laura came over this evening," she said. "She quite enjoyed Mike's little joke."

"Did she now? Scarce a surprise in that," he replied noncommittally as he stood up and took a sip of brandy.

"Quit fencing, Rhys. You were in on it with him, weren't you? You've always been jealous of Charles and disdainful of my father—of all the leading men in town."

He appeared to measure her for a moment. "Just what did Laura tell you?"

"She described the fiasco vividly, right down to the red paint on their . . . er, their hindquarters." She flinched.

"Now who's fencing, Tory? Their asses were shaved and decorated with masterful penmanship."

"Yours?" she accused.

He grinned unrepentantly. *What the hell.* "Mike's inscriptions. I merely supplied the mules."

"And the list of names?" She began tapping her foot nervously as he drew closer.

"No. 'Twas that devilish Irishman, I fear. Senator Gates and Mayor Johnson will have a hard time living it down."

"So will my father and a lot of other men in town," she said gravely, then could not resist asking, "Did you send the messages to Charles and the mayor?"

"Guilty." He threw up his hands in mock surrender. "You should've been there, Tory. Old Johnson was madder than a scalded skunk, and Charles couldn't get his fancy rig away from all his well-wishers. He really shouldn't have made those wild accusations to the *Herald* about vote fraud," he said in explanation.

"No, I suppose he shouldn't." She fought the infectious good humor he radiated. Laura's description of the outrageous event was still vivid in her mind. She could see Charles struggling to control his team in the middle of a throng of whooping, howling miners. Her lips fought a smile . . . unsuccessfully. "Charles may have deserved what he got, but not all the others, especially my father."

"How about inviting your parents for dinner at the Georgetown Hotel Friday night—just to make amends? I have an offer to make Stoddard about the railroad. I think he'll be pleased to be included in the deal." He extended his hand, palm open. "Truce?"

"Truce," she responded, then let a small burble of laughter escape before he set down his brandy and pulled her into his arms.

Snowflakes fell like glistening lace, pressing against the glass as Tory stared out the window of the bedroom. "Can we make it to town?" she asked Rhys as he materialized behind her, reflected in the glass.

He peered into the darkness considering, then looked at her troubled expression. "I think the weather will hold. It's only a light dusting. I know how much you want to act as peacemaker between me and your parents." He kissed her neck affectionately.

Tory turned and stepped away from him, still uncomfortable with the way his physical presence affected her. "More like I need to be an umpire. Some of those mules are still running loose on the outskirts of town."

"Not the one with your father's name on it, I trust? I sent one of my hands to look for that one first thing yesterday morning."

She was not mollified. "Papa nearly had apoplexy when Charles came storming into Mama's front parlor that evening. I'm afraid he told the story with considerable embellishment, blaming you for it more than Mike Manion."

"And your dear mother delivered one of her icy set-downs to you while I wasn't home. Did her highness deign to darken our door, or did she summon you to court?" He could see Tory stiffen with anger as she always did when he attacked her family. "I'm sorry, love. I promise to be the soul of charm and humility tonight."

"The charm I'll believe, but no one will ever humble you, Rhys," she retorted.

His face was unreadable, all the teasing laughter gone from his eyes. "Don't bet on that, Tory."

Chapter Twenty

When Rhys and Tory entered the massive grandeur of the Georgetown Hotel, she understood why Colorado millionaires like her husband fancied such places. The stone walls were three feet thick and the architecture resembled that of a Norman castle, complete with bronze statuary and ornate fountains in the courtyards on either side of the ivy-covered main entry. The gleaming floors were made of inlaid strips of walnut alternating with maple, and the wainscotting was covered in heavy velvet. The furniture was massive and dark, everything opulent yet comfortingly masculine, right down to the paintings of Western scenes on the walls and the oversized linen napkins at the dinner tables. The Georgetown proclaimed exclusivity in an unusual blend of European and Western styles.

Hedda and Stoddard were seated in a private

alcove off the dimly lit dining room at the table always reserved for Rhys. When her son-in-law and daughter appeared at the large arched doorway across the room, Hedda watched the subtle interchange between them as they walked around the trout pond in the center of the room and wended their way to the table. The young couple stopped to exchange a few words with several other diners along the way. Hedda's eyes narrowed at the possessive gesture of Rhys's arm circling his wife's waist. Tory, rather than minding the proprietary intimacy, seemed to accept it, laughing and talking with friends as if her husband were as suitable a mate as Charles Everett would have been.

Stoddard, too, had been observing the way Davies treated Tory. He had never seen her so animated and glowing . . . almost as if . . . His mind refused to imagine his daughter in bed with any man, least of all the arrogant, hateful Welshman. He turned his attention to Hedda's cold demeanor. Still niggling at the back of his mind lay the question, *What has he done to Tory that I could never do to her mother?* Instantly appalled, he turned his mind to practical considerations. "Let's not have any of your theatrics tonight, my dear. We're in no financial condition to sneer at the hand that feeds us. He's offering me a chance to invest in the railroad spur into Starlight."

"Money. That's all that ever concerns you, isn't it, Stoddard?" Her voice dripped scorn.

He surveyed her elegant mauve velvet gown and the amethyst necklace at her throat. "Crass as it may be, my beloved, money is what clothes and shelters you in the style to which a lady of good breeding is accustomed."

Hedda did not deign to reply. Tory and her foreigner were approaching the table. Stiff greetings were exchanged as Rhys solicitously seated Victoria, and the owner, Georges Dubay, came over to personally take their orders for dinner.

No one mentioned the fiasco with the mules, or the election. When Hedda turned the conversation to Charles's new thoroughbred race horse, Rhys smiled innocently and asked rhetorically, "I wonder how a man who was destitute only a few months ago was able to afford such an expensive new toy."

"His investments have finally proven successful, I imagine," Stoddard said, wanting to shift the subject away from Tory's ex-fiancé. "About that right-of-way for the railroad . . ."

Tory stifled a yawn as her father and her husband droned on about dull business matters. Her mother's conversation was even less stimulating. Why had she never noticed before that Hedda discussed only frivolous social events, fashions and small-town gossip? *Was I that shallow?* When Tory brought up the work that she and Laura were doing to raise funds for the hospital, her mother was dismayed. When she mentioned volunteering as a nurse, Hedda was shocked. She finally settled for discussing the new winter wardrobe she was having made by Starlight's leading modiste. "The velvets and that brocade were imported all the way from Paris—"

Hedda's eyes followed Tory's as the flow of conversation was abruptly broken. Ginger Vogel, expensively dressed in a green satin gown that amply displayed her cleavage, was being escorted to a table across the room.

"The people they let in here," Hedda hissed in outrage.

"Her escort is a wealthy cattleman. I'm certain the hotel never turns down Lemuel Bolt's money," Stoddard said peevishly.

"I thought Mr. Bolt was a gentleman. Obviously if he's willing to be seen with *her*, my estimation of him was far wide of the mark," Hedda replied maliciously.

Ginger did not wave at Rhys or do anything to indicate that she even knew he and his wife were present in the crowded room. She was the soul of decorum, with her fiery hair coifed smoothly and her makeup subtly applied. Her gown, although cut low, was in stylish good taste.

She looks as good as Flavia, even if she does lack the polished diction, Rhys thought in wry amusement. He enjoyed his in-laws' annoyance for a fleeting moment, then turned to Tory. All pleasure fled. His wife sat rigidly in her chair, her delicate hands clenched tightly about her knife and fork as if she expected to do battle with the trout on her plate. Her face was pale, but her cheeks were flushed. She met his eyes with a stricken, accusing glance, then let her thick gold lashes shield her vulnerability and anger. She methodically cut the fish and vegetables into tiny pieces, then slid them about her plate, unable to eat.

Rhys considered several conversational gambits and rejected them all. Flattery or teasing would not work, nor would pretending that nothing had happened. He had to get Tory away from her parents so that he could talk with her. Then he looked out the leaded-glass window into the courtyard and found his reprieve.

"The snow is really worsening. I had planned for us to stay at the hotel if it got too bad."

"I'd really prefer to go home," Tory interjected with quiet resolution.

"I thought you would, love," he replied softly. He watched Hedda's eyes narrow as he touched Tory's hand in a fleeting caress. Ignoring his mother-in-law, he turned to Stoddard. "We've gone over the basics on the railroad deal. I'll send my secretary to the bank tomorrow with some papers for you to look over. Meanwhile, I think we'd be wise to forgo after-dinner coffee and head home."

"Our house is closer, Victoria," Hedda suggested maternally, with a frosty dare in her eyes for Rhys.

"I thank you for the kind offer, but my wife and I prefer the accommodations at Dragon's Lair," Rhys said brusquely as he pulled back Tory's chair. His hand on her elbow was firm and protective.

Tory positively hated herself for betraying her emotions, even though she was uncertain about what they were—jealousy? hurt? anger? humiliation? She focused on her mother's cold, hostile face. "Mama, I'll see you Sunday at Smithtons'."

Hedda gave her daughter a glance of pitying solicitude. "I should hope you'll be in church first." She paused and turned to Rhys with venom in her eyes. "That is, if your husband can escort you so early in the day. I understand his mornings are usually occupied elsewhere."

"I'll see you in church, Hedda," Rhys replied levelly. His lips smiled, but his eyes did not.

As they prepared to face the snow storm outside, Rhys murmured in her ear, "She does it to bait you, love."

"Which 'she' are you referring to—my mother or your business associate?" Tory asked, proud of the steadiness in her voice.

"You sound like a jealous wife, Tory. I like that—even if you have no cause." He glanced around the empty cloakroom and pulled her into his arms for a swift embrace.

She shoved against his thick topcoat with her

palms. "I am not jealous, merely affronted by that . . . that woman's presence."

"So am I, but what can I do? She's my mother-in-law," he said laughingly, glad her painful embarrassment had shifted to jealous anger. He watched her eyes shoot blue-green sparks. This was the Tory he could spar with.

Tory pulled the ermine hood of her coat up about her face, careless of her elaborate coiffure, and stalked toward the cloak-room door. "You are insufferable," she said between pinched lips. "A good thing you refused Mama's offer of shelter for the night!"

He snorted. "A night she'd have us spend at opposite ends of the hall, or I miss my guess. It may be cold outside, Tory, love, but I have very warm plans for us tonight." As the doorman swung open the heavy front door, Rhys scooped her into his arms and braved the icy blast of wet snow.

"Are you sure we can make it up to Dragon's Lair?" The wind blew her words away as she yelled them in Rhys's ear.

Their carriage was enclosed, back and sides, and they had lap robes of thick wolf pelts to bundle in, but the snow quickly whitened the dark gray fur. Big fat flakes stuck to their eyelashes and burned their cheeks. Tory huddled against Rhys as he slapped the reins and sent the team into a brisk trot.

The carriage moved easily through the frozen streets of Starlight. But once they were clear of town, heading up the winding open road to Dragon's Lair, the snow drifts began to deepen. Fixing his attention on the rutted road, Rhys slowed the horses, careful not to let the carriage wheels bounce from the only moorings they had.

Every few minutes the wind would die down,

allowing him to see the winking lights up the hillside, beckoning them to the warmth and safety of home.

"Hold on, love. Not to worry. We're almost—" A sharp, roaring wind cut off his words as a blast of snow blanketed the carriage, throwing it off the rutted trail. It teetered for a moment, then righted itself. As suddenly as it had risen, the wind stopped and with it the lashing snow. Although the lights of Dragon's Lair were only a few hundred yards away, the buggy could not reach its destination, for the sudden squall had left it buried to the wheel tops in a drift. The horses were also belly deep in snow, restively pulling against Rhys's steadying hold on the reins.

"We can't wait this out. I'm going to free Bruno and we'll ride him up the hill, then send some men down for Brady."

Tory watched fearfully as he climbed down and sank to the waist in the drift. "Is the snow this deep from here all the way home?" she asked worriedly.

"No. It's only blown across a few yards of road. See the rocks over there?" He pointed to several rounded boulders visible in the moonlight. The storm was over, leaving ridges of wind-driven snow piled in erratic patterns across the valley, as if some giant with a broom had run amok, sweeping randomly through the whiteness.

She sat with her teeth chattering, burrowed beneath the pelts while he unhitched the larger and calmer of the two geldings and struggled to lead the big beast clear of the drift. Then he retraced his path through the deep snow to his wife and reached up to lift her from the carriage.

"You'll have to leave the robe behind, Tory. It's too heavy to carry. We'll be home quick enough now."

Reluctantly she dropped the snow-covered pelts. "The air's so cold it hurts to breathe," she gasped as she went eagerly into his arms.

"Hang on just a bit longer," he said soothingly.

The snow clung to her full skirts and cloak. Tory reached out to brush it away, helping Rhys traverse the narrow pathway to where Bruno waited patiently. "Now, let's get the hell up this trail before another squall blots out that moon!" He grunted as he heaved her, snow-laden skirts and all, onto the horse. "Hang on," he said as she clutched Bruno's mane with mittened hands. He swung up behind her, straddling the big brute's bare back. Steadying Tory's precarious balance, he enveloped her in his arms as he kicked the horse into a slow walk.

Feeling her shivering, he murmured, "I know it may offend your ladylike sensibilities to undress a man, Tory, but if you unbutton my coat and pull it around you, we'll both be warmer."

She yanked at the big buttons clumsily with her fur mittens, then snuggled against his chest like a kitten. He smiled and rubbed his chin against the soft ermine of her hood.

When they rode up, Fuller had the front door wide open and was issuing curt commands to the maids, who scurried to obey.

"Send Lee down to fetch a couple of stable hands. Our carriage is at the foot of the hill with the other horse." Rhys dismounted stiffly and lifted Tory into his arms.

When they reached the foyer, he set her on her feet and helped her pull off her cloak and mittens, then shrugged off his coat and handed the sodden mess to the patient butler.

"I've ordered warming bricks for your bed, sir. Would you care for anything else?" Fuller inquired politely as Rhys carried his shivering wife toward the stairs.

"No, thank you, Fuller—oh, you might send up a second brandy snifter. And have Rufus build a big fire in the fireplace."

"The fire is already laid and set, sir. I saw to it when I heard you arriving. I'll fetch the glass." He headed directly to the crystal pantry.

"Punctilious sort of chap, but he does grow on you," Rhys said philosophically.

"T-two glasses?" Tory echoed his orders through chattering teeth. "I n-never d-drink s-strong s-spir-its."

"You never unbuttoned my clothes before tonight either," he replied cheerfully. "I'm nearly frozen stiff, and so are you." He paused midway up the stairs to their bedroom, then said with a devilish leer, "We'll have to help each other out of these wet clothes, lest we take a chill."

She gave him a suspicious look. "I have a maid to help me," she murmured primly.

"Well, I don't. Unless you want May or Zenia to undress me, I'd say you have your work cut out for you, love. It'll restore your circulation if you exercise a bit," he teased.

She muttered something indistinct between chattering teeth as he opened the bedroom door. A blazing fire crackled on the hearth, casting a golden glow about the big room. He sat her down on the edge of the bed and began to pull off her slippers.

"You're blue with cold," he said, furious with himself for endangering her. He peeled off her silk stockings and chaffed her slim little feet with his hands. "Tory, love, I'm so sorry. You could've been killed out there in the snow. All because of my—"

A knock sounded, interrupting his hoarse apology. He rose and strode quickly to the door. When he opened it, Fuller stood there with the snifter. Tory felt the warmth of the room begin to thaw her numb hands and feet until they tingled painfully. She watched Rhys set the brandy bottle and glasses on a low fireside table. His face, usually so unreadable unless he was teasing, looked incredibly vulnerable. He felt guilty for bringing her home in the storm. "I'm all right, Rhys," she said softly as he poured brandy into the snifters. "You had the hard task. I only had to hang on to you."

He turned to her, his eyes anguished. "I risked your life, Tory! I'm your husband. It's my job to protect you, not put your life in danger because of my stubborn pride. We should have stayed in town."

"Even if it meant sleeping in rooms at opposite ends of the hall?" She was the one teasing now. What had come over her, to say something so brazen? One look at his face gave her the answer. The old familiar devilish glint returned to his eyes and a seductive smile slashed across his mobile lips.

He brought the brandy glasses to the bed and handed her one. "Even rooms at the opposite ends of your mother's big house." He paused and considered a moment. "Or, do you suppose she'd have let me in at all? I might have had to spend the night in the stable." Now he was teasing. "Drink your brandy. It'll warm you."

She held the glass gingerly, looking down at the pretty amber liquid that looked like molten lava. She took a whiff of the bouquet and coughed. It burned her nose as if it *were* molten lava! "I can't drink this, Rhys."

"Yes, you can. It'll be good for you. Trust me, love." His voice soothed her as he took a swallow from his glass, then instructed, "Don't breathe in as you drink. That's what makes you cough. Exhale." He tipped the glass up, guiding her hands until she did as he instructed and took a tiny swallow.

Her eyes widened in surprise. It left a fiery trail down her throat and the heat seemed to curl in her stomach. "It only burns for a moment," she said as he smiled.

"Another sip," he coaxed. When she warily complied, he resumed undressing her. "Your skirts are soaked. Stand up. There's a love." He assisted her in rising from the bed and turning around, then expertly unfastened the buttons on her gown and peeled it over her shoulders. Wordlessly he took her glass and placed it on the bedside table next to his, then slid the gown from her arms. Before she realized it, the rustling peach brocade dress and petticoats were pooled about her feet. Rhys handed her the brandy glass with an admonition to sip some more. He drank from his snifter. She emulated his action. Each swallow brought more tingling warmth and a strange, heady lethargy.

When he brushed hot wet kisses across her shoulders as he unfastened the last of her sheer underclothes, she leaned into his embrace, clutching the nearly empty snifter in nerveless fingers. His fingertips brushed her arms, then traveled the curve of her hips to her tiny waist and up to the swells of her breasts. When he cupped one in each hand and pulled her bare back against his chest, she involuntarily arched the tingling hardened nipples into his palms and rubbed herself against his body like a purring cat. She almost dropped the glass.

Rhys murmured soft, indistinct love words as he eased the silk pantalets over her hips. When the undergarment caught about her ankles, he scooped her up in his arms. She kicked the pantalets carelessly onto the bed before he carried her to the big thick rug in front of the crackling fireplace. Setting her down, he reached for the brandy bottle and refilled her glass, then sipped from the very spot on the rim where her lips had touched.

Tory found herself rimming her lips with her tongue as she watched him perform the small intimacy with her glass. "Now you drink," he said hoarsely, handing her the glass.

She turned it carefully to where his lips had touched it, took a sip, then another. All the while her eyes locked with his. Mesmerized as she was by the brandy and the leaping flames, Tory scarcely realized that she was standing naked before Rhys, who was fully clothed. She felt a heady pleasure in his bold admiration of her sleek little body, with its pale silky skin glowing in the firelight.

He broke the spell when he took the glass from her and commanded, "Now it's your turn, love. Finish the job you started out in the storm. I'm fearful hot with all these clothes on."

A small smile curved her lips. "I suspect you'll be hotter when you're undressed."

He laughed softly, pleased beyond words with her boldness even though he knew it was the liquor that loosened her inhibitions. "Undress me, Tory."

Slowly, like a sleepwalker, she stepped closer and began by untying his cravat, then unfastened his shirt studs and cuff links. When she peeled the fine white silk over his shoulders, his body gleamed like bronze in the light from the leaping fire. She put her hands on his chest and felt the crisp mat of hair tickle her fingertips. His heart pounded, and his skin was as scorching as the flames.

Rhys resisted the urge to embrace her and sink to

the soft, warm carpet. With one hand he brushed and teased her pert upthrust little breasts. Then, moistening his tongue with a sip of brandy, he softly laved each hardened nipple until she moaned and sank her fingers into his hair. "You taste better than brandy," he whispered against her racing heart.

Slowly he stopped the caresses and stood back, waiting to see if she would take the next logical step. His trousers were growing increasingly uncomfortable. He moved his hips suggestively and her eyes caught and fastened on the unmistakable bulge at his fly. Her fingers were trembling when she reached out to unbutton the pants. "For courage," he said, offering her another sip from the glass he was holding.

Tory swallowed it and resumed her task. When she had the trousers unbuttoned, they, alas, did not fall in a simple whoosh as her petticoats had. Encasing his long, muscular legs tightly, they had to be peeled down. She began to work them lower, taking his underwear along with them. She would have to kneel to complete the task. As she did so, she looked down in dismay. "Boots," she croaked inanely.

"They're soaked and cold, too," he replied with a faint hint of amusement. He had to concentrate on something else, lest he slip over the brink.

"Lesh figger"—she paused to correct her strangely errant tongue, "Let's figure this out," she articulated carefully. "If you lie down, I can pull them off."

It was unclear to Rhys if she meant the boots or the trousers, but in any case he was more than willing to oblige. He stretched out on his back and raised one leg. Tory studied it a moment, then grabbed the boot and gave a hard yank. It slid free, catapulting her onto her rump in the center of the fluffy rug. A look of surprise crossed her face. He stifled a chuckle and watched her rise to her knees and rub her sleek little posterior.

Helpfully he raised the other foot. This time she took hold of the boot with considerably more care. A tug of war ensued as she twisted on the boot as he pulled his leg back. Tory giggled, Rhys chuckled. Finally the boot popped off, and once more she landed on her backside. While she held the tooled leather boot in her hand, a bemused expression on her face, he quickly slid the offending trousers the rest of the way down and peeled off his hose. With lightning speed he tossed the pile of clothing onto a chair and knelt in front of her, taking the boot from her hands and sending it after its mate.

Tory knelt up, facing him, her eyes wide. He was so splendidly beautiful in the dancing light—bronzed and muscular, so dark next to her pale, soft skin. Her hand stretched out to cover his, and he raised it to his lips in a bone-melting kiss.

"Warm now?" he asked.

"Mmm," she murmured dreamily as her arms curled around his neck. She began to kiss him, letting her lips roam over his mouth, up his cheek to his eyes, then over to his temple. She explored every strong, angular plane of that arrestingly handsome face as she molded her slim curves against his hard, hairy length.

Rhys let her explore, holding his maddening desire in check. A primitive thrill coursed through him as she touched and tasted, finally centering her lips firmly against his. He opened to her questing tongue and met it in a brandy-flavored kiss that nearly singed his eyebrows. Slowly he sank down with Tory clinging to him, deep in the kiss, until he was lying on his back with her atop him.

The heat from the flames licked at her skin, but the fire on the hearth was as nothing compared to the inferno of her husband's body beneath hers. She could feel his hard shaft pressing insistently between her thighs. Experimentally, by instinct, she squeezed them tightly. He rewarded her with a sharp gasp of pleasure. It gave her a fierce sense of power. She wriggled and he moaned. His hands played up and down her back, then his fingers dug into her buttocks as she once again centered her mouth on his for a languorous kiss.

Their tongues tasted, twined, danced. Tory held tightly to him as he rolled across the big rug nearer the blazing hearth. His hand roamed down her side as her backside heated in the golden glow of the flames. He gently disengaged and pushed her onto her back. Her hair splayed in tangled, gilded glory above her head. Her arms fell to her sides and she lay open to him, taut, hungry, waiting. He let his hand trail over her breasts, then down her concave belly to the pale curls below. He knelt up and reached for the brandy glass on the low table, then took a sip and replaced it. When he lay beside her again, he kissed her breasts, then let his tongue trace exquisite patterns over her nipples. The delicate instrument of pleasure traveled lower to her navel, ringing it, then dipping in until she arched in abandon. But when his mouth brushed lower to nuzzle the curls where his hand had just rested, she gasped, the dreamy trance broken.

"No, you can't!" she whispered in amazement.

"Yes, I can," he murmured as one hand held her slim hip and the other parted her legs. She attempted to scissor them closed, but he was too quick for her. He rolled between them and stretched her silky thighs wide apart.

She watched his mouth descend with growing alarm, yet she did nothing more to stop his lips from reaching their target. Would the brandy burn?

Chapter Twenty-one

The jolt of raw pleasure was like nothing Tory had ever imagined. His mouth worked blistering, fiery magic on her. She lay immobilized as her senses reeled out of time and space until she became a mindless creature whose pure animal instincts controlled every fiber of her being.

Rhys could sense her motionless body as he tasted of her sweetness. For an instant he regretted his actions. Was she frozen in shock? Then she let out a gasp of unmistakable pleasure. Her legs remained splayed wide. He persevered slowly, gently. As if in reward for that perseverance, her fingers curled in his hair and dug into his scalp, pulling him closer, urging him onward.

With everyone else Victoria was a lady. But with him, alone like this, she was learning to be a woman. His blood raced with triumph as he felt her begin to arch her hips. Her head thrashed from side to side and she moaned as she peaked. He could taste her honeyed sweetness, feel the convulsive rippling pleasure of her climax, and it gave him joy. Although turgid and aching with unfulfilled need, he raised his head and simply gazed at her satiated body, watching the fire's licking dance reflect on her satiny skin, now glazed with a fine sheen of perspiration. Golden. She was his golden, perfect dream. His love. His life.

As the haze of ecstasy began to fade, Tory opened her eyes slowly and locked gazes with Rhys. She was benumbed by this strange new experience, so wickedly, wonderfully different than what they had shared before. *I must be depraved.* The fleeting thought was obliterated as he slid up and covered her. The heat of his body was scorching and the brush of his crisp chest hair on her damp silky skin set off another barrage of sensations, not new as that other had been, but nonetheless intensely pleasurable.

"Hold me, Victory," he whispered as he kissed her throat and tangled his hands in her hair, wrapping it about his fists and inhaling its violet fragrance.

Her arms closed about him and she let out a low, familiar moan as he slid into her waiting warmth. She felt him shudder and hold still for a moment, buried deep inside her. Her legs wrapped snugly about his narrow hips, urging him on.

Rhys struggled to regain control of the wild desire to spill his seed in her. He could feel the wanting renewed in her. Slowly, carefully he began to stroke. Tory caught his rhythm and pulled his head to hers for a fierce hungry kiss.

She could taste herself as he ground his mouth over hers. She matched his desperation with her own, bucking and writhing, urging him on, harder, faster. When his shaft swelled and plunged one last deep desperate time, she felt him go rigid with the surge of his release, pulling her over the edge with him. They swirled in pure exploding sensation, blind to everything but the incredible intimacy they were experiencing.

Rhys collapsed on her and she clung to him. By the time he regained his breath enough to roll over and nestle her against his side, she was asleep. Heavy-lidded with satiation, his eyes slowly closed and he drifted into the warm cocoon of sleep, whispering, "Victory."

Tory awakened to joyous barks. Mudpie raced across the wide bedroom floor to bathe her face with wet slurping licks. The little dog danced about her head, continuing his sharp, high yipping. She sat up and then immediately flopped back down, hitting her head on the floor. Her head! It must have swollen to ten times its normal size to accommodate the pounding pain inside. Tory held her hands over her ears to soften Mudpie's barking and to keep her fragile skull from shattering. As the raggedy pup pranced about, she shoved him off. "Go away! Ooh, I'm sick. Take pity on me."

Rhys stood in the doorway, admiring the view of his tousled, naked wife. Even hung over she was exquisite! The quilt he had tossed over her in the wee hours of the morning was being systematically pulled away by Mudpie's deviltry. The little mutt had one corner of the cover in his sharp little teeth and was dragging it off her, revealing those delectable breasts.

Shivering as the cold air hit her sleep-warmed body, Tory sat up and hugged the quilt about her, staring with growing horror at the room. Around her on every side lay Rhys's boots, her slippers, petticoats, brocade gown, his silk shirt and trousers. Clothing was strewn everywhere, in piles on the floor, draped across chairs and flung on bedposts—and she lay naked on the hearth clutching a quilt for dear life, feeling as if she had been poleaxed.

"This might help your headache, love," Rhys said as he strolled toward her huddled figure, so small and forlorn. Then she looked up at his knowing grin.

Everything from the past night's bacchanal focused in her mind! Her cheeks crimsoned and her eyes squeezed shut, then opened wide with mortification and righteous anger. "You did this," she croaked, then coughed.

Mudpie did not relent in his attack on the quilt. What a delightful new game. She turned to the dog, unable to meet Rhys's smirk as he sat down beside her, depositing a tray of coffee and hot rolls on the rug. She scooped up the scampering mutt and held him tightly just to keep him from barking and jarring her aching head any further.

Rhys poured the coffee from a big china pot into a dainty cup and offered it to her as casually as if they were seated in the dining room of the Georgetown. "Drink this and you'll feel better."

"I'll never feel better," she murmured, her face buried in Mudpie's thick fur. "Sit still, you mangy mutt, or I'll skin you and make you into gloves! Ooh." It hurt to talk. Her tongue had a dry, fetid coating, as if she had been chewing mouthfuls of the dog's fur. Her stomach was not faring much better as Mudpie rooted and wriggled, trying again to kiss her good morning.

Rhys set the cup down, took the bundle of writhing fur patiently from her, and then again offered her the coffee. "I'll fend him off while you recover."

Still not meeting his eyes, she took the cup and sipped. Heaven! She blew on the steaming liquid and then slowly drained the cup with a series of steady swallows. When she reached for the pot to pour herself seconds, the quilt slipped to her waist. She bit her lip in vexation as he chuckled, watching her struggle to pull it back over her breasts. "Don't you dare laugh at me," she whispered fiercely, despising her fiery blush. "You got me drunk last night. This— all this—" she waved her arm about the dishabille of the room, "was your doing."

"I'm not laughing about last night, love. It was wonderful—at least what went on here was." He eyed the strewn clothes with fond memory. "I'm sorry about setting out in the storm. I placed you in danger with my poor judgment. That was a terrible mistake."

"This was all a terrible mistake," she whispered, remembering the wanton abandon with which she had undressed him. And worse, far worse than that, she remembered what he had done to her afterward, right here on the floor. She had allowed him to do it—no, she had pulled him closer, urging him to perform an . . . an unnatural act! Tory squeezed her eyes closed against the hot, stinging tears. Shame coursed through her.

Rhys scooped the dog up and quickly deposited him in the hallway with a roll to appease him. Then he closed the door and returned to the small figure huddled on the rug. Kneeling beside her, he took her in his arms as she struggled to rise, holding the quilt wrapped around her. She tried to push him away, but his greater strength won out and she knelt limply in his embrace. "What we did—what I did last night wasn't terrible, Tory. I made love to you and gave you pleasure. That's what husbands are supposed to do to their wives."

"And I suppose that . . . doing it that way gave you pleasure, too?" she choked out.

"As a matter of fact, it did. Very much," he replied quietly. He could feel her stiffen.

"You enjoy debasing me, playing with me as if I were some saloon whore!"

"That's not true, Tory. You're lying to yourself. Your inhibitions were loosened by the brandy, but you loved what we did every bit as much as I."

"You got me drunk or I'd never have . . . I'd never let you . . ." She sobbed, then hated her show of weakness. She pounded on his chest in frustration. "I am not your whore. I won't be treated like Ginger Vogel."

He jerked her chin up roughly so her tear-glistened eyes met his. "You're really naïve, Tory, if you think a man does what I did last night to a whore."

She shook her head and put her hands over her ears in angry denial. "I don't care! I don't want to know about you and your women!"

Rhys sighed. He supposed he should not have made love to her that way so soon. But dammit, she was his wife. "You're my woman, Victory—my only woman."

She hiccuped and sniffled, hating the unladylike way she was blubbering. "Your woman, indeed! Your 'business partner' humiliated me in public last night in front of my parents!" If only her head would cease its pounding so she could think before she blurted out what she did not intend to reveal.

"So we're back to Ginger, are we now? You are jealous, Tory, whether or not you'll admit it. Ginger was at the Georgetown with another man. My dealings with her are *only* business."

"And we all know what her business is, don't we?" she asked coldly. "My head is splitting, my body is sore, and I'm in desperate need of a bath. Would you be so kind as to postpone this discussion? I'm at a distinct disadvantage right now." She shoved him away and this time he released her.

Rhys let her gather the quilt and the remnants of her hurt pride about herself. He watched as she stood up and walked toward her dressing closet to grab a robe.

"I'll tell the maid to run you a hot tub before I leave for town," he said matter-of-factly. As he walked toward the door, he stepped over the pile of petticoats and brushed against one of his boots. He could not resist adding, "While you wait for her, you might want to pick up this evidence."

Tory sucked in her breath in embarrassment. That very thought had crossed her mind.

Rhys watched Rufus clean a wide path through the fluffy white snow, lifting the big shovelfuls as effortlessly as swinging a dust mop. The morning was brilliantly clear. The winds had died down and the air was brisk and dry. He waited patiently at the stable door while Lee saddled Blackjack and led the big stallion to him.

"Snow's drifted deep down the road. You sure you'll be all right, Mr. Davies?" the boy asked anxiously.

Preoccupied, Rhys nodded. "Blackjack can get through. I'll be back before dark. Watch you don't get lost in a drift yourself," he admonished the round-faced little Chinese boy, then rode off.

The black was used to heavy snow and churned through it with ease, allowing his master to mull over his problems. "I rushed my fences with Tory last night. Damn fool thing to do, especially after that run-in with Ginger at the restaurant," he muttered to himself and the horse.

When he passed the deep drift where the carriage had been stuck, he swore at his own stupidity. The men had to dig the buggy out. He and Tory were lucky the snow had stopped when it did or they could've frozen to death a half mile from home.

He rounded a curve in the road where a sharp outcropping of rock jutted upward and the stallion snorted and shied. "Easy boy, easy." He leaned forward to croon to the animal just as a bullet whistled past his head, missing him by inches. As the bushwhacker in the rocks squeezed off another shot, Rhys rolled off the horse and into a snowbank by the roadside. He had grabbed his rifle from its saddle scabbard and now clutched it tightly as he dodged several more bullets. Floundering through the snow, he finally found cover behind a boulder and crouched, rifle ready, scanning the hogback from where the shots had come.

Luck was with him, for the brilliant morning sun was at his back. His attacker would have to squint into it as well as face the blinding whiteness of the snow that surrounded Rhys everywhere. If the man appeared, Rhys would be able to see him clearly, but the would-be assassin was probably climbing down the back side of the hogback to make good his escape.

Rhys waited a moment, then heard the crunch of loose rocks. The hunted became the hunter as Rhys jumped up and began to run through the foot-deep powder. He headed toward the jutting ridge of rocks and scrambled up it as his adversary was sliding down the opposite side.

341

Ricky Barlow heard the deadly sound of the Winchester being levered on the ridge above him. He had almost made it to his horse when he slipped in loose gravel, ending his flight. Davies would kill him! He whirled and fired off another round at the man hazily silhouetted on the top of the hill. The sun blinded him and he missed.

Rhys knelt and took swift aim. The impact of the slug knocked the card cheat into the snow at the foot of the hogback. His horse bolted at the loud report, but stopped a few feet away. All was silent as Rhys climbed down the hill to inspect Barlow's body.

"You damn fool. A hell of a price to pay for revenge just because I caught you dealing from the bottom of the deck," he muttered, thinking that he owed Blackjack an extra ration of oats for saving his life. If the stallion hadn't shied, Rhys would be the one lying dead in the snow.

"Who'd have thought Barlow was that good a shot?" Rhys asked rhetorically. The near brush with death was beginning to sink in and he felt in need of a drink. "Well, at least I'm headed for the right place."

Although it was early in the day for the madam of a bordello to be up and about, Ginger Vogel descended the stairs of the Naked Truth Saloon. Her hair was smoothly coifed and she wore a brown velvet gown with rich ivory lace at the cuffs and neckline. On anyone with less than her voluptuous endowments, the dress would have been almost demure. The colors flattered her fiery tresses, but the rounded neckline was cut low, revealing the milky swells of breast.

As she ran her fingers lightly over her pompadour, Ben the bartender laughed and said, "He'll think ya look great, Miz Ginger."

Her bright green eyes flashed over to Ben, giving him a quelling look. "This is strictly business."

Several low chuckles emanated from around the room, but no one met her steely glare. Rhys stood in the doorway dusting snow from his coat. He had overheard Ben's remark and the reaction to it. Ginger met his eyes as he tossed his heavy coat effortlessly over a chair. He shoved the flat-crowned black hat back on his head and nodded to various customers as he strolled casually toward Ginger, who stood midway down the stairs. "Send up a pot of coffee and tell Kelly not to boil hell out of it," Rhys instructed Ben as he passed by.

Ginger turned and headed back upstairs as Rhys followed her. When a voice from the front table called out, "Don't talk bizness too long, now," several men snickered in their beer.

Rhys froze with his hand on the heavy walnut newel post, then turned and directed a tight, chilly smile to a man seated at the table. "You have something you want to say to me, Asa?"

The burly miner watched the gambler shove his expensively tailored frock coat away from the holster on his hip. Now Davies's smile was beatific. "I already had to shoot one man this morning. I wouldn't want to have to shoot another—at least not before I've had my breakfast."

"I got nothin' ta say, Rhys, honest. Jist a mistake."

"Don't make it again." Davies turned and strode up the stairs after Ginger, following her into the office that fronted the apartment in which he had formerly resided.

Ginger's eyes were filled with concern. "You mean that about shootin' a man?"

"Ricky Barlow decided he was pissed because he lost his swell job with Emmet Hauser, I suppose. He

343

tried to ambush me. I had to kill him. Forget Barlow.
The marshal's handling that mess. We need to talk
about other things." He closed the door and sent his
hat flying to land on a big leather sofa. "You see that
our arrangement with this place can't continue, don't
you?"

She shrugged helplessly. "Don't pay Asa Brighton
no mind, Rhys. He's drunker 'n a ox."

"You want me to shoot him and put him out of
his misery, then?" he asked grimly.

"He didn't mean nothin' by what he said. Neither
did Ben. You're God-almighty touchy these days.
What's goin' on . . . or not goin' on with you 'n' that
wife of yours?"

"Leave Victoria out of this," he said coldly. "I can't
come here every morning—or every other—or any
time to collect receipts without half the town speculating about what we're doing up here all alone."

"If it wasn't for her you wouldn't give a damn!
Everything you do is because of her. No way to leave
her out of anythin', but I guess I ain't got the right to
even speak her name, bein' as I'm just saloon trash
'n' she's a lady."

"You mean I'm saloon trash, too. Not 'her kind,'"
he said wearily, rubbing his eyelids with his fingertips.

"That ain't so 'n' you know it! You married into
the high 'n' mighty Laughton family. I seen your
tony in-laws, all actin' like I was poison last night."
She looked hurt and bewildered for a minute, then
stared at him defiantly and said, "Ain't I even got the
right to have Lon take me out for a rest from Kelly's
Gawd-awful cookin'?"

He smiled apologetically and walked over to where
she stood in the center of the large office, hugging
herself like a child expecting chastisement for some

misbehavior. He took her cold hands, peeling them from her arms, and pulled her over to sit beside him on the sofa. "Ginger, I don't want to hurt you . . . at least not any more than I already have, but I have to end our business relationship. You deserve to own the saloon as well as the bordello. The bank will work out the terms for you to repay a loan over several years. Then it's yours, free and clear. No charity involved."

"And you're out of the saloon business for good?" Her smile wobbled.

"Yeah, for good. There's plenty for me to do with my other businesses. I have to go straight, Ginger," he said earnestly. He waited for her reaction.

She studied his face, assessing what he had said and what he had not. "You got it bad, Rhys, 'n' that's a fact. At first I told myself it was just the idea of her havin' a fancy pedigree 'n' your wantin' to show her off, but then after a while I quit lyin' to myself. I seen the way you look at her."

Rhys sighed. "The gossip in a little town like this, it hurts a woman like Tory. She has pride and more insecurity than I ever guessed."

Ginger snorted. "She's jealous! And her without a reason. You'd pull your boots off 'n' walk over hot coals for her."

"I'll sell the Naked Truth to someone else—for a loss if I have to. Please, I want you to have it, Ginger."

Her eyes glazed over with tears, but she blinked them back. "I reckon you got yourself a deal, Rhys. And a clean break from your old life. Send them papers by as soon as you want. I'll sign 'em."

"Thank you, Ginger," he replied gravely. Then he stood and looked down at her. "Let's count last night's take. Did the storm hurt business too bad?"

"Ha! All them randy miners wanted was to thaw out their wangs with my girls, then bet what money they had left on a turn of cards."

She walked over to the desk and opened the ledger while he unlocked the heavy iron safe in the corner. She listened to the tumblers click and fall in place in the silent room, watching those deft, familiar hands on the dial.

The eight-inch-thick iron door opened with a creak, and Rhys extracted several sacks filled with hard coin and currency. Within a half hour they had tallied the money. He took the sacks and placed them in a leather satchel sitting on the desk. "I'll send this back with Rufus tonight. Starting tomorrow, Grange can make the deposits for you."

She stood up and braced her hands on the desk. "Good-bye, Rhys."

"I'll miss you, Ginger. Take care of yourself, and if you ever need help, you send me word. I don't forget my friends"—he grinned sheepishly— "even if I can't do business with them." He turned toward the door, but her voice stopped him.

"If you ever need a bed to sleep in or a woman to warm it, me 'n' this place ain't goin' nowhere, darlin'."

After a long soak in the big marble tub, Tory felt physically refreshed. Perhaps she should go to town and reassure her mother that Rhys's liaison with that saloon tart was nothing to be concerned about. She peered out the window at the brilliant azure sky and glistening snow. "If Rhys can ride into Starlight, so can I," she said with resolution.

It was nearly noon by the time Tory arrived at her parents' house. A groom assisted her down from her filly and took the reins, leading the horse to the stable. She brushed snow from her beautiful wool riding habit and fur cloak. The sun was warming and she had enjoyed the exercise. Her spine stiffened as she admitted that she had needed to work off her anger at Rhys. Hedda must never guess the cause of this particular spat between husband and wife!

She knocked and Ralph opened the door, ushering her into the parlor where her mother sat.

Hedda inclined her head coolly. "I just finished luncheon. If you like—"

"I've already eaten, thank you," she replied woodenly. *Why can't we ever seem to really say what's on our minds, Mama?*

"I assume you've not yet heard the news. Though Charity Soames has doubtless spread the disgrace from here to Lake City by now," Hedda said with a sniff.

"What news?" Somehow Tory knew it concerned Rhys.

Hedda repressed a shudder. "Your husband killed a man this morning." She was rewarded when Tory sank into the nearest chair and paled visibly. "Some cheap, tawdry saloon quarrel. A boy named Ricky Barlow."

Tory's mind spun. "He was jailed over in Silverton months ago, for cheating at cards," she said. "Rhys was the one who caught him in the act. Barlow was a dangerous card sharp, no mere boy! Was Rhys hurt? Where is he?" She began to rise, but Hedda dismissed her fears with a wave of her hand.

"Your gambler is quite unscathed. In fact, he's with Ginger Vogel in their brothel," she said with venom in her voice. "The shooting took place outside of town. That new marshal ruled it self-defense, thank God. As if our reputation isn't in shreds enough, all we'd need is to have Rhys Davies on trial for murder."

Tory's heart was frozen as the winter landscape. *He's with Ginger Vogel in their brothel.* Hedda's cruelty cut her, but Rhys was the real cause, she reminded herself. Here she was ready to run to his side, while he was cavorting with that dreadful red-haired harlot. *And I'm no better than her,* she accused herself, once again remembering what they had done last night and wondering if he shared similar intimacies with Ginger Vogel.

Hedda was studying her daughter's distraught face speculatively when Stoddard opened the parlor door and entered. If Victoria was pale, he was absolutely ashen. Fixing his attention on Hedda, he failed to notice his daughter sitting quietly in the shadows.

With a premonition of dread, his wife stood up. "What are you doing home in the middle of the day?" she asked.

Stoddard walked slowly over to her and took her hands, a most uncharacteristic gesture. He sank onto the brocade sofa behind him and pulled his wife to his side. His face was creased with anguish as he replied hoarsely, "Charles's agents found Sanders in Denver. He's been murdered, Hedda."

Chapter Twenty-two

Tory fought waves of dizziness as she heard her mother's hysterical screams. "He did it! He murdered my baby! That foreign trash! That monster! He wanted Victoria, and Sanders had our money— if he killed Sanders, he could keep her."

That was insane! Tory shook her head in denial, but Rhys's friendship with Blackie Drago rushed into her mind. She forced it aside. Her father could not calm Hedda's shrieking, so she stood up and walked woodenly to the sofa where her hysterical mother sat.

Stoddard looked at his daughter and whispered brokenly, "Get Bessie to send for Dr. Runcie."

She went to the door and opened it. The plump maid was already scurrying toward the sound of Hedda's cries.

Tory stayed at her mother's bedside until the sedative the old physician had given her worked. Hedda's pale, ice-cold hand was still clamped about Tory's wrist even as the older woman slept. Gently, Tory pried her hand free and rubbed the bruises her mother had unknowingly inflicted. She looked down on the beautiful, ravaged face, oddly serene in sleep. "Oh, Mama, you can't be right! Rhys couldn't have—" She choked back the whispered words and bit down on her knuckles until she drew blood. Hedda had shed all the tears. Like her father, Tory was dry-eyed, numb with grief and shock.

Pacing about the cluttered, expensively furnished bedroom, she picked up a heavy gilt-framed photograph of Sanders. A cherubic face smiled winsomely at her. What had gone wrong with his life? Even as a boy he had been self-destructive, always in trouble, always coming to her for help. Entertaining the thought that she might unwittingly have been the reason for his death made her shudder.

Victoria looked around her mother's room. As a child she had rarely been allowed to enter it. Over the years of growing up in boarding schools, she had become an outsider in her parents' home, estranged even more when they had arranged her marriage with Rhys. "I don't belong anywhere," she said forlornly, quietly closing the door, leaving her sleeping mother to a few hours of peace.

But there was no peace for Victoria, and nowhere to turn. She never considered resting in her old room. Rubbing her temples, she leaned against the cool wall in the long, wide upstairs hallway and tried to think.

Stoddard waited for her downstairs. She would read the report the detectives had sent, help her father decide on tentative funeral arrangements, then return to Dragon's Lair and wait for her husband.

* * *

Tory looked at the Charles X ormolu clock on the mantel in the front parlor. Nearly dark. Rhys should be back any moment. She had spent the afternoon in an agony of indecision, afraid to face him, yet knowing she must learn the truth. Tory didn't want to return to Dragon's Lair, but she knew it was the only place they could have this confrontation.

Oh, please, let it not be so, some inner voice screamed. She looked warily at the liquor bottle on the cabinet and considered fortifying herself with a drink. *I'm beginning to reason like Sanders.* She stopped short and nearly gave way to tears. Sanders, poor luckless Sanders. How could she have spoken ill of him—her own brother?

Rhys walked up the front steps, resisting the urge to reach down and thump one of the stone dragons in jubilation. The parting with Ginger had been painful, but now that it was behind him, he felt free—free of his old life, free of all the misery of his childhood and stigma of his birth. The future held boundless promise. The marshal had cleared him of any guilt in Barlow's shooting. And from now on, saloons and their patrons would no longer be his problem.

Tory should be greatly pleased when he broke the news that he was out of that business. Rhys smiled as he patted his coat pocket. He had gone to the best jeweler in town and selected an exquisite gold brooch and bracelet, which would be set with diamonds as soon as Tory made a choice. She could select the stones while the two of them were back East. They deserved a honeymoon, and his railroad venture provided the golden opportunity to combine pleasure with business. It would also serve to get her away from her parents for a month.

Fuller took Rhys's topcoat with a smile as wintry

as the twilight, but Rhys had learned that it was merely the old man's way. He was fiercely loyal and quite efficient beneath the facade of pomposity. "Mrs. Davies requested you meet her in the front parlor, sir."

With a smile slashing his face, Rhys nodded and headed toward the closed door. The moment he opened it and stared at his wife's strained expression, he knew that something was very wrong. The smile died on his face. "Tory, love, what is it?" He crossed the room to where she stood like a frozen statue.

I can't let him touch me! her mind screamed, but before she could speak aloud or move away, he took her in his arms. She did not fight him, but pushed firmly away from him.

He released her with a dark scowl. "Don't you think you're being rather melodramatic about last night now that your hangover is gone?" Then he remembered the shooting and swore to himself.

Tory walked several paces away, placing a small oval table between them, then replied, "I'm a bit too preoccupied to even consider last night,"she began very carefully. *Please, Rhys, be innocent.* "Something so important has happened that your saloon liaisons or my . . . moral concerns pale by comparison."

He opened the humidor on the liquor cabinet and extracted a cigar, then lit it as she spoke. "Ever since we met, my saloon liaisons and your moral concerns seemed paramount to you, Tory," he said with a hint of bitterness creeping into his voice.

"Not as much as my only brother."

His head snapped up and his eyes narrowed. "Exactly what is that supposed to mean?"

"Sanders is dead, Rhys. To quote the report of Charles's detective, 'His throat was cut in a professional manner, causing almost instant death.' He was found in a Denver back alley . . . near Blackie Drago's saloon." She waited a beat, trying desperately to read his facial expression. Damn that gambler's mask that he dropped over his features whenever it suited him!

Rhys took steady breaths, calling on a lifetime of practice to keep the pain and humiliation from overwhelming him. "You think I had Blackie's men kill him." His voice was flat, devoid of emotion.

Tory swallowed and felt her throat close. "I don't know, Rhys. Mama and Papa are so certain, but I . . . I . . ."

"Why? Because I can't abide weaklings or drunks?" he asked brutally. "If that were motive for murder, I'd have been out of the saloon business before I turned twenty."

Tory's hands balled into fists. "You always despised my brother and told me to forget him. He wasn't just another 'drunk' as you so kindly put it. He was the only man who could've released my family from your control."

"Let me get this straight," he said with a dispassion that amazed even him. "You think I wanted Sanders dead so your father would never be able to get his money back and whisk you away from me? And, of course, being a crony of the infamous Blackie Drago, I could have had Sanders killed by snapping my fingers."

With a snap of his fingers. Her father's very words about Rhys and Blackie! She fought the tears back. "You killed a man yourself this morning on the way to town," she blurted out, still trying to see beyond his accusatory anger.

He stared at her coldly. "Pity Barlow's little ambush failed. If he'd shot me, think of all the disgrace it would save the Laughtons."

"I don't care about what outsiders think—just about my family." *You're part of my family, Rhys.*

"Your family. Your fine, pedigreed, ice-blooded family who had to stoop to admit me, to let me touch their princess. That's what this is really about, Tory. You don't want to be the wife of a gambler from the Denver underworld. That's all I'll ever be to you— a vulgar nouveau-riche foreigner who makes you think and feel the way no real lady ever should!"

He ground out his cigar in a cloisonné bowl with insulting thoroughness as Tory stood speechless with hurt and a welling anger. "You've used me, Rhys, just as you accuse my family of using you! You want a lady for display, a curiosity to experiment with. Damn you, you delight in controlling me and laugh at me when you succeed."

He resisted the urge to walk across the room and show her just how thoroughly he could bend her to his will. "Oh, I can control your beautiful little body, can't I, love?" he taunted. "We both know how well. Pity you have neither heart nor soul to give along with it!"

In that moment, Tory almost believed him innocent of Sanders's death. He was so coldly furious that he might well be genuinely surprised by it. But he was right about their hopeless relationship, which was a thing of lust, not love. If she had no heart to give, neither did he. Everything between them was based on mistrust and manipulation. "What do we do now?" she asked wearily as he walked to the door and yanked it open.

His lips slashed in that old familiar smile, but it did not reach the arctic blue of his eyes. "Why, love, you'll be happy to know I'll never humiliate you with my lecherous touch again. The house is yours. You're my wife and I'll continue to provide for you." He reached into his coat pocket, took out the velvet case, and tossed it at her feet. "A small token. Maybe Charles can afford stones for the pieces. I'd planned on diamonds, but then I have such poor taste. Good-bye, Victoria."

"Where—where are you going?" The question seemed to ask itself as she crossed the floor, ignoring the dull gleam of the gold brooch and bracelet scattered on the floor.

"Since you're tired of being my 'whore,' I'll seek out more welcome accommodations—with Ginger."

The door slammed like a closing crypt. Tory sank into a heavy velvet-upholstered chair nearby and buried her face in her arms. The tears she had held at bay all day now poured forth, wracking her body.

The wind was icy, cutting a man to the bone in the depths of the night. Starless and black, it suited his needs. No one must see him with that one. No one must ever connect the two of them. He reined in his horse and dismounted by the filthy cabin. How did people live this way? Wrinkling his nose in distaste, he climbed the steps. No smoke appeared from the chimney. Just as well not to draw attention. He hunched beneath his coat and entered the dark room.

A light flared as his cohort put a match to a filthy kerosene lamp. "'Bout time you got here. You bring my money?" His eyes glowed dully in the flickering light.

"I have half of it. You only did half the job," his employer stated with cold finality.

"It ain't my fault Barlow got hisself killed." He swore a series of inventive oaths as he grabbed the money from the other man and began to count the wad of bills with expert thoroughness. "This is hardly 'nough fer my expenses. Denver's a long ways away 'n' I had ta be real careful doin' the job."

His companion let out a scornful bark of laughter. "As if killing a sot like Sanders Laughton was any trick."

"Keepin' clear of Drago's men is always a trick 'n' don't you ever forget it! When do I get the rest of my money?"

"When you do the rest of the job right and kill Rhys Davies yourself."

Ginger stormed into the room, flung open the heavy drapes, and yelled at the snoring man sprawled across the big bed. "Damn you, Rhys, you may be willin' ta let her kill you, but I sure as hell ain't!"

He blinked at the obscene brilliance of the sun and the scarlet-clad woman silhouetted against it. Both hurt his eyes. He rolled over with a muffled oath and pulled a pillow over his head.

Ginger was across the room kneeling on the bed in a trice. She yanked the pillow away from him and pulled down the heavy comforter. The room did not possess the amenity of central heat like Dragon's Lair. He had let the fire die out last night and he was freezing. With a surly oath he grabbed at the covers, but Ginger was wide awake and much faster.

"Your goose pimples are getting high as the San Juans, darlin'. Now I got you a nice hot bath next door. Why don't you scoot into it 'n' soak while I bring us up some breakfast. You 'n' me got us some talkin' ta do. I figure we'll both do it better sober and on full stomachs."

An hour later, the man who faced her across the table looked a bit like the old Rhys, but for bloodshot eyes and several nicks from a careless shave. His hair was damp from his bath, and that endearingly errant lock, as usual, had fallen over his forehead. He wore a brown velvet robe belted loosely about his waist and nothing beneath it. The old devilish smile slashed his face as he asked, "Since when did you take up social work, Ginger?"

"Since you became your own best customer. It's bad for business." She studied the haunted pain in his eyes as he sipped his coffee. He had returned with only a few meager suitcases of clothing over a week ago, saying that he was taking her up on the offer of a bed to sleep in. So far, he had done nothing about the rest of her offer of a woman to warm it. He had been too busy trying to drown himself in whiskey.

"You leavin' your wife's got somethin' ta do with her brother bein' killed, don't it? Real fancy funeral," she continued when he ventured no reply. "All them friends of the Laughtons turned out like old Sandy was the salt of the earth. Hell, everyone knew he was only a spoiled rich lush who died in a saloon back alley."

"She thinks I had him killed," Rhys said bleakly. He ran his hands through his hair and held his head as if he could squeeze back the memories of that awful day.

"That's crazy! Why'd you wanna kill that punk? He wasn't worth a bullet."

"It's a long story, Ginger, love." He paused and searched her face. Without makeup, bathed in the morning light, she looked younger, more earnest and vulnerable than he had ever imagined. Sighing he said, "Seeing as you have the time to listen and want me to unburden myself . . ."

As Rhys told her about his marriage, Ginger knew there was a great deal more that he was holding

357

back. *He's crazy in love with her 'n' he thinks she despises him!*

Looking at the splendid male specimen seated across from her, Ginger considered. Either Victoria Davies was blind and stupid, both of which, alas, the madam doubted, or else Rhys was mistaken about his wife. She decided to bide her time and see what happened before she interfered. *I got me no sensible interest in playin' matchmaker.* Pain radiated from his soul, and Ginger knew one way to console a man better than any other.

"I reckon this all means your offer to sell me this place is off," she said without regret when he finished his story.

A wistful smile played about his lips. "No, love, but maybe you could take me in as a boarder?"

"I said I'd be here if you needed a bed to sleep in or a woman to warm it . . ." She paused and studied his face. "You just let me know when."

He reached over and took her hand, raising it to his cheek. "I don't want to hurt you again, Ginger. I can't give you love."

A wicked yet oddly sad smile played across her mobile lips. "I'll settle for the next-best thing, Rhys." She moved her soft palm to his mouth and let him plant a kiss on the sensitive skin. Then she reached over and tugged his robe open, pulling him up as she rose. They embraced slowly. After a long exploratory kiss, she chuckled low and whispered, "Consider this your first rent payment."

But as the weeks rolled into a month, Rhys did little else but drink, gamble, and occasionally make love with Ginger. Wylie ran the Lady Victory and reported to him at the saloon. His foremen from the ranches did likewise. He went to the bank for a few hours a week and took care of essential matters, but canceled his plan for backing the railroad spur to Starlight. Stoddard was furious, but without his son-in-law's approval, he could do nothing. That pleased Rhys.

It did not please Mike Manion. The little Irishman stormed into the Naked Truth the day he heard the news. Rhys sat, as was his wont, at a back table, engaged in a casual game of five-card draw with several stockmen and the owner of the Rose Theater. Mike's furious brown eyes impaled him from across the room, but he did not interrupt the game. Stalking to the bar, Mike ordered whiskey with a beer chaser. Rhys folded his cards, scooped up his winnings, and excused himself. When he approached the bar, Mike had downed the shot in one fiery gulp and was working on the beer. "That stuff's pretty potent for a skinny Mickey."

"You ought to know. I hear you've been downing enough of it to float Red Mountain," Mike replied sourly.

"Why is it I have a feeling I'm in for another lecture?" Rhys sighed. "What this time, Mike? You've surely given up trying to get me to reconcile with Tory."

"Bad enough you wreck your own life and let your businesses go to hell. You'll be damn lucky if Charles Everett doesn't end up buying and selling you."

"Charlie boy has had a bit of a reversal in his fortunes here lately," Rhys said without interest.

Mike snorted. "He's attending to his investments like you ought to be doing. He's got a piece of the railroad. If he can get Senator Benson's backing, he can bring it into Starlight without you!"

"Think he'd turn Democrat to do it?" Rhys speculated idly.

"You're talking about my town—our town, Rhys

Davies. A place that's been damn good to you. You can't let a weasel like Everett get a stranglehold on it just to spite your father-in-law." Mike watched his friend's face darken.

"I'll admit to a bit of perverse delight in thwarting the pompous old bastard," he admitted.

"Only in the short run, boyo. He and Charlie boy are still thick as thieves. If Tory divorces you, she might just end up married to that thief." Mike waited for some reaction.

"They deserve one another," Rhys said without emotion as he downed the shot Ben had silently set before him."

"Well now, I'm real glad to hear you feel that way, boyo, seeing as how old Charlie has been a frequent caller at Dragon's Lair the past couple of weeks. He's there right now." Finally, Mike had engaged Rhys's interest. He watched as his friend's knuckles whitened on the shot glass.

Rhys turned and headed for the door, then paused only long enough to say, "Thanks for the information, Mike."

"What about the railroad?" Mike called after him, but Davies did not reply.

Rhys reined up a lathered Blackjack next to Charles Everett's fancy rig. He took the front steps two at a time in long-legged strides. When he shoved open the front door, he could hear their voices. Tory's was softly remonstrating, Charles's increasingly insistent.

"You really must understand, Victoria, that I have your best interests at heart."

"My name has been dragged through the mud enough, Charles. It isn't proper for you to call here without my parents or some chaperone," Tory said.

Rhys stood in the open parlor doorway, fighting

the insane desire to rush to her and bury his face in her pale gold hair. Instead he said insolently, "And my wife is a stickler for what's proper, Charlie boy. I should know."

Tory froze at the sound of his voice. She was so absorbed with getting rid of poor bumbling Charles, she had not heard him arrive. She turned and looked at him with stricken eyes, wanting to be angry and coolly impervious as her mother would be. But instead she felt a rush of absurd longing assail her. Her mouth was dry and her knees weak. Here he was, come from his whores to tear her heart out all over again. "Why have you come, Rhys?" She hated the plaintive sound in her voice.

His eyes skewered her for a moment, then moved to Everett. "Don't fear that I plan to degrade you with my unworthy attentions again, love. Let's just say I plan to insure that no one else touches what's still mine."

"Now see here, Davies—"

"Do you want to play the gentleman and step outside?"Rhys interrupted. "Or we can break Tory's expensive furniture in here."

"No, Rhys! This is absurd. You can't fight Charles." Tory took a halting step toward him, then paused as an implacable wall of cold fury stopped her.

He didn't even look at her, but his eyes burned into Everett. "Your pleasure, Charlie boy, but don't wait too long and wear out my patience. It's much softer landing in the snow."

"This is precisely the sort of barbaric barroom behavior I'd expect from you, Davies," Everett sneered. He strode toward the door. "Let me warn you, however, I boxed in college."

Rhys grinned evilly. "I boxed in grammar school."

"He's not joking, Charles. I've seen him beat a

muleskinner insensate," Tory cried in frustration. Men, stupid, violent, arrogant, insufferable . . . Fearing what was coming, she watched as they filed out into the front yard. As obnoxious as his solicitude had become, Charles did not deserve this. And she did not either. To be fought over like a cheap trophy! Still, Tory could not stay inside. Furious with Rhys's high-handed possessiveness, she watched in humiliation from the porch as the men squared off.

Charles raised his fists in the best Marquis of Queensbury stance, desperate to put on a good front for Victoria. He detested the crude ruffian who had cost him so dearly. Perhaps this was a chance—

Rhys came in under Everett's first punch with a hard right, left combination that snapped Charles's head back and bloodied his nose. They were evenly matched in size, but it was quickly evident that Tory's assessment had been correct. Charles was no match for her husband's street-honed skills.

They danced about the shoveled pathway, jabbing and weaving in the cold afternoon air, emitting little puffs of vaporized breath. Charles landed one glancing blow to the cheek, but Rhys quickly recovered and smashed his fist into Everett's nose and jaw, sending him reeling into the snow.

"College champ, eh?" he taunted, playing with the stupid politician. He had held back, letting Charles swing, rusty and awkward, just so he could administer a sound thrashing.

When Charles heard Tory's gasp of dismay, he rallied and rose in a red haze of anger, only to be again pummeled. For every blow he could land, the powerful Welshman punished him with three far more telling ones. As his right eye closed and his stomach began to ache abominably, he grasped just how uneven the contest was.

"You're doing this because you've lost her to me, aren't you?" He gasped the insult, hoping to catch his foe off guard.

"No, I'll never give my wife to any man, Charlie boy. I'm doing this . . . for . . . pure . . . pleasure," Rhys replied as he delivered a final brutal series of punches that sent the dark-haired man sprawling, bloody and unconscious on the front lawn.

Wiping a small drop of blood from his lips with a linen handkerchief, Rhys instructed Tory, "Have a couple of the horde of servants who are doubtless watching toss him in his fancy rig and drive him home. He's creating a bloody mess on the front lawn."

"You have no right—"

"I have every right. This is my house and you're my wife, no matter we live apart, Tory. The next time I find you with a man, I'll kill him." He turned and walked away.

Tory could feel the eyes of the whole staff on them. Once that would have shamed her to tears. Now she did not care if her namesake the Queen of England was watching.

Chapter Twenty-three

Victoria walked down the bustling street from Dr. Runcie's office, nodding absently to anyone who greeted her. She was too preoccupied to notice the whispers and stares of other passersby. As the estranged wife of the silver millionaire who had returned to his saloon, Tory lived in limbo, with only a few close friends standing by her, like Laura Everett, and ironically enough, some of the men who had worked with her at the mud slide last summer.

Social ostracism was a thing to be dreaded by the girl she used to be, but that Victoria was gone forever. She had been a spoiled, sheltered child before her marriage. Tory realized for the first time that morning how monumentally and irreversibly Rhys Davies had changed the course of her life. She could blame him for the gossip and cruelty of shallow acquaintances who now snubbed her. She could

364

hate him for her estrangement from her parents, who had become nervous and polite strangers. She could even accuse him of her brother's death. But was he guilty? Tory had to know the truth.

Mike Manion's dingy old newspaper office, citadel of Democratic politics and gathering place for all the people her parents considered their social inferiors, was a most unlikely destination for Mrs. Victoria Laughton Davies. Working up her courage, she opened the door and walked in the dim interior.

Wrinkling her nose at the pungent odor of linseed oil, she scanned the clutter. Mike sat with his short legs propped improbably high on a stack of boxes, leaning back in a rickety chair with a tablet and pencil in his hands. He had paused in his writing, obviously deep in thought. Nervously Tory cleared her suddenly dry throat, and addressed him. "Hello, Mr. Manion—Mike?"

Mike nearly tumbled backward at the sound of her low, cultivated voice. The only lady ever to set foot in his office was Laura. He knocked over the packing boxes as he scrambled to his feet.

"Tory—Mrs. Davies, what an unexpected pleasure."

"Please, call me Tory. That is, if you still consider me a friend after all that's happened."

Mike frantically cleared a chair with all the aplomb of a starving squirrel searching for buried nuts in a blizzard. Finally, dusting off the sturdiest seat in the house, he offered it to her with a flourish. "Please sit down, Tory." He paused, studying her pinched face and the fathomless pain in her blue-green eyes. She may not have been drinking, but she looked as bad off as Rhys. He gave her his most disarming Irish smile and said, "Now, I'm reasonably certain you haven't come to drop off a garden club column for Laura."

She returned the smile hesitantly. "Hardly, in the dead of winter."

"Can I get you a cup of coffee? Not the freshest, but it's strong and hot. Virgil reboils part of last night's grounds every morning. Says it only gets good with a starter. Kinda like sourdough bread."

Tory nodded. "Yes, please. It sounds . . . interesting."

"Wait till you taste it!" He poured coffee for each of them and then pulled his chair up to hers. "Now, what is it you need, Tory? Anything I can do for you, I will."

Her eyes filled with sudden tears. God, she hated these unexpected bouts of crying that she had been subjected to lately. "I appreciate that, Mike. Especially considering how close you and Rhys are. I imagine—"

"What's between the two of you is for the two of you to talk out, not for the likes of me or anyone else to gossip about. I assume your visit has something to do with that rascal though, doesn't it?"

She nodded, clutching her mittens in a death grip as she drew a deep breath. "Laura once said you could find out anything that went on in Colorado if you put your mind to it."

"A bit of exaggeration, perhaps, but I do have quite a few contacts in southwest Colorado," he replied with a smile, guessing what she wanted.

"How about Denver? You do have contacts there?"

"I know the infamous Blackie Drago, even if not as well as Rhys does."

"I want you to find out who killed my brother." Her voice was low and intense and she met his eyes steadily.

"Even if you fear there's a chance that it was your husband?"

She fought to breathe for an instant. Wide-eyed, she asked, "Do you think there's any chance he was involved?"

"No." His level brown eyes met hers. "Rhys wouldn't kill a helpless lad even to hold on to you. As desperately as he wants to keep you, Tory, that isn't his way. Neither is paying hired assassins to do his dirty work."

She breathed a sigh of relief and looked at him gratefully. "I don't believe so either, now that I've had time to get over the shock and think things through, but . . ."

"But there's always that niggling doubt," he added for her.

"He's your friend, Mike, but he's my husband. I'm too closely involved to be able to sort through this. I don't trust my own instincts these days. *Especially* these days," she added beneath her breath.

Mike nodded in understanding. Considering her background, she had been through a lot in the past months. "I sent word to several friends in Denver as soon as I heard of your brother's murder, Tory."

Her head snapped up. "And no word of who did it?"

He reached over and patted her hand. "Not yet, but they do have several leads. Sanders had only a few thousand in a local bank when he was killed. Either he or someone else transferred it out of Denver. Steve Loring's working on that end of it. Blackie's working on the thug who did the actual deed. There are a few other loose ends, but until we get it all put together, I don't have much."

Tory nodded thoughtfully, her mind racing as she stood up and took Mike's hand in hers. "I have every faith in you and your friends, Mike. I don't know how to thank you."

"Seeing you and that Welsh rogue back together will be thanks enough," he replied with the sparkle returned to his liquid brown eyes.

Tory mulled over the Irishman's words as she retraced her steps to where she had instructed Lee to wait with her carriage. She had a great many things to ponder. As she approached the rig, Lee began to climb down. Tory waved him back into the driver's seat and told him that she was going for a walk through town before returning to Dragon's Lair. *It's so lonely in that big house without Rhys.*

"Seeing you and that Welsh rogue back together," Mike had said. Did she want that brawler back in her life, beating insensate every man who looked at her? His fierce temper and intense jealously had surprised her. Considering his current life-style, he certainly had no right to be making threats!

After working off her anger with a long tramp through the melting snow, Tory was no closer to putting her tumultuous thoughts in order than she had been yesterday when Rhys had stormed off, leaving poor Charles unconscious in the yard. But she was feeling decidedly hungry. Catching sight of a small, unpretentious, but clean-looking lunch room, she decided to rest her weary body and try the food, which smelled heavenly.

Ma Brennan's was not the sort of place Hedda would consider for luncheon, but the plump old woman who ran it was friendly and efficient. Odd, Tory mused, how many things she did lately that her mother would disdain.

Deep in thought, Victoria sipped her hot tea and devoured a rich scone with tart wild raspberry preserves. When another customer entered and walked to her table, she did not notice until the familiar voice rudely jarred her attention.

"Ain't this outta your neighborhood, milady?" Ginger sneered.

Tory stared at her nemesis, dazed by the harlot's audacity. She could feel the heat steal into her cheeks.

Ginger smirked. "Afraid of the gossip, bein' seen with me?"

"Since everyone in southwest Colorado is already gossiping about Rhys's two women, I doubt this will make a fig's worth of difference." She took another sip of tea to fortify herself, wondering what Ginger was going to do.

"Aintcha the cool one. Rhys always liked that . . . your bein' such a lady 'n' all." Her voice was peculiarly wistful and earnest. She sank uninvited onto a chair across from Tory and began to fiddle with the scarred tin spoon and fork. "He come back all bloody yesterday. Beat up somethin' awful."

Tory's lips quirked in a smile at the gross exaggeration. "You should've seen the other fellow."

Ginger's green eyes narrowed in anger. "He charged out there soon's he heard that prissy-ass ex-boyfriend of yours was sniffin' round you. This ain't no joke, *Mrs.* Davies."

Tory sobered. "No, *Mistress* Vogel, it certainly is not. If it's any consolation to my husband, Charles Everett won't ever return to Dragon's Lair. Rhys's fists are a persuasive deterrent."

"He only done it 'cause he's in love with you," Ginger said, hating herself for the admission.

"He wants to protect his possessions," Tory countered gently.

"Then why'd he move outta his own house 'n' give up everything he worked for? He stayed drunk for a week after you accused him of muderin' your brother."

"He never gave me a chance to explain anything," Tory defended herself. Then she sighed. "We never could really talk. All he does is accuse me and say cruel, hateful things to mock me." Now she was getting maudlin.

Ginger watched the beautiful woman fight back tears with a grace and dignity she could only envy, never emulate. "You never said anythin' cruel or done nothin' hateful to him? Just called him a back-stabbin' killer."

"I didn't mean it—that is, after I had time to weigh everything, I didn't believe he was responsible, but by then . . ." Tory shrugged helplessly, then looked at Ginger. "Why on earth am I defending myself to you of all people? Why are you here?"

It was Ginger's turn to shrug. "I seen you come in here all alone."

"Spying for Rhys to see if I was having an assignation? Considering your relationship with my husband, I think that's a lot of nerve." As her surprise faded, her anger began to grow.

"You got it all wrong as usual," the madam said as if explaining to a half-wit child. "I been feelin' a need to talk to you—to tell you how much he's hurtin' 'cause of what's happened. I guess after yesterday's fight 'n' all . . . well, when you come in here and I saw my chance, I just had to say my piece." She stopped and stared into Tory's eyes, woman to woman. "I just want you to know it wasn't easy, neither."

"You're in love with him." It was not a question. Watching the way Ginger averted her eyes and nervously fidgeted with the flatware elicited a surge of empathy from Tory.

"Question is, are *you*? I told him you wasn't our kind, that he shouldn't marry you, but I was wrong. I ain't his kind . . . not the kind he wants or what he deserves. But I'm gonna warn you. Don't keep hurtin' him. Either take your man back right now or cut him loose. Don't play with him. Cause if you do, I'm gonna fight you with everythin' I got."

Tory looked into the blazing emerald eyes and said quietly, "I imagine your arsenal is most formidable."

"Don't you forget it." Brushing suspicious moisture from her eyes, Ginger quickly rose and walked out the door without a backward glance.

"Perhaps we're both to be pitied," Tory whispered to herself.

For weeks he had stalked his prey with cunning and patience, determined not to fail this time. Now success was within his grasp. He had been waiting for what seemed like hours in the gloom of the stable behind the Naked Truth. *Damn! Mighta been better to make my try on th' trail.* But then, he really had never been all that good with a gun, especially not a long-arm—but Davies was. Knives were his specialty and darkness was his ally. But Rhys seldom went out nights, preferring to spend them in the saloon with Ginger, damn the bitch's green eyes.

Just then he heard the corral gate swing open and the sound of boots scuffing toward the stable door. He peered through a chink in the wall. That dumb stable boy!

The intruder pressed back into the shielding darkness as the skinny youth entered, closing the door behind him. He muttered something to himself and then, as his eyes adjusted to the darkness, called out toward the big black stallion's stall at the far end of

371

the stable. "All right, Blackjack, hoss, time to earn your feed."

The assassin slid forward with a sense of elation. His information had been right. Davies was going to inspect the Lady Victory mine this morning. His hand closed over the thin youth's mouth, then pulled back his head, exposing his victim's throat, which he slashed with one practiced stroke. Sammy made a muffled, gurgling noise as he thrashed, but soon ceased. Without ever letting the body touch the floor, the big man carried it easily to a side wall and covered it with a heap of discarded burlap sacks.

As the assailant returned to his post next to the door, he cursed softly. The stallion was snorting and moving about restlessly in his stall. The man crouched silently in the darkness. If that stallion began to smell blood, he'd really start a ruckus. "Come on, ya Welsh bastard! Come 'n' get it!"

Blackjack settled down just as the sound of boots once more crunched on the gravel. The killer peered through a chink in the wall to see Rhys approaching the corral. He could not see the Welshman's face because his head was tipped slightly forward. Apparently, Davies was lost in thought.

The murderer grinned at his own deviousness. He had been right again. Easier to take him here, close to home, where Rhys would feel safe enough to let his guard down, than to make a try on the trail, where he'd have his eyes peeled. But the killer's grin faded as he watched the ease with which his intended victim swung open the heavy corral gate. As he speculatively measured the breadth of Rhys's shoulders, he thought, *That Welsh bastard'll be a lot harder to take than that puny Laughton kid.*

He began to perspire. He would not be able to man-handle Davies as he had the stable boy. The gambler might be able to launch some counter move in the split second between the time he was grabbed and the time the knife got to his throat. As the sound of boots grew closer, the assassin's self-congratulatory grin again spread malevolently across his face. He turned his fist so that the cutting edge of the big Bowie was parallel to the ground. The blade was heavy and razor-keen; a snapping flick would be all that was necessary to slice through the carotid artery. *The first thing he'll feel is th' knife 'n' then the blood shootin' outta his neck as fast 'n' hard as a cow pissin' on a flat rock.* If the Welshman had enough presence of mind after that to try for his gun, the killer could easily control the gun hand of a dying man and finish him off. He tensed as the door opened and closed.

Rhys moved into the darkened stable before he realized something was wrong. Thoughts of Tory and Charles Everett suddenly fled. Damn. He had expected to see the alley doors at the back of the stable open and Blackjack saddled and waiting, but the stable was dark as a cave. Senses honed in the warrens of Five Points made him crouch and start to spin around. A sharp, searing pain lanced across his chin and jaw. He heard his assailant's muffled oath and then felt a burning agony in his side. *Jesus!*

Rhys grabbed the knife hand before his attacker could pull out the blade for a second thrust. Instead of risking a try for his gun, Rhys threw a short chopping right at what he hoped was the man's throat. It landed on his adversary's cheek, but the Welshman followed the blow with a knee aimed at his opponent's groin. It landed on a beefy thigh and knocked Rhys off balance. As he fell backward, he could feel the blade slip out of his body.

In agony, Rhys was dimly aware of the sounds of retreat. The rear doors of the stable creaked open and gravel crunched beneath racing boots. He fought to roll over and get to his knees, then clawed for the Colt Peacemaker on his hip. When he raised it, his pain-dazed eyes saw only the emptiness of the alley. His target had vanished. The last sounds he heard were the neighs of his enraged stallion and the ringing of a shot he managed to squeeze off before he sank face forward into the straw and blessed oblivion.

Ginger heard the shot the same time as Kelly, who was cleaning up the kitchen after breakfast. "That come from the stable?" the big cook asked, dropping his dishcloth into the washpan.

"Rhys just went out to get Blackjack a couple a minutes ago," Ginger replied. She set her coffee cup in its saucer with a sharp crash, gathered up her brocade robe, and dashed out the back toward the corral.

Kelly followed as fast as his bulk allowed. Ginger was struggling with the heavy stable door when he caught up to her. Blackjack and several other horses were nickering loudly as the cook swung the door open. Brilliant morning sunlight bathed the interior.

"Rhys! Darling!" Ginger ran across the straw to where his body lay crumpled near the alley door. She rolled him onto his back and sucked in her breath. He was covered with blood. "Get Grange quick," she instructed Kelly as she pulled back Rhys's heavy sheepskin jacket to inspect the seriousness of the wounds.

The fat cook was back in a couple of moments with a half-dressed Grange, who had been roused from sleep by the shot. "He ain't been shot. He's been cut—across his jawline and his side. Woulda gone deeper if'n he weren't wearin' th' coat."

Ginger shuddered to think what would have happened if the assassin had hit his original target—Rhys's throat! "Pick him up real careful."

Grange and Kelly lifted Rhys up and began to carry him to the kitchen door. Rhys revived groggily with a string of mumbled oaths. "Son-of-a-bitch, easy, easy. You're tearing me apart."

"Take him upstairs for now. I'll try 'n' stop the bleedin' while you go for the doc, Grange." Ginger pulled her blood-stained robe about her waist in the freezing early morning air and led the way.

"Where's Sammy? He was supposed to saddle . . . Blackjack," Rhys gasped out, gritting his teeth.

A dark look flashed between the two men carrying him. "I'll see if I can find him soon's we get you taken care of," Kelly replied. The cook had seen the youth enter the stable a good while before Rhys had left the house. He was not optimistic about the chances of Sammy being alive.

Ginger had already turned back the covers and gathered emergency medical supplies when Grange and Kelly laid their boss on his bed. "Get the coat off him. I can cut the shirt away," she instructed briskly. They complied as Rhys groaned, semiconscious now. Ginger set to work while Ben raced for the doctor and Kelly went in search of the stable boy.

Fortunately, Ginger had witnessed her share of barroom mayhem and was adept at stopping bleeding and binding up knife wounds. Doc Runcie was across the Uncompahgre River delivering a baby at a ranch. His wife was uncertain about when he would return.

Word of the unsuccessful attempt to cut Rhys's throat in his own stable spread like fire in tinder. By noon Laura Everett had heard the news.

"Thank God he's alive," she told Mike, who had just come from the Naked Truth. "Are you certain he'll be all right? I do wish the doctor were here."

"Ginger Vogel is nothing if not devoted to him, Laura. She's seen her share of cut and shoot and knows what to do," Mike replied.

"I only wish Tory were with him," Laura said softly.

"I wonder what devil did this. Got clean away."

Laura looked at Mike with a sudden flash of insight. "Didn't you say in that grisly news story about Sanders Laughton that his throat was cut?"

"I'm way ahead of you. The question is what enemy would Laughton and Rhys have in common." He stroked his chin in consideration.

"While you ponder that and write your story for the paper, I have some business of my own to attend to. A man should have his wife by his side when he's been injured."

"Matchmaking again, Laura?" Mike teased.

She snorted. "As if you haven't been trying to do the same these past weeks! Maybe this monstrous attack will shake some sense into both those head-strong young fools."

"Tory'll have to beard Ginger in her own lair," Mike said with a twinkle in his eye. "That'll put Hedda into high dudgeon, indeed." A wide grin made his cherub's face turn devilish with delight.

Chapter Twenty-four

Tory stood in front of the Naked Truth feeling her heart slam frantically in her chest. Half afraid it would leap up into her throat, she swallowed. "I have to be calm. And brave," she whispered, straightening her spine and holding her chin high. She felt neither calm nor brave as she shoved open the heavy oak door and stepped inside.

Mid-afternoon business was brisk. The crowd of miners, stockmen, and townsmen mingled with Ginger's gaudy harlots, laughing, drinking, and playing cards. Her eyes swept the room, catching a glimpse of the much-touted nude hanging stage center across from the bar, but she quickly looked away and fixed her attention on the stairs leading up to the bedroom where Rhys lay gravely injured.

As she began to walk deliberately across the big room, the noise quickly died. "Gawd damn, if'n it ain't his fancy uptown wife," one drunken cowboy whispered. "Miz Ginger'll send her packin'," a griz-zled old miner said, belching loudly. The piano play-er sat with his hands frozen on the keys, and Ben dropped a bottle of expensive bourbon, spilling its pungent contents the length of the bird's-eye maple bar.

Every eye in the place was on the pale, beautiful blonde in the expensive sable cloak. Tory looked to neither left nor right, but steered a course toward her destination with single-minded determination.

"Damned if I'd want to be in Rhys Davies's boots." Grange muttered beneath his breath after Tory walked past him. He had just returned with word that the doc was on his way to the saloon. Prudently he decided not to pass that information along to Ginger and Rhys just now. Let old Doc Runcie deal with two spitting hellcats.

Tory felt her knees wobble when she began to climb the imposing staircase. It looked a mile high. Closing her ears to the whispers and guffaws below, she persevered. *What will he say to me?* She ago-nized with each footstep. Would he send her away in humiliation after she had destroyed her reputa-tion and abased her pride by coming to him? "I just won't let him, that's all," she whispered fiercely. The brass doorknob felt ice cold in her sweaty palm. She clutched it in a death grip and knocked.

Ginger Vogel's voice called out, "That you, Grange? Come in. You got the d—" The whore blanched as the words died on her lips.

"Hello, Rhys," Tory said, ignoring her husband's mistress and looking at his drawn face. He was propped up with a mountain of fluffy white pil-lows behind his back, obviously naked beneath the sheets but for the thick wad of bandaging around his waist.

"You got some nerve, yer ladyship, sashayin' in here now. Afraid you'll get cut outta the will?" Ginger put her arm intimately around Rhys's shoulders and glared at her rival.

"Why don't you leave us alone for a minute, Ginger, love?" he said, his eyes never leaving Tory's face. The tension between the two women crackled across his bed.

"If it takes you nearly dyin' ta get her here, Rhys, she ain't worth it," Ginger protested. He turned his head and gave her a steely look she knew well. Reluctantly she stood up and rounded the big bed, careful to let her robe gape open, flaunting her dishabille in front of the prim, lovely woman. She walked past Tory, hips swaying defiantly, but paused at the door long enough to say, "Just call if you need anything, darlin'. I'll be right next door."

Tory forgot the angry whore the minute she noticed that his jaw had been cut, too. Dear God! He'd almost died the same way Sanders had! The breath left her body and she stood speechless with horror.

The silence thickened. Rhys's face remained unreadable as ever while he studied her. Finally he asked, "Why did you come, Tory?"

"Not to secure my place in your will," she replied tartly, twisting a glove in her hands, then nervously stuffing it into her cloak pocket. She gazed around the big, masculine room. All the furniture was dark and heavy, oversized, as was the bed. *The bed he shared with Ginger Vogel.*

"Your reputation's in shreds," he said almost conversationally.

"And so, almost, was your throat," she snapped, fighting tears and trying to remember the rehearsed speech that had fled her mind the instant she had come face to face with him.

"If I were dead, you'd be free, Tory. You could marry Charles and have the kind of life you always wanted."

The threatening tears finally bested her, overflowing at last. She dashed them away with small tightly balled fists. "I'd never marry Charles. I despise him. Oh, Rhys! W-when Laura told me someone tried to murder you, I was so afraid. I realized I'd been a fool to wait this long . . . a coward."

"Tory—aah!" He swore as the pain lanced through him when he tried to swing his legs over the side of the bed.

She rushed to the bed and sat beside him, stroking the dried cut across his jaw after he collapsed back on the pillows. "You're still no gentleman, swearing in the presence of a lady," she said with a wobbly smile. Her fingers caught the lock of hair falling over his forehead and brushed it back. "But I love you anyway." She held her breath.

His hand shot up and imprisoned her wrist with surprising strength. "Don't play with me, Tory."

"Odd, that was the warning Ginger gave me last week." At the look of incredulity on his face, she explained, "I was in town and she accosted me in Ma Brennan's lunch room."

He began to rub a soft, rhythmic pattern on her sensitive inner wrist, all the while measuring the way her pulse raced. "But it took an assassin's knife to bring you here."

"A pretty dramatic way to get a woman to see what everyone's been telling her is true."

"And what has everyone been telling you?" Her pulse speeded up as he held her wrist.

"That you didn't kill Sanders. That you loved me . . . and that I loved you, too." Her eyelashes fluttered wide and she looked into his face, trying to read it.

A wry smile curved his lips. "Somehow I doubt that your parents were part of this 'everyone.'"

"Mama will be furious, but I don't care, Rhys. I had to tell you how I felt, to ask you to come home to Dragon's Lair." She waited as he continued to stroke her wrist, studying her face silently.

"You could have sent word by Mike," he said softly, brushing her wrist against his lips.

"Maybe I wanted to see your famous lady—the one hanging across from the bar. Maybe I needed to see for myself that you were all right. I realized what it would mean if I lost you—really lost you." She put her head against his shoulder and sobbed.

Rhys's hand curved around her head and he buried his fingers in her soft silky hair. "You always smell of violets, even in the wintertime," he murmured, kissing the top of her head.

She raised her face and asked with a tear-thickened voice, "Is it too late to start over again?"

"Ginger said you were—"

Dr. Runcie stopped in the doorway, mortified to have burst in unknowingly on Rhys and his wife. Damn that jealous harlot Ginger for not telling him!

Rhys had just started to reply to Tory, but the words died on his lips. Reflexively he tightened his arm around her as he spoke to the old man. "I think I'll live, doc, but you can look me over if you want."

"More like stitch you up, from what I heard," the gruff physician grumbled as he put his leather bag on the bedside table. "Knife wounds can be pretty ugly, young lady. But I believe you saw worse at the mud slide."

"I'll do whatever you need to help," Tory replied.

He grunted in assent and said, "Best begin by unwrapping that packing so I can take a look." He took a needle and thread from the bag, then extracted a bottle of disinfectant and some cotton, all of which he carefully arranged on a clean linen square he placed on the bedside table.

Tory's hands trembled as she unfastened the tight bandages, trying desperately not to cause Rhys more pain than necessary. She gasped when the long, bloody slash was revealed.

"Good," the doc said casually. "It's not too bad." He probed and Rhys swore. Tory tried not to wince in empathy as she felt his muscles bunch and quiver with the pain. Finally satisfied, the doctor doused some cotton with the evil-smelling liquid and began to cleanse the wound.

When he had finished, Runcie said cheerfully, "Now if you think that hurt, just wait until you feel my fine stitchery."

Rhys bit his lip, then gritted his teeth as the doctor sewed the slash tightly closed. It would leave a bitch of a scar, but it would scarcely be his first.

Tory held tight to his hand, feeling each puncture and pull of the needle as if it were her own flesh. She bathed his sweaty brow with a cool cloth, praying for the doctor to finish.

"There, that should do it." Runcie pronounced his work good as he wrapped a much lighter bandage about his patient's waist. "Shouldn't bleed anymore to speak of. Lucky for you they stopped the bleeding so quick—even luckier that fellow missed his mark. Here, let me disinfect that chin." He swabbed the nick on Rhys's jaw, muttering something about his Welsh luck saving his life.

"It wasn't luck so much as street instinct. I turned and crouched just in time."

"Well, still damn lucky all the way around." Dr. Runcie looked over at Tory and smiled. "Especially considering the blessed event. A man oughta live long enough to see his first child born."

Tory felt Rhys go very tense, but his face gave nothing away. Quickly she interjected, "How soon can my husband travel back to Dragon's Lair, doctor?"

Runcie shrugged. "No bleeding. Wound's not deep. If he's game to walk—with a couple of those strapping fellows downstairs helping him—I don't see why he couldn't ride in a buggy tonight. I'll be out to check on the patient tomorrow. Keep him quiet and feed him lots of hot liquids."

With that bit of advice, he snapped shut the bag he had just efficiently repacked and stood up. "Good day, Rhys, Tory."

As soon as the door closed, Rhys said, "How long have you known?"

Her face heated beneath his cool scrutiny. "Last week . . . the day I, er, encountered Ginger."

"But you waited until now—you *were* going to tell me today, weren't you, Tory?"

"Yes, of course, but there was so much else going on, things to settle between us first," she whispered, feeling that something was wrong. She looked into his eyes. "Don't you want the baby, Rhys?"

His hands clamped over her shoulders and he nearly shook her, then he sighed and released her. "Yes, Tory, I want the baby. The question is, do you?"

She felt as if he had slapped her. "How can you ask such a thing?"

He stroked a violet-scented curl that had come unpinned. "I may have trapped you, Tory, but know this—I'm coming back to Dragon's Lair with you and I'll never let you go again!"

*   *   *

I may have trapped you . . . I'll never let you go . . .
Tory stood outside their bedroom door, a tray in her
hands, working up the courage to face her husband.
He thought she was only pretending to care about
him because he had trapped her with an unwanted
pregnancy. How wrong, how cruelly wrong he was,
but Rhys was not the only one who had made cruel
mistakes. She had to own up to her share of them
as well. *So now you're paying for yours,* she thought
sadly as she opened the door and walked inside, a
bright good-morning smile pasted on her lips. It did
not reach her sad aqua eyes.

Rhys watched her gracefully carry the small silver
tray to a bedside table and deposit it. Smells of coffee, hot corn bread, and scrambled eggs filled the
air, but it was the delicate violet perfume that held
his attention. He watched her fuss nervously with
the food. "Why didn't you sleep with me, Tory?"

"Yes, you're used to a woman in your bed—if
not Ginger, then me. You were feverish and needed
to sleep. Doctor's orders," she replied briskly. "So
is this. Eat," she commanded, placing the tray on
his lap.

"So this is how it's going to be," he said wearily
as he stared without interest at the food. "You're
willing to pretend wifely devotion now that you've
done your duty. You'll give me my heir, and in return
I'll go straight and not embarrass you with Ginger
Vogel."

Tory fought the urge to pick up the tray and hurl
coffee and eggs at his face. "I won't ask anything of
you, Rhys. If you prefer Ginger's company to mine,
go back to the Naked Truth." She felt her nails biting
into her palms as she awaited his reply.

He set the tray back on the table, wincing in pain

as he turned sideways. "I told you I was here to stay with you. I'll never let you go again, Tory."

"But you'll never trust me either," she said sadly. "You believe I only came to you because of the baby, that I lied when I told you I loved you and wanted to start over again."

He studied her with his expressionless gambler's face, giving away none of the turmoil inside. "I don't know, Tory. I honestly don't know what to believe."

She swallowed and turned away from those fathomless blue eyes, pacing across the big bedroom to stare out the window. "I told you the truth yesterday. And my motives were not self-serving. In time you'll believe me,"

"Perhaps," he echoed softly.

"You will." She paused, then turned to face him. "We're nothing like my parents. Our marriage may have started out all wrong, but even so, it's going to work out differently."

"Is that so?" he taunted.

"Yes, it is. You see, I plan to disregard my mother's advice and start taking Laura Everett's."

"What's that supposed to mean?" Rhys had a fair idea, but damn, he wanted her to say it.

Cheeks burning, she replied, "I hope your stitches can stand it, because I won't spend another night freezing in the guest bedroom. I'll be sleeping in my bed, with my *husband*."

"Once I would've given all the silver in the San Juans to hear you say that," he said bleakly, realizing that manipulating her this way brought him no satisfaction.

"But now, you don't care anymore?" She refused to accept that.

"Oh, I care, Tory. I care too damn much! You're in my blood. I'll never get free of you."

"And you resent it? So did I, at first. You'll get over it. I did." She walked to the bed and scooped up the tray, shoving it back on his lap. "Eat and regain your strength. Those aren't only the doctor's orders!"

He gave her a slumberous look that used to infuriate her, then silently began to devour the breakfast. Tory left the room without another word, feeling emotionally drained.

"You've hurt his pride, and he won't make it easy for you, Tory," Laura had warned her yesterday before she had worked up her courage to go to the saloon and fight for her husband.

"Laura, you were more of a prophet than even you imagined," she muttered beneath her breath.

But he had admitted, even if it was with bitterness, that he could not stop loving her—there was a chance for their marriage. A chance on which she would gamble everything. She thought of tonight, and a slow smile spread across her face. If only Dr. Runcie's prognosis for Rhys's recovery was as optimistic today as it had been yesterday! "Soon, Rhys Davies, soon," she promised, as much to herself as to him.

"A note, madam," Fuller said, handing her a heavy vellum envelope she instantly recognized as her mother's stationery. Seated in the solarium, she had been reading an order catalogue for tropical plants. By next winter this glass room would be a mini-paradise. Nervously she tore open the envelope.

Her mother had been inconsolable with grief for several weeks, adamantly insisting that Rhys had murdered her son. Tory could well imagine how the news that her daughter had walked into the Naked Truth and dragged him back to Dragon's Lair would sit with Hedda.

She scanned the missive—summons, really—commanding that she appear to discuss "the most distressing news I heard this morning." Tory was emotionally and physically exhausted and unwilling to deal with Hedda. Dr. Runcie had explained to Tory that she could expect to tire easily and find her moods a bit unsteady, especially during the first few months of her pregnancy. Of course, he never anticipated she would have to deal with the threat of someone trying to kill her child's father!

Tory rang for Zenia and requested pen and paper. She composed a brief note, explaining that she was too concerned with Rhys's health to come today but would call on her mother within the week. "Perhaps when I tell her that she's to be a grandmother, she'll believe Rhys is innocent," Tory temporized. But she did not really think that probable.

After all, her pregnancy had not even made Rhys happy. The last thing she would have considered when she confessed her love was that he would think she did so because she was "trapped" by their child. That had wounded her deeply, but after she had spent a restless night mulling everything over, she supposed it was no worse than she deserved. They both had to learn to trust. Love without trust simply would not work.

Cass Loring inspected the small ramshackle cabin, hidden in overgrown weeds. An hour's ride outside Denver, it was isolated and looked unoccupied. Dubiously she asked, "This is the place?"

"Blackie's informants are always right, Cassie. Do you want me to go in with you?" Steve asked.

"No, I can handle her. We agreed it would be better if she talked woman to woman."

"She's a nasty little bitch, from what Blackie told

me about her," Steve said grimly.

A wicked smile spread across Cass's face. "Remember how I handled Selina Ames?" She caressed the blacksnake whip coiled against her shoulder as if it were a house pet. "She talked to me . . . woman to woman."

Steve returned the smile. "From the looks of this place, I doubt there are any china vases or fancy furniture for you to bust up with that whip."

"Yes, but Selina was rich and worried about her pretties. This one's poor—and greedy. I think that'll make my job just as easy," she said with cool confidence.

Steve gave a fond chuckle. "To borrow a line from Rhys's theatrical repertoire, 'Lay on Macduff,'"

Cass dismounted from Angelface, while her husband stood guard. He watched her knock on the cabin door and enter.

Tory stepped from her bath and toweled dry. The steamy vapors were redolent with the essence of violets. *Rhys loves the fragrance*, she thought as she began to brush her hair dry with long, slow strokes. "After all the courage it took to walk into that saloon, this should be simple by comparison," she reassured herself.

Dr. Runcie had examined Rhys's side that afternoon and pronounced it healing remarkably well. Of course, he left no instructions about whether or not they could resume conjugal relations, and Tory would have died of embarrassment to ask. Nonetheless, she felt reassured that it would be safe for her to sleep in the same bed with her husband tonight. She would bide her time and let nature take its course. Within a week or so, his resistance would weaken and her courage grow stronger.

She belted her heavy white velvet robe over a demure white silk nightrail. If not blatantly seductive, the gown was soft and innocent. That had always appealed to him. When she opened the door to their bedroom she heard splashing from the master bath. Doc had said Rhys would benefit from a nice long soak. She had used a guest-room bath while Rufus assisted him into their longer sunken tub. After dismissing all the servants, Tory planned to act as nurse and valet for her husband.

Rhys lay with his head against the heated marble of the tub. His side ached, as much from the drying stitches as from the cut. He swore and shifted in the hot water. Doc was right. Soaking really eased the stiffness of the wound. He wondered if Tory had meant what she said. Would his prim little puritan actually climb in bed with him? He refused to dwell on her motives for this reunion and dreamed instead of how it would feel to touch her silky skin and smell her delicate essence. Feeling himself hardening, he chuckled ruefully, still letting his imagination run wild.

Tory stood in the doorway, the tip of her tongue moistening her lips as she gazed raptly at his naked body. His eyes were closed, making him look boyishly appealing and vulnerable. His magnificent chest rose and fell with soft laughter. The hot water revealed as much as it concealed. That male part of him was standing upright like Excalibur breaking through the waves of that old English lake.

"You're having pleasant dreams, I see," she said sweetly, entering the large room with a fluffy towel on her arm.

His eyes snapped open and he sat up abruptly, splashing water all about. Then, seeing her flushed cheeks and deducing what she had been doing, he lay back with a smile. "How long have you been peeping?"

"Long enough," she replied as she knelt by the tub.

"I suppose you're right," he said smugly as he glanced down at his hardened shaft protruding from the water.

"You'll shrivel to a prune if you don't get out of there soon," she admonished, ignoring his ribaldry.

"And we wouldn't want me to shrivel, would we, love?" he asked as he began to climb from the tub.

A smile twitched at the corner of her lips. This was the old devilish Rhys she remembered. She enveloped him in the towel, careful of the ugly stitched-up gash in his side. "*We* wouldn't want you to do anything to impede your complete and rapid recovery."

Before she realized what was happening, he had her wrapped in the towel along with him and was unfastening her robe. He wrapped his hands in her hair and brought it to his lips, then buried his face in the curve where the slender column of her throat met her shoulder. "Let's work on that sweet dream I was having," he murmured.

"Rhys, you're not strong enough—your side—the stitches," she remonstrated, growing breathless. "I might injure you."

"I'll take my chances. After all, I am a gambler, love."

Chapter Twenty-five

"I only planned to sleep with you tonight, not for us to . . . to . . ."

A wry smile twisted his lips. "Somehow, Tory, cuddling chastely with you doesn't seem to be biologically possible for me." He tugged off her robe and let it drop carelessly on the bathroom floor along with his towel.

"Even when you're stitched up like a Christmas goose?" she asked with breathless exasperation.

"Gander, love, gander," he corrected with a chuckle. "Anyhow, the goose analogy isn't very apt . . ." He nuzzled her neck, murmuring against it, "After all, who'll be stuffing whom?"

A chuckle, half shock, half mirth, shook her as he continued caressing her with soft kisses. "At least let me bandage your side first," she managed to say. "You might break open the stitches."

"Mind you, be gentle with me, love," he admonished as he pulled her after him, holding fast to one slim wrist as he walked to the bed and sat down, completely comfortable in his splendid nakedness.

Tory took the long strips of bandaging in shaky fingers and began to bind his waist. Every time she reached around him and touched his hot flesh, a frisson of pleasure shot through her body. When she felt him tremble in response, she hurried to complete the task. "That should protect you," she said uncertainly, looking up into his eyes.

A wistful smile hovered about his lips. "A suit of armor, Tory love, couldn't protect me from what you do to me. Come here."

He drew her up from her kneeling position between his legs and slid his hands beneath the hem of her white silk gown, running them up her slim legs until he cupped her silky little buttocks. She was so delicately boned and slim-flanked, a stab of worry assailed him. What if she had problems carrying his child? If anything happened to her . . .

Tory felt him go suddenly still. Her fingers splayed in his curly hair, gently tugging and caressing. "What is it, Rhys?" she whispered softly.

He must not frighten her, but still, he had to know. He hesitated, then asked, "Have you asked doc about whether our making love will hurt you or the baby?" He looked up into her face, now blazing with embarrassment.

"Now who's worried about whom?" she managed to say. "When Dr. Runcie told me I was with child, the issue didn't exactly seem pressing, considering our separate living arrangements." Tory tried unsuccessfully to keep the rancor out of her voice.

Rhys knew from several of his married friends that

their wives did not need to abstain from making love during pregnancy, but a woman as hardy and tough as Cass Loring was a far cry from his pale and delicate Victoria. "I told you I wasn't going back to Ginger—or anyone else, Tory," he said, trying to reassure her. "But for now, until I can talk to Dr. Runcie, let's just sleep, nothing more strenuous." He lay back and pulled her with him beneath the thick covers. Lord, it was going to be a long, miserable night! He took a deep breath and tried to relax.

Tory lay very still, almost dazed by his sudden reversal from randy stud to solicitous gentleman. This was not her old Rhys. Was he really concerned for her and the baby? Or did he now find her body, thickening in all the wrong places, less appealing than the voluptuous Ginger's? Had he been dreaming of Ginger when she interrupted his bathtub reverie?

She curled against his hard body, feeling the sexual tension coiled in it. No, he wanted her—and badly! She could abase her pride more and seduce him. He would not long be able to resist, but she decided against it. *I need time to think this through, and he needs time to heal,* she thought. Then in misery she wondered if healing was not only required of his body but of his soul as well. *What have I done?* The chill night air held no answer. She drew closer to Rhys and tried to sleep.

When Rhys arose from a long, restless night, he was still weak and disoriented from yesterday's ordeal. Tory was gone. He felt her pillow. Cold. She had been up and about for some time. He pondered the enigma of his beautiful lady, whom he loved with all his heart but feared to trust. "First thing I have to do is talk to Doc Runcie," he muttered, throwing back the covers. After a night abed. the stitches had tightened up again. The sharp, stabbing burn caught him unaware when he tried to swing his legs over the edge of the bed.

Tory opened the door just in time to hear his colorful stream of oaths. Rhys was doubled over, holding his side. Mudpie raced ahead of his mistress, barking a furious morning welcome. He bounced as if his short, shaggy legs had springs, licking Rhys's face with an amazingly oversized tongue.

"Well, you must be feeling better," she said briskly as she watched him scoop up the pup and deposit him on the big bed. Tucked neatly against her hip she carried a tray laden with fragrant hot rolls, fresh coffee, and a bowl of oatmeal steeped in thick sweet cream. She set the tray on the bedside table and gently shoved him back beneath the covers. Before he could do more than swear again, the dog was at his face with more slurps.

He laughed and held Mudpie at bay. "I surrender to you both!" When the pup hopped nimbly over him and began to sniff at the tray, Rhys looked at its heaping contents. "You and that doctor want me to get fat?" he groused.

"You need strength to heal. I'm the one who'll get fat. You're in pain and white as a ghost," she added crossly.

"I just moved too fast and pulled the drying stitches, that's all," he protested, feeling oddly elated as she fussed, arranging the tray on his lap, then plumping up pillows behind his back. While she sat at the foot of the bed and held the greedy pup, he dug into the hot oatmeal and took a sip of coffee.

After she was satisfied that his appetite was up to snuff, Tory tossed the pup back onto the bed and headed for the bathroom. She could hear Rhys and Mudpie negotiate for bits of buttered sweet roll as she knelt to turn on the steaming hot water. "You'll feel better when you soak again," she called out.

"I hope so since I have to go to town today," he said, feeding bites of crumbly sweet roll to the dog.

"You'll do no such thing," Tory cried out as she turned off the water, then stood up and walked back to his bedside. "You're in no condition to be bouncing around in a carriage."

"I'm fine. There's something I have to do."

"What?" Her heart squeezed with dread. Surely he did not regret his precipitous move from the Naked Truth.

"Er . . . Mike. I have to see Mike. The marshal from Lake City is supposed to be investigating the attempt to kill me, but I want to do some checking on my own. Mike can handle it for me." He also planned to drop in for a talk with Doc Runcie before another night went by, but he was not going to tell her that and worry her unnecessarily.

"Speaking of Mike," she temporized, "I talked with him last week . . . about who killed Sanders." That got his attention. She met his piercing blue stare levelly, then picked up Mudpie and held him tightly as she once more sat down on the bed.

"And what did that Irish font of information have to say?" he asked expressionlessly.

"He sent word to Denver to find the murderer as soon as he heard the news."

"And?"

"And he has every friend you both know in the city working on it. Lots of leads, but nothing definite yet. But I've been thinking . . ."

"Always a dangerous proposition," he said with a hint of his old teasing ways. He coaxed Mudpie with one outstretched hand and she released the dog.

"No, really, Rhys," she protested, wanting desperately for him to believe that she trusted him. But hadn't she herself gone to Mike for proof of his innocence? Her conscience smote her, but she continued, "I read the detective's report about my brother's murder. His throat was cut." Her eyes fastened on the cut across Rhys's jawline.

His hands stilled on the dog's shaggy fur. "And you think the same fellow who wanted me dead killed Sanders?" He hesitated, then resumed stroking Mudpie and said, "Frankly, the same idea did occur to me, but damned if I can see any common enemies we might share." He forbore to mention that any street tough in Denver would happily kill a drunk like her brother for the price of a bottle of forty rod.

"Emmet Hauser and my brother knew one another. They were on the verge of a fight when I came upon them in the park on July Fourth. I think . . . well, I'm afraid Sanders could have been involved with Hauser's niece Ella. She acted awfully familiar with him."

"And I won the saloon from him. That for sure puts me on Hauser's list." He digested that, vaguely recalling the man's niece being at the altercation in the park. "Damn!" He suddenly stopped petting the dog and sat up in bed. "Barlow! I thought he was after me because I had him sent to jail for cheating at cards. He was doing Hauser's dirty work then. He might have been hired by him to kill me."

"And when he botched the job, Emmet came after you himself. No one has seen him or Ella in months." Tory worried her lower lip with small white teeth, then looked at Rhys. "You stay here. I'll send for Mike. You're in no condition to fend off another attack by a brute like Emmet Hauser."

He polished off the last of his coffee, then set the tray on the floor. The dog was off the bed with his front feet planted in the dishes in a single bound. "First I'll soak, then, nurse, you can bind up my wounds and I'm going to town," he said with finality.

"Then I'm going with you."

"The hell you are. You're staying right here and rest. You look pretty peaked yourself. You have the baby to consider now." He yanked off the covers, but exercised more care in sliding out of bed this time.

Tory watched him stand up and raise his arms. Then he commanded her to unwrap the bandages so he could get on with his bath. "And if I refuse?" she asked mutinously.

"Then I'll do it myself," he replied, reaching down to tug at the wrappings.

She conceded defeat and unfastened the bandage, knowing it would do no good to argue further. He shrugged free of the last of the wrap, and she touched the puckered stitches gingerly. "The wound does seem to be healing well," she said grudgingly. Mudpie wagged his tail in agreement.

Just to show her he could, he stretched languorously, but very carefully, then walked briskly to the bath as the dog cheered him on with yipping and tail wagging. He knelt and turned on the tub to finish filling it.

As Tory rummaged through his armoire playing valet, she mulled over his actions. He had sworn never to let her go and was furiously jealous of Charles. He had returned with her to Dragon's Lair because of the baby. Now he did not want her overtaxing herself because of her pregnancy. She smiled in spite of her troubled thoughts. Once, just saying the word "pregnant" would have caused her to flush with embarrassment. What a stupid little prig she had been! But that was exactly what Hedda Laughton had raised her to be—a perfect lady. That was what had attracted Rhys to her in the first place. He wanted his wife and child, but would he ever trust her—or even desire her again?

"I'll get fat and shapeless and he'll go back to Ginger . . ." She struggled with tears. Her pregnancy was playing havoc with her emotions. "I've never cried as much in my life as I have in the past month," she mumbled to Mudpie as she laid out Rhys's clothes.

Tory needed to talk to another woman. As soon as Rhys left for town, she would take the other rig and make a hurried visit to Laura's. She did not allow herself to dwell on the possibility that she might follow Rhys to the *Plain Speaker* . . . or to the Naked Truth.

As soon as she pulled up in front of the lovely old frame house and saw the front crowded with carriages, Tory could have cried with frustration. Laura's endless charitable and social functions left her little free time. This was garden club day. The intrepid woman would have a houseful of chattering guests all afternoon. Scanning the carriages for her mother's covered buggy, she did not see it. Laura and Hedda had become increasingly estranged ever since Tory had gone to the mud slide last fall. Her mother blamed Laura for encouraging such unseemly behavior.

Tory sighed, saddened beyond words because of her own deteriorating relationship with her parents. She looked down at Mudpie, huddled beneath the thick fur lap robe. The sun was brilliant and the snow glistening, but the temperature was quite cold. "Laura loves to see you, Mudpie, but somehow I doubt that Mama will share her sentiments," she said ruefully.

As if he understood, the pup barked once in agreement and scuttled deeper beneath the furs. "Ah well, I might as well not waste this trip to town. Maybe it will help Mama accept my reconciliation with Rhys if I tell her about the baby." As she drove across town, she did not really believe that anything would mend the breach, but visiting Hedda was much preferable to her other impulse. She resolutely refused to go to the newspaper office to check on her husband.

While Tory proceeded to the Laughton home, Rhys sat in Doc Runcie's waiting room nervously rubbing his injured side. The soak had helped ease the tightening stitches, but now the infernal things had begun to itch like hell.

"What are you doing up and about, you blasted Welsh mule?" Runcie's white hair was finger-combed back from his forehead and his shirt sleeves were rolled up. "I just finished sewing up another thick-headed foreigner. Some damn German brewer tried to pick a fight at your saloon. Mr. Grange can be most persuasive with that twelve-gauge. I dug enough lead out of that fool's ass to take down a grizzly." He motioned impatiently for Rhys to follow him in where his nurse was cleaning off the examining table. "If you think I'm taking out those stitches just because they itch—"

"I didn't come here for myself, doc." Rhys paused and looked over at Mrs. Whaley. "Er, doc, could we talk in your office, in private?"

The old doctor nodded irascibly. He had spent a

chaotic morning, and muttered, "If this is the winter slow season, God deliver Starlight from the spring." He motioned for Rhys to follow him down the hall to his private quarters.

"Any luck finding another doctor to help out here?" Rhys asked as they walked.

"Yes. I may just take her up on the offer, too."

"Her! A female doctor?" Davies was incredulous.

Runcie chuckled. "Medical school's been turning them out for around forty years. Twice as hard for a woman to make it through because men don't want the competition. Might make this Dr. Elizabeth Denton Gantry the offer of a job. Seems her mother's been practicing in San Francisco since the fifties."

"Well, I'll be damned," Rhys said as he sat down in a big leather chair across from Runcie's desk.

"Yep, you young Welsh pup, you most probably will, but that's not why you're here," the doctor said as he closed the door.

For a moment Rhys Davies felt acutely uncomfortable. He could discuss anything about himself with the doctor, but to discuss his wife seemed so painfully personal. He began hesitantly, "It's about Tory . . . she's so small and delicate . . . I'm worried about her."

Saul Runcie fixed Rhys with a measuring eye. "I've known Tory Laughton since she was born. I ought to. I delivered her. She may be fine-boned and prone to sunburn, but she's squirrel tough. She'll come through this pregnancy with no trouble at all. You really helped me out though, right off."

"How's that?" Rhys looked baffled.

"You ordered her out of her damn fool corset! Best thing in the world for all women is to throw those damned torture racks on the trash heap, especially when they're expecting a child. I told her to get plenty of fresh air and exercise, gave her a sensible diet, and told her not to pay a lick of attention to anything overprotective or dumb you might tell her."

"Thanks a lot . . . I think. You're sure she's not going to have any problems?"

The old man flatly assured him, "Tory's like her mother. Hedda always was strong as a steel band. Both her deliveries went easy as could be. Of course, she carried on to Stoddard like he'd sawed off her arm, but that's just how she is—cussed! Thank your gambler's luck Tory doesn't think like her mother. Tory's a throwback to some ancestor or other, not like Hedda or Stoddard. Maybe a great-grandma back East." His eyes twinkled.

Rhys's face reflected immense relief. "Then, it would be safe for me . . . for us—"

"Right up till she tells you it's time to ride into town and fetch me," Doc interrupted gleefully. "Or, on second thought"—he paused and watched Rhys's face fall again—"you might just be fetching that new female doctor. Tory might really take a liking to another woman delivering her baby."

Rhys left the office in pure bliss. A smile twitched about his lips as he recalled Runcie's parting advice about making love with his wife. "Just don't go doing anything out-of-the-way acrobatic like swinging from that fancy chandelier of yours." He climbed into the buggy and eagerly headed home.

Tory walked toward the kitchen door of the Laughtons' brick house with Mudpie tucked beneath her coat. She had pulled up the alley and cut across the back yard, hoping to leave the pup in Tess's warm kitchen while she told her parents her news, after which she was sure she would be facing their angry questions about why she had disgraced them by entering a saloon. "As if Rhys would ever have come crawling back to me," she whispered forlornly.

Mudpie barked once, but she shushed him sternly. "Now you must be quiet or it's out in the snow with you. Tess will be in terrible trouble for letting you in the kitchen if you bark and give yourself away."

As if anticipating the bribe of a juicy steak bone, the pup silently wagged his tail. Tory climbed the stairs and shoved open the heavy back door.

Tess was hard at work in the cheery warmth of the big room, rolling out crust for a dried-apple pie. Her face wreathed in a welcoming smile when she saw Tory and the raggedy little dog. "Ain't he the cutest little dickens! You always did want a dog, Miz Tory. Here, let me hold him while you take off your coat."

"Tess, meet Mudpie," Tory said with a chuckle. "Is Mama home? I need to talk with her, but I don't want her to know this rascal is with me. She has less than fond memories of their first encounter."

"I'll keep him happy 'n' quiet," Tess promised. "Your mother's upstairs in her parlor." Her expression darkened. "It's the maid's day off. Even got the back stairs fresh painted this morning. Man said it won't be dry until late tonight. House was empty until that friend of your pa's come over. Your pa got back from the bank early. Him 'n' Mr. Everett are in the study."

"Oh, I see," Tory said awkwardly. The last man alive she wanted to see was Charles Everett. Rhys would never understand. As if things weren't already tense enough between her parents and her husband. "Maybe I should come back another day."

"Your ma . . . she ain't actin' right, Miz Tory. She's been real poorly ever since, well, what happened to your brother, God rest him. She seemed real upset yesterday. Maybe you could cheer her up."

"I guess I could walk past the study very quietly and go upstairs," Tory said uncertainly. Hedda had always been so coolly in command of everything, but the family's penury, her marriage to Rhys, and now Sanders's death had destroyed her mother's orderly world.

"Please, Mudpie, you be quiet and do as Tess says," she implored. The dog snuggled against the big woman's ample bosom and wagged his tail.

Tory set off down the long hallway after carefully closing the stout kitchen door. Even if the dog barked, there was little chance that anyone in the front of the house would hear him. She neared the door to her father's study and heard the indistinct drone of voices. How odd that they had left the door ajar. Then she recalled that it was the servants' day off, except for Tess, whose domain was strictly the kitchen. *I'll just have to slip by without them seeing me.*

She neared the door and the voices grew clearer. Her father was speaking.

"Dammit, Charles, when we began this thing you told me Davies would be dead in a month. Now he's still hale and hearty, rubbing my nose in the dirt, and we're no nearer to getting control of his money than we were when Tory married the bastard."

"Just calm down, Stoddard. Barlow was Hauser's mistake. I didn't even know he was using the stupid boy. I'm meeting Emmet shortly at the cabin to give him a good dressing-down about that debacle in the stable. Next time he won't fail. That damn Welsh trash will be dead, and you'll be back in control of your bank." Charles's voice was quiet as it wafted into the hall on fragrant cigar smoke.

Tory stood with her back against the wall, fighting waves of suffocating nausea. *They plan to kill my husband!* Her own father and the man she had been affianced to. They had planned it all along—ever since she had married Rhys! She choked back the bile rising in her throat. *I have to get away and warn Rhys!*

She turned and dashed for the kitchen, forgetting the Louis XVI side table with its Sevres vase directly in her path. Her hip caught the edge of the table with wicked impact, toppling the vase to the floor and sending Tory flying against the opposite wall. The pain was punishing, but she gritted her teeth and shoved off again limping. She had nearly made the safety of the kitchen when strong fingers clamped over her mouth and an arm wrapped about her waist, squeezing the breath from her.

Charles lifted her kicking, struggling body up and turned to Stoddard. "Damn, this is a wonderful mess!"

"What will we do?" Stoddard asked, his eyes straying toward the front stairs and Hedda's sitting room above it. He looked at his daughter struggling in Charles Everett's grasp like an enraged fury.

Charles's face, black with rage a moment earlier, took on a slow, ugly smile. "I guess you and your dear daughter will have to make a trip to your summer cabin out of season."

"You can't mean to harm her, Charles," Stoddard protested, aghast.

"You moron! Of course I won't harm my future wife." He felt Tory struggle with renewed fury and winced as she succeeded in kicking him, but his cruel grip on her never slackened. "She'll make excellent bait for her present husband. If Davies thinks she's at the cabin, he'll come running to her rescue—right into Emmet Hauser's open gun sights."

Chapter Twenty-six

"Since we don't have any chloroform at hand, my dear, you will forgive me," Charles said, shoving Tory roughly toward Stoddard, who caught her before she nearly knocked him down. Just as she sucked enough air in her lungs to scream, Charles's fist connected with her jaw. She slumped against her father, out cold.

"Good Lord, Charles, did you have to do that?" Stoddard struggled to hold his daughter's unconscious weight.

Impatiently Everett grabbed Tory, slung her over his shoulder, and returned to the library with Stoddard following, wringing his hands. "What would you have me do? Let her scream her fool head off and bring that damn cook flying down the hall with a rolling pin in her hand? We have to get her out of here quickly and quietly. She's in no mood to listen to reason," Charles added sarcastically as he gagged Tory with his linen handkerchief. "Give me your handkerchief," he commanded.

When Stoddard complied, Everett took the linen and tied her hands tightly behind her. "Now, get a hold of yourself. We'll make this up to Victoria after she's been relieved of that barbarian husband. Once she's a wealthy widow, we can cajole her around. Anyway, she'll be up to her pretty little eyeballs in the murder of a man who the whole town knows deserted her for a saloon doxie." He laughed mirthlessly. "Most of Davies's good friends, incited by that imbecile newspaper editor, will doubtless want her hanged for collusion in his death. Your daughter will see things our way, believe me." As he spoke, Everett poured a stiff belt of Stoddard's fine whiskey in a glass and shoved it at the ashen-faced older man.

"This isn't at all the way we planned it," Stoddard said, drinking down the bourbon with a shudder.

"Sometimes one has to improvise,"Charles replied as he picked up Tory's unconscious body and slung her once again over his shoulder. "You check to see that no one is about. I'll follow with her. If we go out the side door, we can use the hedge as cover to get to your stable."

In the kitchen, Tess pulled the first batch of apple pies from the oven. Looking at the dog quizzically observing her, she speculated aloud, "You got a sweet tooth?"

As if in answer, Mudpie eyed the steaming flaky crust and wagged his tail. With a shake of her head she walked to a large pie pantry and opened it, then scooped up the pies and placed them inside. Quickly losing interest in the unattainable, the pup went back to the bone she had given him earlier.

When that proved boring, he scampered across the big room to a door left ajar, which led into a storage area where Tess kept supplies. Smelling his way around, he found nothing of interest amid sacks of flour, tightly sealed barrels of molasses, and pungent herbs. But a small window at the end of the long room beckoned him. It was open a tiny crack to let fresh air into the stuffy storeroom. He scrambled onto a pickle barrel with difficulty and peered out, tail thumping.

Tess, checking on her charge and finding him safely occupied, decided a trip to the privy was in order. Grumbling about rich people who had indoor conveniences only for themselves, she slung on a coat and walked out the kitchen door. "I gotta freeze my tender parts off in this cold. It purely ain't fair," she muttered, cutting across the back yard in the opposite direction from the high row of snow-covered hedges that concealed Stoddard, Charles, and their prisoner.

Tess couldn't see Tory being carried out, but Mudpie did. In spite of several furious barks, he heard no reassuring sound from her. The mutt jumped from his perch and headed into the kitchen. Finding it empty, he raced to the rear door and began to scratch frantically. As soon as Tess opened the door, he shot past her, crossing snow that had drifted deeply along the hedge.

The cook watched him race toward the stables, bounding up and down through the drifts. "Guess you got the same urge as me," she said with a chuckle, expecting that the mutt would get cold and return as soon as he found a clear place in which to transact his business.

Charles saw Tory's buggy tied out back, and his eyes narrowed. "See if that stupid drunk of a stableman is about," he commanded Stoddard as he dumped the awakening girl into her small conveyance.

Stoddard returned saying, "He's asleep by the stove inside."

"Good. You drive her carriage up to your cabin. Let's just hope the trail is clear."

"Look, Charles, I don't like—"

Stoddard's remonstrance was cut short by a raggedy bundle of growling fury that launched itself at Everett's pants leg. He quickly released Tory, causing her to crumple to the floor of the carriage. One reflexive kick sent the little dog flying across the snow, but Charles's pants leg was ripped all the way up to the knee. With a snarled oath, he lunged after Tory's unlikely rescuer. Mudpie danced just out of reach, barking furiously. Quickly realizing he was getting nowhere, Charles turned to Stoddard, who was standing helplessly by the carriage, and snapped, "Get the hell out of town with her. Stand on her if you have to when she wakes up. I'll keep this little bastard from following. You know what to tell Hauser when he gets there. Hurry, dammit!" He practically lifted Stoddard into the carriage and shoved the whip into his hands.

Tory could hear Mudpie's angry barking through a haze of pain. She was lying in a cramped position with her hands tied behind her. Her jaw ached, and when she tried to cry out, she became aware of the gag in her mouth. Her memory returned in an avalanche of terror as she heard Charles commanding her father to drive. She let out a muffled sob and struggled to sit up, but her terrified father took Everett's advice and placed one foot across her shoulder, shoving her down. The buggy took off with a sudden lurch, slamming her head against the hard wooden surface below the driver's seat. Everything went black.

Charles fleetingly considered shooting the mutt as he kicked and grabbed at the furball, while Stoddard flew down the alley. But a shot would bring unwanted attention, and killing Tory's pet would be difficult to explain. When Laughton's stableman Barnie stumbled out, rubbing sleep from his eyes, Everett yelled, "Grab that damn dog! It attacked me." Thank God the carriage had got away without the pup being able to follow it.

Barnie had no better luck than Everett in catching the nimble animal, who finally eluded his pursuer and bounded down the alley. The carriage with his beloved mistress's scent was long gone. Lost, cold, and bereft, Mudpie began to scout in widening circles, looking for someone friendly in this suddenly hostile town. Then he caught a familiar scent. There was one place his mistress often took him, and it was nearby!

Rhys climbed out of his carriage, still elated over the news from Doc Runcie. He was greeted by the efficient Fuller, who opened the front door just as he reached for the knob.

"Good afternoon, sir. I trust your morning in town was productive."

Rhys fairly beamed. "More than you could ever guess, my friend. Is Mrs. Davies about?"

Fuller had the good grace to look flustered, "Er, I assumed you knew, sir. The mistress went to town just after you did. She took the pup with her." That fact obviously pleased the tidy butler immensely.

"Did she drive herself?" Fuming, he already knew the answer. Headstrong woman.

At Fuller's affirmative nod, he stormed back down

the steps and yelled to Lee, who had begun to lead the horse and carriage away. "Saddle Blackjack before you rub down that gelding." If she had her buggy in town, he would drive it back and no more nonsense from her. Swing from chandeliers, indeed! All he wanted was to keep her safe, tucked in their nice warm bed.

As he rode to town, Rhys considered where his errant wife most likely had gone. Either to Laura's or to make peace with her parents. Since the Laughton place was closest, he would try there first. As he rode, his side ached. To take his mind off the discomfort, he mulled over the situation with his in-laws. Although he did not give a damn for their regard, Tory was cruelly caught in the middle. By coming to the saloon so openly and asking him to return home, she had chosen him over them, but should he require her to abandon them?

In time she might come to resent losing her only remaining family. His old insecurities still nagged at him as he remembered how he and Stoddard had bargained for Tory as if she were a piece of thoroughbred livestock. Now he had bound her to him with the child, but he knew that was not enough. *I want her to believe in me!*

Rhys was so deep in thought that Blackjack nearly overran Laura Everett's small carriage, which was rounding a corner near the Laughton house. "I see we're both bound for the same place," she called out. "Are you well enough to be riding after what happened yesterday?"

"I'm up on this big devil, am I not?" he said with a weak smile.

At the sound of that familiar voice, Mudpie's ears pricked up and he worked his head above the tight confines of the lap robe in which Laura had wrapped

411

him. He let out several sharp barks.

"Keeping an eye on Mudpie, Laura?" Rhys asked in amusement. "I know Hedda detests the rascal, but—"

"No, as a matter of fact, I was returning the runaway. I found him scratching at my back door and assumed he'd left Hedda's place, sensing how unwelcome he was." Her smile faded as she added, "Not that I'm exactly persona grata myself these days."

"Of course, my in-laws just love me," Rhys said drily. "I owe you for sending Tory to me yesterday, Laura."

"She would've come sooner or later. I just helped work up her courage for sooner."

"Still, since I owe you so many favors, let me repay a bit. I'll take that rascal and beard the lioness in her den to get my wife back."

"Are you sure you wouldn't rather change places and wait while I extract Tory from Hedda's velvet clutches?" she asked with a twinkle.

"I have to face them eventually." He shrugged carelessly. "Might as well be now. Anyway," he said as he reached down for the wriggling pup, "Tory and I have a few things to settle ourselves."

"Oh-oh. I detect the brewing of another tempest in a teapot," she said without great concern as she handed over Mudpie.

As Laura turned her small rig around and headed home with a cheery farewell, Rhys rode toward the Laughtons. Tory's buggy was not out front. Perhaps in the rear? "Did you escape from Tess? Odd you'd go so far from your mistress," he said to the pup. "Well, we won't skulk in the back door this time, bucko." Rhys dismounted in front of the imposing brick edifice and walked boldly up the stairs with the little dog tucked beneath one arm. He was amazed when Hedda herself opened the door. His eyebrows raised as he pushed back his hat and gave her a startled, "Hello, Hedda. Ralph quit?"

Her lips thinned with fury as she looked from the smiling ruffian to the nasty little beast. "How dare you show your face in this house! You murderer! You'll hang for having my son killed. I swear it!"

Rhys walked insolently past her, ignoring her outburst. She flinched back when Mudpie's tail touched her sleeve. Then a look of cunning suffused her face, replacing the rage of a moment earlier. "If you're searching for Victoria, she isn't here."

Rhys turned and looked at her measuringly, alarm registered on his usually impassive face. "She's not with Laura and she's not at home. Where the hell else would she be?"

Hedda's eyes glowed a pale silvery aqua. "There's no need for your disgusting profanity, you child killer! It would seem Victoria is coming to her senses. She's gone with her father to our summer cabin. She needs some time to reconsider her rash actions of yesterday." Triumph fairly radiated from every pore in her body.

"You're lying," he said in a cold, deadly voice. She hissed in outrage as he took a step nearer, letting Mudpie jump to the floor. "Tory wouldn't leave me now. And she wouldn't leave her dog to wander lost in the cold, either."

Hedda looked at the mutt with disdain, then backed away from the menace of the man looming over her. "You're a fine one to call me a liar! Why wouldn't Victoria want to be rid of you after all you've put her through?"

He skewered her with his icy gaze. "Because she's carrying my baby. That's what she came to tell me

413

yesterday. Now where is my wife, dammit?"

Hedda literally staggered back against the wall in horror. "Your child. Oh, God, God," she whispered brokenly, then looked up at him with loathing. "Even that won't do you any good. It's too late. Charles told me Stoddard has taken Victoria to our cabin. I never spoke to her, or she would've told me about the tragedy of carrying a murderer's baby." She paused for effect, then said spitefully, "Perhaps she's going to have an abortion at the cabin. Her father might be able to arrange it!"

Rhys never in his life so badly wanted to strike a woman. "Give me directions to that damn cabin or so help me God I'll beat them out of you!"

A few minutes later, Rhys stalked out of the house with Mudpie at his heels and a rough map in his hand, leaving a softly sobbing Hedda Laughton in her parlor. Grabbing up the dog, he mounted Blackjack and rode quickly to the Naked Truth.

Ginger Vogel's jaw dropped. So did the deck of cards she held in nerveless fingers. She watched Rhys stride into the saloon and head for the stairs. He barely paused to nod at her as he took the steps two at a time. Skirts held high, she raced after him. His face was grim and his movements tense as he raided the desk in his old office and yanked his Winchester from a case in the corner.

"You got real trouble to be up and runnin' after near bleedin' to death yesterday," she said from the door.

The small dog he had carried in barked excitedly at her feet. She ignored it until he turned and said, "Would you mind keeping an eye on Mudpie here?" He motioned to the mutt as he jammed cartridges into his pockets.

"Would you mind tellin' me what the hell's goin'

on?" She rounded the desk and her hand on his arm.

"Something's happened to Tory. I need my rifle," he replied tersely. "Hedda says she's gone up to a cabin on Gold Leaf Mountain with Stoddard—to get away from me. I don't believe it."

"Rhys, it's a setup to kill you! It's gotta be."

"Maybe," he said flatly. "But whoever's doing it has endangered my wife." He looked at her, and she could read the desperation in his eyes. "Tory's pregnant, Ginger. She wouldn't leave me now."

Ginger swore. "Some lowlife bastard's usin' her to get to you. You can't just ride up there and take a bullet with your name on it!"

"I can't just sit here while she's missing." He buckled his gunbelt about his hips and checked the .45 caliber Peacemaker.

"You think her own pa would hurt her?" she asked incredulously.

"Hell, I don't know. Charles Everett's involved. Probably Hauser, too."

Ginger blanched. "Emmet's snake mean. Jesus! Him 'n' that weasel lawyer together—you need help!"

"I don't have time. Anyway, if I go alone, there's less risk they'll hurt Tory." He walked past her, shaking off her restraining arm. "Watch the dog, will you? Tory loves him."

"Where is this cabin? I'll send someone after you," she called out, racing behind him as he stalked down the stairs.

"I've survived when the odds were a lot worse. This time I know they're after me."

Mudpie was barking at his heels. He stopped in the saloon door and picked the dog up, thrusting him into her arms. "Lock him up." With that he was gone.

From the window she watched him ride out of town heading west. "Any of you fellers know about a place ole man Laughton's got up on Gold Leaf Mountain?"

Tory lay on the big soft bed, her hands bound securely. In spite of her exhaustion, terror and discomfort kept her wide awake. She stared across the room to where her father knelt, building a blaze in the large open fireplace to combat the chill. They had been forced to abandon the buggy on the narrow snowy trail several miles down the mountain. Stoddard had unhitched the team and tied her to one horse, then mounted the other and led them the rest of the way to his hunting lodge, riding bareback.

He had not removed her gag. *He's afraid I'll talk him out of Charles's mad scheme.* But looking at the driven desperation in his eyes, Tory did not really believe it was possible. Stoddard Laughton had become a stranger to her. Her eyes followed him about the room as he closed all the curtains and then threw the bars on the front and rear doors.

He had said very little up until now, but with everything in readiness for Emmet Hauser, he had to attempt to reason with his daughter. She had not fought him when he moved her from the buggy to the house, but only because she was dazed. Stoddard studied her surreptitiously as he began to prepare a simple meal from stores that Charles had provided Hauser in the cabin, which was their secret rendezous point.

He sliced part of a smoked ham and opened a jar of strawberry jam to soften the stale biscuits. While he worked, he considered Tory's relationship with Davies. Hedda was convinced that the trashy foreigner had won her allegiance, or at least turned her into someone other than the biddable ladylike daughter Tory had been trained to be. He had seen the blatantly sexual electricity that flashed between the two of them, even before their marriage. Indeed, it was one reason he had first considered the possibility of using his daughter to recoup his fortune.

Victoria obviously did not share her mother's aversion to the bedroom. Hedda would never have couched it in those blunt terms, but he knew it was a fact. His daughter was physically in thrall to the arrogant Welshman. Accepting that distasteful thought was one thing, but if Tory's loyalty ran deeper, they were in serious trouble. He would have to test the waters. Filling a plate with food and pouring a cup of coffee, he set them on the sturdy table in the center of the room. Then, looking at the rigid way she lay on the bed, dirty, disheveled, and bruised, he quickly brought a cloth and a basin of water to her side.

Very carefully he removed the gag. Tory swallowed, but she did not say anything, just gazed at him with those accusing turquoise eyes. He had always thought they were her mother's eyes. Now he knew that only the color was the same. When he bathed the bruise on her temple, she flinched and drew back, not as much in pain as in revulsion.

"You'd better let me tend you, Tory," he admonished sternly.

"Kiss the bruise you yourself inflicted," she said accusingly.

"You are going to listen to me, young lady. What I have to say may be unpleasant, but this past year we all of us have had to deal with a great deal of unpleasantness."

"I scarcely consider that murdering my husband falls in the category of mere unpleasantness," she said flatly.

"You were the one who hated Rhys Davies. You protested your horror at marrying saloon trash. Now Charles and I are offering you a way to escape."

Her bound hands clenched into fists behind her back. "And I suppose once I'm a rich widow, Charles will expect that I'll marry him in gratitude for his masterminding my freedom." This had to be a nightmare. Surely she would wake up any moment, safe in Rhys's arms. The curt nod of her father's head quickly brought her back to brutal reality.

"Charles was the man you chose to wed," he said with smug assurance.

"Charles was the man you and Mama chose! The man who killed Sanders!" At Stoddard's look of incredulous disbelief, she continued quickly, "Yes, if he hired Emmet Hauser, it must be true! Sanders had his throat cut. The same way Rhys was attacked. My husband didn't kill my brother. Emmet Hauser did!"

"That's the most absurd thing I ever heard in my life. Charles had no reason to kill Sanders. Your husband, my dear, had every reason—his obsession with you. I'll hear no more girlish fantasies!" He towered over her, furious with her obstinacy and frightened by what might happen if she persisted with her absurd accusations.

Tory watched his struggle with his inner demons. For the first time in her life she realized what a weak man Stoddard Laughton really was. He had always been manipulated by Hedda. Now he was being used by Charles. *He's afraid of what will happen to him if I don't agree to Charles's plans.*

"I'm hungry, Papa. Please, my arms hurt. Could you untie me and let me eat?" No cajolery, just a simple request. She must proceed carefully and think this through or he would turn on her even without Charles's promptings.

Stoddard looked at his small, delicate daughter. She could go nowhere in this snowbound wilderness. Although only an hour from town, the cabin was isolated and Hauser would soon arrive. "Very well. I hope you'll be amenable to reason." He untied her wrists and watched her rub circulation back into her numb hands.

Her arms ached as if wrenched from their shoulder sockets and her fingers burned and tingled. She rubbed her jaw and felt the swelling from Charles's love tap. *A lifetime and I never knew him at all.* Of course, she had never known her parents or even Sanders, if she were to be truly honest. *Maybe I saw in them only what I wanted to see.*

Tory stood up and walked slowly to the heavy table where the food beckoned her. She was always starved these days—when she wasn't nauseous—but eating now was simply a ruse to reach the table and a possible weapon. As she bit into a slice of ham, Tory debated telling Stoddard about the baby. She simply could not gauge how he might react. The news might make things better or worse. What could she do to escape? Her mind raced in circles.

"When will Emmet Hauser arrive?" she asked between bites.

Stoddard sat down across from her, careful to keep the knife well clear of her as he dug into his plate of food. "Soon. Long before Davies gets the note at Dragon's Lair instructing him to come here," he said guardedly, watching for her reaction.

Tory averted her eyes and forced herself to keep eating. The ham lodged in her throat. She sipped coffee in desperation, trying to swallow it and remain calm. Remembering Hauser's sour-smelling body pressed against her that day in the park, she decided to gamble. "There's something you must

419

know that will seriously upset your plans. I'm going to have Rhys's child in the spring, Papa." She held her breath a moment as his fork clattered onto the plate. "Your grandchild," she whispered pleadingly, but the expression of enraged horror on his face told her she had lost the gamble.

"You expect me to hand you over to that back-alley murderer and walk off to prison and total disgrace simply because you're going to have his sprawn!"

Tory held on to the sides of her chair seat to keep from flying across the table and slapping him. *How can I escape?* She no longer gave any thought to her father's safety or even his life, just so long as she escaped. "Charles won't marry me now," she said coldly, stalling as she inventoried the room for a possible weapon.

Stoddard laughed coarsely. "To get Davies's fortune, Charles would marry a gargoyle impregnated by Satan himself." He looked into her face, now composed, unreadable. "I need Charles to control you, I fear, Victoria. You've not proven any more dutiful than your brother. I always told Hedda she mollycoddled the boy. You were both indulged too much," he said bitterly.

"Yes, I suppose from your point of view we were," Tory said softly, eyeing the sharp butcher knife beside her father's plate while he stared into the fire, lost in his twisted reminiscences. No, he would easily overpower her before she could grab it. Just then a log in the fire burned through and slipped with a loud hiss onto the stone hearth.

Stoddard stood up, careful to reclaim the knife and slip it into his belt. She made no move but sat sipping her coffee. Coffee! As he walked to the hearth, she looked at the heavy granite pot, filled with scalding hot coffee. Steeling herself, she silently placed her cup on the table and watched as he bent over the fire with the poker in his hand, shoving the heavy log back into the blaze. Without allowing herself to consider that he might topple into the fire, she grabbed the pot with a heavy quilted holder and lunged up, wrenching the lid off as her father turned and straightened, poker in hand. The scalding liquid spashed full in his face, and he screamed in rage, raising the iron implement to strike blindly at her.

Tory quickly sidestepped and used both hands to bring down the heavy granite pot. It connected with his temple. Desperation had given her amazing strength. Stoddard dropped the poker from limp fingers and crumpled to the hearth inches from the licking flames. The knife in his belt clattered to the floor and bounced into the corner near the bed, but Tory did not notice in her frantic haste. She threw the pot to the floor and then pulled her father's unconscious body away from the fire with one fast yank of his arm.

Once she had him clear of the fire, Tory reached inside his jacket and grabbed the Navy pocket pistol from his belt. Rising, she quickly scanned the room for the blanket they had thrown about her when they abducted her. Wrapping it around herself, she ran to the front door and slipped the heavy bar, then raced into the chill afternoon air. The horses stood tethered down the slope in plain view. Tory gathered up her skirts and began to slog through the snow determinedly with the pistol clutched in one hand.

She had just grabbed Annabelle's reins and was ready to haul herself up on the horse's back when a strong pair of gloved hands clamped on her waist.

"Well, what have I got me here?" Emmet Hauser asked with a nasty chuckle as he knocked the gun from her hand.

Chapter Twenty-seven

Mike Manion had put in a long day. The afternoon edition of the *Speaker* was sold out and he had earned a rest. Keys jingling in his hand, he considered tidying up the place—but only for a moment. Only a madman or a *Sassenach* would disturb the sublime chaos of his office, although Virgil now and then made a stab at it. The Chinese woman who scrubbed the windows and floors monthly, whether they needed it or not, replaced every slip and balled-up wad of paper exactly where she found it. Perhaps someday when life grew peaceful in the San Juans he would really clean out this firetrap. Shrugging, he turned to the door.

"Don't lock up yet unless you want to buy me dinner," Steve Loring said with a broad grin.

Mike tossed his keys onto his desk, where they vanished in the quicksand of papers. "Well, news must be mighty good to bring you all the way from

Denver," he said, rubbing his hands in gleeful anticipation of a hot story. "Who did in the Laughton lad?"

Steve doffed his heavy sheepskin jacket and tossed it on the coat tree, then shoved a box to one side of the desk and sat on the edge with one long buckskin-clad leg swinging carelessly. "You're going to love this, Mike. What do you think about Charles Everett being fitted for a noose?"

"Saints be praised," Mike breathed in pure delight. "Do go on." He fished through a drawer and pulled out a pencil, then grabbed his note pad from the seat of his chair.

"It's a long and twisty tale. One I'm sure your readers will relish, even if Stoddard and Hedda won't. Blackie sent a few of his trusty minions out, as per your request, to check on Sanders's activities before he met his demise. While he was still in Denver the first time, before he went to Cheyenne, he made a few very interesting fiscal transactions."

"And that's where you came in," Mike said, pen poised.

"His daddy's money was placed in an account in San Francisco. Quite a tidy sum. For a sot, the kid was damn bright—he sent me on a paper trail that took some fancy unraveling."

"Not to mention pulling a few strings back East," Mike suggested with a twinkle. Steve Loring was the scion of one of Philadelphia's wealthiest and most influential banking families.

"Uncle Robert came through for me all right." Steve grinned. "The old man may be seventy-three, but he's still cagy as they come. Sanders's loot was stashed in the Union General of San Francisco, but only until the day before his death. Then the account was closed out."

Shirl Henke

"By Charlie boy."

"Yes, but only after someone in Cheyenne had persuaded Sanders it was in his best interests to sign a power of attorney. Then Charles went to work. A lawyer is well equipped to be a first-rate bank embezzler."

"Almost as well equipped as the banker's son," Mike interjected. "I wondered at Everett's sudden prosperity here of late, buying that new thoroughbred race horse. Lots of things didn't add up."

"They added up—to his having gotten his hands on all Stoddard's money from Sanders. That's a lot of addition, believe me."

"Which still leaves us with the mystery of who did in poor Sandy. Charles hates mussing his clothes, much less getting them bloodied," Mike said, recalling the day at the mud slide more vividly than he would have liked.

Steve chuckled. "We have Cassie to thank for, er, prying that bit of information from Ella Hauser." Mike's eyebrows rose, but he said nothing, just continued taking notes. "When Blackie first checked on Sanders's arrival in Denver, he found that a big man, fat and tall with odd-colored yellow eyes, had been asking questions in posh bars about the kid.

"Emmet."

"None other. He finally gave up and took a train to Cheyenne, but not before he tucked his dear sweet niece into a scrubby little cabin on the outskirts of Denver."

"Probably no worse than she lived in here," Mike muttered as he wrote.

"One big difference. She's very uncomfortably pregnant now—and very unhappy being deserted, first by her true love, Sanders, then by her only kin, Emmet. By the time Blackie located her and Cass had a little discussion with her, the sweet thing was ready to tell the world how everyone in southwest Colorado had done her wrong—including Charles, who hired her uncle to find Sanders, promising him a handsome reward for beating the whereabouts of the money out of him."

."Charles, of course, knew old Emmet hadn't the connections to get at the money."

"Right. Apparently, once he reported back to Everett about where the money was, Charles set about his irregular transfer of the assets, then told Emmet to lure Sandy back to Denver and kill the kid. The rub is, Emmet did such an outstanding job of it, Charles offered him a second assignment."

Mike dropped his pencil with an oath. "To kill Rhys! He already made one attempt yesterday. Hauser must be in Starlight!"

Steve swore. "Well, Hauser has an old grudge against Rhys Davies—being paid for doing the job would only sweeten the deal. But like Sanders and Charles, Emmet's too greedy. He decided he didn't need to bother with his niece, whose connection with the banker's son had never panned out the way he wanted. He left her with a few hundred dollars and a promise to return."

"When he didn't come back, she talked to Cass."

Steve nodded. "Even if Rhys is forewarned that someone is after him, I'm going to ride out to Dragon's Lair and tell him it's Hauser and Everett. I've already tried to reach the marshal here in town, but he's gone somewhere on business. I sent word to the authorities in Lake City. As soon as they send someone, Everett will find himself in jail. You tell the Lake City marshal to start looking for Hauser, too." As Steve stood up, a blast of icy air caused him to turn toward the front door. Ginger Vogel had shoved it open with blind haste. She was out of breath and looked terrified. "Emmett Hauser and Charles Everett are going to kill Rhys!" she gasped, collapsing against the door as she closed it.

"What the hell are you talking about?" Steve strode over to her and held her shoulders firmly as she struggled to talk and breathe at once. She had run flat out from the saloon to the newspaper.

"He rode outta here for Stoddard's place in the mountains. Wouldn't listen to reason and get help." She fought to stay calm.

"I know Laughton's hunting cabin up on Gold Leaf," Mike said.

"I prayed you did! No one else in the saloon had more than a vague idea," she hiccuped. She turned to Loring, noticing the gun casually strapped to his hip. "You going to help him?"

"Yes, but first, tell me what's going on," Steve said. Ginger explained to him what had just transpired at the Naked Truth.

"Mike, you wait here for that marshal and then follow me. I'm going after Rhys. Give me some fast directions to that cabin. He can't be far ahead of me."

Ginger breathed a sign of relief as Steve left the newspaper office. "He oughta catch up with Rhys real quick."

"Believe me, he'll even up the odds," Mike said drily.

Charles Everett was on the way to his club to set up an alibi. When Rhys Davies was killed, every man of account in Starlight would know he could not have been the one who shot the sorry son-of-a-bitch. Stoddard could then bring his widowed daughter home in shock, and her former fiancé would console her in her loss. Nothing would be considered amiss if he married her in a few months. Everyone knew they had been affianced before her family's financial straits caused her unfortunate marriage to the gambler.

He congratulated himself on his careful planning, now finally on the verge of fruition. Suddenly he caught sight of Davies's Denver friend Loring striding purposefully from Manion's newspaper office. Charles stepped quickly into an alley to avoid detection, then watched Loring check the rifle on the saddle of his big gray stallion and swing up. When he rode off in the direction of Gold Leaf Mountain, Charles began to sweat.

When he saw Ginger Vogel being consoled and assured by Manion as she left the office, he began to shake. How could they have learned about the trap? The note was only being delivered to Davies's place, telling him to ride alone to the cabin for his beloved wife's sake.

"The dog! That son-of-a-bitch of a mutt! He must've found Davies," he muttered, his mind racing. But how would Davies have known where to go? How would Loring? Maybe he was jumping to conclusions. He had been worried over having Tory dragged into the plan unwittingly, but that had worked out reasonably well. Perhaps the arrival of Loring was just a fluke. To be safe, he decided on a brief detour, just in case everything did not go according to plan.

"Th' way I figger it, he oughta get here in an hour or so, all worried 'bout his little ladylove." Hauser leered at Tory, who lay on the bed with her hands tied behind her, covers pulled up to her waist as if she were injured.

Although gagged, Tory glared with open hatred at the filthy killer who sat across from her father.

Hauser wolfed chunks of the ham directly from the bone, cut with his Bowie knife. It was probably the same knife he had used to kill her brother—the same knife he had used on Rhys! Her eyes shifted from the big greasy thug to Stoddard, who sat with a cold compress over his burned face and bruised temple. *I should've let him burn in the fire*, she thought vengefully as she remembered how he had stood by coldly while that brute lasciviously manhandled her. Then he had the gall to tell her snidely that after Emmet, Charles ought to look better to her!

She lay partially on her side, straining at the bindings on her wrists with little success. Hauser was far better with knots than Charles had been.

"She's right worried 'bout her man, Laughton. 'N' I don't mean Everett. Lookee how them eyes er glarin' at you."

"I'll handle Victoria. You need only concern yourself with Davies when he arrives. I certainly hope you have more success than you had in the stable."

"He's a foxy one, that Welsh bastard. But I got me a hole card this time." He sucked on a knuckle from the ham bone and studied Tory. "He'll be so afraid for her, he won't be thinkin' straight. Besides"—he patted the .44 caliber Colt at his waist—"I ain't gotta be quiet this time. When he knocks on that barred door, you answer, all scared, sayin' your daughter's been hurt. I'll—"

"Yes, yes, we've rehearsed the damn thing over and over. I know what to do," Laughton said angrily. Damn, but his head hurt. To think his own Victoria had nearly killed her father—and for that trashy scum who had her own brother murdered! What kind of sexual hold did Davies have on her that she would turn her back on family, position, respectability—just to save his miserable life?

428

Images of the two of them, his prim, cool girl-child entangled naked with that big Welsh animal, flashed through his aching head. He threw the cloth on the table in disgust and forced the thoughts aside. For reassurance, he patted the gun in his coat pocket. Lucky for him, Hauser had taken it from her before she was able to shoot them both! To think the stupid chit actually believed that Charles had hired Emmet to kill Sanders. How absurd!

At this point Stoddard knew she would do anything to save her lover. How the deuce Charles would get her to marry him posed a real problem, especially since Rhys had gotten her pregnant. But the problem would be Charles's. Stoddard was the one here, taking all the risks with this vile, smelly assassin. Lord knew that Tory herself had done enough damage. He was badly burned and had a terrible goose egg on his temple. And Charles was safe at his club in town!

Tory had loosened the cords, but they were still double-looped around her wrists. *I have to get this gag out so I can warn Rhys when he rides up!* Her hands worked frantically at the ropes as she listened for the sound of Blackjack's hoofbeats pounding up the mountainside. She knew he would come, just as they'd planned. Rhys loved her—and he would die for it.

Tears burned her eyes but she blinked them back. Just then a dull gleam caught her attention in the shadows between the bed and the hearth. The knife her father had placed in his belt just before she knocked him unconscious! If only she could get to it. But with both men in the small cabin there was no chance. Still, she had to try. Using her feet, she began to ease the covers down so she could swing her legs over the side of the bed. If only they would not look her way!

Stoddard began to cough. "That fire's throwing out smoke, Hauser." He swore in misery as his burned face stung from the smoke inexplicably pouring into the room.

Hauser stood up with an oath and overturned his chair. "You damned fool. The chimney's probably got birds nestin' in it!" Coughing, he knelt by the hearth and tried to peer up into the fire wall. "Unbar the back door 'n' get this smoke out afore we suffocate," Hauser choked, his eyes filled with tears.

Tory rolled from the bed and knelt in front of the knife, her hands frantically scrabbling for it behind her back. Both men ignored her in the chaos.

"The damn bar's stuck!" Stoddard yelled.

Hauser swore and groped his way toward the rear door. "Keep yer voice down. You'll warn that Welsh bastard if he's within ten miles of here." Shoving Laughton out of the way, he heaved the swollen wooden bar up and yanked the door open.

"I'm a lot closer than ten miles, Emmet," Rhys said softly as he swung his Winchester in Hauser's face.

Smoke-induced tears streamed down the killer's face, incongruous with the rage that contorted his mouth in a snarl. "You stopped up the chimney!"

"Where's Tory?" Rhys shoved the rifle barrel into Hauser's gut.

Tory saw her father behind the door and tried to cry a warning through the gag, but Stoddard shoved the door against the barrel just as Rhys caught sight of her through the smoke. In that split second Hauser lunged for the rifle, jerking Davies forward into the room. The two men rolled on the floor, punching, gouging, and kicking. Tory sawed furiously at her bonds with the knife she had finally secured, fighting for air with every breath in the billowing black smoke.

Finally she felt the last of the frayed rope separate. Quickly she unknotted the cloth that secured the gag in her mouth and spit out the wadded handkerchief. She stood up and gripped the knife in her hand, approaching the no-holds-barred fight on the cabin floor. Stoddard stood across the room from her, coughing and watching the combatants.

Rhys knew he had undone all Runcie's careful stitching, but didn't give a damn as he and his opponent regained their feet. The Welshman landed a solid right jab to Hauser's throat. Tory was alive. That was all that mattered—that and killing Hauser. He hit the man again, knocking him against the bed. The big ox was surprisingly resilient, considering the roll of fat about his middle. He came back with a roundhouse swing that narrowly missed Rhys, whose timing was off because of the agony in his side. Gritting his teeth, Rhys danced to one side, then sent a volley of blows to his foe's face. Hauser was nearly out. Rhys clubbed him to his knees and stood over him, right hand clenching his victim's shirt front while pounding him senseless with his left.

Stoddard could see that Hauser was done for. He groped frantically in his pocket for his gun.

Damn the gambler, saloon trash, no better than his opponent! Rhys Davies had killed Sanders, taken Victoria and turned her against her family—even made her pregnant! Now Davies would ruin everything and send him to prison and disgrace. He raised the gun and cocked it awkwardly.

Tory screamed at her father as he aimed at Rhys's back. She could not reach him to deflect the shot, but she could stop him from hitting his target. Tory threw herself over Rhys's body just as Stoddard fired.

The force of the bullet slamming into Victoria staggered her husband. Rhys dropped the unconscious Hauser and turned as she slipped to the floor. "Tory!"

"Laughton, you son of a bitch," Steve Loring yelled from the open door, gun raised.

Stoddard whirled and began to squeeze off a shot. It went wild. Loring's .45 slug hit dead center, knocking the older man across the sooty floor. Steve spared him barely a glance once he was certain the man was dead. Rhys was cradling Tory in his arms. She was bleeding profusely.

"Tory, my love, my Victory, don't you die—you can't, I won't let you! You took that shot meant for me, oh, darling. I love you, please." Rhys sobbed in anguish.

Tory could feel his arms around her. He was alive! Miraculously the nightmare was over. She looked up into his tear-streaked face and said softly, "Now do you believe I love you, you mule-headed Welshman?" Then she fainted.

Steve quickly stepped outside to get fistfuls of snow and packed them into the towel left on the table. He knelt by Rhys and placed the ice pack over the blossoming red stain on her black dress. "Press this to the wound while I tear that sheet to bandage it," he instructed Rhys.

The Welshman held the icy rag to her slim waist, all the while crooning love words to her. Steve was back in a moment with strips of sheeting to bind up the wound.

"If we keep it cold enough to slow the bleeding, we can get her down the mountain safer."

"Tory, my Victory. You have to live, love. I have to tell you I believe you. . . . I love you."

* * *

Charles walked toward his study, intent on picking up the documents he needed and riding away as fast as his best thoroughbred could carry him. His stable boy was saddling it right now. The marshal had ridden into town and then had set out with Manion hell-bent for Gold Leaf Mountain. It took no genius to deduce that they knew about the plan to kill Davies. He opened the door with one hand, the other clutching a hastily packed valise with a change of clothing.

"Hello, Charles. Are you planning a trip?" Hedda's voice was brittle and cold. She sat behind his desk, holding the power of attorney giving Charles access to Sanders's San Francisco bank account.

Everett froze, then slowly put down the suitcase. "What are you doing in here, going through my things, Hedda?" he asked with exaggerated patience. He had no time for a hysterical woman.

She smiled glacially and replied, "I came to tell you I'd sent Davies to the cabin. Imagine my surprise when your butler informed me you were upstairs packing. I decided to wait here and have a discussion about the change in plans."

"I can explain, Hedda. I just got word from a San Francisco bank—"

Her laughter interrupted him. Its eerie sound sent chills down his spine. Hedda snapped the paper in front of him. "How stupid do you think I am?" she hissed furiously. "'Just got word'—this is dated several days before Sanders was killed! You had my son murdered—and then you took the money! *Our* money. You were using us—"

"I used you the same way you used me—and that poor sorry bastard you married," he said nastily. "Who came to me with a plan to kill Davies? Who

433

browbeat Stoddard to go along with it?"

"You were supposed to find my son and return him, not kill him!" she said with deadly intensity.

He smiled sarcastically. "I merely rearranged your master plan to suit myself, dear Hedda. Just call it a short-term loan."

"Your *loan* cost my son's life. That is not acceptable, Charles, not acceptable at all."

"And I was supposed to ask your permission like Stoddard and Sanders always have?" he sneered. "Give me credit for more intelligence, madam."

"I'll give you exactly what you deserve, Charles," she said quietly. "You will hang. Stoddard and I shall testify at your trial about how you hired this Hauser person to murder Sanders and our son-in-law. How you deceived us, robbed us." Her face took on a beatific glow. "You really did a terrible thing, leaving my poor daughter widowed. Stoddard and I shall be her sole consolation . . ."

"You're mad," he said with dawning horror. When she raised the Smith & Wesson he kept in his desk drawer and pointed it at him, he swallowed. "Now, Hedda—you can't shoot me. Then *you'd* hang! Think of your plan," he coaxed, but she did not lower the gun.

"I am thinking of my plan. Take your suitcase and attempt to flee, Charles," she commanded with disdain. "I'll not give you the opportunity to do to me what you did to my son."

For an instant her eyes scanned all the incriminating evidence she had spread out in front of her. In desperation he dove across the desk and grabbed her wrist, but instead of deflecting the shot, he only succeeded in raising the muzzle of the weapon from his chest to his face. The explosion was deafening.

Hedda felt his grip on her wrist suddenly slacken as his body was thrown back by the impact of the bullet. He flopped onto the floor face up—except that now, he no longer had a face.

She quickly averted her eyes and looked at her dress of black silk faille. "This was my best new mourning gown. Now it's quite ruined. Bloodstains can't be removed from silk . . . at least I don't think they can. I shall ask Bessie . . ."

By the time Charles's valet found his body sprawled in front of the heavy oak door in his study, Hedda Laughton had vanished.

Laura Everett stood at the front door of the Laughtons' imposing home, waiting for Ralph to respond to her knock. She still could scarcely believe the news that Mike Manion had brought her. How on earth could she soften the blow for poor Hedda? Squaring her shoulders, she greeted Ralph and stepped inside when he opened the door. *No one else is closer to Hedda. I'm the nearest thing to a friend she has left.*

"I'm so glad you've come, Mrs. Everett. Mrs. Laughton's locked herself in her room," the butler said, concern lining his wizened face.

"I'll go up and see what I can do," she replied.

When Laura reached the door to Hedda's room, she knocked. There was no response. Wondering how literally Ralph had meant "locked herself in," she tried the knob. It turned.

Hedda sat stiffly on a delicate balloon-back armchair, facing the window, staring sightlessly into the gathering darkness outside.

"Are you all right, Hedda? It's Laura. I must speak with you." Hedda did not answer. Had she already received word? Was she in shock?

"Tory is going to be all right, Hedda. Doc Runcie says the wound is not too serious. Steve stopped the bleeding."

"There was so much blood." Hedda shuddered. "My dress is quite ruined."

Laura stood in the doorway, almost afraid to enter the eerie pall of the room. Only the snow outside the window, casting a reflection on Hedda's face, broke the darkness. "Hedda, you do know Stoddard is dead?" she asked gently.

"Rhys Davies and Charles Everett are dead," Hedda intoned quietly.

"No, Hedda, Rhys is quite all right. It's Stoddard who's dead," she said patiently. A prickle of warning climbed the hair at her nape. What was this about Charles being dead?

Suddenly Hedda turned, as if Laura's words had just registered. Her face was a twisted mask of hate. "Rhys Davies is dead! He must be. I planned it that way—to free Victoria for Charles . . . but Charles killed Sanders . . . he shouldn't have done that." Her voice went from venomous fury to icy calm.

Laura walked slowly into the room and turned up the gaslight. Its dim flicker illuminated Hedda's bloodstained dress and the spatters on her face and hands. She sat still once more, staring sightlessly at Laura.

"Dear God in heaven, what have you done?" Laura fought to control her breathing, then pulled a bell summoning the maid.

Rhys sat by Tory's bedside watching her even breathing. She looked so vulnerable and pale in Dr. Runcie's bleak infirmary cubicle. She would be all right. Doc had promised. She had slept soundly all night. Now it was early morning. The old physician had also ordered Rhys to climb back in bed himself. His side had been restitched and he'd lost some blood, but the wicked throbbing only served to help him stay awake until he could tell her.

Tory felt the pain pulling her like a magnet back to consciousness. She moaned and then heard Rhys's voice soothing her, his hands touching her. Her eyelids fluttered open. "You're alive," she whispered in awe.

"Only because of you," he said hoarsely. "Tory, my Victory, my love, if you'd died before I could tell you how much I love you—that I believe you. Damn woman, you didn't have to kill yourself to prove your point!" His hand gently cupped her bruised face.

She smiled at him and reached up to stroke his jaw, then gasped as the pain lanced from her waist all the way to her fingertips.

"Easy, love, easy. You've been shot, but you're going to be fine. I have Doc Runcie's word on it." He placed her hand back on the bed and caressed her arm reassuringly.

"Rhys! The baby! Is it—Have I—?"

"The little devil rests undisturbed in spite of everything. You didn't lose our child, Tory."

She closed her eyes for a moment in a silent prayer of gratitude. "Thank God. You and our baby—all safe." Then her face crumpled. "Papa . . . he would have killed you."

"He's dead, Tory," Rhys said gently, not knowing how to tell her the rest—or if he should wait until she was stronger. "Steve had to kill him."

The violent scene at the cabin flashed through her mind and she shuddered. "He would have killed you if Steve hadn't . . . I never realized how much they hated you. How they used you."

"They used us both, love. Hauser is in jail in Lake City."

"But Charles will just hire someone else—"

"Don't worry about Charles," he evaded. "Just concentrate on getting well so we can raise our family. Tory, I love you, and now I know you love me. It's more than I ever dared dream." He caressed her face and leaned down to place a soft kiss on her lips.

This time she reached up more carefully and placed her hand on his beard-bristled cheek, looking deep into his eyes. "Tell me the rest, Rhys. You're keeping something from me."

"It can wait until you're stronger, love."

"After all I've survived, don't you think I'm tough enough?" she asked reasonably.

He sighed and held her hand, stroking the pulse in her wrist unconsciously. "Charles is dead, too. You have nothing to fear from him again."

"It was Mama, wasn't it?" she said, startling him.

"How did you—?"

"Papa never did anything without her approval. If he was helping Charles with his plan to kill you and claim your money through me, then it was only logical that he and my mother acted together. But they would never have knowingly let Charles kill Sanders."

"They didn't know—until your mother went to Charles's house and found incriminating evidence about how he had Sanders killed. Apparently Charles tried to grab a gun away from her and it went off." He shrugged helplessly.

"What will happen to her?"

"We'll have to make some kind of arrangements for her care. The law won't prosecute her. Tory, she's . . . she's lost her reason. Laura found her sitting alone in her bedroom. I'm afraid Doc thinks

438

she'll never recover. I'll hire the best nurses to care for her. She'll always be protected."

"Just so she's not allowed to get free. She might . . . oh, Rhys, she might try to kill you again!" she broke into sobbing. "Both my parents, murderers! You ought to hate me," she choked as her hands held his tightly.

"How could I? I love you too much. If one person has told me, half this town has—you're nothing like your mother or father. You're a throwback, lady, to some distant ancestor. A real blueblood from New England who can probably trace her ancestry all the way to Queen Elizabeth. You were named for Queen Victoria, after all."

"No queens, no blue blood, Rhys," she said, smiling through her tears. "I'm a gambler's woman and that's all I ever want to be, my love."

He kissed her with exquisite tenderness. "You are a gambler's *lady*—always believe that, love."

Epilogue

Tory inspected herself in the full-length pier looking glass, wiping the steam from her bath that obscured the surface. "Why I want to see my body in this condition, heaven knows," she chuckled as her very well rounded abdomen appeared in the mirror. Critically she turned this way and that, noting with approval the vibrant healthy glow of her skin, freshly toweled and oiled after her bath.

"Pleasingly plump," she said, then chuckled once more as she reached for her nightrail lying across a chair. The sheer aqua silk whispered about her skin after she slipped it over her towel-wrapped head.

She rubbed her long hair vigorously with the towel. Still damp, it looked a darker blonde, almost the gold of old minted coins. Soft curls framed her face and the tangled mass fell down her back to her waist—if she'd had a waist. With one final look at herself in the mirror, she made a rueful little moue and threw the towel across the chair.

Rhys lay stretched out on the bed with their three-year-old son Steven sitting on his chest. The little boy squealed in delight, bouncing up and down as his father held him about the waist. Their laughter blended as Rhys lifted the child high over him. Steven's arms and legs flailed wildly in midair.

Tory watched them cavort. Soon there would be another little boy or girl to join in their play. But for now, it was time for her sort of play. "It's well past your bed time, Steven Michael Davies," she said with mock sternness.

"Aw, Mama. C'n I sleep wif you 'n' Papa?" His curly brown hair and dark blue eyes were cherubically appealing.

Rhys before the devil won him over, she thought, then wondered if this youthful replica wasn't developing a few devilish wiles already. Her lips twitched. "You know the rules, Steven. Boys sleep in boys' beds, mamas and papas sleep in their bed."

"You heard your mama, you little rascal," Rhys said, swinging his legs over the side of the bed and sitting up with his son still held high in his arms. "Off to bed with you."

"Mudpie sleep wif me?" the boy wheedled.

Rhys's lips curved into a smile as he looked at Tory. "I suppose that would be all right." He stood up and held the boy close. Steven laid his head on his father's shoulder and wrapped his arms about Rhys's neck. With a flourish Rhys said to Tory, "Lead the way."

Mudpie was already sitting in Steven's bed when the trio walked into the gaily painted and papered room. Tucking in their son was a shared nighttime ritual. After the toddler had a story, a prayer, and a long drink of water, the adults tiptoed out, leaving the snoozing dog to guard his charge.

"Steven is getting big. You take care not to carry him when I'm not around," Rhys said as he patted her rounded belly. "After all, we wouldn't want his baby sister complaining, would we?"

"You're so certain it will be a girl this time," she said with a smile. "What do you know that I don't?"

"Celtic intuition," he replied with cocky assurance, tapping his forehead.

She snorted. "You've been listening to Mike's blarney too long—not to mention Sister Frances Rose, the old charmer."

He paused in the doorway to their room, smiling in reminiscence. "It was good seeing her again. She adores you and Steven. I think she'd be pleased to know his little sister was conceived on our visit to New York. Should I write that in my next letter?"

Tory chuckled. "Yes, I expect she would enjoy that tidbit. Oh, Rhys, the work she does with those children—it's just wonderful. Not to mention the whole new building a certain benefactor donated to St. Vincent's."

He looked at her with laughter in his eyes. "And would a staunch Episcopalian girl such as yerself be wantin' ta convert?"

"I don't think it's required in order to support such a worthy cause. I'm just so grateful that she saved your rascally hide and sent you west to me." The teasing good humor softened to love as she brushed the lock of hair falling across his forehead, then reached up and kissed him lightly on the nose. "My belly's in the way, but I've been giving that some thought . . ." She let her hand trail suggestively across his bare chest, inside his robe.

He followed her into the bedroom and closed the door. "You have, have you? And what has that perverse little mind of yours come up with now?" Leaning against the door with one shoulder, he looked incredibly sexy and eager to have her demonstrate.

She moistened her lips seductively with the tip of her tongue. "Come here and find out," she invited, standing with her arms outstretched, her body silhouetted by a dimmed gaslight. The sheer silk nightrail revealed her lushly plump curves.

"You are beautiful," he breathed as he walked into her arms.

"And you are blind, but I love you for it," she murmured as she kissed him teasingly, then slid from his embrace and took his hand to lead him to the bed. She tossed back the covers, then knelt on the cool white sheets and reached for the belt of his robe. Untying it, she peeled the navy brocade from his shoulders and he shrugged it off. "My, oh, my," she said softly, appraising his big naked body with a boldness that once would have brought crimson to her cheeks, even in her innermost imaginings.

He waited to see what she would do next.

With one seductive swish, she pulled her silk nightrail over her head, letting the pale golden splendor of her hair fall about her shoulders like a cloak. Her breasts, full and heavy, peeked from between the curls. She moaned as he cupped them, hefting their weight in his hands. When he bent down to tease and suckle them with his mouth, she arched each one in turn for his searching lips. Her fingers combed through his hair, pulling his head closer.

After a few moments of the exquisite torture, her hands moved to his shoulders and she pulled him onto the bed. "Lie down," she whispered. Rhys obeyed, stretching out as she knelt at his side. Her busy fingers teased, touched, and tantalized his flesh from his chest down to his belly, skittering past his straining staff, then stroking between his hard thighs. Finally she gave a low throaty chuckle when he bucked and arched in desperation. She took his shaft in both hands to stroke its velvety length.

He moaned. "Have you no mercy, woman?"

"None whatsoever," she whispered with glowing eyes. "Now roll on your side and face me," she commanded, guiding him with a most persuasive handhold. Then she released him and lay back, raising her legs over his hip. As he slid into her, she arched her hips forward to meet his thrust. "Like this . . . my belly . . . doesn't get . . . in the . . . way," she said in gasping little whispers.

"Not at all," he murmured, holding one curving little calf aloft as he thrust his hips forward and threw his head back in ecstasy. He let her set the pace, guiding the depth and swiftness of his strokes with her hand rocking his thigh. Slowly the languorous tempo accelerated until she cried out his name, the way she always did now when she climaxed. Just hearing her voice that way was enough to send him over the edge along with her. This was bliss, this was paradise, this was his Victory.

As breath and conscious thought returned, they disentangled and she cuddled against him and gave him a soft brushing kiss of satiation. "How did that way work?" she asked impudently.

"How the hell do you think it worked, you bold siren?" he chuckled in reply.

"Some siren, more like that walrus we saw in the New York Zoo," she snorted.

"But an inventive little walrus . . . or is it walrusess?" They both laughed as he massaged her belly. He raised up on one elbow and leaned over to look in her eyes. "This is glorious. Once, you would have died of embarrassment before you'd have lain here so beautifully naked, letting me hold this plump little belly."

"I remember a time when you had to ply me with liquor just to get me to undress you," she said mischievously.

"And you hated yourself in the morning," he teased, his hand still on her stomach. He felt a kick. "We disturbed her."

She smiled lazily. "She—if it is a she—won't grow up to be a prude like her mama used to be. After all, she might not be lucky enough to find a man like her father, who would put up with such a straightlaced lady."

"And unlace her corsets?" he asked with a tender kiss to her forehead.

"Corset? What's a corset? It's been so long, I forget," she replied dreamily and faded off to sleep in his arms.

Author's Note

After finishing the first of the "Colorado Couple," *Terms of Love*, we had hoped the research for *Terms of Surrender* would be a matter of simply going over the notes. We were wrong. Rhys and Tory's story had to take place later in time, and the setting had to be a small town. Then I stumbled upon the beautiful and historically rich area of Southwestern Colorado during the silver boom of the 1880s. That meant investigating a totally different environment from Denver and the freighting routes south into Arizona. We knew the hero was a Welsh immigrant who grew up on the mean streets of New York City, which entailed two additional sites to research.

In doing the general background reading on southwest Colorado, I rediscovered a favorite tale of mine, the legend of the infamous Alfred Packer, man-eater. We must beg the reader's pardon in that we used the details of his macabre trail in this story set in the spring of 1884, when in fact the first Packer trial took place in the spring of 1883 and the overturn of his conviction by the Colorado Supreme Court occurred in the fall of 1885. The grisly elements of humor in newspaper coverage of the trial were simply too good to pass up, even though we had to compress and rearrange the dates a bit. An additional apology must be made to the eminent Georgia jurist, Melville Gerry, who passed sentence on Packer not only in grammatical English, but with great eloquence. The popular newspaper accounts were vastly more amusing and served the purposes of our story. Gerry's fellow Democrat Mike Manion would be sympathetic to the liberties we took. Although a great deal has been written on this fabulous bit of Colorado lore, the best source for our purposes proved to be *The Case of Alfred Packer The Man-eater* by Paul H. Gantt. Residents of the Centennial State took political partisanship seriously in the early decades of statehood. For further information on Democrat/Republican alignments, *The Politics of Populism* by James Edward Wright is excellent.

Rhys Davies was a Welshman, a man who never lost the lilt of the language in his voice or the roguish charm of the Celts in his manner. For the background information to create his childhood, *Wales Through the Ages, Volume II*, edited by A. J. Roderick, proved a solid source. The incredible hardships endured by immigrants to America in the late nineteenth century were detailed with great clarity in *New York; The Centennial Years 1676–1976*, right down to the sewage-filled, rat-infested warrens of Five Points. Rhys was raised in an orphanage. For the concept of Sister Frances Rose as his tutor and boxing coach, we are indebted to Jim Henke, who knew several real-life counterparts during his childhood. For the details about the Daughters of Charity, *The Catholic Encyclopedia, Volume 3*, provided essential information.

The resources on Colorado are as numerous as peaks in the Rockies, but a few worked particularly well in meeting our needs with this story. Since Rhys was a saloon owner, we found quite a bit of unique anecdotal information in *The Saloon on the Mining Frontier* by Elliot West. A good source of descriptive details on Colorado saloons is *The City and the Saloon* by Thomas J. Noel. For technical information about the mining aspects of the Colorado silver boom, *Leadville, A Miner's Epic* by Stephen M. Voynick dispels a great many myths about the hard-rock miner. The best overview of the era of gold and silver barons in Colorado is without a doubt *The New Eldorado* by Phyllis Flanders Dorset. The book itself is a gold mine of local color, outrageous tales, and even more outrageous people. In old Colorado, truth was stranger than fiction.